TRUTH, LIES, AND THE QUESTIONS IN BETWEEN

TRUTH, LIES, AND THE QUESTIONS IN BETWEEN

L. M. ELLIOTT

LITTLE, BROWN AND COMPANY
New York   Boston

> THIS BOOK IS A WORK OF FICTION. ALTHOUGH THE HISTORIC, CONTEXTUAL FACTS OF 1973, WATERGATE, ELECTED AND APPOINTED GOVERNMENT OFFICIALS, AND THE DEBATE SURROUNDING THE ERA ARE REAL, THE CHARACTERS, THEIR CIRCUMSTANCES, AND THEIR DIALOGUE IN THIS NOVEL ARE PRODUCTS OF THE AUTHOR'S IMAGINATION.

Copyright © 2025 by L. M. Elliott

Cover art © Shutterstock. Cover design by Kayla E. | designaltar.org.
Cover copyright © 2025 by Hachette Book Group, Inc.
Interior design by Kayla E.

Hachette Book Group supports the right to free expression and the value of copyright. The purpose of copyright is to encourage writers and artists to produce the creative works that enrich our culture.

The scanning, uploading, and distribution of this book without permission is a theft of the author's intellectual property. If you would like permission to use material from the book (other than for review purposes), please contact permissions@hbgusa.com. Thank you for your support of the author's rights.

Little, Brown and Company
Hachette Book Group
1290 Avenue of the Americas, New York, NY 10104
Visit us at LBYR.com

First Edition: January 2025

Little, Brown and Company is a division of Hachette Book Group, Inc. The Little, Brown name and logo are registered trademarks of Hachette Book Group, Inc.

The publisher is not responsible for websites
(or their content) that are not owned by the publisher.

Additional copyright/credits information is on page 346.

Little, Brown and Company books may be purchased in bulk for business, educational, or promotional use. For information, please contact your local bookseller or the Hachette Book Group Special Markets Department at special.markets@hbgusa.com.

Library of Congress Control Number: 2024033477.

ISBNs: 978-1-64375-282-2 (hardcover), 978-1-5235-3069-4 (ebook)

Printed in Indiana, USA

LSC-C

Printing 2, 2025

To Megan and Peter, brave believers
in truth and where it leads.

CONTENT ALERT

1973 was a sexist time. While great care has been taken to handle these scenes in a non-sensationalistic manner that is sensitive to survivors, this novel does depict several instances of gender-based violence. The United Nations defines this as sexual, physical, mental, and economic harm inflicted in public or in private—power and control over someone else brought through threats or acts of violence, coercion, and manipulation.

Tragically, our National Institute of Health (NIH) estimates that one-third of college women in America will experience IPV (Intimate Partner Violence)—gender-based violence from someone they know, are dating, or love and trust.

If you experience gender-based violence, please know you are not alone. Reach out for help. You can call the following hotlines:

- 800-799-7233 (National Domestic Violence Hotline)
- 800-656-4673 (National Sexual Assault Hotline)
- 866-331-9474 (love is respect teen dating abuse helpline, or text LOVEIS to 22522)

You can also learn more at https://www.justice.gov/ovw, the Department of Justice's Office on Violence Against Women.

"A LIE GETS HALFWAY AROUND THE WORLD BEFORE THE TRUTH HAS A CHANCE TO GET ITS PANTS ON."
—WINSTON CHURCHILL

"IF YOU CAN'T LIE, YOU'LL NEVER GO ANYWHERE."
—PRESIDENT RICHARD NIXON TO A POLITICAL ASSOCIATE

"THE TRUTH WILL SET YOU FREE. BUT FIRST IT WILL PISS YOU OFF."
—FEMINIST GLORIA STEINEM

PROLOGUE

WELCOME TO 1973

1973—the year of Watergate, the Equal Rights Amendment, *Roe v. Wade*, and the end of our fighting the Vietnam War.

A year of political intrigue when many Americans say, do, and accept just about anything to maintain their status quo. When Congress, the president, and the courts get into a checks-and-balances slugfest that hinges on unexpected heroes: a young, bespectacled "turncoat"; a stubborn, gruff judge; two rookie reporters and their shy but steely widow publisher; secretaries who brave telling truth to their bosses' power; a "miniskirted" lawyer; and a handful of influential politicians putting country over party.

A year when women have constitutional equality within reach only to have it unraveled by some housewives and their home-baked bread, mobilized by fear of being shoved out of their traditional roles as wives and mothers.

A year when Americans' willingness to ask hard questions, to recognize truths and lies—or not—defines all that follows.

In many ways, 1973 is a culmination of what came the decade before and a backlash against it: the 1960s civil rights and Great Society programs; the youth movement, its anti-establishment, anti–Vietnam War peace trains, and mantras of Flower Power, Make Love Not War, and Power to the People; plus the sexual revolution and the liberation of contraception.

So, before we plunge in, welcome to a quick Magical Mystery Tour of how what *was* leads to what *is* in 1973. It'll blow your mind.

NIXON'S

1968: AMID ESCALATING ANTI-VIETNAM WAR DEMONSTRATIONS and protests following Martin Luther King Jr.'s tragic assassination, presidential candidate Richard Nixon promises a return to "law and order," to bring the war "to an honorable end." **A FRIGHTENED AMERICA NARROWLY ELECTS HIM—BY A MERE 1 PERCENT OF THE POPULAR VOTE.**

But Nixon doesn't end the war quickly. In fact, his Vietnam policies will ultimately **COST THE LIVES OF 22,000 MORE AMERICANS.**

By 1970, five years into the war and one year into Nixon's first administration, young Americans are frustrated and angry. Peaceful flower-child protests haven't worked. **YOUNG MEN LIVE IN DREAD** of their birth date being pulled out of a plastic container on TV to be drafted to fight a war they don't believe in. **HORRIFIC SCENES OF BATTLES AND INJURED VIETNAMESE CIVILIANS FLOOD AMERICAN HOMES EACH NIGHT** via network news. Sit-ins and rallies on college campuses grow more rebellious.

At this point, **MOST POLLED AMERICANS AGREE THE VIETNAM WAR WAS A MISTAKE.** But the majority remain critical of the students' antiwar movement, many adults damning them as spoiled ingrates or debauched hippies. **NIXON FUELS THEIR RESENTMENT BY CALLING STUDENTS WHO DISRUPT CAMPUSES "BUMS."**

THE COUNTRY IS A TINDERBOX.

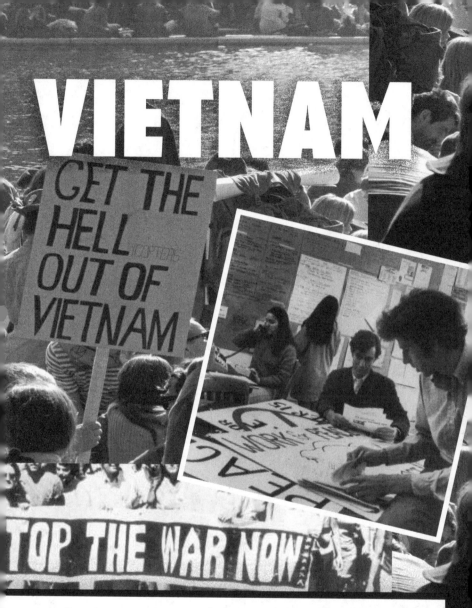

VIETNAM

APRIL 20, 1970: <u>**NIXON ANNOUNCES A WITHDRAWAL OF 150,000 TROOPS.**</u> Americans rejoice. Finally—an end in sight.

But ten days after announcing that troops are coming home, <u>**NIXON ADDRESSES THE NATION AGAIN, ANNOUNCING THAT HE'S ACTUALLY EXPANDED THE FIGHT BY ORDERING AMERICAN SOLDIERS OVER VIETNAM'S BORDER**</u> into Cambodia to "clean out enemy sanctuaries." Cambodia, he says, is harboring secret Viet Cong hit squads. The United States cannot act like a "pitiful helpless giant." "We will not be humiliated."

<u>**COLLEGE CAMPUSES ERUPT.**</u>

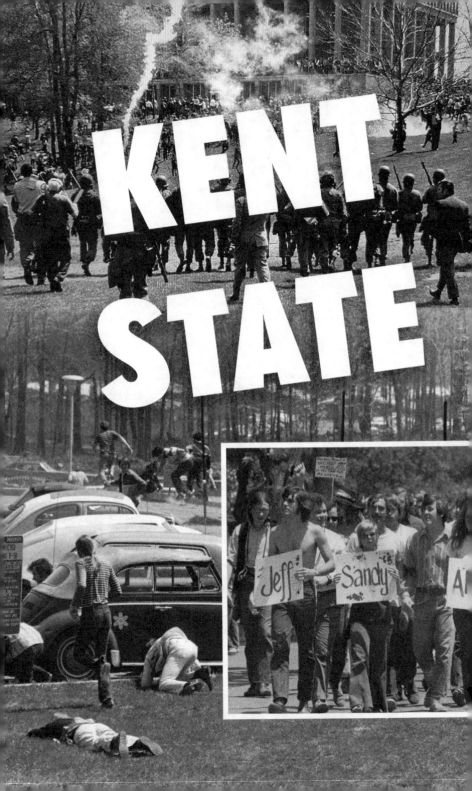

Feeling duped, chanting the now familiar "ONE, TWO, THREE, FOUR, WE DON'T WANT YOUR STINKING WAR," some student demonstrations grow desperate and destructive. At Ohio's KENT STATE, one group sets fire to the ROTC building.

MAY 4, 1970: Fitted with gas masks and bayoneted rifles, 100 NATIONAL GUARDSMEN—MOST AS YOUNG AS THE STUDENTS THEY ARE SUPPOSED TO SUBDUE—FIRE INTO A CROWD for thirteen deadly seconds. How it begins is unclear. But four undergraduates die, and nine are wounded.

IN HORRIFIED REACTION, STUDENTS AT 400-PLUS COLLEGES AND HIGH SCHOOLS GO ON STRIKE. Thousands of sympathetic adults join them. In Mississippi, in the heat of overturned cars set ablaze, police open fire on a JACKSON STATE dormitory, thinking a sniper is inside—killing two more innocent college undergraduates.

IN NEW YORK CITY, hundreds of high school and college students crowd onto the steps of the old Treasury Building in lower Manhattan to protest the campus shootings. Infuriated by who they feel are unpatriotic "peaceniks," **CONSTRUCTION WORKERS FROM NEARBY SKYSCRAPER PROJECTS GRAB CROWBARS AND PLANKS AND WAVE THEM THREATENINGLY AT THE STUDENTS.**

The **"HARD HAT RIOT"** is about to explode.

A non-student protester reportedly spits on a flag a worker carries, and **THE HARD-HATS SWARM UP THE STEPS TO DISLODGE THE "LONGHAIRS."** They also attack bystanders trying to help the teens.

A Wall Street secretary is hit repeatedly as she shields an injured student. **"IF YOU WANT TO BE TREATED LIKE AN EQUAL, WE'LL TREAT YOU LIKE ONE," HER ASSAILANT SHOUTS, SPEWING HATRED FOR THE GROWING FEMINIST MOVEMENT.**

Other Wall Street traders cheer the workers for "cracking heads." Eyewitnesses report police just stand by. **SEVENTY PEOPLE ARE INJURED. ONLY SIX ARRESTS ARE MADE.**

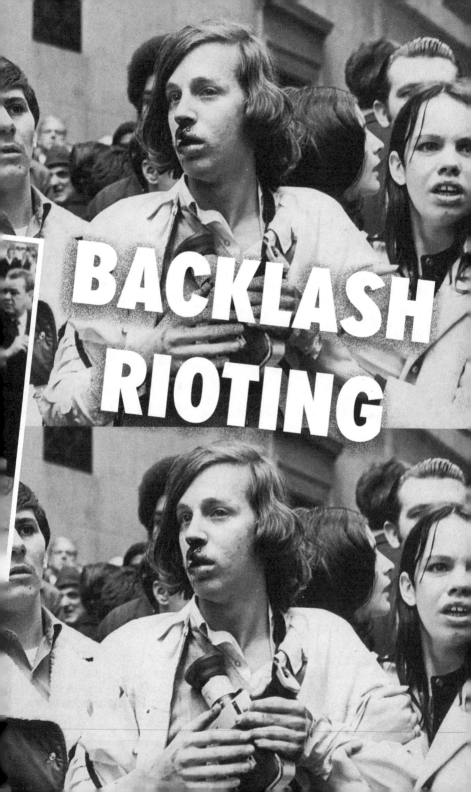

THE HARD HAT RIOT reflects in sickening vividness a Gallup poll finding that 58 percent of Americans believe the slain Kent State students responsible for their own deaths: "They were warned." Only 11 percent blame the National Guard.

Twelve days after the Wall Street melee, **BLUE-COLLAR WORKERS MARCH THROUGH LOWER MANHATTAN, BRANDISHING FLAGS AND SIGNS SAYING THINGS LIKE "WE BUILD THE SCHOOLS THEY TEAR DOWN."**

It is a culture clash and generation gap of epic proportion. **AND NIXON EXPLOITS IT.**

Praising working-class Americans as being the long-suffering, hard-working "Great Silent Majority," Nixon plays on their grievances, their fear of cultural changes, their sense that America is leaving them behind, and their disdain for any anti–Vietnam War "dove"—like his 1972 presidential opponent George McGovern.

HISTORICALLY DEMOCRATIC, BLUE-COLLAR WORKERS SWING TO THE REPUBLICAN PARTY AND NIXON IN THE 1972 ELECTION—despite the leaked Pentagon Papers that revealed Nixon (and his two predecessors) had continued to send the sons of working-class America to Vietnam, even as it became clear the U.S. could not win the war.

TO THESE DIEHARD NIXON SUPPORTERS, ANY REVELATION OF HIS WRONGDOING WAS SIMPLY HIS ENEMIES TRYING TO SMEAR HIM.

WATERGATE AND THE POST

JUNE 17, 1972: FIVE BURGLARS ARE ARRESTED INSIDE THE DEMOCRATIC NATIONAL COMMITTEE HEADQUARTERS at the Watergate complex. Dressed in suits, they carry elaborate bugging equipment, cameras, pen-sized tear-gas guns, and $2,300 in $100 bills.

The *Washington Post*'s Bob Woodward, a city-section reporter who's been at the paper only eight months, covers the arraignment. He overhears three of the men describe themselves as Cuban exiles and "anti-communists." One, James McCord, admits to being ex-CIA.

"HOLY SH—," WOODWARD MUTTERS.

The next day, he shares the first of many bylines with Carl Bernstein. Their report: McCord was not only ex-CIA but "the salaried security coordinator" for the Committee to Re-elect the President, or CR(EE)P, as Nixon's detractors call it.

THUS BEGINS AN UNLIKELY AND HISTORY-MAKING PARTNERSHIP between a reserved, Ivy-League, former naval officer (Woodward) and Bernstein, who'd become a copyboy at sixteen, hadn't finished college, and had almost been fired for lack of discipline.

ADDRESSES

Name **MRS. HASTINGS**
Street
City
Phone 642-5776
Name HH 347-0355
Street WH-202-456-2282
City Home: 301-299-7366
Phone
Name 11120 River Road
Street Potomac Md. 20854
City Robert R Mullen & Co.
Phone 1700 Pennsylvania

JUNE 21: WOODWARD IS TIPPED OFF BY THE *POST*'S VETERAN POLICE-BEAT REPORTER THAT ONE OF THE BURGLAR'S ADDRESS BOOKS HAS AN ODD NOTATION—"H. H. at W. H."—and another lists "Howard Hunt." Piecing the clues together, Woodward calls the White House switchboard, asks for Hunt, and is connected to the office of the president's Special Counsel.

"Good God!" Hunt responds, when Woodward eventually reaches him at home and asks why his name is in a burglar's address book. Hunt slams down the phone. **THE *POST*'S HEADLINE THE NEXT MORNING: "WHITE HOUSE CONSULTANT LINKED TO BUGGING SUSPECTS."**

"Three days into the story," Executive Editor Ben Bradlee brags, "and we're already into the White House. **NOT BAD FOR THOSE TWO KIDS."**

City 861-0130
Phone RGD 6-17-72

Despite the break-in's shocking implications—that **NIXON'S RE-ELECTION WORKERS AND MAYBE EVEN WHITE HOUSE STAFF ARE ILLEGALLY SPYING ON HIS DEMOCRATIC OPPONENTS**—few other reporters latch onto the Watergate "caper." The country is preoccupied with Vietnam and the presidential race.

THE *POST*'S REPORTS ARE DENOUNCED AS FAKE, biased, a "witch hunt" designed to undermine Nixon's re-election. Its publisher, Katharine Graham, a homemaker who has only recently inherited control of her family's newspaper after her husband committed suicide, is threatened.

"KATIE GRAHAM'S GOING TO GET HER T-- CAUGHT IN A BIG FAT WRINGER IF YOU PRINT THAT," explodes John Mitchell when asked for comment on a Woodward/Bernstein report that he'd controlled secret funds for covert intelligence-gathering against Democrats while he was attorney general.

BUT GRAHAM HOLDS FAST—JUST AS SHE DID THE PREVIOUS YEAR WHEN THREATENED WITH JAIL TIME FOR PUBLISHING LEAKED, TOP SECRET PENTAGON PAPERS THAT REVEALED the Kennedy, Johnson, and Nixon administrations had all known the Vietnam War was unwinnable yet still sent Americans to fight and die.

WOODWARD AND BERNSTEIN—(OR "WOODSTEIN" AS EDITOR BRADLEE DUBS THEM)—CONTINUE REPORTING, INCLUDING:

(1) $89,000 was deposited into a Mexican bank account belonging to a Watergate burglar. Included was a $25,000 check—a donation to Nixon's re-election, made out to the campaign's Midwest finance chairman—that was diverted from CR(EE)P to the burglar, without that financer's knowledge.

(2) The FBI established that the break-in was part of calculated political sabotage aimed at the Democrats' leading presidential primary contenders. A year before the Watergate burglary even happened, a thirty-one-year-old lawyer, Donald Segretti—hired to work for Nixon's campaign by a college friend, Dwight Chapin, Nixon's appointment secretary—had been masterminding "dirty tricks" to undermine potential opponents. The stunts ranged from sophomoric pranks to more insidious disinformation, from setting off stink bombs at rallies to stealing candidates' stationery to fake damning letters about other Democrats. Like using stolen Senator Edmund Muskie letterhead, for instance, to forge and "leak" these lies: that one primary rival senator was employing call girls, another had fathered an illegitimate baby with a seventeen-year-old, and that Congresswoman Shirley Chisholm

"WOODSTEIN" KEEP DIGGING

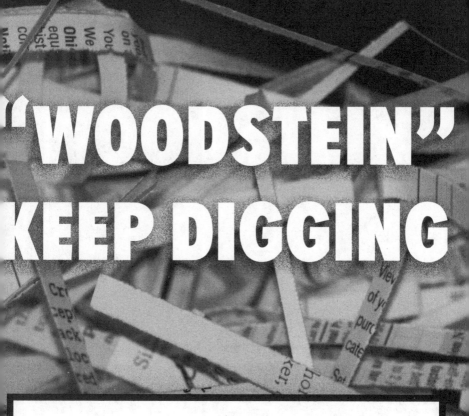

had been confined in a psychiatric hospital.

Once again, the trails lead straight to CR(EE)P and the White House, suggesting Nixon's people were involved in financing the break-in and okaying election misdeeds.

Nixon denies these reports as "absurd fiction." And according to polls, 57 percent of Americans believe Watergate is "just more politics," nothing "serious."

Nixon defeats McGovern in a historic landslide.

But, as Nixon prepares for his second inauguration, "Woodstein" keep digging, cross-referencing lists of White House and CR(EE)P workers, then knocking on their doors to ask questions. Many are secretaries, who confide that incriminating documents are being shredded. That former White House employees working at campaign headquarters knew all about the bugging. That large amounts of hush money are being paid out.

The reporters are stunned to learn federal investigators haven't interviewed these workers. When asked why not, one prosecutor responds, "Why are you believing those women?"

Such was the country's attitude about women's judgment—few states allowed women to serve on juries in 1972—that was igniting feminist demands for change.

FANNIE LOU HAMER

GLORIA STEINEM

WOMEN RISE UP:

ALITY OF RIGHTS UNDER THE LA
THE UNITED STATES OR B

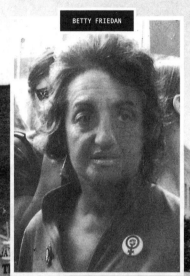

THE EQUAL RIGHTS AMENDMENT

MARCH 22, 1972: AFTER 43 YEARS OF WOMEN LOBBYING, THE U.S. SENATE VOTED OVERWHELMINGLY—84 TO 8—TO ADOPT THE ERA. Thirty-two minutes later, Hawai'i became the first of 38 states needed to ratify. The next day, Delaware and New Hampshire follow suit.

PREVIOUS SENATE VOTES HAD FAILED BECAUSE OF SOCIAL CONSERVATIVES like Sam Ervin, a North Carolina "Dixiecrat," who insisted the ERA "went against God's plan" and "would have serious impact upon the social structure of America."

That kind of sexist political obstruction convinced feminists that while changing public perceptions was vital, **IT WAS EVEN MORE CRUCIAL FOR WOMEN TO HOLD OFFICE. ONLY THEN COULD THEY WRITE LAWS TO BRING PERMANENT**, legally binding changes. In 1971, of 535 members of Congress, only twelve were women.

ACTIVISTS FROM BOTH PARTIES— INCLUDING DEMOCRATIC CONGRESSWOMAN BELLA ABZUG, REPUBLICAN SPEECHWRITER JILL RUCKELSHAUS, *MS.* MAGAZINE EDITOR GLORIA STEINEM, FEMINIST AUTHOR BETTY FRIEDAN, AND CIVIL RIGHTS ACTIVIST FANNIE LOU HAMER—FORMED THE NATIONAL WOMEN'S POLITICAL CAUCUS (NWPC). Its purpose: to teach women how to run for office at all levels.

Quickly organizing, wearing buttons proclaiming "Make Policy Not Coffee," caucus members gained enough delegate credentials to vote the ERA into both the Republican and Democratic 1972 party platforms. **DEMOCRATS ALSO PROMOTED THE LANDMARK PRESIDENTIAL BID BY CONGRESSWOMAN SHIRLEY CHISHOLM**.

Given their success at both conventions, the growing clout of the National Organization for Women (NOW), and the stunning popularity of the new feminist *Ms.* magazine, the equality of opportunity promised by the ERA's simple 40 words seemed to enjoy an unbeatable groundswell of support.

Within ten short months, **22 STATES RATIFY THE ERA**. Only sixteen more are needed.

As 1973 dawns, feminists are giddy with hope, predicting final ratification will take only two of the allotted seven years. Finally, American women would have universal protection of rights rather than having to undo discrimination state by state, one lawsuit at a time.

No one anticipates the backlash of anti-ERA suburban housewives that will be marshalled by an affluent Illinois mother of six named Phyllis Schlafly, who masterfully plays off their fears of becoming obsolete in a society rocked by the women's movement.

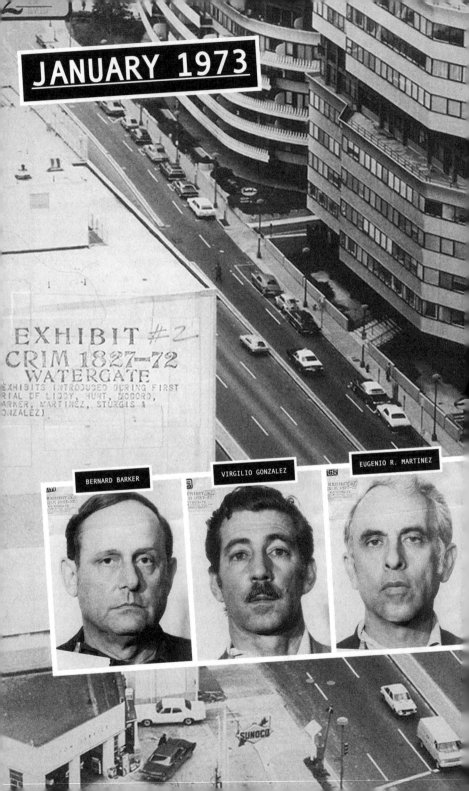

WATERGATE

THE SIXTEEN-DAY TRIAL of the Watergate burglars begins. **ALL PLEAD GUILTY** except their handlers Gordon Liddy and Howard Hunt, who nonetheless are also convicted of burglary, wiretapping, and conspiracy.

Chief Federal District Judge John Sirica presides. Despite overwhelming public opinion, Nixon's landslide re-election, and unwavering White House denials of any involvement in the scandal, **JUDGE SIRICA DOESN'T BELIEVE THE BUGGING WAS SOLELY THE IDEA OF THE BURGLARS** or overly zealous campaign aides. He chastises the prosecutors for not pushing harder to learn more about the higher-ups he suspects ordered and financed the break-in.

SIRICA POSTPONES SENTENCING for eight weeks until late March, giving the defendants time to stew and consider his offer that they can lessen what he implies will be very long jail time if they will be more forthcoming and name others Sirica is convinced are involved.

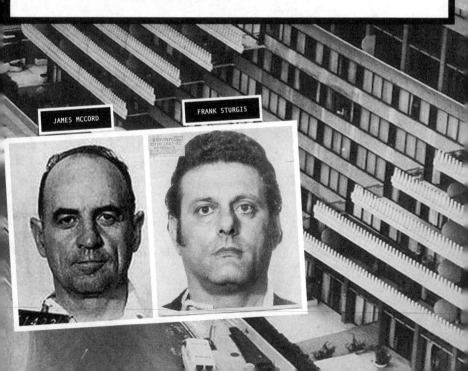

JAMES MCCORD   FRANK STURGIS

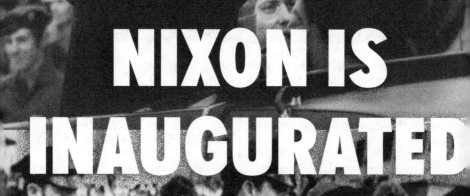

NIXON IS INAUGURATED

NIXON IS INAUGURATED FOR HIS SECOND TERM. His parade is interrupted by anti–Vietnam War protesters throwing vegetables at his motorcade and chanting, "Nixon, you liar, sign the cease-fire."

When treaty negotiations with the North Vietnamese collapsed in early December, **NIXON ORDERED ONE OF THE MOST CONCENTRATED BOMBINGS** in world history—decried by critics around the globe as barbaric. But by the end of January, Nixon's administration will reach a tenable peace agreement. Finally, **AMERICANS WILL NO LONGER BE SENT TO FIGHT IN VIETNAM**.

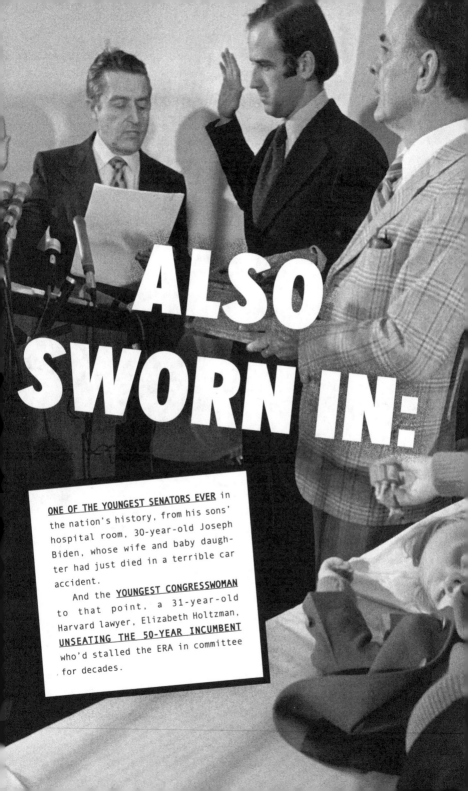

CHAPTER ONE

JANUARY

She'd give just about anything for that boy's socks. What was his name? Patty glanced at the teenager sitting to her left and smiled.

He grinned back. It was a good smile—big like his voice was loud, honest, the corners of his mouth disappearing into those ridiculous, curly sideburns he kept stroking.

Abe. That was it.

Embarrassed that she was wondering how big a smile she'd have to bless him with to get those socks, Patty abruptly turned back toward the parade route. When the heck would things get rolling? She tried to wriggle her toes that prickled sharply from the cold. Were they actually moving? Or had they frozen into immobile chunks of flesh?

Don't be so melodramatic. One of her parents' favorite reprimands filled Patty's mind.

Patty looked down at the black patent-leather go-go boots Simone had lent her the night before. As if the thin, slick-shiny plastic was any kind of protection against winter temperatures. Her godmother's daughter had meant well, of course. Her attempt at the friendship being forced on them. Or maybe it was pity at Patty's mother insisting she wear L'eggs pantyhose instead of the cream-colored, cable-knit, knee-sock-warm tights Simone had offered. They were very hip—like the type Twiggy wore under her miniskirts in fashion magazines. Patty had almost drooled over them.

"Certainly not. Ladies wear stockings—especially to important ceremonies," Patty's mom said as she looped the last loose strand of Patty's dark hair around a pink curler and thrust a bobby pin into it to hold her hair taut, so tight her scalp throbbed and ached. "Tomorrow, nothing but ladylike deportment. Make your father proud." Then she'd doused Patty in a fog of Final Net hairspray, adding, "And remember—pretty is as pretty does." The gospel according to Dot Appleton.

Easy enough for her mother to say, Patty had fumed. Because her father was a high-profile Republican fundraiser for Nixon's campaign, her parents had been invited to the glassed-in VIP reviewing stand to watch the inaugural parade. Where her mother could easily back her slim, meticulously maintained size-four tush up to a heater.

Another blast of wind gushed up Patty's A-line skirt to her girdle, saturating her own butt in icy cold. She clamped her teeth against their chattering in the ripple of shivers that followed. She should have sat on a lower rung of the metal bleachers, where these constant frigid gales would have been less likely to storm straight to her underwear. But this is where other congressional pages had wanted to sit, so they could better view the horse cavalries, marching bands, and floats passing along Pennsylvania Avenue toward the White House.

She'd just joined their ranks the previous week. Most of the teenage pages had been working the floor of the Senate and the House since September, coinciding with the school year. She figured sitting among them to watch the parade was a good way to meet more of her fellow pages quickly.

Patty looked back to Abe. Bet his socks were wool, thick, cozy. But what she *really* wanted—after that last wind gust—were his corduroy pants.

Abe frowned. "You okay?"

Oh God, caught lusting after slacks. If only nice girls could wear them and still be considered "nice." Patty forced the bright smile she'd flashed at countless cocktail parties her parents hosted. "Oh yes, just excited. I feel like I'm part of history!"

Squinting a little, Abe cocked his head in a *really?* expression. So, he was the cynical type. Or pretended to be. Surely he wouldn't give up the usual all-American adolescence to be a page, working ridiculous hours to run notes back and forth from the Senate floor to congressional offices in service to his country if he was truly some Doubting Thomas.

But Patty adjusted her wide-eyed patriotism accordingly, trained to shift, chameleon-like, to reflect the hues of opinion of people around her, especially those of boys. "Maybe not part of it exactly. A *witness* to history." She paused. "My godmother's daughter is actually in the parade, though. She's the one I'll be spending my weekends with—in Old Town Alexandria. My parents didn't want me in D.C., unchaperoned at my residence hall, when Congress wasn't in session. Her high school marching band has been mixed in with a bunch of other local schools to create a band of 1,776 players. To match the theme for today's parade. You know, the spirit of 1776."

Abe snorted. "Leave it to Tricky Dick to exploit the feel-good imagery of a bicentennial that's not even happening until three years from now," he muttered. "Given Watergate, I wonder how George Washington—Mr. I-Cannot-Tell-a-Lie—would feel about Richard Nixon being sworn in again as president."

"Hey now," the boy sitting on Patty's other side said, leaning forward to speak around her toward Abe. Friendly, earnest. "Don't be badmouthing Mr. Nixon. Not today, roomie. Today's sacred! When our government resets in a peaceful transition of power. Accepting the vote, the will of the people, even if our guy loses. That's democracy!" He grinned. "Besides, it's clear the president didn't know anything about the break-in. It was just a bunch of overly enthusiastic campaign knuckleheads."

Abe shook his head in mock sorrow at what he clearly viewed as his friend's naivete. "The whole thing reeks of dirty tricks, buddy. The more they dig, the more they're going to find, mark my words," he concluded.

"But . . . but he's saying precisely what my father does," Patty surprised herself by jumping in. "That there's no way President Nixon can know of everything going on during a campaign. Too many workers all over the country. Daddy handled contributions from hundreds of people in Illinois, Kansas, Missouri—way too many to keep track of."

"That's right. Listen to the lady," the boy beside her spoke in a soft drawl. Like Abe's slightly brassy northeastern accent, his friend's southern intonation was another distinctly regional way of speaking Patty had never heard in person before, growing up in the Midwest. "Don't forget, the indictments stopped with the five burglars."

"And their two wacko handlers," Abe countered. "Calling themselves anticommunists. Seriously? Some are ex-CIA. Experts in lying and hiding things. Doesn't that tell you something? Plus, a couple had direct ties to the White House. Don't you read the *Washington Post*?"

"Naw," said the boy with a mischievous grin. "Vice President Agnew calls those reporters 'nattering nabobs of negativism.' I go for the *Evening Star*."

Abe rolled his eyes. "Well, I've obviously got my work cut out with you."

"And I with you," the boy answered good-naturedly. He elbowed Patty. "I pray for his sorry atheist soul all the time. I'll get him before we graduate." He extended his hand. "I'm sorry, I haven't introduced myself. I'm a House floor page—"

Abe interrupted, "The lesser chamber to yours and mine—"

"—Will Ferguson. And that depends on how you look at things," he tossed back at Abe.

Patty shook his hand, marveling at the boys' amiable banter when clearly they had serious political disagreement. In her parents' house, only one line of thought was allowed—Nixon's—and Americans who questioned the president were savaged as being radical Left, lily-livered commie-lovers. "Patty. Patty Appleton." Oh, how his wool mittens hugged the thin kid leather of her gloves in warmth.

"Golly. You're shaking. Here." Will pulled an emerald-colored scarf off his neck that took some time to dredge up entirely out of his peacoat. "My mama knit it for me, worrying Washington, D.C., was as cold as the North Pole or something. I tried to tell her the weather wouldn't be all that different from North Carolina. Today is an exception. WMAL radio says the windchill's yanked us down to twenty degrees."

Without worrying about propriety—or what her hometown boyfriend would say about her wearing some other guy's clothes—Patty grabbed the lovingly crocheted scarf and wrapped it around and around and around her thighs. It was long enough to reach below her knees. "Thank you sooooo much." Feeling her shudders subside, she sighed contentedly.

"I teased Mama that thing made me look like Linus carrying around his blanket, she made it so long." Will pushed up his collar to cover his throat, now sans woolen muffler, momentarily revealing on one wrist a nickel-plated POW bracelet, engraved with the name and capture date of an American prisoner of war. "She didn't want me to leave home. Fourth son—baby of the family and all." He paused. "But now I can tell her she made it just the right length to rescue a damsel in distress and help me look like Lancelot or something."

"Ha! You wish!" Abe reached around and swatted Will on the back.

Precisely Patty's thought. She needed no rescuing, but she reflexively looked up into Will's face and murmured—in jest, mostly, "Thank you for your kindness, good sir."

Will beamed. He did have dreamboat big blue eyes.

Now that her teeth were no longer chattering, Patty started to ask Will if his POW bracelet honored someone he knew. Back home, a few of her classmates had purchased and worn the thin metal cuffs as a way of supporting awareness of American soldiers imprisoned by the Viet Cong. None of them actually knew young men who'd been drafted. Their brothers and beaus were college boys. Safely deferred. But the parade interrupted Patty asced the first military band passed Sixth Street down by the National Archives and came into view.

"Finally!" the three of them exhaled. En masse, all the pages around her leaned forward and craned their heads toward the domed Capitol, where the swearing-in had taken place and the parade route began. The metal bleachers groaned a bit with their simultaneous shift.

"What took them so long to start?" a page in front of Patty grumbled.

"Antiwar protesters," said another, who moments before had jogged up to the bleachers to push his way into the next row down. "Dressed in shrouds, carrying fake coffins and signs calling Nixon a killer. Police had to clear them out before the motorcade could roll. Some even threw rocks at the Secret Service."

The page whistled. "Wow. That took nerve." Then he cursed, putting his hand to his mouth. "Dammit. Cracked open my chapped lips. This wind is murder."

Reaching into her coat pocket with one hand, Patty tapped the teen on his shoulder with her other. "Take my ChapStick. It's fresh. I haven't used it yet. Hope you don't mind it tasting like cherry."

"Thanks!" The boy took the tube gratefully and rubbed his lips with the ointment, leaving a ring of ruby atop the baby-fine hair trying to sprout into a mustache. He held it back toward her.

"Keep it," she answered. "I'm more a Lip Smacker girl."

At that, the entire row of boys turned around to look up at her.

"It's . . . it's a new lip balm." *For pity's sake, Patty.* She'd need to get used to being around so many boys, who might misinterpret brand names and references that other girls would immediately know. The cloistered, social narrowness of her all-girl Illinois prep school was suddenly showing.

Sousa's *Semper Fidelis* saved her.

"Marines!" Will abruptly stood, respectful, solemn.

"All three of his brothers are marines, deployed in Vietnam," Abe explained in a quiet aside to her. "One MIA, one still fighting, one held prisoner in the 'Hanoi Hilton,' going on a year now. Pretty tough on Will."

Patty glanced up, thinking she should say something. But if Will heard his friend, he acted like he didn't.

The band drew closer, their drumbeat beginning to echo through the metal stands.

Even over the approaching cymbals keeping the 4/4 beat, the trumpets and trombones, the drums, Patty could hear one of the guys lean over to the teen with the chapped lips to snicker, "Wonder what else she has hidden in her coat that tastes like cherry."

Patty had been what her mother called an early bloomer. By fourteen, she'd already developed, rounding and filling out in womanly curves. Over the last four years, she'd grown accustomed to the sideways glances from boys (and their fathers) at the country club, the stupid but comparatively innocuous comments about mountain ranges coming from guys thinking they were simply flirting, the uninvited wolf whistles on the street when she and her mother went shopping in Springfield.

But this boy's comment was so . . . so gross. And so . . . overt. Her face flamed red in fury and in an additional sensibility she didn't know how to completely describe. Disgust? Fear? Sullied, for sure. Searingly self-conscious. Thank God neither Will nor Abe seemed to have heard it. She didn't want them thinking she invited such "repartee." They seemed gentlemanly—like they could be friends. Patty pretended the offensive innuendo hadn't happened.

That she was invisible.

Of course, that didn't work for long.

Notebook in hand, a newspaper reporter was wading through the pages, asking their feelings—as young Americans—about the inauguration.

"*New York Times* guy," Abe announced. "I recognize him. He's always hanging around in the halls, buttonholing senators' staff." He waved and called out, "Wanna talk to the home team?" He pointed at himself and gave a thumbs-up.

But the journalist approached Patty instead. "Hey, miss! You're one of those new girl pages, aren't you? What's that like?"

Again, a sea of teenage boys turned to eye her, their noses red from the cold.

Patty felt her heart bang fast in her chest at being singled out. Automatically, she used phraseology her mother had coached her to say: "Oh, it's a great honor. I'm just thrilled and grateful to be here."

"There's only a handful of you, right?" the reporter pressed.

"Yes, sir."

"And none yet in the House?"

She nodded. "No, sir. I mean yes. I mean . . . you are correct. No female pages in the House yet. Just boys on that side of the Hill."

The reporter waited, his pen held to the paper. His eyebrows shot up in an unspoken *anything else?*

Patty smiled demurely and remained silent. She'd learned that from her mother, too. Dot Appleton at her doctor-husband's side always, her delicate hand tucked into the crook of his arm, as he fielded overtures from wannabe buddies while wooing Republican donors at countless receptions.

The reporter waited hopefully for a few more beats before he gave up and turned to the boys surrounding Patty. "So . . . What do you guys think about having girls around?"

"Swell!"

"Great to see their pretty smiles in the morning—better than a cup of coffee."

"They'll keep us civilized—less farting!" A roar of laughter.

Chortling, the writer jotted down their answers. Then he looked back up at Patty and considered her for several beats before he pushed with, "A bunch of senators really fought having girl pages. Thought you couldn't carry heavy reports. That sitting on the rostrum's steps would make girls look undignified. That your presence would wreck the easy congeniality between senators and pages because they'd have to censor any off-color language. Hell, they even had a two-hour debate about what girl pages would wear, worrying you might choose distracting outfits. A lot are still annoyed that you're breaking two centuries' worth of tradition.

"So, how do you feel about being a pioneer? A symbol for the women's movement, for female liberation?"

"Oh. Oh my gosh. I'm not some big libber," Patty blurted. Her mind filled with all the derisive comments her psychiatrist-father had made about no one liking libbers or how "hard on the eye" most feminists were. "Except that Gloria Steinem," he'd say. "Something must be wrong with her, something we can't see, that she's not married. A repressed something. After all, she's certainly got the looks. She's probably a closet . . ." and at that her father would trail off, as if *lesbian* was a dirty word or a term Patty—at almost eighteen years old—didn't know.

The reporter didn't move, just waited.

Taking a deep breath, Patty tried to say something articulate. "I haven't experienced any discrimination or sexism." But she paused, suddenly thinking of her first day in Washington when one of the guy pages sent her to retrieve the *Congressional Record player*. She felt herself flush once again with embarrassment, remembering the senators' guffaws when she'd appeared at their cloakroom doorway to ask for it, and was told the *Congressional Record* was the official printed transcript of a day's debates and proceedings. That had just been a prank, though, one the more senior pages put every newbie through, female or male. Wasn't it?

The boys continued staring at Patty in expectation of her saying something else. Catching the eye of the teen who'd made the vulgar joke moments before, Patty felt her face turn even redder. Come to think of it, she hadn't experienced really blatant sexism, the kind that made her this embarrassed, this uncomfortable, until now. Even so, she bit her lip, fretting under her breath, "It's not as if I'm some bra burner."

But the reporter heard her. Brightening, he scribbled fast at that last sentence. "Great. Thanks, miss." He swam back down through the boy pages, some of them whispering and looking at Patty over their shoulders.

Sugar! she exploded inside.

That would be her quote—about bra burning, which naturally piqued the imagined image (and salacious, off-color comments) of bared or mostly visible breasts—because of course it would be. In the *New York Times*!

Pretty is as pretty does? *What will Mother say?* She knew Dot Appleton adhered to the adage that a lady appeared in newsprint only five times in her life: at her birth, debut, marriage, child-birthing, and death. Patty caught her breath. And Daddy. Oh God. *Daddy.*

Shooting to her feet, she furiously unwrapped her legs and handed Will's scarf back to him without looking at him directly. Burning with mortification, Patty was anything but cold now. "I promised Simone to take a photograph of her band. She's going to be in the back, with a hundred piccolos and flutes. I think I'll be able to spot her better from the sidewalk."

Murmuring, "Excuse me. Excuse me, please. So sorry. Excuse me," she carefully picked her way through the boys and fled the bleachers.

"You . . . said . . . what?"

Dot Appleton put down the Belleek teacup from which she was sipping the next day with a loud *clink*. A tiny slosh of coffee spilled over the wafer-thin rim into the shamrock-painted saucer. Her hand trembled. It had been doing that a lot recently, ruining the watercolor notecards she painted.

Despite obvious annoyance, however, her tone remained quiet. Patty's mother never raised her voice. Not that Patty had witnessed anyway. Ever. When Dot Appleton was angry, that silky-smooth voice of hers simply grew terrifyingly icy and soft. So soft, in fact, the person who had offended her had to lean in close to hear her words. More than once Patty had wondered if that was how spiders lured flies into a web.

"I . . . I said . . . that I wasn't some kind of bra burner," Patty squeaked. "It just came out, Mother. I'm sorry."

They were sitting in Sunday-morning sunbeams in her godparents' kitchen. Patty would be staying with them—her "Aunt Marjorie" and "Uncle Graham," and their daughter, Simone, the owner of the mod Twiggy tights—for her year of paging. Her own parents had stayed over for the inauguration. Aunt Marjorie was at the kitchen sink, whisking eggs in a bowl, prepping them to scramble as she gazed out into a courtyard garden asleep for the winter. Bacon sizzled on the stove. Leaning over the counter, Simone was reading the *Washington Post*, its sections spread out in a horrendous mess.

Simone and Aunt Marjorie both wore flannel pajamas and fluffy slippers, their matching honey-blond hair yanked up in sloppy ponytails—which Patty found shocking. She'd never seen her own mother in a robe past her parents' bedroom doorway. But maybe it was because both dads—hers and Simone's—were still snoring upstairs. Patty's father had evidently had a little too much Chivas Regal at the inaugural ball. And Uncle Graham had pulled a week of near all-nighters prepping for a court case for the IRS, where he was a prosecutor.

Her mother didn't respond to her apology, just continued to stare down Patty, the corner of her left eyebrow shooting up at an angle as steep as a playground slide.

Patty squirmed.

Still whisking, Aunt Marjorie turned around, leaned her backside against the sink, and said after a sympathetic laugh, "Sounds like the reporter caught you unawares, sugar. My friend Jill says they like to do that—startle you into giving them a good . . . what was the term she used?" Aunt Marjorie trailed off for a moment. "Oh! a sound bite. A catchy quote readers or listeners will remember. She and the other caucus members are trying to learn to speak in them."

"Something readers will remember?" Patty's mother repeated sarcastically. "*Precisely*. Now you're labeled as a girl who'll discuss women's unmentionables in print. It's so . . . unbecoming. Couldn't you think of something nice to say? Like how beautiful the Capitol is?"

"Oh, Dottie, *pshaw*, we certainly talked about underwear when we were at Wellesley. At least I know I did. 'Cause I always envied yours." Aunt Marjorie winked at Patty in a theatrical aside. "Pink and lacy. Always." She put down the bowl of eggs and turned the bacon.

"Marj! For pity's sake!"

"Your mama was my guide to all things feminine and chic," Aunt Marjorie continued in affectionate teasing of Patty's mother. "Helped me buy my first push-up bra, as a matter of fact. Shooed away that hovering saleslady at Filene's who was embarrassing me so much, and showed me how to lean over so that I plopped properly into the cups to fill them up after latching the back. Of course, I don't have your mama's lovely figure, so all I did was slide right out. Now your mama, she—"

"Marjorie, whatever you're going to say next, just stop!" To Patty's amazement, her mother actually laughed. "You were absolutely hopeless with clothes."

"That I was."

"Until you came back from Paris—then you were far more sophisticated than I could have ever hoped to be. Those hats!"

Aunt Marjorie pulled the last piece of bacon out of the skillet and sighed dreamily. "That year abroad was such a revelation. I wish you'd come, Dottie. You'd have fit right in with those sidewalk artists of the Montmartre."

Patty realized her mouth had been hanging open during the women's exchange and snapped it shut. The college-aged Dot

Appleton her godmother described was a total stranger to her. And she'd never before seen her mother happily joking around or so at ease with another woman.

"Besides," Aunt Marjorie added as she poured the eggs into the skillet and started stirring, "aren't you proud? Patty *is* a trailblazer. It's so exciting what she's doing. Jill says that we will never get real change for women until we have more of us holding office ourselves—not just activating the phone tree or sticking stamps on envelopes for male candidates. Right now, of the nation's five hundred and thirty-five senators and representatives, only sixteen are women. It's so small a number I can't even calculate what infinitesimal percentage that would be.

"But just think. Patty's having an experience that before was only granted boys. Watching Congress work firsthand is perfect training for running for office herself one day." She smiled encouragingly at Patty.

"Oh, gosh, I would never presume I—" Patty started to say she'd never be confident enough to run for office herself, but her mother cut her off.

"Good Lord, Marj, don't be putting that idea into her head. Politics are so cutthroat. Maybe her husband one day." She paused. "As a matter of fact, we all have an eye on her beau, Scott. Very promising and articulate young man." Her voice turned singsong, like a mother trying to coax a toddler to walk: "If things go well, he and Patty could be the Republican answer to Kennedy and Jackie one day."

Sitting up straighter at the compliment, Patty noticed Simone shoot a quizzical look her way. Patty ignored it. Instead, she smiled at her mother, hoping to prompt more positive appraisal. But Dot Appleton didn't seem to notice. She stood to pour herself more coffee from the percolator and then opened a monogrammed gold pillbox, taking out and swallowing, one after another, a green, a yellow, a pink, and finally a white tablet. Patty made note that the little white pill was a new addition to her mother's regimen.

"Who is this Jill whose opinion you put so much stock in anyway, Marj?" she asked with her more characteristic coolness.

"Oh, you'd looooove her. Her name's Jill Ruckelshaus. Her husband is head of that new EPA, *but* she's a Republican speechwriter herself, *and* a part-time special assistant in the White House office of women's programs, *and* a co-founder of the National Women's Political Caucus. *And* a mother of five!" Patty's godmother elongated the coordinating conjunctions into breathy two-syllable words.

"I met her last spring because my neighbor's car broke down and she was desperate to get to a caucus meeting she didn't want to miss. We'd carpooled our boys to Saint Stephen's, and I owed her a thousand favors from those days. So, I gave her a lift. Then she convinced me to come into the house and listen to what these ladies had to say. They were strategizing about going to the nominating convention in Miami to argue for things like support for the ERA being included on the Republican Party platform. It . . . was . . . *absolutely* electrifying!"

She paused for a moment to catch her breath. Patty's mother had forewarned her—with considerable impatience—that "your godmother has that infuriating, Faulknerian habit of going on and on with a story." But Patty was actually finding her monologue kind of charming. She swallowed a little laugh as Aunt Marjorie launched into another burble of enthusiastic detail.

"They're all sharp as tacks. And it's truly bipartisan—not some left-wing, hippie-dippie group. The Democrats do outnumber us considerably, but the caucus is working to recruit women of both parties to run for all kinds of office—from Congress to state legislatures to school boards. I've gotten to meet women like Anne Armstrong—Nixon's one and only woman *White House* counselor! Oh! And Betty Friedan." Aunt Marjorie took in a deep breath and whispered conspiratorially, "Friedan is wonderfully . . . shockingly outrageous, Dottie. You should hear her!"

"The woman who wrote the *Feminine Mystique*? Marj! She's such a radical!"

"You mean the feminine *mistake*, don't you?" A disapproving baritone voice interrupted from the dining room door as Patty's father entered. "That woman is responsible for half my female patients, housewives weeping on my couch, saying Friedan opened their eyes to their feeling so unfulfilled. Honestly, those gals were perfectly fine until they read that troublemaking scree. Friedan's like the Typhoid Mary of neurosis." He sat down at the table while running his hand through his salt and pepper hair, his head clearly pounding. He looked to Patty's mother. "Coffee, please, dear."

Hastily, Patty's mom filled a teacup, dumped and stirred a heaping teaspoon of sugar into it, and placed it in front of her husband. Aunt Marjorie went silent and scooped a large portion of scrambled eggs onto a plate, adding bacon and buttered toast before setting it down in front of him. Then she served considerably smaller portions to the rest of them. "Breakfast is ready, girls. Simone, put down the paper now, honey. What are you looking so hard for anyway?"

Folding the newspaper into a semi-tidy pile, Simone brushed back her curtain bangs, leaving a smear of newsprint ink on her forehead. "I wanted to see the write-up of the parade. They didn't mention us at all. You'd think they'd feature local kids who froze their bottoms off to march in it."

"I would think the honor of participating in something like a presidential inauguration was reward enough for any young lady," Dr. Appleton announced through his first bite of bacon. "Outside validation is ephemeral, after all."

Patty squirmed, embarrassed for Simone—a familiar feeling she'd had countless times when her friends unwittingly walked into the gristmill of her father's psychoanalysis. Plus, her gut-punch worry he'd think less of her for associating with them.

"I'm sure in the end you'll find it well worth those few hours of discomfort—a wonderful memory to tell your children someday," Dr. Appleton concluded as he scooped up a heap of scrambled eggs. No question. Presumed fact.

Instinctively, Patty shook her head at Simone, trying to warn her off from answering.

But Simone hesitated only a moment—first twisting an oval, color-changing mood ring around her right hand's pointer finger, then adjusting a peace-sign pinkie ring on her left—before she replied. "Actually, what I found it to be was glacial—in temperature and timing. They made us get out of our buses an hour before the inauguration even began. The wind was so awful, the majorettes were turning blue in those sequined bathing suit uniforms they wear."

"Poor things," Aunt Marjorie sympathized.

Simone smiled at her. "I thought about what you might do, Mom. Bundle them up, right? For once that felt like a good idea and not an annoying one!"

"Goodness, imagine that!" her mother teased back.

Simone laughed.

Patty stared at them, astonished that Aunt Marjorie hadn't flattened her daughter for insolence, as Simone continued, "Elsie and I got the whole band to cluster tight around them, to shield them from the wind, and warm them up—a little anyway."

"That was . . . resourceful," Dr. Appleton commented, just

the slightest touch of acerbic on the adjective, a tone that always made Patty wonder if he truly meant his compliment.

Simone nibbled her toast and considered him a moment, clearly planning what she was going to say next. And it looked to be sassy, given the growing defiance on her face. *Did this girl have a death wish?* Patty wondered.

"When we were finally ordered to fall in, after huddling together like that for an hour, I could barely hold my piccolo, I was shivering so much. And I had on long johns under my uniform! We were all way out of tune from the cold. And shrill? Oh my God. I swear my ears are still ringing from marching in a merged piccolo section from the dozen or so high schools it took to reach that total 1,776 body count. With that many players, the band stretched over three blocks. We were totally out of sync from section to section. The whole concept was ridiculous." She pushed aside her plate, concluding, "Another egomaniac move on the Dickster's part."

Sitting back, eyeing Simone carefully, Dr. Appleton smirked. "Quite the outspoken daughter you have there, Marjorie. Guess the apple doesn't fall far from the tree."

Patty's mother turned ashen.

And Patty realized, for the first time, the probable reason she had seen so little of her godmother before now.

Pressing her lips together slightly, Aunt Marjorie cast a reassuring glance at Patty's mother, then turned back to Dr. Appleton. "Yes, isn't Simone delightfully opinionated?" she warbled. "That's how she held her own, growing up with twin brothers just thirteen months older. And Graham and I encourage it. She's smarter than the two of us put together. Reads everything under the sun. She has a lot to say." She reached over to cup Simone's chin with her hand and added with fondness but also a tad of chastisement in her voice, "As long as she says it respectfully. We wouldn't want to come across as rude or strident, now, would we, sugar?"

Simone forced a made-for-show smile before standing and taking her plate to the kitchen sink. "Hey Patty, wanna come to my room to listen to a new album I just got? The Allman Brothers—I think you'll dig 'em. Word is they're coming to D.C. this summer for a big concert with the Grateful Dead. I'm not that into the Dead, but I love the brothers' 'Ramblin' Man.' I can't wait to see them live!"

Glad to retreat from the kitchen's palpable tension, Patty nodded and hurriedly finished her eggs. She had no idea who the Allman Brothers were, and she certainly wasn't a fan of the LSD-dropping Grateful Dead—her favorite singers were the Carpenters brother-sister duo and Donny Osmond. But she'd listen to just about anything at that point to escape the situation. Her father was definitely in one of his more critical moods. She could anticipate what might come next—his warning her in front of everybody, *Don't be picking up bad habits, princess.*

Meaning Simone.

"Sure, I'd love to," Patty chirped, popping out of her chair and clearing her place.

Still rinsing her plate at the sink, Simone added, "By the way, Mom, that percentage you were trying to think of, of women to men in the Senate and House. Women would calculate to being just 2.99 percent of all Congress members.

"And Aunt Dottie, fun fact: Bra burning is a myth, according to *Ms.* magazine. A lie that guy reporters concocted when they covered the feminist protest of the Miss America contest and saw demonstrators throwing symbols of female objectification into trash cans. You know—girdles, bras, garter belts. Nobody lit a fire in those cans. It's all hype to make feminists seem like dangerous, chest-beating, warrior-women." She shrugged. "Just saying. Come on, Patty."

Turning on her heel, Simone marched toward the staircase. Patty scurried to keep up, before anything else bra related could slip out, alerting her father to her impending *New York Times* quote. From the way she talked, Simone could be one of those flower-child girls refusing to wear a bra at all. God alone knew what might come out of her mouth next.

What did shocked Patty even more.

As Simone climbed three flights of narrow stairs in her family's nineteenth-century row house, she talked over her shoulder to Patty. "I just read a column in *Esquire* by Nora Ephron—do you know her? She's outta sight."

Patty shook her head no. "Isn't *Esquire* a magazine for men?"

"My brothers subscribe. It still comes here rather than to their college dorms. Anyway, Ephron writes about what it's like to be a woman. Pretty daring stuff. There's one titled 'A Few Words About Breasts.' In a magazine *for guys*. So, you really shouldn't be queasy about being quoted as saying 'bra burning.' That's nothing. We need to stop being so timid!

"Ephron described how traumatizing it was for her to be flat-chested. Like me." Simone gestured to her own waifish figure. "How she was told that men wouldn't fall in love with her, that she'd have sexual problems, be frigid, and definitely was less of a woman than girls with nice big breasts." She glanced back at Patty, in an unspoken *like you*. "She did dumb stuff like only sleeping on her back so she wouldn't impede her boobs growing. And splashing cold water on them every night because some busty French actress told *Life* magazine that's what she did to get her perfect C-cup bustline."

They reached the top floor. "Ephron says the size of our breasts and whether or not we wear makeup—and the cultural conditioning surrounding that garbage—puts up terrible walls between us women."

Patty blinked, feeling the weight, minuscule as it was, of mascara on her eyelashes as Simone threw open the door to her bedroom. Inside, the walls were crowded with artwork. A fist inside the female symbol's circle. A "Janis Joplin, Live in Concert" poster written in psychedelic bubble lettering. An enormous photo of a wild-haired flutist gyrating on stage with some band called Jethro Tull.

How was Patty supposed to survive twelve months of weekends in this household that was so different from hers, with this brazenly outspoken, know-it-all girl—who was about as foreign to her as a Martian—without either alienating her hosts or annoying her parents? Patty becoming a Senate page had been her father's idea. He'd lobbied his contacts hard for her to receive that congressional sponsorship. Patty getting it was a real feather in the family's cap, he'd said. It would break her heart to disappoint—or, God forbid, embarrass—him now.

WATERGATE

FEBRUARY 7: ALARMED BY GROWING EVIDENCE that the Watergate break-in was not an isolated mistake but part of a larger, coordinated election interference effort, **THE SENATE VOTES 77 TO 0** to create a Select Committee to **INVESTIGATE THE ACTIVITIES OF NIXON'S PRESIDENTIAL CAMPAIGN**.

WOMEN UNITE

JILL RUCKELSHAUS

THE NATIONAL WOMEN'S POLITICAL CAUCUS (NWPC) holds its first convention. The caucus had hoped for 800 attendees—instead **2,000 WOMEN** come, hungry to lobby for equalizing their rights: Republicans in A-line skirts, kitten pumps, and pearls, and Democrats in jeans, sandals, and halter tops. Houston's Rice Hotel is overrun, compounding problems by at first refusing to page attendees, its management claiming that **RESPECTABLE WOMEN DON'T** receive calls in hotel lobbies.

"THE QUESTION WAS COULD ISSUES ABOUT EQUALITY AND FAIRNESS TRANSCEND POLITICAL PARTISANSHIP," says Jill Ruckelshaus, White House liaison for women's groups.

It did.

From then on, the NWPC answers questions at press conferences in pairs—**ONE DEMOCRAT AND ONE REPUBLICAN**.

NOW & THE ERA

Minnesota, South Dakota, Oregon, and New Mexico ratify the ERA—bringing the total to 27 of the 38 states needed.

A few days after NWPC's assembly, the **NATIONAL ORGANIZATION FOR WOMEN (NOW)** holds its own conference in Washington, D.C., adopting policy statements on **POVERTY, SEXISM IN SPORTS**, the **CIVIL RIGHTS OF LESBIANS**, developmental **CHILDCARE** programs, and raising the **MINIMUM WAGE TO $2.50** an hour. The attendees also propose setting up a **TASK FORCE ON RAPE** to educate the legal system and the public that it is an act of violence, not sex.

Attendees of the NOW conference discuss with alarm the **GROWING OPPOSITION OF SUBURBAN HOUSEWIVES** led by conservative activist **PHYLLIS SCHLAFLY**. A self-published, bestselling author, mother of six, with a master's degree in government from Radcliffe, Schlafly had run for Congress in her Illinois district three times (1952, 1960, and 1970) and lost three times. She took up her campaign against the ERA in 1972, turning feminism into a polarizing political issue about gender roles. Schlafly **PREACHES THAT THE ERA WILL MEAN HUSBANDS WILL NO LONGER BE EXPECTED TO BE A FAMILY'S "BREADWINNER"** or to "provide physical protection." The movement's slogan: **STOP ERA (STOP-TAKING-OUR-PRIVILEGES)**. "American women never had it so good," she says. "Why should we lower ourselves to 'equal rights' when we already have the status of special privilege?"

WOMEN IN FLIGHT

FRONTIER AIRLINES 2ND OFFICER EMILY HOWELL becomes the **FIRST FEMALE PILOT** employed by a commercial airline, in notable contrast to the industry's **TREATMENT OF STEWARDESSES** as "sky bunnies," **DRESSING THEM IN HOT PANTS AND GO-GO BOOTS, REQUIRING THEY BE A CERTAIN WEIGHT, AGE, AND SINGLE**. One airline requires its hostesses to **KISS MALE PASSENGERS ON THE CHEEK** as they get off the plane. Another runs ads featuring pretty flight attendants with suggestive double-entendre taglines like: "I'm Cheryl. Fly me." Some stewardesses begin to organize to **PROTEST BEING MARKETED AS "SEX OBJECTS,"** saying that when employers and the public don't "consider you a professional, you don't think of yourself as one." A dangerous presumption, they add, when in an emergency stewardesses "urgently need the respect, confidence, and cooperation" of passengers.

CHAPTER TWO

FEBRUARY

"Please don't be late, boys."

Patty stared out from behind the glass doors of Thompson-Markward Hall—the Young Woman's Christian Home where she lived during the week—into the 5:30 a.m. gloom, searching for Abe and Will. She patted the pouf of her partial updo and the tight ringlets framing her face, worrying she hadn't used enough Dippity-Do the night before to hold them all day. Exhausted after running miles of errands through the tunnels connecting the Senate chamber and the members' offices, she'd rushed through the nightly task of coating strands of her naturally straight hair with the emerald-green gel before rolling them.

She hadn't slept well either. The twin mattress of her neat but rather Spartan single room was lumpy, the pillow definitely not the soft goose down she was used to. Resting against its unyielding puff, her curlers had pressed hard against her head, poking and jolting Patty awake throughout the night.

Yawning, she checked her wristwatch again, getting antsy. Patty couldn't just head to school on her own. She and her parents had signed an agreement that she would never walk around Capitol Hill in the dark—even the mere two blocks to the Library of Congress, where the Page School's classes were held—without being escorted by male peers. The boy pages—even those as young and vulnerable as fourteen—had no such restriction.

Patty hadn't balked at the double standard, though. For one thing she'd grown up in quiet suburbs and was more than a little unnerved by D.C.'s city streets. Fears about crime and the city's safety in general were running especially high in the past few days after a seventy-one-year-old senator, John Stennis, was gunned down in front of his home, at suppertime, and in a "good neighborhood," where many affluent foreign diplomats lived. Even after the elderly Mississippian handed over his watch and his wallet, and emptied his pockets of change, the two young robbers shot him—once in the chest and once in his leg.

The senator was still at Walter Reed Army Hospital recuperating. Abe's caustic comment that "maybe the old coot shouldn't have voted against the recent gun control bill," had earned him "shut-up, man" shoulder whacks from other pages.

Abe did seem to like stirring up controversy.

Finally! Patty spotted him coming up the street, caught in the little pools of light cast by Second Street's streetlamps, his dark curls bouncing as he waved his arms around dramatically, punctuating some point he was making. He and Simone—two emphatic peas in a pod.

Hastily stepping out the door, she could hear Will warning, "You've got to stop baiting those guys. You're going to get us into deep cow dung with the landlady. She doesn't like fuss among her renters."

"Good morning," Patty chirped. "What's Abe done now?"

"Nothing!" Abe defended himself. "Just spreading some needed awareness!"

"Nothing?" Will shook his head with uncharacteristic irritation. "Nothing except seriously alienate the two FBI trainees living in our boardinghouse. Telling them Hoover was a skunk and engaged in unfair policing of civil rights activists."

"Well, he did, didn't he? And *skunk* and *unfair* weren't the words I used. I said *a-hole* and *racist*."

"Right." Will put his hand on Abe's arm so he'd listen. "Haven't you noticed our landlady has a signed photograph of

Director Hoover hanging in her kitchen? She was a secretary at the Bureau. You also seem to forget we've gotta share a bathroom with these guys." Removing his hand, Will strode forward. "I for one am grateful for what they do. They serve and protect. You. Me. Patty. Besides, Hoover's dead. The new acting director seems like a good guy. He's hiring female agents—for the first time. That should appeal to your liberal heart!"

"Your optimism is nice, buddy boy. But I would remind you what Voltaire said: 'Optimism is the madness of insisting that all's well when we are miserable.'" Abe elbowed Patty. "Eh? Like that?"

"So . . . you were listening in French class yesterday when we discussed the Revolution," Patty said with a small laugh.

The Senate hadn't adjourned until way after dinner the night before, and Abe had laid his head down on his books the following morning in class. An outrageous rudeness, given the fact there were only five students. Back home at her Catholic prep school, getting caught blatantly dozing might have earned Patty detention.

But the Page School's teachers were unusually tolerant, given their students' murderously long days—starting at six a.m., they crammed an entire school day of subjects into three hours, ending with a break for breakfast. Then they sprinted across First Street to get to the Capitol by ten a.m. to set up each member's desk—putting the printed-out *Congressional Record* of the previous day's proceedings and the debate calendar for the coming day into thick notebooks. Then fetching and delivering buckets of ice for drinks to every office.

Patty, Will, and Abe reached the enormous bronze statue of Neptune—flanked by his sons and sea nymphs riding muscular horses—that guarded the white stone stairs sweeping up to the grand entrance of the domed Library of Congress. Patty could hardly wait to see the fountain in the spring when it was working and the dolphins started shooting water. Next time her art-loving mother was in town, Patty should bring her here. Dot Appleton would be impressed, maybe even happy, for a few moments anyway. She paused for a moment to drink in the beautiful scene while the boys jogged up the stairs ahead of Patty, oblivious to its wonders.

Reaching the door first, Will pulled it open, bowing for Patty to go through ahead of him while tossing Abe a memorized quote of his own: "'Optimism is the faith that leads to achievement. Nothing can be done without hope.' Helen Keller. My mama's heroine." Following Patty inside, Will upped the ante of country twang in his otherwise melodious drawl, in joking self-deprecation: "Lord knows I ain't much of a student. But I do like that quote mighty well."

Their hurrying footsteps echoed off the marble pillars and archways, the richly colored mosaics of muses, scholars, and statesmen that decorated the Library's walls and vaulted ceiling, until they reached the tiny elevator that would take them to the third-floor attic where their classes were held.

"I suppose we're going to need both attitudes today, compadre. My healthy skepticism with your aspirational hope," Abe concluded as they squished in and felt the lift dip a bit with their weight. "Today's the debate on Senator Kennedy's resolution that the Senate form a Select Committee to investigate Watergate."

Will frowned. "Kinda a witch hunt, don't you think?"

Patty looked at him with surprise—Will was sponsored by a Democratic member of the House. As a Republican page, she might have such sentiments about any investigation of her president, but shouldn't Will be supportive of Ted Kennedy—such a prominent member of his party? But then she remembered. Some southern Democrats were more conservative than Republicans and consistently voted with President Nixon's agenda. Bipartisanship or contradiction? So much to learn about the Hill's ways.

Rattling, the elevator eked its way upward as Will continued, "They got the burglars. They've been found guilty in a court of law. Doesn't the Senate have more important things to do?"

"Ah, come on, roomie." Abe gave Will a playful shove, making the elevator sway and Patty catch her breath. She hated this contraption. "It's obvious Watergate is bigger than just the break-in and burglars. For one thing, where'd they get all that moolah? And what about Donald Segretti? Forging fake letters on stolen Democratic stationery to make candidates look bad. Releasing mice at one of their press conferences to freak everyone out. That guy was a college buddy of Nixon's appointment secretary! Open your baby blues."

Will scowled.

Abe threw his hands up. "It isn't just me thinking these things, buddy. Judge Sirica doesn't buy it. That's why he's holding off sentencing. To scare them into coughing up some truth. Sirica's convinced someone higher up *told* those bozos what to do. It's not fair to just punish the foot soldiers carrying out bad orders from superiors. You of all people should sympathize with that."

On a roll, Abe didn't notice Will's face go ashen at his alluding to Will's marine brothers. "And if those orders came from the Oval Office? Man, oh man, we better figure that out—fast. That would mean the most powerful man in the world, the guy with nuclear codes, might do anything to stay in power."

Visibly offended, Will shot back, "It's a wild goose chase. President Nixon says he knew nothing about any of this. I happen to respect the word of my president."

"I respect the *presidency*."

"Well . . . what about Chappaquiddick?" Will countered, referring to the tragic accident when Senator Kennedy drove off a narrow bridge into a tidal pool in 1969 and a young female staffer in the car with him drowned. "Why isn't somebody investigating that?"

"Good grief, Charlie Brown. You're not going to resort to that tired-out false equivalency, are you? It's like comparing apples to kumquats!"

"Guys!" Patty interrupted, dismayed by the acrimony between them. She'd been so impressed by what good friends they were despite how wildly they differed in background and opinion and personality. "This isn't a good way to start our day."

Chastised, the boys fell silent and glanced down and away from each other. As the elevator door shuddered open, Abe pointed to her feet and pulled on the bossy tone she'd heard him use as the head Democratic floor page divvying up errands. "Glad to see you're wearing sensible flat shoes today, Pats, and not those stacked platform Mary Janes—as foxy as they are. We're sure to be going on a lot of runs!" He exited and turned down a narrow hall created by file cabinets to reach his first class. Will huffed off in the opposite direction.

Neither said goodbye to her.

As Patty watched the sun rise through the window of her English class, its coppery glow washing the U.S. Capitol in rose-gold light, it didn't feel quite as glorious a sight as the day before.

Snap. Snap-snap.

"Your turn," whispered the page sitting beside Patty on the steps of the Senate dais.

Caught daydreaming again. It was hard not to be distracted by the hubbub in the spectator gallery as reporters and visitors found their seats during the mind-numbing opening chores of Senate protocol. The legislative clerk had just done roll call to discover a sufficient quorum was not present—which had sent pages scrambling to locate members of their respective parties.

Some of the errant senators had simply been gabbing in the cloakrooms adjacent to the chamber. Easy to retrieve. But others were all the way back in their offices across Constitution Avenue. Herding them had taken some doing.

Patty had been part of the mad dash through the halls of the two Senate office buildings (at such moments referred to without much affection as the SOBs). She couldn't take the easier errand of going to the sumptuous Marble Room—the luxurious lounge for senators just off the Senate's lobby—because girls weren't allowed anywhere near it. Not even its doorway. Some of the senators, wanting to keep the crisp crease in their slacks, would strip, hang their pants over the upholstered armchairs to prevent the wrinkles that sitting might bring, and walk around in their underwear as if in a locker room.

What would they do if a woman senator was ever elected again? Patty wondered as the clerk started reading each of the hundred names.

Senator Humphrey? Present.

Senator Inouye? Present.

Senator Jackson? Silence. *Senator Jackson?* Silence. Jackson was marked absent.

"Who snapped?" Patty whispered back as the roll call droned on. She looked up at the forty-three desks on the Republican side of the floor.

SNAP.

"Oh, I see him." A fortysomething man with square wire-rim glasses was holding up his hand. She darted to the second row of mahogany desks, riffling mentally through her crib sheet of names. She hadn't yet done an errand for this member. From Connecticut. *Umm.* She retrieved it just in time. "Yes, Senator Weicker?"

"Water, please." He glanced at her with a slight smile of acknowledgment as he sorted the copious papers on his desktop.

"Yes, sir," she answered, now trying to recall if he preferred bubbly or still. Fellow Republican pages had already warned her to never bring the ultra-conservative Senator Goldwater anything but club soda.

As she reached the water cooler in the outside lobby hall, she remembered. Still water. She filled a glass with ice and returned to Weicker's desk, proud of not spilling a drop on the way or when placing the water on its corner. She was also careful to not stand on the riser behind and above him, appearing taller than he was. She'd made that mistake on her very first day, delivering juice to a senator who was temporarily presiding over the chamber. That senator was short and evidently defensive about his stature. The other pages had teased her mercilessly for the rest of the day about "showing up 'Senator Squat.'"

Patty didn't know whether Weicker had any such sensitivities. But it didn't matter. The senator had turned to chat up a colleague seated behind him, so he didn't notice her as she placed the glass on his desk.

Retreating to the steps, Patty sat back down as the presiding officer announced that seventy-seven senators were present. Which was enough to consider Kennedy's resolution to establish a Select Committee to conduct "an investigation and study of the extent, if any, to which illegal, improper, or unethical activities were engaged in by any persons, acting individually or in combination with others, in the Presidential election of 1972, or any campaign, canvas, or other activity related to it."

The ranking Republican, Tennessee's Howard Baker, immediately stood to be recognized by the chair. "Mr. President, I have an amendment at my desk which I ask the clerk to report."

He held up his typed proposal, and the first page in line skittered over to take the paper across twenty-or-so feet of blue-carpeted space to the legislative clerk, who then read Baker's amendment to the assembled senators. Baker wanted the committee's membership to be equally distributed between the two parties, rather than giving the majority Democrats one extra seat and therefore, potentially, the deciding vote.

The debate on that seemingly simple request dragged on well over an hour.

Flitting about the chamber like swallows, the pages took and delivered notes between the seventy-plus members who remained in their seats as one held the floor to speak: scraps of ideas or proposed wording for potential compromises, counter-arguments to what the speaking senator was advocating, requests to their staffers for info on historical precedent they might cite when it was their turn to talk.

Abe had been right. It was already a whopper of a day. But when she could sit long enough to listen, Patty marveled at the courtly respect the two main and opposing speakers, the proposed co-chairs—Senator Baker and Will's hero, Senator Sam Ervin of North Carolina—maintained.

Said Baker: "I have no doubt whatever about the objective manner, the calm, cool, and judicial manner, in which the distinguished senator from North Carolina will conduct this inquiry as chairman . . ."

Patty assessed Baker's face, looking for a hint of sarcasm on it. There was none in his voice. She'd made the mistake of not detecting subtle disdain before, with her father. But no, the senator's respect for his political adversary seemed sincere.

He continued, "Nor does it suggest that I have any fear that the majority members of the committee—nor the staff, for that matter—will engage in a partisan witch hunt. On the other hand, we must face the fact that, inevitably, this inquiry will be fraught with political implications." To prevent such perception by the public, Baker urged changing "the composition of the committee to three Democrats and three Republicans..."

Senator Ervin rose to argue that equal numbers would paralyze the committee, preventing consensus and "any kind of meaningful action." The seventy-six-year-old North Carolinian drawled on for almost thirty minutes, his bushy white eyebrows wiggling up and down as he cited precedents of past Select Committees for a one-seat majority—going back to 1946. After that litany, he concluded, "I know that it is not the motive of my good friend from Tennessee to have a stalemate..."

Patty couldn't help but wonder, however, even with all the polite niceties between the two men, if that's precisely what Senator Baker was trying to accomplish—to slow or confuse things—to shield the Republican White House. That's what her father would do. He'd said before that the best way to muddy things was to ask for a lot of opinions.

Ervin urged his colleagues to reject Baker's request—if the Senate wanted a Select Committee that would "function instead of being bogged down in indecision and chaos." He added his personal reassurance: "If I had any feeling that Democrats on this committee or the committee itself would seek to crucify people for political purposes, I would vote against the resolution entirely."

Nodding ceremoniously at Baker, Ervin sat his rather ample and imposing self back down behind his desk.

Other Republicans who followed were not so deferential. They demanded the committee's inquiry expand—to also investigate Democratic president Lyndon Johnson's 1964 campaign. Senator Gurney of Florida justified this tit-for-tat but incongruous demand, saying voters across the country considered "the

Watergate affair" nothing more than "a political wing-ding" that happened every election and within both parties. The only way, he argued, to "show the greatest sense of impartiality" was to perform a deep dive on LBJ as well.

Patty frowned, slightly baffled. Sure, most Republicans detested Johnson. Her father constantly railed against LBJ's uncouth manners and his Great Society policies that Dr. Appleton derisively relabeled "the great welfare society." But this senator was talking about an election that had happened ten years and two elections back.

Ervin wasn't having it. In a mellifluous, oh-my-you-simply-don't-understand-do-you-poor-thing tone, he countered, "The senator has quite well said that there have been no charges of any improprieties in 1964 . . ." He paused, like a good Shakespearean actor, thought Patty, waiting to make sure his fellow senators looked up to pay attention to his pointed denouement statement: that adding an unconnected investigation to one that facts and law demanded be done, just so "we can discover if there is any basis for such charges . . . would be about as foolish as the man who went bear hunting and stopped to chase rabbits."

Patty chortled at Ervin's quip as a collective belly laugh rumbled through the chamber.

No wonder Will loved this senator. Leaning forward, she put her elbows on her knees and cupped her chin in her hands, fascinated by the unfolding drama. She was annoyed when the next finger snap interrupted. But then she saw which Republican member it was.

"Yes, sir, Senator Javits?" He'd been the first senator to advocate for female pages—calling it "simply a question of fundamental human fairness." He was a real favorite.

"Water, please. And make a candy run for me, too, would you, Patty? I didn't eat enough breakfast to get through this."

"Yes, sir."

She scurried to the cooler. Wait. Candy? Where was she supposed to get candy? And what kind?

She peeked back into the chamber and saw Senator Javits reading notes just handed to him. Patty hesitated to interrupt. She'd have to ask another page for guidance. Oh God. The only one who was seated on the steps at that moment, waiting for an assignment, was the Lip Smackers guy from the inaugural parade—Jake something. She'd avoided talking to him ever since.

No choice. Maybe the inauguration had simply been a bad moment. Guys sometimes acted stupid when in a pack, trying to impress their buddies and thinking girls couldn't overhear. "Excuse me," she said, crouching down so he could hear her whisper.

"Hey there, Lip Smacker girl."

Patty felt herself blush. Nope, this guy was just plain ol' insufferable. But she stuck to her mission. "Where does a candy run take me?"

Jake leaned in way too close. "For me? Down to the cafeteria for Pixy Stix or Chuckles. Or maybe some wax lips," he smirked, "to suck on."

Gag me with a spoon. Patty glanced around, once again fearful someone might overhear him and judge *her* the flirt, inviting this guy's double-entendre. She stood. *Kill 'em with kindness*, her mother always said—and it was all that Patty had at that moment. She hoped the small, party-perfect smile she gave him was somehow so sharp in its pointed civility that it might cut a hole of self-recognition in Jake's heart, however unlikely. "Thank you for your help."

Her head buzzing slightly from her flushed embarrassment, Patty walked away with all the grace she possessed in case the creep was watching her backside as she retreated. Through the massive, carved doors, their molding so ornate they felt like temple entrances, down three steps of veined, pearly marble to the hallway. There she paused, leaning against one of the palatial Corinthian columns lining the passage—decorum be damned—to wait for her heart to stop racing.

Hurry up, her mind scolded. Getting to the cafeteria and back quickly was going to require a sprint. Without looking, Patty simply bolted—and ran smack into Abe as he rushed out of an elevator, his arms full of folders.

"Oh my gosh!" she gasped.

"What the—"

In their collision, official papers scattered all over the black-and-white tiled floor.

"I'm so sorry!" Patty dropped to her knees to help Abe scoop up and quickly restuff the folders, as other pages and senators' staff bustled past.

Lunging to nab a loose paper that a passerby was about to step on, Abe snapped, "Where were you going in such a damn hurry?"

"To the cafeteria. Senator Javits wants some candy."

"Why are you going all the way there?" Abe frowned. "Just go to the candy desk."

"The candy desk? Jake told me I needed to go to the cafeteria."

Abe rolled his eyes. "He was razzing you, Pats. Want me to talk to him?"

Patty's face reddened again with mortification. No, she didn't want Abe to talk to him—he wasn't her father. Although deep down, she sort of wished Abe could punch Jake for her. But she'd learned the hard way with the clique-y girls at home that having somebody stand up for her only made her seem weaker. "No. Thanks, though."

"O-kay. But you need to stop being so gullible. Some of the guys are still laughing about you looking for a congressional record *player*. Whether you want it or not, Pats, you've got the responsibility of proving girls can be good pages." He patted her shoulder, like an adult comforting a child failing at a game of dodgeball with the implicit warning of *get it together, kid.* "The candy desk is number seventy-four, back row on the Republican side. Some ex-Hollywood musical star, a one-termer, started the tradition. Senator Fannin sits there now. Just tell him Senator Javits needs a little fortification." Abe shook his head. "You and Will, what am I going to do with you two?" He hurried on his way.

Fighting off tears from his reprimand, Patty fully absorbed—for the first time—the fact that if she screwed up as a page, she could ruin the hopes of other female teenagers wanting to follow in her footsteps. That kind of pressure? That's not what she had signed up for. She'd just wanted to come to the Senate to see the wonderment of democracy, to be part of something her father so loved.

Or had her father put that idealistic notion into her head? Or her boyfriend? Scott had seemed so pleased, telling her not to worry about a long-distance relationship. It'd be worth it, he'd said. If things went according to plan, he'd be attending Georgetown University in the fall. They'd be together in D.C. then. Scott even joked that her Hill experience would make her the perfect wife for a man of ambition. And wasn't he always saying he wanted to be president someday?

Do it for Scott. It'll make you more worthy. The Republican answer to Jack and Jackie, her mother had said. Patty took a deep breath—her confidence shot but her sense of purpose restored—and headed for the candy desk, just as the vote on establishing an investigative committee began.

One after another, the seventy-seven senators present rose to call out their decision. In somber voices, they all voted *yay*—without any dissenting amendment about committee makeup or expanded inquiry into a ten-year-past Democratic candidacy being added to a resolution focused on the Watergate scandal. Not a single *nay*. Unanimous.

"I'll be darned," Senator Javits murmured as he took the peppermints Patty brought him. "That was impressive. Let's hope this unity holds."

"You make me feel like a natural woman . . ."

Whoever was sitting in that parked VW Beetle was going to lose their hearing with the radio cranked that high, Patty mused, parroting her parents' reprimand when she blasted the American Top 40 weekly countdown. She was waiting, once again, at the door of Thompson-Markward Hall. Nice tune, though. Pink Samsonite by her side, she was watching for her godmother's wood-paneled station wagon.

A thin girl got out of the bright red VW, music still blasting. In the gloam of the coming night, Patty didn't recognize her until Simone shouted, "Hey! It's me." She waved, the long leather fringe on the arms of her jacket swishing. "Let's go. I'm starving!"

"Where's Aunt Marjorie?" Patty asked as she pulled the passenger seat forward, far enough to shove her weekend suitcase into the Bug's cramped back. "Thanks for coming to get me," she added hastily, realizing her question seemed rude. She felt guilty enough that Simone's family had to pick her up every Friday night, only to ferry her back the next morning and wait for Patty to do her Saturday half day of work when the Senate was in weekend session. Besides, shouldn't Simone have a date? Patty and Scott had always spent Fridays together.

"She's in Houston." Simone flipped her waist-long blond hair over her shoulder and pushed the Beetle's gearshift into drive. Parted in the middle, her hair hung in a sheen of sandy gold, à la Peggy Lipton in the *Mod Squad*. Patty's mother had totally disapproved, privately admonishing Patty to never wear her hair like that. So unpolished, no pride in her appearance, Dot Appleton *tsk-tsked*.

Wait. Did Simone say Aunt Marjorie was in Houston? Was her dad there, too? Were the girls completely unsupervised for the weekend? Patty's parents wouldn't like that. Not at all. "Houston? Did she go with your dad to a business meeting or something?"

"Dad's at home. Mom's at the Women's Caucus convention—the first national political gathering of women since the early suffragists' days. She's psyched." Grinding gears a tad, Patty shifted into third to race through a yellow light on Constitution Avenue, the Washington Monument rising to their left, the White House off to their right across long lawns, somehow green even in winter.

"Your dad doesn't mind?" Patty asked in surprise.

"Nope. Dad's hip." Simone picked up speed as she skirted the Lincoln Memorial to cross over the bridge heading to the George Washington Parkway. It was totally dark now, and the wrought-iron streetlamps lining the bridge were lit up against the night, like a runway pointing to Arlington Cemetery and JFK's eternal flame that flickered into view as they crossed.

Simone sighed audibly. "Seeing Kennedy's flame always makes me sad," she murmured. She hit play on her eight-track, the song she'd been blaring earlier starting again.

Rich piano chords and a woman's slightly raspy voice filled the little bubble of car.

"Who's this?"

Even in the dark, Patty could tell Simone's sideways glance at her carried a where-the-heck-have-you-been expression. "Carole King. Her *Tapestry* album." They were cruising along the Virginia side of the Potomac River now, the Jefferson Memorial coming into view across the glasslike waters.

"*. . . when my soul was in the lost and found, you came along to claim it . . .*"

Suddenly horribly homesick, Patty felt her eyes well up with tears. "After dinner, may I use your phone to call Scott? I'll pay your parents back for the long-distance charge."

"No problem." Simone glanced her way again. "Is calling your boyfriend what this song makes you think about?"

"Oh yes," Patty breathed, unabashed. "Meeting Scott totally changed my life. And me."

"Really? The way I interpret the song's message is that a woman will never be happy—never find that *peace of mind*, as King calls it—until men accept her for who she *naturally* is. Not for anything he changes in her. You know, people getting who you are. Without having to put on some role. It's an anthem for female empowerment, don't you think?"

"Oh yeah." Patty nodded, hoping her faked agreement was convincing. *Female empowerment* was not exactly a phrase she used.

They passed National Airport, wedged between the parkway and the river, as Simone's eight-track clicked and whirred through several songs. Quieting, the girls listened, Patty growing uneasy during "It's Too Late" as King sang about people changing and that souring their romance. She was relieved when the song ended and the edge of Old Town Alexandria with its nineteenth-century clapboard row houses, painted in white, yellow, or Wedgwood shades of blue and green, came into view.

"The really cool thing about this album," Simone spoke again, "is that King has been a relatively anonymous songwriter until now. She wrote 'Natural Woman' for Aretha Franklin in 1960-something, and Aretha—oh my God, you've heard that version, I hope?"

"Oh—yeah," Patty played along again.

"Aretha's rendition just blows your mind! Right?"

Patty nodded.

"It's so strong and passionate. Aretha is the queen of soul for sure! I'll always love her version. But this is Carole King stepping out to sing music that before she hid in a studio writing for others. Just her and her piano, all alone on stage. It's like we're bearing witness to this woman finding herself. I don't know, I really dig that."

Turning left off Washington Street onto Prince, Simone held tight to the VW's steering wheel as the Bug rattled and bucked along a block of cobblestones. "Oh wow—a spot!" Simone whipped the little car into place parallel to the curb in one, quick go.

"Meat loaf tonight," she announced as she got out.

Inside, the warm smell of dinner embraced them. Simone's dad had the table set and ready. Amazed, Patty wondered if her own father even knew where to find their silverware.

As the three sat down to meat loaf, mashed potatoes, and green bean casserole that Aunt Marjorie had made and left for him to warm up, Uncle Graham asked, "So, ladies, how was your day?" Subdued and pleasant, he was quiet and methodical to Aunt Marjorie's vivacious chatter. Simone seemed so relaxed around him. But then again, his question carried no lying-in-wait overtones.

"Same old, same old," Simone answered breezily. "Symphonic Band was really good, though. We're working on an orchestration of Tchaikovsky's Fourth. The third movement's got a terrific piccolo solo in it. Totally exposed. Third octave. Scaaaa-ry. The band director told me Tchaikovsky called the phrases 'capricious arabesques.'" She laughed. "That was no help at all! But I'll nail it. We're going to play it at festival competition."

She turned to Patty. "What about you? Did something momentous happen this week in the sacred halls of Congress? I'm so jealous—you're getting to see it all firsthand. People fighting for our rights and the common good. Well . . . some of them, anyway."

Patty smiled. "Yes, as a matter of fact." Enthusiastically, she described Senator Ervin's humor-laced charisma, his sway over the other senators.

Nodding as she spoke, Uncle Graham sipped his whiskey, listening.

When she was done, he said, "You're right about his influence. The White House better not underestimate old Sam. He pretends to be a backwoods country farmer, but Ervin's a preeminent constitutional law expert. Harvard Law grad."

"And a total jerk, Mom says," muttered Simone.

"What?" Patty had found the senator so gracious. Why did Simone have to spoil things? "You mean because he'll be investigating President Nixon?"

"No-o-o." Simone sat up. "Because he voted against the Equal Rights Amendment last year. Eighty-four senators voted for it. Even that awful segregationist Strom Thurmond! Only eight opposed it."

Her indignation now in full swing, Simone spluttered, "That old fart Ervin is still fighting it, too, trying to convince state legislatures to vote it down. He calls the ERA"—Simone made quotation marks in the air as she spat out Ervin's words—"'a conspiracy of professional harpies!' He claims passing the ERA will undo 'God's plan for us' and—oh no!"—she dramatically waved her hands about her face as if in panic—"might make women delay when they marry or have children, legalize homosexuality, and no longer require a woman to take her husband's family name, which—according to Ervin—would create chaos in government recordkeeping!" She flounced back in her chair. "How narrow-minded can you get? Someone needs to tell this guy it's 1973."

Patty stared at her, stunned by her vehemence.

"He's also in league with that right-wing, nutjob woman from your area, that Phyllis Schlafly. She claims that"—again Simone made quote marks in the air—"'women want and need protection.' Seriously? *And* she says ERA activists like Mom are out to destroy the American family. Mom! Miss American Pie herself."

Simone's anger hung in the air, thick and acrid like smoke.

Listening to Simone's barrage, Patty felt a little breathless. She'd met only one girl like Simone before. So opinionated. So blunt. So darn articulate and sure of her words. Last year's valedictorian. No one liked her. Patty's classmates rolled their eyes and gossiped that her outspoken ways were so . . . so *masculine*. No one was surprised when she chose among her many college acceptances to go to Yale—which had started taking women only in 1969—rather than one of the Seven Sisters Patty's friends only dreamed of being smart enough to attend. That girl had intimidated the heck out of Patty.

She was feeling the same way about Simone.

Her words had left Patty worrying about something else, too—that she was lacking not only in her debating skills but in her family somehow. She'd never had the kind of heartfelt fury or fierce pride in her mother that Simone exuded.

Hesitantly, feeling she should contribute something to the conversation—the way she saw Will and Abe toss opposing ideas back and forth—Patty offered, "Daddy says wives suddenly wanting careers should remember that marriage is a 'we' proposition, not an 'I.' He says his women patients with the most intractable problems, those who cause their families the most heartache, are distracted from homemaking by delusions of grandeur."

Simone looked like she might explode. "You don't seriously believe that, do you?"

"It's . . . it's what Daddy says," murmured Patty, taken aback.

"So what? You can't just swallow—"

Simone's father put his hand on his daughter's to stop her saying anything else. "You know, Patty," he began, his voice gentle and nonjudgmental, "there's an interesting fact we know well at the IRS, analyzing people's tax returns. Half of America's wives who work *have* to. To help pay mortgages and feed their kids. Those women—especially—shouldn't be paid only sixty percent of what a man in the same job is paid. Or be limited to lower-paying clerical work. The ERA will require that laws and opportunities be equal, consistent across all the states, rather than women having to fight for change one lawsuit at a time. That's why your Aunt Marjorie believes in it so much. And why I support it, too."

Leaning back, Uncle Graham crossed his arms and pondered, "It'll be interesting to hear what plan of action the caucus comes up with this weekend to push the ERA through. Only a dozen more states needed, right, girls?"

Patty had no idea. She was still processing the notion that so many wives *had* to work because of financial need and were paid so little. No one she grew up around had such issues. With some discomfort, she was seeing how lucky, how sheltered her world was.

"Eleven," Simone answered her father, seeming to notice Patty was mulling over things and dialing down her indignation as a result. But she couldn't help tossing out the last word: "In any case, Patty, beware Ervin. He's definitely a male chauvinist pig in sheep's clothing." Simone shrugged, adding her usual punctuation, "Just saying."

The hall clock chimed eight o'clock. Patty startled at the sound, then with some relief at having a reason to escape, she asked, "May I be excused, please? I'd like to call Scott, and Mother says I should never telephone a home after eight thirty." Good thing her mother never knew about the prank calls she and her girlfriends had made late into the night at sleepovers.

"The upstairs phone cord stretches into my room for privacy," Simone offered, "in case you get all smoochy."

Was she teasing? Or ridiculing? No matter which, Patty couldn't believe she'd said that in front of a dad!

Dragging the phone into Simone's bedroom, Patty dropped into a bright-orange bean bag beside Simone's antique four-poster bed on which she'd hung a fringe of hippie beading instead of a crocheted canopy. *This girl's taste is beyond questionable*, Patty thought as she dialed. She had to admit, though, the bean bag was incredibly comfortable.

Scott's mother answered.

"Hi, Mrs. Smith, it's Patty. May I speak to Scott, please?"

"Good evening, Patty dear. I'm afraid Scott isn't here. He's gone with your gang to see *The Getaway*."

"Oh." She hesitated, stung that her boyfriend had gone out to a movie without her, and that one in particular, since it starred Ali MacGraw. Scott called Patty a MacGraw look-alike. Even introduced her to his friends and family by asking them to notice her resemblance to the pretty brunette and doe-eyed star of *Love Story*.

You're being illogical, overly sensitive, Patty berated herself. *Unfair to Scott.* By the time she got home during Congress's spring break the movie would be out of theaters. Of course he wanted to see it while he could. That's all. It wasn't like Scott was secretly out on a date or something. Patty forced chirpiness. "May I call tomorrow instead?"

"Of course! But he's playing in a tennis tournament. The club has just put in one of those amazing bubbles to keep the courts warm in the winter. We're all so excited about it. He's signed up for both singles and doubles. I'm afraid he'll probably be there all day, dear."

"Oh." Tennis was how she and Scott had met. Again, she pushed away hurt to sound upbeat. "Did you say doubles, Mrs. Smith? Is he playing with Jerry? If so, they'll be unbeatable."

There was a long pause on the other end. "Nooooo," Mrs. Smith replied. "It's mixed doubles."

"Oh." Again *oh*. *Pull it together, Patricia.* "Who . . . who's his partner?"

"Your friend. That lovely Suzie."

Patty's stomach flopped. Lovely? Suzie was physically gorgeous, for sure. She'd dazzled everybody during their debutante ball last year. She also routinely trounced Patty on the tennis court. Suzie was no friend of Patty's, though. Swallowing hard, Patty said, "Could you please tell Scott that I called, Mrs. Smith? Maybe he can call me on Sunday whenever it's convenient for you?"

"I'm not positive what the plan is after church, but I will be sure to tell him."

"Thank you. Please give my best to Mr. Smith."

"I will, dear."

Patty hung up, her hand trembling a bit, right as Simone walked in. "Done already?"

"He was out."

"Oh."

Oh was definitely the word of the hour, thought Patty glumly.

Waving her hand as if flicking away gnats, Simone said, "His loss. I'm heading over to a friend's to play Boggle. Come with."

Was Simone sincere? Or just being polite? Or—Patty caught her breath a little in embarrassment—was it a pity invite?

Simone seemed to read her thoughts. "Seriously. I meant to ask you before. It'll be fun. My friends are killer Boggle players. And no woman should stay home on a Friday night just because she didn't hear from some guy." There was that shrug. "Just saying."

Patty was terrible at the timed word-play game. The little sandglass made her anxious. She and her friends preferred Twister or Charades. She shook her head. "Thank you, really, but I think... I think I'll just soak in the tub. My feet are so sore from all the running today." She stood and headed to the bathroom that linked Simone's room to her brothers', where Patty slept on the weekends.

Besides, she had a love letter to write, and it better be a good one—as full of the longing to be close and understood as that Carole King song.

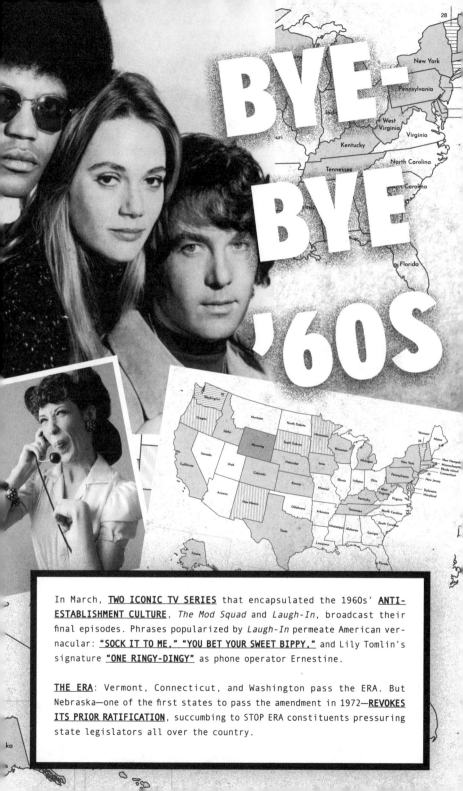

BYE-BYE '60S

In March, **TWO ICONIC TV SERIES** that encapsulated the 1960s' **ANTI-ESTABLISHMENT CULTURE**, *The Mod Squad* and *Laugh-In*, broadcast their final episodes. Phrases popularized by *Laugh-In* permeate American vernacular: **"SOCK IT TO ME," "YOU BET YOUR SWEET BIPPY,"** and Lily Tomlin's signature **"ONE RINGY-DINGY"** as phone operator Ernestine.

THE ERA: Vermont, Connecticut, and Washington pass the ERA. But Nebraska—one of the first states to pass the amendment in 1972—**REVOKES ITS PRIOR RATIFICATION**, succumbing to STOP ERA constituents pressuring state legislators all over the country.

JAMES W. McCORD, JR.
ROCKVILLE, MARYLAND 20850

FILED
MAR 23 1973

TO: JUDGE SIRICA   JAMES F. DAVEY, Clerk   March 19, 1973

Certain questions have been posed to me from your honor through the probation officer, dealing with details of the case, motivations, intent and mitigating circumstances.

In endeavoring to respond to these questions, I am whipsawed in a variety of legalities. First, I may be called before a Senate Committee investigating this matter. Secondly, I may be involved in a civil suit, and thirdly there may be a new trial at some future date. Fourthly, the probation officer may be called before the Senate Committee to present testimony regarding what may otherwise be a privileged communication between defendant and Judge, as I understand it; if I answered certain questions to the probation officer, it is possible such answers could become a matter of record in the Senate and therefore available for use in the other proceedings just described. My answers

[text obscured by "WATERGATE" overlay]

members of my family have expressed fear for my life if I disclose knowledge of the facts in this matter, either publicly for to any government representative. Whereas I do not share their concerns to the same degree, nevertheless, I do believe that retaliatory measures will be taken against me, my family, and my friends should I disclose such facts. Such retaliation could destroy careers, income, and reputations of persons who are innocent of any guilt whatever.

Be that as it may, in the interests of justice, and in the interests of restoring faith in the criminal justice system, which faith has been severely damaged in this case, I will state the following to you at this time which I hope may be of help to you in meting out justice in this case:

1. There was political pressure applied to the defendants to plead guilty and remain silent.

2. Perjury occurred during the trial in matters highly material to the very structure, orientation, and impact of the government's case, and to the motivation and intent of the defendants.

3. Others involved in the Watergate operation were not identified during the trial, when they could have been by those testifying.

A true copy:
Test: Hugh E. Kline, Clerk
United States Court of Appeals
for the District of Columbia Circuit.
By: _____ Clerk

CONVICTED WATERGATE BURGLAR JAMES McCORD—once head of security for Nixon's campaign committee—buckles under Judge Sirica's presentencing pressure. **THREATENED WITH A DECADE OF JAIL TIME**, McCord sends a confession to Judge Sirica.

IT IS A BOMBSHELL.

McCORD REVEALS A LARGER CONSPIRACY of calculated cover-up and obstruction of justice, saying he and the other burglars had been **COERCED TO REMAIN SILENT**, plead guilty, and perjure themselves to protect higher-ups.

Judge Sirica reads the letter aloud in court. On a day **AMERICANS EXPECTED THE WATERGATE "CAPER" TO BE PUT TO BED** with the burglars' sentencing, (sealing the claim that the break-in and other election dirty tricks were simply the acts of overzealous campaign workers), **THE SCANDAL CRACKS WIDE OPEN AGAIN**.

JAMES MCCORD

MARTHA MITCHELL

McCord's letter gives credence to accusations previously dismissed as too outrageous to even consider, such as the claims by the outspoken **TALK-SHOW DARLING MARTHA MITCHELL**. The former attorney general's wife had told reporters she'd been **FORCIBLY DETAINED AND DRUGGED** by her husband's bodyguards the day after the break-in to **PREVENT HER CALLING HER PRESS CONTACTS** to share her suspicions that Nixon had to be involved. Why? To buy time for CR(EE)P, of which her husband was then director, to cover up the break-in's connection to Nixon's re-election campaign. She knew McCord. He'd been part of her husband's protective guard. Martha believed **HE WOULD NEVER ENGAGE IN BURGLARY UNLESS ORDERED TO DO SO**.

But "poor Martha" was **DISMISSED AS "UNHINGED"** and "all mixed up" by Nixon's circles. That perception was bolstered by her husband's resigning from CR(EE)P just two weeks after the break-in, claiming he "loved that little girl" and needed to focus on taking care of her.

"We all fell under the sway of the campaign to make her seem nuts," says CBS's Lesley Stahl. "But she was the canary in the coal mine **TRYING TO WARN US SOMETHING WAS VERY WRONG."**

COMING

Vietnam War veterans return home and **AMERICAN POWs ARE FINALLY RELEASED**, 120 at a time, in two-week intervals. The wounded and sick come first, then the rest in the order in which they were captured. **MANY HAVE BEEN IN CAPTIVITY FOR YEARS.**

HOME

NEWLY FREED AMERICAN POWs CHEER as their C-141A aircraft lifts off from North Vietnam territory and they know they're safely on their way home.

At a White House reception for returning POWs, President Nixon greets **NAVY PILOT JOHN McCAIN, HELD FOR OVER FIVE YEARS**. McCain broke one leg and both arms when his plane was shot down over Hanoi. He was tortured, his injuries not treated until his captors discovered his father was an admiral and commander of all U.S. forces in the Vietnam theater. Offered early release over other captured American flyers because of who his father was, McCain refused. His injuries left him permanently unable to raise his arms above his head.

CHAPTER THREE

MARCH

Arrrrrggggh. Patty yanked her suit jacket from under the Singer sewing machine's bobbing needle and ripped out her botched, meandering seam. How could making a pocket be so hard?

Pressing down on the machine's pedal and pushing the material under the needle as it chugged up and down, she tried again for a straight line of stitches. *Tik-tik-tik-tik-kkkkkkkkkkkkkk.* The thread balled, the pocket puckered.

Sugar!

Wasn't this polyester-blend material supposed to be easier to work with than wool? Of course, Patty wouldn't know, not really. Her mother had always been the one to sew any clothes they made at home. Patty had simply helped pin and cut out the patterns with pinking shears. Dot Appleton was the artist with the needle, not only tailoring beautiful dresses but creating intricate crewelwork pillows, true works of art with painstaking hand stitching—fishbone leaf, French knots, whipped spider, lazy daisy.

Patty had inherited absolutely none of her mother's artistic or seamstress talents.

Suppressing a little scream of aggravation, she stopped herself from slamming the low, slanted ceiling of the attic room and kicking the baskets of material scraps, patterns, and yarn surrounding her. Patty gazed out its small window, across the neighboring row houses' green tin roofs, to a sliver of Potomac River visible through tall, often crooked-from-age chimney stacks.

The only reason she had to be doing this nonsense was that no matter how many pantsuits the character Mary Richards wore in the Minneapolis TV studio of *The Mary Tyler Moore Show*, no stores—including D.C.'s fancy Garfinkle's—sold more than a handful of business-style pantsuits for women. Clinging, sexy cocktail-party versions, sure. But they were of no help. The Senate had designated female pages replicate as much as possible their male counterparts' coat-and-tie de facto uniform. Patty and her mother had scoured the department store, before going to its tearoom for lunch. They'd found all of one that fit her.

Dot Appleton had hastily sewn a second suit, so Patty would have two, one navy blue, one black—but both had only decorative pockets, no truly functional ones. Certainly no inside breast pockets like men's suits had, deep enough to tuck and hide pens or day planners. Patty needed a jacket with real pockets—desperately—for her next time-of-the-month. She wasn't about to get caught unprepared again.

Trying to explain why she needed to be excused to go to her residence hall for an hour to the sergeant at arms—a stern man who hadn't wanted female pages to begin with—was humiliating. "Sick? How sick?" he'd asked. "Are you throwing up? Then no."

If only she was allowed to carry her purse on the floor—the whole debacle could have been avoided. She always had a pad tucked into her pocketbook for emergencies. Totally discreet, especially now that the new pads had adhesive to stick directly to panties, no more needing that thin belt that pinched her skin and always slipped around.

Why couldn't the Senate rules be bent for this reason? Or why couldn't the bathrooms be equipped with feminine products? And why the heck wasn't she regular—so she could just be proactive and preemptively protected the day she was due? All her school friends' periods came like clockwork. What was wrong with her?

Big hot tears slipped down her face. *Sugar! Sugar! Sugar!*

The sound of an audience's guffaws and applause rolled up the narrow stairs from the next floor down. Patty flinched as if they were laughing at her.

One ringy-dingy, came a nasal female voice. *A gracious good afternoon . . . Have I reached the party to whom I am speaking?*

Patty could hear Simone giggle.

Without really thinking what she was doing, Patty stumbled down the stairs, still shedding tears, crumpled pocket in one hand, the trouble-making jacket in the other.

Simone looked up from the floor where she was sitting, the *Washington Post* spread out in front of her, her legs in a perfect ballet split. "Holy moly, what's wrong with you?"

What *was* wrong with her? Patty started sobbing.

Scrambling to her feet as the record went on—*three phones to be installed in the John Mitchell residence, or is that the Mitchell residence john?*—Simone lifted the record player's needle off the vinyl disc to hurriedly say, "I didn't mean that the way it came out." She put her arm around Patty's shoulders and led her to the bean bag.

"I . . . I . . . I . . ."

Awkwardly Simone patted her shoulder, waiting.

"I . . ."

Simone went into the bathroom and came back with a box of tissues.

Patty blew her nose.

"Is that the problem?" Simone pointed to the material Patty still clutched.

Sniffling, Patty finally managed to speak. "I can't get the pocket to attach without bunching." She threw the jacket and pocket to the floor.

Simone picked them up to look. "Oh, I can fix that for you."

"You can?" Patty did not expect sewing to be part of Simone's skills, given her libber attitudes about homemaking.

Laughing—seemingly pleased by Patty's surprise, perhaps validating the hip persona she wanted to project—Simone flopped down beside her. "One of the benefits, I suppose, of staying in my public middle school rather than going to that all-girls private prep alma mater of Mom's. Home Ec was a required class. Just like Shop was for the boys."

"Is that why you wanted to go to T. C. Williams?" Patty wiped her eyes. She'd wondered but not asked since Patty's father had vehemently disapproved of the fact Simone attended a massive city high school. It almost kept him from allowing Patty to stay with Simone's family. *What kind of bad influences might Simone be under?* he'd blustered.

"Is *what* why I wanted to go to T. C.?" Simone asked.

"For Home Ec. It must be great preparation for running a household."

Simone snorted. "No way. I didn't go for Home Ec. I went for music. I wanted a real band program. And the Titans are a great football team. We just won the state championship. So, the crowds are massive, high on school spirit. Playing halftime shows is beyond groovy."

She stretched back into a split and then leaned over, resting her elbows on the floor and pressing her hands together like in prayer. Was that yoga? Patty had never seen anyone do it before. She winced, thinking how much that position would hurt her thighs.

"I also didn't want to go to high school with a bunch of people just like me," Simone continued. "How can you learn how to talk to people if all you've ever done is essentially look in a mirror at school? Besides, maybe because of my brothers, it just seemed weird to be around boys only at dances organized between single-sex schools. T. C.'s more real world, you know?"

She looked at Patty thoughtfully. "You should come to some of the games in the fall." She sat back up, pulling her knees to her chest. "Do you some good."

Patty decided not to ask what she meant by that comment. "What were you listening to?" she asked, changing the subject and still snuffling.

"Oh, the best. Lily Tomlin. You know, the comedienne from *Laugh-In*. It's a recording of a live stand-up show she did as Ernestine the telephone operator."

"Oh, right." Patty recognized the voice now. "She's pretty sarcastic, isn't she, that character? My parents don't like her at all."

"I bet not!" Simone answered, but her tone was empathetic. "They can't argue, though, with how prophetic her political satire is. You walked in during her Ernestine calling Martha Mitchell. Ernestine suggests that Martha jot down instructions on the wall for ordering a new phone since she doesn't have notepaper handy. Then Ernestine says, 'What? There's already too much writing on the wall?'" Simone laughed.

Patty looked at her blankly.

"You know the saying, right? That there are clear signs something unpleasant is coming."

"Of course." Patty rolled her eyes.

Simone studied her. "You know *who* I'm talking about? The wife of the former attorney general, John Mitchell, who ran CR(EE)P when the Watergate break-in happened. The woman always calling reporters from her bathroom to gossip about Nixon's administration."

"Ye-ah." Patty mainly remembered that her father called Mrs. Mitchell a loud, delusional lunatic. And that her husband—one of Nixon's best friends and a very important lawyer—had had to resign to take care of her. "Poor guy," her father had muttered after hearing that report.

"Well, it looks like that unpleasant something is about to happen." Pointing to a section of the spread-out newspaper, Simone said, "Turns out James McCord—the convicted Watergate burglar who used to run Mitchell's protective detail—has confessed to Judge Sirica that he was *pressured* to plead guilty and *not* identify others involved in the Watergate operation." Simone paused, raising her eyebrows meaningfully and emphasizing her words: "He committed perjury . . . to protect higher-ups—like Martha's husband, John Mitchell."

Simone leaned back against her bed. "I've been reading the *Post* front to back since all this started. Last summer Woodward and Bernstein reported that Mitchell controlled a secret stash to fund clandestine spying on Nixon's opponents—when he was AG, the nation's highest official tasked with *protecting* the rule of law. When they called him for comment, Mitchell threatened Mrs. Graham, the paper's publisher, with—well"—Simone pointed to her breast—"that her you-know-what would get 'caught in a big fat wringer' if she printed the story. But she did. Brave woman." Simone nodded thoughtfully. "Looks like McCord might corroborate allegations about that illegal slush fund and about Mitchell. So . . . stuff's about to hit the fan."

Patty tried to imagine what her father's response might be to all this. He always put his opinions so succinctly. Probably that McCord was just making things up to save his own skin and avoid jail. She rubbed her forehead. She really didn't want to wander into political debate right then. Her head already hurt from crying, and during the week Patty got an earful about Nixon and Watergate from Abe as it was. She shifted the conversation back to *Laugh-In*. Safe territory. "My favorite character of Lily Tomlin's is actually Edith Ann."

"Oh my gosh. Mine too!" Simone smiled back. As if on cue, the girls put on a squirmy five-year-old facade and simultaneously intoned, "and that's the truth," sticking out their tongues to blow spitty raspberries at each other à la Edith Ann.

They laughed—their first shared joke, a glimmer of friendship. It felt good.

"I'm sorry I was such a mess when I came down." Patty explained why she needed pockets.

"Oh wow. That would make me cry, too," sympathized Simone. "But . . . you know the outline of a pad might show through that pocket. They can be so bulky. Tampons are so much smaller. There's a new one with a rounded plastic applicator that doesn't hurt as much—"

"Oh!" Patty shot to her feet like she'd been stuck with a needle. "I could never use those. I'm a virgin."

Looking both stunned and amused, Simone said, "I am too. It doesn't—"

"You are?" Patty blurted.

Simone's mirth disappeared. "Yes. Why do you think differently?"

Given Simone's liberated woman opinions, all the Woodstock, free love, hippie music she listened to, Patty had just assumed that she . . . Well, that she might . . . Her face turned red. She sure hadn't meant to let on she thought Simone was . . . *that* kind of girl. "I just meant—"

"I know what you meant." Simone's voice turned cool. "Listen," her tone now was purely instructional, "you should know that using a—"

Flustered, Patty interrupted again, "I just don't want my husband to question anything on my wedding night—I want an unimpeachable white wedding."

"Like—I—was—trying—to—say," Simone began again, emphatically speaking each word. Then she stopped. "Never mind." Shaking her head, she stood as well. "You need to borrow this."

She pulled from her shelf *Our Bodies, Ourselves: A Book by and for Women*. In the cover photo, what looked like a grandmother and her granddaughter held up a sign together: "Women Unite." "The book explains better than I can. It's brand-new. Written by twelve feminist researchers. To empower us by learning about our own bodies. It has anatomy charts, for one thing, that will show what I'm trying to tell you. It'll explain a lot of other stuff, too, like PMS."

"What's that?" It sounded horrible.

"A physical cause for the blues some of us feel each month. Fluctuating hormones. The male medical establishment poo-poos the theory. But it makes a lot of sense to me. Read the book." Simone shoved it into Patty's hands and then scooped up the rumpled jacket and pocket. "You have to guide the material through the sewing machine slow and gentle. You can't be impatient. Come on. I'll show you."

What a good little hostess, Dot Appleton would say about Simone's helpfulness.

But Simone's friendly warmth was gone. Patty had insulted it away.

"You look pretty today, Patty." Will slid into the desk beside her. "Is that a new outfit?" Will had only seen her bundled up against the March winds on the way to classes that morning.

"Thank you." She smiled, tugging a little at the rose-colored scarf she'd double wrapped and then tied in a small bow around her throat to look like the choker necklaces models in *Seventeen* wore. "It's not new—I just accessorized."

She'd gotten the idea after Simone graciously finished adding the bothersome pockets to her jacket—even after Patty had stuck her foot in her mouth, up to her kneecap. From leftover material scraps in her mother's baskets, Simone had also created a multicolored tie-belt that not only gave the jacket some pizzazz but cinched its waist, making the suit fit Patty better, even flatter her figure.

When Patty had gushed her thanks, Simone had given her signature shrug and replied, "It was pretty lame before. Made you look like some automaton. Don't let the patriarchy do that to you. Gloria Steinem says feminism is about our being equal as we are, not having to become them." She turned off the sewing machine. "Like Mama Cass sings. You know: 'Make your own kind of music.'"

Humming the tune, Simone started down the stairs, tossing back, "Just saying," before closing the door to her bedroom and disappearing into a muffled concert of the Mamas and Papas folk group. Totally disinviting Patty—before she could find a way to apologize for insulting Simone earlier.

Patty just hadn't been able to find the right words. How to make up for basically insinuating a girl was easy? How would Patty respond if one of the guys who'd assumed she was fast simply because of her appearance apologized to her? What would she say? "Oh, that's okay you decided I'd go all the way just because I filled out a C-cup nicely." No, that kind of mistake was impossible to unsay. Bringing it up to apologize might only make matters worse. Maybe letting it lie and trying to make nice in other ways would balance the scale out.

"Hail fellow—and mademoiselle—well met!" Abe threw down his books, rattling the wooden tabletop, and sprawled into his chair, interrupting Patty's worry. "Where's teach?"

"She was here when I walked in," Will answered, opening his notebook to pull out his homework. "But the principal came and got her."

"That's weird," Abe replied. The pages' daily class schedule was such a breakneck race, a teacher not locked in place, raring to start talking the instant students assembled, was unheard of. He opened his spiral notebook and took out his homework as well—a neatly completed page of equations and numbers, pristine and precise, like Patty's.

She couldn't help noticing what a mess Will's math sheet was. It looked like he'd erased and scratched a hundred times. There was even Scotch tape running diagonally across the paper, holding it together. And his answers? Those that Patty could make out in the morass of his scribbling were wrong. All wrong.

Scowling, Will perused his calculations and chewed on his pencil. It was as pocked with teeth marks as a corncob at an eating contest. He'd recently gotten back a *D* on homework that Patty had seen. This was sure to be another one—or worse.

"Will," she whispered to catch his attention but not others. Patty happened to be very good at math—something she didn't usually show off. Not many other girls she knew liked the subject. And boys could be so strange about girls who enjoyed chemistry and calculus. But Will was going to flunk Trigonometry the way he was going unless he got some tutoring.

At the sound of her voice, Will looked up from his paper, putting a hand over it as a cloud of pink embarrassment colored his dusting of freckles.

She felt a little tug of pity at her heart. Patty certainly knew what it was like to feel mortified. She'd felt it plenty since coming to the Hill. *Don't make it worse by being a bull in a china shop about it*, she cautioned herself. *Or a smug know-it-all like Abe. Or— God forbid—Simone. Be respectful.* She opened her mouth, closed it. Good grief. All Patty really knew about talking to boys was how to flatter them.

Putting his other arm over his homework, totally shielding it now, Will smiled sheepishly and whispered back, "Cat got your tongue?"

Just say it.

Patty thought about Simone's unsparing honesty and how it made her so uncomfortable at first but then, eventually, helped her. That shocking book, for instance. Patty had to admit the text and diagrams of female private parts *were* illuminating—explaining things she never had the words to ask about before. She *was* comforted to learn that her mood swings before her cycle might be explained physiologically, that other women felt them, too. Before, Patty had worried she was becoming like some of her father's "hysterical" patients who needed "to calm the hell down," as he put it. She was going to try eating ripe bananas and drinking raspberry-leaf tea the way the book suggested as help for her cramps, too.

The material on "sexual independence," desire, consent, "reproductive rights"—those chapters just felt too scandalous to look at. Birth control for unmarried women hadn't even been legal until just last year! And the recent Supreme Court decision, that *Roe v. Wade* case—she knew very well what her father and the teacher-nuns at her old school would say about abortion. And how they'd chastise her for looking at the book to begin with—there were photos of naked women dancing together!

Patty took a deep breath and focused on Will. "Looks like..." she faltered.

"Like what?" Will asked, encouraging.

He was always such a gentleman to her. Would he continue to be if she managed to insult his intelligence? Then a way came to her. "This semester is pretty much a repeat of math I had back home last year." Total truth. "I can help you with your homework problems." Also truth. "If you let me."

Will bit his lip.

"I... I had trouble with these kinds of problems at first, too." She tossed in a little white lie. What could it hurt?

"You?" Will seemed to relax. "That's hard to believe, you're so brainy."

Nodding, she leaned toward him and gently pushed his hand away from his paper. "Take this first problem. It's just a right triangle question. 'If the sun is twenty-two degrees high in the sky, and it casts a shadow on a building that's sixty meters high, how long is its shadow?'"

"I don't know why I need to be able to calculate the length of a shadow," grumbled Will, "if I go into politics."

"You never know," she teased him. "Catch a political opponent lying about a building project, maybe? Here, look at this, you've set up your diagram right, but you've used the wrong function. You've used cosine to find the distance to the building, but you really should be calculating the tangent, opposite side over adjacent side. That's why your answer doesn't seem quite right."

"Oh, I get it now." Will sat back in his chair. "Thank you, Patty. You should be a teacher. My mama always said how much she loved teaching before she had my oldest brother and had to quit."

"Mr. Ferguson?" Their teacher had quietly reentered and put her hand on Will's shoulder.

Startled, he looked up. "Yes, ma'am?"

"I need you to come to the principal's office."

Patty panicked. Had she gotten Will in trouble somehow by correcting his homework? "Miss Bennett, I was just trying to—"

But Will and their teacher were already out the door, leaving Abe, Patty, and the handful of other pages staring at their backs.

A few seconds later the bell rang for class change.

"What the hell?" Abe muttered as he gathered up his books. "What do you think that's about?"

"I don't know," Patty answered hesitantly. "You don't suppose the teacher thought Will was cheating on his homework, do you?"

"Will?" Abe guffawed. "No way. Everybody knows the guy's dead honest. He'll fall on his sword of incompetence before ever doing anything wrong."

Reflexively, Patty punched Abe's arm. "That's mean."

"It's just fact. I love the guy. But he ain't headed for Harvard. Maybe one of North Carolina's state schools."

Hearing put to words her own sentiments about the hierarchy of colleges suddenly sounded so . . . so superior and snooty. Like her father's assumption that a big public high school would be inferior to private preps. Patty's stomach churned. Did she come across as that much of a snob, too?

Abe kept talking as they walked into their history classroom. "I'm pretty sure none of his brothers went to college. Just straight into the military. So, there isn't exactly a family tradition of—" He stopped in his tracks. "Oh *shhhhhhhhhhh—it*."

"What?"

"His brothers." Concern replaced Abe's more typical quick-to-make-a-joke response.

"But the treaty's signed. The war's over for us. Finally, thank God. They're coming home, aren't they?"

"Supposedly. Although I don't trust Tricky Dick's word, given his cover-up of troop deployment, and all the lies about the war the Pentagon Papers revealed." Abe paused and his tone turned from snarky to worried. "A few days ago, Will heard that one brother—the one who's on his second tour in 'Nam—was scheduled to be flown back to the States by the end of the month. But Will's still waiting to hear about the one who's been a POW and about the one who's MIA—his oldest brother. His family has been praying that son's name will show up on a previously undisclosed list of POWs. The Viet Cong have been notoriously evasive about listing captives." Abe reverted to his acerbic voice. "Of course, who can blame them—after all our bombing raids with napalm.

The burned villages. The civilians killed. We weren't exactly Boy Scouts over there."

"For pity's sake, Abe." Patty swatted him again—harder this time. "How unpatriotic can you be. And how—" she started to say *incredibly insensitive*. "I hope you haven't said anything like that to Will."

He frowned, silent. Clearly trying to remember.

"Oh, Abe, surely you haven't. That would have been terrible to—"

"Miss Appleton. Mr. Schmidt."

Abe and Patty whirled around. There stood their math teacher. "Come with me, please."

Silently threading their way among other pages scurrying to their classes, Miss Bennett led them through a labyrinth of tall shelves to the principal's small office. Before knocking, she turned to them. "He's asked for you two. Please walk him back to his room to pack—quickly. Then over to Union Station. His mother wants him home and has him booked on a train to Raleigh. It leaves in an hour. You need to help him hurry. He's quite upset."

"Is it—" Abe breathed.

"One of his brothers is dead."

Tapping the door lightly with her knuckles, she swung it open. The principal stood beside an arched window overlooking the Capitol grounds, his eyes averted outside. Will was hunched over his stack of books, shoulders quaking, still holding the cord of a telephone, its receiver resting on the floor, beeping a busy signal.

Red-eyed, Will stumbled to the elevator. Stumbled through the Library of Congress's vaulting beauty. Stumbled down its stairs. Turned right onto First Street, right again at the Supreme Court onto East Capitol. Dead quiet.

Abe and Patty dogged him. Neither speaking. What could they say, other than their initial "I'm so sorry"? Seeing their friend's anguished expression, they knew how hollow the condolence rang in Will's ears. It was too soon. Too soon for him to take in anything. And this boy was supposed to get on a train for a five-hour journey of mourning by himself?

Finally, Will's stumbling threw him down onto his hands and knees on the pavement, his books and papers skittering. "Dammit!" he shouted, rubbing at the pain in his shins.

Abe scrambled to collect Will's things before everything blew away while Patty dropped down beside him, instinctively reaching out to hug him.

But Will flinched away, looking toward the sky. "Damn you, God!"

Stunned, Patty sat back on her heels. Will was the most sincerely religious friend she had.

Will hollered his curse again. And again. Raising his voice louder with each outcry.

They were right in front of the Folger Shakespeare Library, and people approaching its tall art deco doors stopped to stare.

"We're okay. Thanks for your concern," Abe said, waving them off. He shoved Will's things into Patty's hands and hauled Will to his feet. "Come on, buddy. Let's get you off the sidewalk." He herded the trio toward the marble benches in front of the entrance, ornamented by an enormous carved Greek mask of tragedy. "Fitting," he muttered as he settled Will onto the stone slab and glanced up at the woeful, stony face.

"This stinks, man." Suddenly Abe was angry. Furious about the politics. Livid for his friend in a way Patty hadn't seen before. "You shouldn't have to go through this. Your brothers shouldn't have been there in the first place. It wasn't our fight. And what an effing boondoggle! How many thousands of Americans dead?

Because Nixon didn't want to be the first American president to lose a war. Remember his insane reasoning—'We will not be humiliated.' He—"

"Stop!" Will held up his hands. "Stop! I can't live with this—this god-awful loss—if people say it wasn't worth it. That the war and what my brothers went through wasn't morally justified." His blue eyes were agonized. "Just shut up! For once in your life, shut the hell up!"

Gaping, Abe quieted.

Will covered his face. "I'm sorry. I'm sorry. I'm sorry."

"It's okay, man. I deserved that."

Patty checked her watch. Forty minutes until Will's train left Union Station, four or five long blocks from where they sat. Will and Abe's boardinghouse was another two blocks down East Capitol. "Abe, I think you better run to your room and throw some things together for Will."

"But—"

"He needs to sit for a minute." Patty bossed Abe for a change. "Hurry!"

Abe bolted.

She put her arm over Will's shoulders. This time he let her. "I'll hang on to your books for you, Will."

"Thank you," he mumbled into his sleeve. After a moment, he raised his head, but his gaze went past her.

She turned to look where he did. Will seemed to be staring at the enormous stone-relief sculptures lining the building's wall. Nine scenes of Shakespeare. She'd marveled at them before—especially the one of Titania, leaning up against Bottom the ass.

Silent, Will gazed for a long time. Long enough for Abe to materialize again, a tiny figure way down the street, sprinting, a knapsack banging against his hip as he ran.

"There's Abe," Patty said, pointing. "Ready?" But Will was still transfixed by the stone scenes along the building.

"Today's the Ides of March," he murmured. "*Et tu, Brute?*"

Surprised, Patty turned to him. Will recognized Julius Caesar's assassination in the carved marble and knew that line?

"*Et tu*," Will breathed again. "Brutus was like Caesar's brother, wasn't he? Before he stabbed him to death." He rubbed his forehead, hard. "I think . . . I think I killed my brother, Patty." His words were so soft, so tremulous, Patty had to strain to hear them.

"What? Oh no, Will. You aren't thinking straight. It was the North Vietnamese."

A single tear slid down Will's cheek and off his chin. "I prayed and prayed for my brothers," he whispered. "The longer my youngest brother was held prisoner, and we heard stories of . . . of torture." He pulled in a shuddering breath. "The Viet Cong got Jimmy the very first week he was in country. He's . . . he's only nineteen. Jimmy is the kindest, the best of all of us, Patty. Gentle. He's not like my other brothers. He's no John Wayne. I've been so afraid that he couldn't hold up against on-purpose cruelty. So, I started bargaining with God. Promising Him all kinds of things if He would just save Jimmy. To please give him the will to stay alive. Jimmy's my best friend. I even"—a river of tears now flowed down Will's face—"I even . . ." His voice was barely audible. "I even said if . . . if You must take one of them, Lord . . . take . . . take . . ." He broke off, sobbing.

"Oh no. No, no." Patty held him tighter. Will only wept harder.

God Almighty, what should she say? What would the nuns at her school back home tell her? Patty racked her brain for some scripture they'd taught her that would assuage Will's pain, his illogical sense of guilt. Something about mercy, about forgiveness. But she could come up with nothing to ease the anguish of a teenager who so fervently believed in the power of prayer that he thought he'd managed somehow to pray one of his brothers into a terrible death.

After a fruitless moment, Patty simply said, "I don't believe God works like that, Will." Then with a rueful laugh, she said, "I know what Sister Margaret would say. She'd tell me that I was placing far more importance on my ability to negotiate than I had any right to—if I thought I could tell God what to do."

Will managed a laugh. He wiped his face on his sleeve. "I've never met a nun." Their eyes met. "Thanks, Patty. You're pretty darn cool, you know."

Their gazes held. He really had the most soulful blue eyes she'd ever seen. And there was such a new, awful sadness in them. Without thinking, Patty kissed Will on the cheek. She meant it as a friendly, supportive, sympathetic peck. But she felt him shudder, felt herself linger—her face pressed against a wisp of his soft hair.

Then she heard Abe's shoes against the pavement. She jumped up, away.

"Whew!" Abe threw Will's knapsack down to the ground and leaned over, winded.

Twenty-five minutes left.

Will stood. Hesitated. Glanced shyly at Patty, his face flushed.

"We better hurry," she said.

"I've got him, Pats." Straightening back up, Abe clapped Will on the back. "I'm coming with you, man. I'll just train down and back. Keep you company. Least I can do after being a jackass. Besides, I've never been below the Mason-Dixon Line."

"You're standing below it right now," Will replied.

"Oh yeah?" Abe winked at Patty. "There you go. I'm just a dope from New Jersey. Seriously, though, Will. I'd like to go with you. You shouldn't make this trip alone. I'll keep my mouth shut and just sit beside you. That okay?"

Will managed a wobbly smile. "Okay. Thanks."

Abe turned Will toward Union Station. "Explain where we are to the sergeant at arms?" Abe asked Patty.

"Of course. Take care, Will. I'll be thinking of you."

Will nodded, raised his hand to his forehead, and gave her a half-hearted salute.

Watching Abe and Will jog away together, Patty felt an inexplicable pang. She waited until her friends disappeared past the fountains and trees of the Senate gardens that separated the train station from the Capitol grounds before turning back to the Library of Congress—wondering what in the world was wrong with her.

"Heads up! Excuse me, please!"

Later, still distracted by a jumble of thoughts, Patty didn't notice the slender woman dashing down the hall outside the Senate chamber, followed by a cameraman.

"EXCUSE ME!"

A strong hand grabbed Patty's arm from behind to yank her back, out of the way, just in time. "Head in the clouds again, Lip Smacker girl?"

Him.

Still reverberating from Will's raw grief, she had no patience, no energy to muster polite appeasement for jerks making trouble for the heck of it. Not after having just witnessed the impact of *real* trouble and the pain it brought. "The name's Patty," she shot back.

Jake let go, throwing his hands up into the air as if at gunpoint. "Geez, okay, *Patty*. Relax. Don't be so sensitive. It's just a joke. C'mon, smile."

Another knot of reporters dashed by, trying to catch up to the woman, who outpaced them even in her heels.

"Who's that?"

"Connie Chung, CBS."

A second TV crew bustled by.

"What's going on?" Patty couldn't help her curiosity. Simone's voracious newspaper reading and the pages' collective urge to be in the know—always—were seeping into her as well. Before coming to Washington, she'd never seen teenagers fight over daily newspapers like the pages did or truly read them front to back like Simone.

Patty was even beginning to jockey for the pages' most desired chore: standing by the wire feeds for the Associated Press and United Press International, cutting off intriguing news bulletins as they ticked loudly out of the large gray machines and cascaded to the floor in rolls of paper, thick with urgent typing. Abe had claimed it was like having a finger on the pulse of the world as the machines rattled and spewed the latest happenings.

"They're chasing Senator Ervin's staff."

"Why?"

"They caught wind of a secret meeting in Ervin's hideaway office. With McCord—you know, the guy who puffs himself up as being"—he made quotation marks in the air—"the chief of security for Nixon's re-election committee."

The man Simone had been talking about. Patty nodded. "The Watergate burglar who wrote Judge Sirica claiming he'd been pressured to keep quiet. That he'd perjured himself but now was willing to share more information."

Jake looked at her with a bit of grudging respect. "That's right. After seeing that letter, Senators Baker and Ervin subpoenaed McCord. He came in today. But the senators were trying to keep the session on the down-low until they knew if McCord really had anything legit to say."

"Did he?"

"Word is he squealed like a stuck pig. Whether what he said is legit or not, or just fighting the chopping block with last-minute begging is up for debate."

Jake sounded like Patty's father.

"Guess we'll read more in the papers tomorrow from the looks of this chase," he continued. "But I know this much: I took Senator Baker his lunch and overheard McCord claim that Mitchell approved the break-in and a whole bunch of other political espionage. McCord is trying to convince Senator Baker that he was in the right place at the right time to know—meeting daily with Mitchell about his family's security. Claims he even drove Mitchell's daughter to school.

"But . . ." Jake paused dramatically. "Mitchell just issued a statement calling McCord a liar. Saying he barely knew the guy."

Patty couldn't believe she was asking Jake this, but she did: "Do you believe McCord?" If any of it were true, that meant people in the White House had been involved in a crime, a serious one, and then . . . then tried to hide it. Men a few feet from the Oval Office. Trying to manipulate and put the fix on an election. That . . . that would be . . . awful. So . . . un-American.

"Are you kidding?" Jake gave her a how-stupid-can-you-be grimace. Then he held up his hands like counterweight scales and said, "Let's see, the word of an important, successful lawyer, the onetime attorney general, one of the best friends of one of the smartest presidents we've ever elected"—he lowered one hand as if weighted with evidence—"versus a clown. A so-called security expert who got caught red-handed, like some dumbass kid trying to shoplift at a candy store right in front of the owner."

Another clutch of reporters hurried by.

"But the game's on now." Jake nodded toward the reporters with disgust. "Jackals. They've caught the scent of blood in the water. It'll be more than just those *Washington Post* hit men hounding staff now." Jake sauntered off, cocky as always. "Catch ya on the flip side, Peppermint Patty."

Patty chewed on all Jake had said. She didn't want to believe any of McCord's claims. Her father had worked so hard to help elect Nixon. Her parents and all their friends were fervent believers in the president, his foreign policy, his domestic philosophies, his patriotism and intellect. There was no way a man like that would cheat on an election. But would people around him? It just didn't make sense. Nixon had won in a landslide. McGovern's campaign had been a disaster. *Why* would they do it?

Watching Jake turn the corner, Patty realized that this was the first time she'd been able to hold her own with him. Because she knew about McCord.

Whether Patty liked to admit it or not, she had Simone to thank for that.

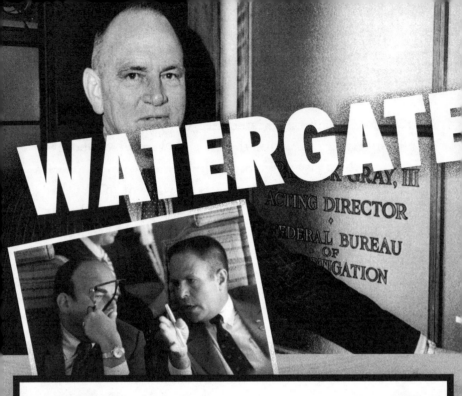

WATERGATE

IN HIS APRIL CONFIRMATION HEARINGS— (unrelated to Watergate at first)— **ACTING FBI DIRECTOR** Patrick Gray admits **BURNING DOCUMENTS TAKEN FROM THE WHITE HOUSE** safe of convicted Watergate conspirator Howard Hunt.

Eleven days after the break-in, he'd been handed envelopes of "political dynamite" by John Dean, counsel to the president, in the presence of Nixon's chief domestic policy adviser, John Ehrlichman. **THE MATERIAL "SHOULD NEVER SEE THE LIGHT OF DAY,"** said Dean, implying they endangered national security.

In truth, the envelopes contained faked documents and damning gossip about Senator Ted Kennedy when he was a possible presidential Democratic candidate.

GRAY RESIGNS FROM THE FBI.

Ehrlichman denies instructing Gray to destroy the documents. But two days later, **UNDER A TSUNAMI OF PUBLIC OUTCRY, EHRLICHMAN RESIGNS AS WELL.**

SO DOES NIXON'S CHIEF OF STAFF, BOB HALDEMAN, accused of ordering campaign donations be used for hush money payments to the burglars.

In response, Nixon gives his first televised speech addressing Watergate. Saying he had accepted the resignations of "the finest public servants it has been my privilege to know," Nixon stresses that doing so was **NOT TO IMPLY WRONGDOING**, but to restore public confidence that legal and ethical standards "are being enforced by the president of the United States." Even so, **NIXON COMPLAINS HE'D BEEN THE VICTIM** of people he trusted lying to him.

HE FIRES DEAN, and the spotlight of blame snaps onto the 34-year-old lawyer.

BATTLE OF WITS

PHYLLIS SCHLAFLY STEPS UP HER STOP-ERA CAMPAIGN. Deluged with Valentines, home-baked bread, and face-to-face pleas from her followers, legislators in **TWELVE STATES HAVE REJECTED THE ERA**.

Pert, poised, and polished, **SCHLAFLY HAS BECOME THE DARLING OF TALK SHOWS**, a sound-bite maven of conservative opposition with her rapid-fire hyperboles and **HER INSISTENCE THAT THE ERA WILL DESTROY THE AMERICAN FAMILY**. Some talk shows pair her with pro-ERA feminists, like **NOW PRESIDENT WILMA SCOTT HEIDE**, who **DOES HER BEST TO DEBUNK** Schlafly's claims. One example: Schlafly's assertion on the *Mike Douglas Show* that the amendment would "take away a mother's right to stay home with her children. It will *require* her to work and produce 50 percent of a family's income, since, under the ERA, **A HUSBAND WILL NO LONGER BE OBLIGATED TO SUPPORT HIS CHILDREN**."

ANOTHER BREAK-IN

GORDON LIDDY

In ironic coincidence, **PROSECUTORS IN A FEDERAL TRIAL AGAINST DANIEL ELLSBERG**—the military analyst who'd leaked the Vietnam War **PENTAGON PAPERS**—discover that Hunt and fellow Watergate conspirator Gordon Liddy had broken into the office of Ellsberg's psychiatrist. **AS "PLUMBERS"** tasked by Nixon's administration with "fixing" leaks, **THEIR GOAL WAS TO STEAL MENTAL HEALTH TREATMENT RECORDS** that might damage Ellsberg's credibility and weaken his defense. At the time, both Hunt and Liddy were employed by the White House, reporting directly to Ehrlichman. Citing government misconduct, **THE JUDGE DISMISSES ALL CHARGES AGAINST ELLSBERG**.

CHAPTER FOUR

APRIL

Abe was skipping. Skipping! And singing a *Mary Poppins* song wildly off tune: *"Let's go fly a kite. Up to the highest height."*

What a goofball.

He tried to jump up at an angle to kick his heels together. Totally missed.

Patty laughed at him. "Face it. You are no Dick Van Dyke."

"Aww, c'mon. I've got a little bit of Bert the chimney sweep going here." Abe faked a soft-shoe tap as their newly made kite flapped around him.

"Hey, be careful!" Patty pulled the kite away. It'd been a battle to cut the thick paper into a precise quadrilateral shape so that the geometry of it would catch the wind correctly. His silly cavorting could tear it or knock its stick-ribs askew.

Patty's competitive nature was getting the best of her. She and Abe were on the Mall for the annual Kite Carnival the Smithsonian had started a few years back to coincide with the Cherry Blossom Festival. "We might win best-made if you don't break it!" she fussed.

Looking at the crowds of people gleefully dashing around the Washington Monument's wide-open grounds and launching a flock of colorful and creative kites—there was even a paper eagle fluttering in the breeze—Abe shook his head. "Best made? Not a chance, Pats!" He reached for the kite's string ball. "You hold, I'll run."

"Wait a second." Patty held the kite out of his reach. Running with the kite was the best part.

"The wind's coming and going, Pats. It needs real speed and a hard yank to lift."

"You think I can't sprint?" She'd seen him bolt down the Hill's tunnels—Abe was definitely faster than she was. But still. Coming today had been her idea. She should do the honors.

Tugging on his sideburns as he considered, Abe said, "Lady's choice. But if ya wanna maybe win highest-flying..." He pointed toward two National Air and Space officials with clipboards, jotting down notes as they watched a young boy race across the lawns, whooping, his bright red kite getting smaller and smaller as it climbed higher and higher toward the wispy clouds—his mom clapping excitedly.

With a bit of stubborn defiance, Patty kept her hold on the kite.

Abe laughed. "Right on, sister. Go for it." He took the kite as she unfurled the first few feet of twine, getting ready to run. "We'll make a feminist out of you yet, Ms. Appleton."

Patty ignored his teasing. What did feminism have to do with flying a kite? "Ready?"

Nodding, he held it over his head. "Go!"

Patty darted, feeling the kite dip and bob on the line.

"Go, go, go!" Abe shouted.

The kite swerved and rattled. The string wasn't pulling taut. The breeze was erratic—first strong, then tepid. Dip and bob. Dip and bob. The kite felt like it was going to trip and plummet. *Sugar!* She didn't want to hear Abe's ribbing if she failed to get it up into the air.

Patty leaned forward into her best fifty-yard dash.

"That's it! GO!" Abe's voice was getting distant as she ran farther and farther.

Suddenly she felt a sharp yank and then consistent tugging as their kite filled with wind. Patty let the string unspool and the kite swam upward in zigzags . . . up . . . up to peacefully settle and skim along the air, its tail of red-white-and-blue bows sashaying prettily behind.

"Well done!" Abe called, jogging up to her.

Flushed and exuberant, Patty grinned her thanks, still a little breathless from her run.

Abe glanced up to the sky, back down at her, and then up again.

"Is . . . is something wrong?" Patty brushed her hair off her face. Did she look disheveled or something?

"Nope." Abe crossed his arms, uncharacteristically succinct. Of course, that lasted only a few seconds. "Anyone ever tell you that you look like Julie Andrews?"

"What? No!" Patty frowned. "Gross. She's old. She must be forty! Do you think I look like . . . like someone old enough to be our mothers?"

"I'm talking about ten years ago when she was in *Mary Poppins*. Beautiful, big eyes. Great smile." He looked back up to the clouds.

"Thank you. I guess?" Patty made a face. "My boyfriend says I look like Ali MacGraw, you know, from *Love Story*."

"Oh yeah?" Patty felt rather than saw Abe take an arm's-length step away from her as he asked, "We ever going to meet your Romeo?"

"In the fall. He's been accepted to Georgetown." Patty beamed.

"Oooooh. Georgetown. That's impressive." Abe's convivial tone felt a bit forced.

More kites vaulted into the low blue heavens and began sailing beside theirs.

"Keep an eye out for crossing lines," Abe warned.

Mmm-hmm. Why was it suddenly feeling so awkward? "Too bad Will isn't here," Patty murmured. "He'd have enjoyed this. Do you know when he's coming back?" She startled at the feel of her stomach squiggling with butterflies at her mention of Will.

"In a couple weeks. Not until next month probably. He wants to help his mom settle. She's taking his brother's death hard. And the one who was a POW? Will won't say much—you know how he is—never wanting to say anything bad. But I'm getting the sense that brother came home pretty beat up in all sorts of ways."

"Oh gosh. Is Will's dad helping them cope?" Patty was having a hard time envisioning her psychoanalyst father in that kind of situation. Would he be loving and reassuring to her mother? Or cool and analytical? He could be so dismissive of her mother's "annoying histrionics," as he called them, when Dot Appleton's controlled veneer finally cracked and she showed actual emotion. Her father was so much the center of everything about their family, Patty had always instinctively absorbed his take on things—including how to interpret her mother. But now Patty was beginning to wonder whether if her father was different—maybe a little less imposing, maybe more like Simone's dad—her mother might be less withdrawn and on edge.

"You didn't know?" Abe broke into her thoughts. "Will's dad died back in '65. He deployed with the first combat troops we sent—thirty-five-hundred marines to Da Nang to protect our airbase. A drill sergeant. Meant to just be advising South Vietnamese troop training. Will's dad was a few months off from retirement when he was blown up by a Viet Cong ambush. Will was only ten years old at the time. That's when they had to move back in with his grandparents, in a farm east of Raleigh." He sighed and added, "There's a family we as a nation screwed but good."

Hit with a wave of sadness for Will and unease with Abe's biting comment, Patty handed him the spool of string, wanting to regain the morning's sense of fun. "You fly her for a while."

Abe went silent, concentrating on gently tugging the string to keep the kite up in the air. "Sooooo..." he murmured.

"Sooooo?" Patty echoed.

"So, where's this girl you want me to meet? You plotting something, Pats? What's she like?"

Inconsequential banter—thank God. In truth, Patty was plotting a little—hoping that introducing Simone to a really nice guy she clearly had much in common with, politically and philosophically, at least, might thaw the frostiness she'd caused the previous month with her presumptions about Simone's sexual experience and possible lack of... well, what Patty defined as virtue. "She's a total lefty, a real smarty-pants, like you! A bit... mmm... blunt." Patty laughed lightly. "I never know what's going to come out of Simone's mouth next!"

"My kinda girl. So where is she?"

Patty checked her watch. "She should be here soon. She and her mom are picking up my mother at National on the way."

"Your mom's coming to town? I'd love to meet her."

"No, you wouldn't." The words just popped out of Patty's mouth. "I mean... She... You two wouldn't agree on anything." The last thing Patty needed, frankly, was for Dot Appleton to get a whiff of Abe's politics. She'd label him a socialist or worse. Patty would never hear the end of it. Simone was just as bad as Abe, but her mother tolerated her because she was Aunt Marjorie's daughter. Flustered, Patty rushed on, "I'm not really sure why she's here, to be honest. Easter break is next week, so I would have seen her at home in a few days anyway."

"Maybe she wants to experience the cherry blossoms. People come from all over the country to see them, you know." Abe nodded toward the lacy, rippling line of pink on the horizon, where the three thousand cherry trees Japan had given the United States back in 1912 were in riotous bloom along the Tidal Basin.

The pages had trooped down Constitution Avenue together a few nights before to stand beneath the small, graceful trees at twilight—holding up their hands to catch petals shaken loose by the evening wind, falling like rose-colored snow flurries. It had been totally enchanting.

Maybe, Patty conceded, although her mother hadn't said that.

"Is she going to fly a kite, too?" Abe grinned. "We could agree on that!"

Patty smiled ruefully and shook her head at the absurd visualization of her mother flying a kite. "She and my godmother are heading to the National Gallery of Art after dropping Simone with us. The NGA evidently just purchased a new Picasso that Mother is all excited about seeing. She was an art major in college." Patty paused. "She actually is a really good painter." Why the heck were her eyes misting up thinking about her mother's garage apartment studio, filled with landscapes and still life paintings that stayed locked up there?

"I didn't know that about your mom. I only hear you talk about your dad. Do you draw, too?"

"Not even with crayons."

"There you are!" called a female voice. "I've been looking everywhere for you. We should have walkie-talkies or something, like those Watergate burglars."

Patty turned. There was Simone, her face a pretty pink from the slight chill of the early April wind that was lifting her long hair in billows of gold. Abe's mouth dropped open in bedazzlement before he snapped it shut with an audible click of his teeth.

Well, she'd been right about Simone being Abe's type, given his reaction. But Patty had been dead wrong about something else. Simone wasn't single, like she'd thought. Simone was with a guy. Holding hands. And something else Patty never would have anticipated—he was Black.

"This is Julius," Simone introduced him.

Patty stared.

If Abe was disappointed that Simone had come with an unknown beau when he was expecting to be set up with her, he didn't let on for a second. "Hey man." Abe held his hand up and out, level with his face, waiting.

Julius grinned at the soul-power gesture. "All right. My white brother's hip." He put his hand below Abe's to receive a slap before the boys shook hands side to side, thumb to thumb.

"Glad to know you," Abe said to Julius, then turned to Simone. "You must be the famous Simone. I've heard wonderful things about you. A pleasure." Left hand to his heart, he bowed as he shook Simone's hand with his right.

Oh, he was smooth. Abe was sure to be a senator one day. Should be, anyway—if the electorate had any sense. The Republican Party would need to watch out for him. Patty might even consider the sacrilege of crossing party lines to vote for him.

Following Abe's lead, Julius held his hand toward Patty. "When Simone said she was hanging out with you today, I asked to tag along, so we could meet. Hope you don't mind my showing up unannounced."

Patty slipped her hand into his. Grasping hers firmly—not the way some men took a woman's hand gingerly, as if she might break—Julius patted it with his other. Up, down, up, down, lingering for several seconds. An earnest, embracing double handshake.

With a feeling she could not define, Patty realized Julius was the first Black person with whom she'd ever shaken hands.

After a half hour of kite flying, the foursome headed to the National Gallery to meet Patty's and Simone's mothers. Strolling along the Mall toward the Capitol, the guys walked up front, laughing loudly and punching each other's shoulder in some shared joke. Given the sidewalk's limited width, Simone and Patty fell in behind, side by side.

"I hadn't realized you had a boyfriend," Patty said, trying to be careful in how she approached Simone's love life, given her inadvertently insulting her before with her stupid assumption Simone was no longer a virgin. "Where did you meet?"

Simone looked sideways at her, suddenly defensive. "School."

"Oh, right. Of course. I just . . . Sorry. My school was all-girls," Patty reminded Simone. "He seems really nice."

That softened Simone. "He is." She smiled. "He's in band, too. Plays trumpet. First chair. Crazy good. He's waiting to hear if he's got a full scholarship to one of the country's best music conservatories. Fingers crossed. He won't be able to go if he doesn't get that money."

"How long have you been dating?"

"A while," Simone added with her usual shrug. "We're not going steady or anything."

"But you were holding hands," Patty blurted. Why in the world would they risk so much if they weren't serious enough to go steady?

Patty had seen the movie *Guess Who's Coming to Dinner*. The screen daughter introduces her Black fiancé, Sidney Poitier, to her disapproving father—who worries about the challenges they'll face as an interracial couple in a country where more than a dozen states still outlawed mixed-race unions. Eventually the father blesses their marriage, seeing how much they love each other. But still. Real life rarely worked out as neatly as movie scripts.

Patty's own father had given her quite a lecture to that very point when he found Patty watching a special broadcast of the movie on TV. With the Black Panthers' increasing militancy following MLK's terrible assassination, her father and his friends were expressing real hostility to Black Americans and people who advocated for them. It was pretty embarrassing to hear them talk the way they did. And her father's take on the Hill's Black pages—who were as small in number as females like her—was not to say they didn't belong, but that they were at Congress as "window dressing." Thank God he hadn't said it where any of them could hear him.

He'd also about had a fit when he learned Simone's high school was busing students to redistribute Alexandria's racial ratios and integrate T. C. Williams. Dr. Appleton had added "liberal idiocy" to his list of negatives about Aunt Marjorie, for being okay with Simone "being a pawn in a sociological experiment."

Simone's dating a Black guy would be a bridge too far for Dr. Appleton. Patty could easily imagine the ugly labels he'd use. It was the kind of thing that might make her father decide it was better for Patty to be at home than in Washington. He'd already been making noises that she could only attend a college that wasn't overrun with "ungrateful hippies."

All that rushed through Patty's mind before she realized Simone was glowering at her. "You going to imply I'm some promiscuous Jezebel again?"

"NO!" Patty protested loudly enough that Abe and Julius both glanced back at her, questions on their faces. "No," she said, lowering her voice. Maybe this was her opportunity to apologize. "Listen, I didn't mean anything when—"

"Sure you did," Simone cut her off. Then with a wicked grin, she needled Patty, "Want me to tell you how good a kisser a trumpet player is? You know they change octaves and notes mostly by shifting their lip position against their mouthpiece—they've only got three valves, not like all the keys I have for different notes on my flute. Gives them very subtle embouchure. Make-out heaven. Sexy as hell."

Patty turned crimson.

"Oh geez," Simone chortled, and put her arm through Patty's. "I'm sorry. I don't mean to push your buttons. Well, maybe I do. God knows you need some shaking, Patty Appleton, some serious waking up." She shrugged. "My brothers tease me all the time. I instinctively relate to other people that way. Maybe I shouldn't."

Patty started to pull away, but Simone kept their arms locked and walking forward, like Parisian ladies perusing shops along the Champs-Élysées in photographs Aunt Marjorie had taken and shown her.

"My mom wants us to be friends," Simone continued, "like she and your mother are. Don't think we'll ever get to their bosom-buddy level. Let's be honest: We probably would not gravitate to one another if we met at school. I mean, you're nice, even sweet sometimes, but . . . you could use some serious consciousness-raising, you know? And . . . well, seems like you're establishment all the way and I'm kinda counterculture."

She broke off to laugh at the face Patty was making, the question "*kinda* counterculture?" all over her face. "Yeah, yeah, okay. We're just diametrically opposed on a lot of things, right?" She waited for Patty to nod. "But Mom's very into sisterhood right now, no matter differences of opinion or style between women. Sticking together is how change will happen, she says. And," Simone added with a rebellious smile, "totally disappoint all the men who harbor fantasies of catfights between us."

Abe and Julius had stopped in front of the beautiful wide, white staircase of the National Gallery of Art. The city really seemed all glistening-pearl marble and domes. Simone slowed their approach and whispered in Patty's ear, "You know that guy Abe is sweet on you, don't you? There." She pulled back and said, "I don't have many friends. I seem to intimidate people for some reason—but I think that's the type of revelations girlfriends are supposed to share. Jane Austen certainly seems to think so."

She let go of Patty's arm before Patty could whisper back, *is not!* about Abe, or *hell yes* about Simone being intimidating.

Simone approached Julius and took his hand. "Mom said to look for them in the Picasso exhibit. You coming, Abe?"

Patty didn't know whether to insist he come or shoo him away. What the heck would Simone say next? She didn't want Abe to get any kind of wrong idea. She was devoted to Scott.

Maybe sensing her hesitation, Abe declined. "Naw, I need to do laundry. Next time though. Thanks for the kite flying, Pats. See ya Monday. Rest up and be ready to run! You never know these days what could happen next on the Hill with Watergate. All hell could break loose this week!" Promising to give it back on Monday, Abe kept the kite, turned and strode away, once again singing, "*Let's go fly a kite . . .*"

Inside, the trio passed through the museum's rotunda with its centerpiece fountain and statue of Mercury, gracefully balanced on one winged foot as he sprinted. It was crowded. Patty couldn't help but notice as they winnowed through bodies that Julius was the only Black person she could see in that sea of white art lovers. Did he note it as well? Neither he nor Simone seemed the least self-conscious if they did. They had, however, stopped holding hands.

Following signs to a gallery promising paintings by Pablo Picasso and fellow cubist Georges Braque, they found Patty and Simone's moms standing in front of a tall, thin canvas of brown, gray, and cream interlocking patterns. Both women had their heads cocked sharply to the right as they looked. Like Simone had done with her, Aunt Marjorie held Dot Appleton close by the arm, the onetime college roommates talking in animated whispers.

Something about their embrace stopped Patty in her tracks. She'd never seen her mother linger in such an affectionate stance. Even with her father. Even with Patty.

With a strange pang of jealousy, Patty turned away to read the gallery's description of the recently purchased Picasso, completed by the artist in 1910, that the mothers were admiring. "An extraordinary transformation of the human figure to an almost complete abstraction expressed in fragmented planes." *Femme Nue*. That was supposed to be a woman? To Patty, the painting simply looked like a jar of geometry shapes had been dumped in a pile atop one another.

She followed Simone and Julius across the room to a more traditional image in soft pastel colors—a delicately outlined couple standing in front of a window, the man's arm around the woman's shoulders. The woman looked down, modestly but also . . . Patty inched closer, edging around other patrons gazing at this Picasso. On the woman's face, a shy hint of hope.

The Lovers was the title. Patty nodded. *Yes*. Picasso had captured a heart-stopping aura of guileless anticipation, of unexpected, nascent chemistry between the two. The way the man was looking at her, the way the woman had taken his hand, the painting promised a coming kiss, one that was gentle, reverent, perhaps even their first. Oh, it was lovely.

Clearly spellbound as well, Simone sighed. Without turning from the painting, Julius reached out and took Simone's hand. Rapt.

Patty caught her breath at the sight of them, their mirroring the romance depicted in the painting. They might not be going steady, but there was an obvious commitment, a sweetness, a tenderness between Simone and Julius that was palpable. Beautiful. Pure.

Hussy.

Patty whirled around. She stared at a phalanx of older women, perfectly coifed, pearls at their throat, brooches shaped like blossoms on the lapels of their tweed jackets, right above pins that indicated they were donors to the gallery. They seemed to be looking straight ahead at a painting of a mournful family, all in blue, next to *The Lovers*. Austere, but silent.

Had Patty imagined the hissed slur? Simone didn't seem to have heard anything. Patty turned back to the painting.

Then she heard the voice again, answered by others. *This is what the world is coming to. Give them an inch. What did her mother teach that trashy girl?*

Patty turned on her heel again. But this time Aunt Marjorie was walking briskly toward them, head high, saying "excuse me" with pointed iciness to the doyennes as she brushed past.

"There you are, sugar," she burbled, hugging Simone. Then, in a stage-loud voice, "I'm so glad you came to see the collection, Julius. Aren't the Picassos breathtaking?" She put her hand on his shoulder and smiled at him, gracious, warm, even protective.

The grande dames shook their heads and *tsk-tsked*.

"How about some lunch?" Aunt Marjorie herded the trio toward Patty's mother. "Shall we, Dottie?"

Patty's mother did nothing to hide the fact she was appalled by Simone's choice of beau. It was smeared all over her perfectly made-up face.

Seeing it, Julius let go of Simone's hand.

Patty felt her stomach turn with a terrible recognition—that her mother's sour expression was a physical manifestation of what Patty had been feeling when she first saw Simone with Julius: fear of what others would say. The thoughts were that ugly.

"Mom! It's starting!" Snapping on their television a few days later, Simone fiddled with one of the rabbit-ear antennas to sharpen the set's image before pulling off her purple suede boots and plopping into the chintz-covered love seat next to Patty. "This ought to be good," she pronounced. "I'm stoked to hear the president of

NOW take on Madam anti-lib, anti-choice, anti-empowerment. Schlafly's somehow managed to run roughshod over other people. I think it's because they just can't believe the whoppers coming out of her mouth."

She pulled her feet up and hugged her knees, sinking into the soft cushion so much that she listed over onto Patty's shoulder. "MOM! You're going to miss it!"

Wiping her hands on a bright-pink apron, Aunt Marjorie hurried into the small living room. She'd insisted on making a special Julia Child dinner—the PBS French Chef's signature beef bourguignon—for Patty and her mother before they flew out together the next morning for home and Easter vacation.

Patty wondered if her godmother would be going to so much trouble if she knew where Dot Appleton had been the previous day.

Somehow, at some luncheon back home, Patty's mother had met and been charmed by Phyllis Schlafly, joining her housewife crusaders who'd descended on the Illinois State House the previous month to lobby its lawmakers. Her mother had baked a dozen loaves of her delicious banana bread, attaching handwritten love notes dictated by Schlafly: "From the bread-bakers to the breadwinners. Please defend motherhood."

What had been anticipated to be a sure win vote for the ERA was reversed—the bread-bakers prevailed. Wanting to impress their leader, Patty's mom had shared the fact her daughter was a Capitol Hill page. So she could always schedule a visit to D.C., if she could be of help in any way while in town.

That was why Dot Appleton was in D.C. *really*—not the cherry blossoms, or the Picasso. It seemed Senator Sam Ervin—the powerful chairman of the Watergate Committee whom Patty so admired for his seeming courtliness—was continuing his campaign against the ERA. Just like Simone had accused him of doing that night at dinner. He was using Schlafly's mailing lists to send out his own anti-ERA speeches paired with her missives—adding the clout of his Senate office to the STOP ERA argument and his postage-free, congressional franking to mail them. Patty's mother was hand delivering a new batch of Schlafly addresses.

"This is so exciting," her mother had purred as she drove Patty to Capitol Hill in Simone's borrowed Bug. "I never thought I'd step into a political debate. That's for your father to do. But"—she reached for her purse and put it in Patty's lap—"open it, and read Phyllis's newsletter. You'll see why I'm doing this. Our very way of life is being threatened."

Patty unfolded a cream-colored paper titled *The Phyllis Schlafly Report*, with an eagle outstretched over the word *Report*, and an oval, sorority-style portrait of a beaming Schlafly to the left. The essay was long, peppered with church dogma—about family being the most important unit of society, that women gave birth and men didn't, and if anyone didn't like that fact "they'd have to take up their complaint with God." Patty mostly glossed over it until she reached *"A noisy movement has sprung up agitating for 'women's rights.' Suddenly, everywhere we are afflicted with aggressive females . . . yapping about how mistreated American women are."*

Whoa. Aggressive? Yapping? Simone, maybe, thought Patty, but not Aunt Marjorie.

She read on through Schlafly denigrating Gloria Steinem and *Ms.* magazine as being pretentious, shrill, antifamily: *". . . a series of sharp-tongued, high-pitched, whining complaints by unmarried women . . . to sow seeds of discontent among happy, married women so that all women can be unhappy in some new sisterhood of frustrated togetherness."*

Patty felt carsick. Or was it a little shock at the vitriol? Simone read *Ms.* religiously. She had every copy ever printed in her room. Patty had picked it up a couple times to thumb through. It was liberal and pointed, sure, but she didn't see anything as . . . as spiteful as this in the magazine's articles. God, women could be so hateful to each other.

"See what I mean?" her mother said.

Patty wasn't so sure she did.

Driving back to Alexandria that evening, her mother was almost giddy about the three-minute encounter she'd had with Ervin: "What a charming gentleman," she'd cooed. Then she admonished Patty to not tell Aunt Marjorie. "We've never really agreed on politics. A bleeding-heart, your godmother. And in this case, what Marj doesn't know won't hurt her. I'm going to say I revisited the Picassos. And I did, half the day. So, it's not a fib."

Patty had been unable to do anything but stare at her mother. She'd never seen her so energized. And rarely did her mother let Patty in on her thoughts.

Now, in her godmother's cozy family room, with Simone practically sitting on her, Patty squirmed with guilt at keeping a secret from people who were being so nice to her. As if Simone might hear her thoughts, pressed together this close, Patty scooched away to lean against the tiny sofa's rolled arm as Aunt Marjorie shouted, "Dottie! The talk show I wanted you to see is starting."

"Here, I'm here." Patty's mother swept into the room—still clutching a folded sweater, obviously mid-pack—just as the show's host, Mike Douglas, announced he had two guests, representing the opposing sides of the ERA argument, which "has stirred controversy throughout the United States." First up was national chairwoman of the STOP ERA committee, Phyllis Schlafly, an author, a wife, and a mother of six.

The studio pianist struck up "I Enjoy Being a Girl," as the stage doors—painted in enormous flower-power daisies—parted dramatically. In glided Phyllis Schlafly, trim in a blood-orange suit-dress, the gleam of the gold eagle pin on her lapel outshone only by her beaming, beauty-queen-worthy smile.

"There she is," the two moms said simultaneously, their tone of voice completely different from each other.

But only Patty seemed to note it.

"Good grief," muttered Simone. "You could bounce a dime off that beehive." She elbowed Patty and pointed to the screen. "At least she's not wearing one of those obnoxious stop-sign buttons. You know what her STOP ERA stands for? Stop Taking Our Privileges. She just wants to stay queen of her suburban castle. Not every woman is married to some rich lawyer or lives in status-symbol land. Julius's mom used to clean house for a Pleasant-Valley-Sunday woman like that—imperious and oblivious—before she finished night school and got her job at the library. Mrs. Allen loves working with books. But she *needs* the income. Working is not some lark like this woman Schlafly insinuates a woman having a job, or a career, is."

Aunt Marjorie nodded in agreement, while Patty's mother settled into unreadable stone.

Patty felt her gaze swivel back and forth between the mothers: How in the world was she to please both her mother and her godmother, who hosted and encouraged her with such kindness? Honestly, Aunt Marjorie may have already complimented Patty more in the last three months than her own mother had in her entire life. Where could she safely land during this political debate?

On the television, Douglas explained that Schlafly had seven minutes to detail her position. When she heard piano music, she had one minute to wrap up. "Fine," Schlafly replied, smiling, blinking, her white eye shadow shining.

With an on-camera savvy that a seasoned broadcaster would admire, Schlafly turned to directly face the TV audience. She explained that when she first heard of the ERA, she thought it might be a good thing. But then she realized the Civil Rights Act of 1964 and the Equal Employment Opportunity Act of 1972 promised all Americans equal pay for equal work. So, if any woman felt discriminated against, she could simply file a complaint with the government.

"And then hope the EEOA commission will actually do something," murmured Aunt Marjorie. "And that it won't take years to resolve."

But more importantly, Schlafly continued, the amendment would have many unfortunate consequences. "For example, the laws of every one of our fifty states *require* the husband to support his wife and family." She reached behind her chair to pull up a massive law encyclopedia—American Jurisprudence 2nd, volume 41, which "spells out all these wonderful rights that the wife has to be supported by her husband and to be provided with a home by her husband. Things that are very precious to women."

"Precious indeed," Patty's mother breathed. Barely a whisper.

But Patty heard.

The ERA, Schlafly grew emphatic, would invalidate those protections. "Because under the ERA no longer can you have any law that imposes an obligation on one sex that it doesn't on the other... This is what the proponents want... to take away from the wife her legal right to be a full-time wife and mother."

"Oh, for pity's sake." Aunt Marjorie crossed her arms. "That's not what we want at all. We—"

Dot Appleton held up her hand for silence, before sitting down slowly into an armchair, mesmerized—as one does when getting bad news.

Schlafly talked on for another four minutes about a dangerous, "unisex" world the ERA would create, where women could be thrown into prison cells with male inmates, about women being "just as smart" but certainly "not able physically to compete with a man," about the possibility of wives' Social Security benefits being denied.

With each dire prediction, Patty's mother slumped further into the chintz armchair. Patty had never before seen her sit without ramrod-straight posture.

Aunt Marjorie paced.

Chewing on her fingernails, Simone grumbled about being able to lift a bass drum as well as any guy.

Patty anxiously watched them all, trying to plan out what she'd say that could appeal to them all if asked her opinion, as flummoxed as a chameleon thrown atop a paintbox of hues.

During her remarks, Douglas had leaned toward Schlafly, frowning slightly, trying to eyeball the various reports she held up as supposed corroboration of her claims. "Ooooo-kay," Douglas said as she concluded, sitting back in his chair. "The other side after these messages."

"The next woman is who I'm excited for you to hear," Aunt Marjorie explained to Patty's mother. "She's so even-keeled and smart. A mother herself. Not like some of the more radical feminists you find offensive, Dottie. I think she'll impress you. And help you understand why I'm volunteering with the caucus." She smiled hopefully. "Maybe she'll convince you, too. We could use you! An elegant, moderate, articulate Republican."

Ha! Thought Patty. *If you only knew, Aunt Marjorie.*

Harp music fit for a Disney princess movie filled the sitting room as the TV screen flickered to an ad of a woman in a miniskirt and heels sashaying alongside a vacuum cleaner. *"Glide through your housework with a Hoover . . ."*

Next up, a cuddling couple in their pajamas, sitting on the edge of their bed. The man talked, the woman remained silent, smiling.

"My wife's incredible."

"Oh my God!" Simone jumped out of the love seat as the TV man went on about his wife being able to take care of their baby all day, make a great dinner, go to a PTA meeting, and still look "better than any of her friends."

"This is that unbelievably sexist ad! NOW wants us to boycott Geritol because of this baloney!" Simone tried to dash to the set to turn off the volume but stumbled on her boots. "Arrrrggggh!" she growled, finally reaching the dial just as the ad ended with the husband saying, *My wife—I think I'll keep her.*

Patty's mother looked baffled. "What's wrong with that? I take Geritol."

Simone stared at her, literally biting her lip, before glancing toward her own mom.

"Well, Dottie, it's that he's objectifying her," Aunt Marjorie said gently. "Honestly, I might not have seen it before myself. I take Geritol, too. You and I both want to stay attractive, especially to our husbands. But what my Women's Caucus friends would say is if the wife in the ad wants to take a vitamin supplement, that's great, but—"

"She should do it for her own health," Simone interrupted. "Not to give some guy bragging rights."

Inwardly, Patty winced. At every cocktail party Dot Appleton had hosted for his Republican cronies, her father inevitably put his arm around her when a male guest commented on the evening's success, and said, "Thanks, I think I'll keep her." His way of giving her mother credit for the event. Direct compliments or thanks were not his style.

Her mother had always seemed pleased by the comment. And whenever she witnessed it, Patty had thought it nice, too. That her father was showing appreciation for all she did to create and sustain his aura of importance within their community.

"I'll keep her?" Simone rolled her eyes. "Like some hat? Or pet dog? Grown women should have more self-respect." She shrugged and tossed out her usual "Just saying."

Simone might as well have lobbed a grenade into the room.

Patty's mother drew herself back up, sitting straight as a flagpole. "Do you always allow your daughter to belittle your existence, Marjorie?" Her voice was steely. "I happen to be proud of my role as helpmate and homemaker. But perhaps you don't take that as seriously as I do." She glanced pointedly around the cozy, jumbled room, the books lying about, the faded slipcovers.

Patty wanted to fade herself to undetectable—embarrassed by her mother, embarrassed *for* her godmother.

Taken aback, Aunt Marjorie stiffened. "That's hardly what Simone is saying," her voice uncharacteristically frosty. "She—"

"It's back on!" Simone interrupted, turning up the volume. She flopped onto the sofa, bouncing Patty and seemingly oblivious to the sudden arctic chill between their mothers.

"Now speaking for the ratification of the Equal Rights Amendment," Douglas announced, "is a homemaker, parent, registered nurse, and president of the National Organization for Women, Ms. Wilma Scott Heide."

The daisy-decorated stage doors parted again, the piano played, this time something bland and schmaltzy. NOW's new leader entered briskly, wearing a blue pantsuit with white piping and bright white shoes, her bobbed hair soft in its graying curls.

"Awwwww. She looks like Nurse Edmund in the pediatrician's office," Simone said. "Doesn't she, Mom?"

Still distracted and eyeing her college best friend with sharp questions in her expression—which Patty's mother was studiously ignoring—Aunt Marjorie didn't respond.

"Mom? Doesn't she look like—"

For her daughter, Aunt Marjorie regained her congenial composure. "She does. You're right, sugar. Now, there was a saintly woman. Nurse Edmund convinced all children to get their shots without a whimper."

"Could they find anyone more frumpy?" Patty's mother sniped.

Aunt Marjorie startled, frowned again, but kept quiet.

Douglas gave Heide the same instructions. Instead of facing the camera, Heide turned to him, and in earnest tête-à-tête, said, "First of all, let's state what the amendment—already overwhelmingly passed by Congress and supported by the last four presidents, including the incumbent, and both parties—what it says." She recited the ERA: "Equality of rights under the law shall not be denied or abridged by the United States or by any State on account of sex."

Without this simple, succinct amendment, Heide explained, "as a matter of law and fact, women are not included in the intent or the content of the constitution, which is the basic legal document of the land." She paused to let that sink in, before adding that because the Supreme Court had never "declared unequivocally that women are to be considered persons under the law," women "can be and have been denied due process and equal protection."

She listed some of the most detrimental ways women were treated as second-class people—as if incapable by virtue of their sex of being responsible, independent citizens. Women could not open a business on their own, and were denied loans and credit cards unless their husbands or fathers cosigned. Many universities and colleges denied women admission, greatly reducing their educational opportunities.

"Exactly!" Simone sang out. "It's outrageous—UVA only started admitting female coeds three years ago. And there's still only four hundred and fifty women in a class of six thousand–plus students. My brothers say a lot of professors won't even call on girls in their classes."

"Shhhhh, honey." Her mother put a finger to her lips and then pointed to the TV as Heide addressed the most inflammatory of Schlafly's statements: that the ERA would upend a wife's "so-called right to support." Such support was only stipulated when a woman had to sue for divorce, Heide explained. The same was true with pay inequity. The discrepancy between a man's paycheck and a woman's for the same work, or with what kind of job a woman was allowed to even apply for (typically clerical) was addressed only if a woman took her employer to court and convinced the judge that her boss had engaged in discriminatory practices.

By comparison, the ERA would *codify* equal pay for women—eliminating reliance on costly, time-consuming lawsuits and the opinion of judges—whose decisions could be unpredictable or influenced by their own personal prejudices.

The piano played and Heide summed up: "When we look back to this time in our history, we will probably consider it primitive—if not barbaric—that we even considered it debatable in a country that pretends to be a democracy whether or not the majority of its citizens should be included in the basic legal document of the land." She ended with a small, expectant smile, waiting for what was to come next: Q and As, direct rebuttal between the two women.

Schlafly went straight for scare tactics, saying the ERA would require women be drafted.

Really? Patty sat up, alarmed—she didn't want to fight in a war.

"All I can say is thank goodness that Congress had the good judgment not to ratify this amendment ten years ago, or instead of having fifty thousand boys killed in Vietnam, twenty-five thousand of them would have been girls," said Schlafly, her tone less silky now. "I don't think this is an invasion of my rights that women weren't snatched up and killed in Vietnam."

Pointing out the draft was ending in June and the armed forces would become all-volunteer, Heide countered, "The fact that we are willing to have our boys and our men killed and maimed" says something wrong about "what we think of boys and men."

Patty found herself nodding with Heide on that point—remembering Will describing his POW brother as the kindest and gentlest of his family—terrified that he would not be able to survive the cruelty of his captors. Why assume a sensitive boy like that was suited for combat just because he was male? Then Patty caught herself and stopped mid-nod, worrying her mother would see her agreeing with the feminist.

Heide was about to go on, but Douglas noticed Schlafly's itchy urgency and leaned toward her. "Mrs. Schlafly?"

Abruptly changing topic, Schlafly spouted, "Well, I think the ERA will give husbands who want to get out of their marriage obligations a great opportunity to do so . . . Marriage is a contract . . . If you buy an automobile and you make your payments on time, the court doesn't interfere . . . Most people fulfill their contracts because it's the honest thing to do. But quite a few of them will only pay up because they don't want their car repossessed . . . If we pass the ERA, we will be proclaiming to all the world that this contract no longer includes the obligation of a husband to support his family."

"You see," Patty's mother said, pointing toward the TV screen, "under the ERA, Philip could just up and desert me—leaving me with nothing."

"Oh, Dottie, Philip would never leave you—"

What? Patty turned to her mother. Was that something she feared? Should . . . should Patty be concerned about her father abandoning them?

"*Shhhhh*," Simone shushed. "Is Schlafly trying to compare women to used cars?"

It was Heide's turn.

"C'mon, nurse-lady," Simone cheered, "dish it."

"The truth is—and we stick to the truth here—" Heide added politely but pointedly, clearly impatient with Schlafly's fear-mongering. The truth: No law specifically required a husband to support his wife. The question only came up during divorce hearings. With the ERA, that decision "will be made—not on the basis of sex—but on the basis of individual resources and needs."

In her final salvo, Heide said, "I find it interesting, even amusing, that Mrs. Schlafly is going around the country arguing *against* the right of choice provided by the ERA, when she is herself exercising free choice." Schlafly's extensive travel and lobbying seemed very "liberated" from a traditional homemaker's role.

"Ha!" Simone erupted. "Go for it!"

Heide concluded with asking if it felt right "for one sex to be excluded from the basic legal document of the land and denied the right of choice?" She paused before finishing with, "Let us leave it to individuals to make choices about how they will live their own lives."

"Right on, sister!" Simone jumped up and raised her fist in salute.

Patty's mother also stood, her expression thunderous in its disapproval. She smoothed her skirt, picked up her sweater, and left the room without a word. Aunt Marjorie watched her go, shaking her head, her face sad and frustrated.

Patty filled with dread at the thought of the long plane ride home with her mother. How in the world was she going to hide that a lot of Heide's arguments made sense to her? A fact that startled the heck out of her.

Her foreboding only increased that night when her mother downed a cobalt-blue pill at bedtime—a new addition to her rainbow of meds—and icily responded to Patty's surprised *another-pill?* look that *your father* had prescribed them to help her sleep. Patty's worry skyrocketed as she watched her mother fumble about in the bathroom to brush her teeth and then listened to what sounded like muffled crying as her mother tossed in the bed next to Patty's before finally falling silent in a heavy, drugged slumber.

Patty lay awake a long time, disturbed and discombobulated.

WATERGATE

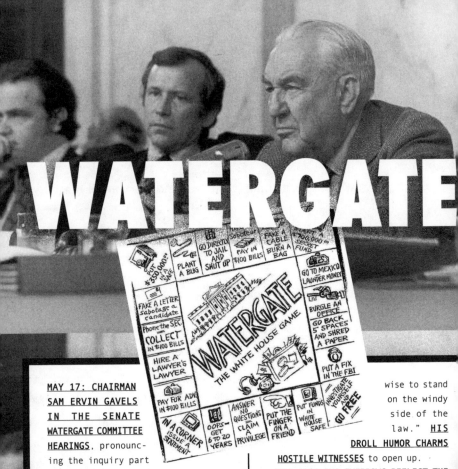

MAY 17: CHAIRMAN SAM ERVIN GAVELS IN THE SENATE WATERGATE COMMITTEE HEARINGS, pronouncing the inquiry part of America's "eternal struggle to govern ourselves decently."

Americans are instantly captivated by the cat-and-mouse drama of testimony and cross-examination, and the **GROWING EVIDENCE OF A LARGER CONSPIRACY**. People bring portable TVs to their offices. TVs in bars and department stores and taxi radios blare the hearings. **SATIRIC CARD AND MONOPOLY-LIKE GAMES ARE QUICKLY CREATED**, tied to the deadly serious national crisis.

PART OF WHAT ENTHRALLS VIEWERS IS ERVIN HIMSELF. A Harvard law grad and strict constitutionalist, the North Carolinian maintains a folksy wit, often quoting scripture, Shakespeare, and countrified wisdoms like, "It's not wise to stand on the windy side of the law." **HIS DROLL HUMOR CHARMS HOSTILE WITNESSES** to open up.

HIS WAGGLING EYEBROWS REFLECT THE ASTONISHMENT AND INCREASING OUTRAGE THE NATION FEELS with each shocking revelation—like that of burglar James McCord, who testifies that convicted conspirator and onetime White House consultant Howard Hunt not only offered him hush money but "executive clemency" if he stayed quiet and went to jail. And that Hunt's partner Gordon Liddy had proposed muggings, kidnappings, and luring Democrats to boat parties with sex workers to film their encounters.

The disclosures become so alarming, **THE SENATE REFUSES TO CONFIRM NIXON'S NEW ATTORNEY GENERAL UNTIL HE APPOINTS A SPECIAL PROSECUTOR** to lead a Justice Department investigation.

SUING FOR RIGHTS

Director of the ACLU's Women's Rights Project **RUTH BADER GINSBURG ARGUES HER FIRST SUPREME COURT CASE**. Air Force **LIEUTENANT SHARRON FRONTIERO HAD BEEN DENIED A HOUSING ALLIANCE** and other benefits for her husband that military wives automatically received. "I went to the pay office thinking it was just an administrative error," says Frontiero. "I was told I should be glad I was in the Air Force at all. **NICE GIRLS DON'T MAKE DEMANDS, DON'T CAUSE TROUBLE.**"

Ginsburg argues that discrimination based on sex "assumes that all women are preoccupied with home and children . . . [Such practices] keep women in their place, **A PLACE INFERIOR TO THAT OCCUPIED BY MEN IN OUR SOCIETY.**"

CREDIT FOR WOMEN

When American Express tells **BELLA ABZUG** that she can't get its credit card, even as a U.S. congresswoman, unless her husband cosigns, **SHE INTRODUCES THE EQUAL CREDIT OPPORTUNITY ACT**. The legislation would **PROHIBIT CREDIT COMPANIES AND BANKS DENYING WOMEN LOANS OR CREDIT CARDS**—for married women, unless their husbands cosign, and for single women, unless their fathers cosign.

Part of the creditors' justification for that discriminatory co-signature is the fact that the 1973 median income for men is $11,468 and for women $6,488. Ironically, **THE MORE EDUCATION A WOMAN HAS, THE GREATER THE PAY GAP** between her earned income and that of a male worker with an equal amount of education.

| Mr | Mrs | Miss | Ms |

Mr. Smith | Mrs. Smith | Miss Mary | Ms. Betty

No reference to marital status | Refers to a married woman | Refers to an unmarried woman | No reference to marital status

MS. = MR.

THE GOVERNMENT PRINTING OFFICE INCLUDES *MS.* ON FEDERAL FORMS. Previously, they included one choice for men (*Mr.*) and two for women (*Mrs.* or *Miss*). The new term **ALLOWS A WOMAN TO LEGALLY IDENTIFY HERSELF WITHOUT REFERENCE TO HER MARITAL STATUS**, just as men always have.

CHAPTER FIVE

MAY

"Wow." Abe stopped in his tracks at the same time Patty gave a little gasp. "Look at that."

Crowding the white granite steps to the Old Senate Office Building—leaning, sitting, standing, gazing up at its two-story Doric columns and stone balconies—were a hundred or more people. Spectators. Presumably wanting to get into the Caucus Room to watch Watergate burglar James McCord give his second day of testimony.

"This is wild," he muttered. "C'mon. We'll have to wade our way through."

He took Patty's hand to lead her into the throng to reach the tall French doors. She didn't fight it. The crowd hadn't left any kind of pathway, and she was a bit unnerved by how annoyed the people were about having to move, even an inch, to let them pass.

"Excuse us," Abe politely but firmly announced their presence. "Excuse us, please."

"Hey, man!" a college-aged boy with shoulder-length hair looked up from the card game he and a buddy were playing. "We've been here since sunrise. Take a seat and get in line."

"We work here," Abe answered. "We need to get inside. Excuse us, please."

"Oh yeah? Who for?" asked the cardplayer's friend, who sported a pouf of tight curls, dark glasses, and a shirt that looked like it was made from the American flag, à la the famous anti–Vietnam War yippie Abbie Hoffman.

"We're congressional pages," Abe answered.

"What's that?" The guy pushed his sunglasses down his nose to get a better look at Abe and Patty.

"Messengers for the senators," Patty said, more defensively than was warranted, but she was conditioned to see the guy's shirt as desecrating the American flag. His eyes were big and dark, too. She'd never seen a pot smoker in person, but she suspected his pupils looked so enormous because he was stoned. That's what her father had told her anyway.

"You too?" he asked her.

"Yes."

The guy nodded approvingly. "Right on. How's it feel to be upsetting the old-boy establishment?"

The crowd grew silent to listen to their exchange.

Not this again, Patty groaned inside. "I'm just doing my job, sir."

"Sir?" The guy laughed. "Okay. I dig it. Tell me, though, Ms. I'm-Just-Doing-My-Job Senate Page, what did you think of Friday's testimony? All that cloak-and-dagger stuff about phone calls in highway telephone booths from some unidentified goon telling McCord to keep silent and plead guilty."

Patty frowned. What had she thought? That it sounded like something from a mobster movie. She couldn't believe—or maybe just refused to—that anyone connected to the White House would engage in such thug-like coercion.

She opened her mouth to say so, but Abe took her arm and said, "We're just pages, pal. We aren't supposed to share our opinions." He tugged on Patty gently. "Excuse us, please," he began again.

"But whose side are you on, man?" the guy shouted after them.

"Democracy," Abe called back over his shoulder, "and truth. Wherever it leads."

Inside, he and Patty had to wade through even more people sitting on the cool marble floor beneath the building's airy, coffered dome—all the way to the first steps of the twin Beaux Arts staircases leading to the second-floor Caucus Room, where the hearings were being held. There guards had stopped the line. Abe finally let go of her. Patty trotted up the steps behind him, her hand sliding along the banister's polished bronze railing.

Outside the Caucus Room waited another gaggle. This one of twentysomethings, looking as exhausted as if they'd pulled a month of final exam all-nighters. They carried enormous notebooks of papers they'd assembled throughout the early morning. Patty knew those binders were stuffed with summations of the previous day's testimony, background info on the day's witnesses, and lines of inquiry, plus potential questions for the seven senators sitting on the committee to ask a witness after his or her opening statement.

These were the go-get-'em legal staffers and investigators for the Watergate hearings. Mostly law students. About eighty of them working pretty much round the clock, crammed into an auditorium in the new Senate office building that had been hastily converted into a labyrinth of cubicles, both Republican and Democratic. Patty had recently picked up materials from them for Senator Weicker—one of the committee's three Republicans. She'd been overwhelmed by the bedlam of the place—phones ringing, staffers shouting over the tops of their cubicles to one another, typewriters clattering—all in a haze of pipe and cigarette smoke.

"I'd give anything to be one of them," Abe muttered, gazing at the ardent young men and women. "If only I was turning twenty-one this weekend instead of eighteen. I could join up." He turned to Patty, his eyes shining with admiration. "Now those guys *are* part of history."

Patty recognized his ribbing her dewy-eyed idealism at the inaugural parade. She smiled. "Hey, by the way, what happened with that grad student you let crash in Will's bed?"

About two weeks ago, Abe had noticed a young man sleeping in a dusty Ford Pinto, parked in front of his boardinghouse.

Hearing that the Watergate Senate committee was staffing up "like crazy," the grad student had jumped in his car and started driving, all the way from Berkeley's campus—stopping only for a few hours' sleep here and there on the three-thousand-mile journey from California. The man was that determined.

"They took him," Abe answered. "Honestly, I think they took just about anyone who could prove they're good researchers and were willing to accept peanuts for pay. He found a place with a couple other staffers. They're sleeping on cots in a studio apartment, cooking dinner on hot plates. I couldn't smuggle him past my landlady anymore. She's very opposed to these hearings. Thinks they're"—he adopted a high-pitched grandma voice—"'horribly disrespectful.'" He shrugged—just like Simone. "I've gotta watch myself with her. Or she's going to boot me. Thank God Will got back last night to run interference. He's got her totally charmed."

There it was—that perplexing flop of her stomach. "Will's back?"

"Yeah. Came back with his mom and brother. The one who was captured. Jimmy. He's been invited to that big White House shindig Nixon is hosting for all returning POWs on Thursday. Jimmy can only bring one guest. He's taking his mom." Abe smiled, a thoughtful look on his face. "Sweet guys, that family."

Before Patty could ask if Will was doing all right, shouts of "Senator! Senator Ervin!" echoed through the wide, marbled halls. A phalanx of TV reporters—corralled behind rope lines, holding microphones, the one tall antenna from their headsets making them look like some sort of land-narwhals—began clamoring for attention. Their camera lights snapped on, as bright as fog lamps, blinding some of the staffers.

"Senator, can you tell us what your committee will ask today?"

Without acknowledging their presence, Ervin strode into the Caucus Room, his congressional aides bustling along behind him.

"Game on," said Abe. "See ya tonight, Pats. Will and I will wait for you right outside on the corner to walk you."

"It's only a block to my residence hall, Abe. The sun sets later now. You don't need—"

He waved her off. "Will was pretty determined we three meet up. I think he wants to introduce his mom and brother to us. Gotta go." He scurried to join the wave of people cramming themselves through the Caucus Room's grandiose mahogany doorway.

"Did you hear McCord say *the wife* of Howard Hunt—you know, the ex-CIA man who directed the break-in—was calling him too, trying to persuade him to keep quiet? You don't suppose, do you, that Mrs. Hunt was delivering bribe money as well, like . . . like a bagman in that movie that came out last year . . . Oh, you know, our husbands both loved it . . ."

"*The Godfather.*"

"Yes," she breathed, aghast. "Imagine . . . asking your wife to do something clandestine like that."

Patty was stuck behind a group of women spectators ambling out from the hearings, chattering excitedly about what they'd heard that day—as if trying to piece together whodunit in a delicious Agatha Christie murder mystery before getting to the novel's end where all was revealed.

Usually, she might have been intrigued by the gossip and lingered to eavesdrop. The women were all about her mother's age, clad in the affluent wife's signature garb of matching sweater jacket and skirt, sensible heels, diamond rings, and gold bracelets, speaking with the timbre of social rank and education. But this late afternoon Patty scooted around them, nervous about meeting Will and his family.

It was, of course, one of the few days she hadn't bothered to curl her hair, yanking it back into a ponytail, tied with a long, rainbow-striped scarf. If Ali MacGraw could get away with the look, then she could, too, Patty had decided as she'd yawned and fallen into her bed the night before. If only she'd known. Now she just felt unkempt. Unattractive. And baffled about why the heck it mattered to her. It was just Will.

Outside, she paused on the landing, peering over the exiting mass for him and Abe.

"Hey! Patty!" Her friends shouted at the same time, waving at her from the street corner.

Waving back, she felt her heart suddenly pound at having to walk down the steps while the two of them and Will's brother and mother all watched her descend. She should have left the Caucus Room faster. *Pretty is as pretty does*, came her mother's voice. Patty made herself glide in her best cotillion deportment.

"Hey yourselves," she said self-consciously as she neared the boys. She smiled at Mrs. Ferguson, her breath snagging a tad at how Will's mother clung to her sons, her arm through the older brother's, her hand holding Will's and swinging it slightly as if he were a little boy. As if they might blow away in the wind if she let go.

And Will's brother? His freckled face was as softly handsome as Will's, his honey-colored hair as thick, his eyes as luminous blue. They could almost be twins. But as he greeted Patty with a strong, soldier-sure handshake, she could feel an awful gauntness emanating from Jimmy—even though his mother had clearly been fattening him up for weeks.

"My, aren't you just the prettiest little thang," Mrs. Ferguson purred in a mellifluous drawl that echoed Will's. And it was clear where his azure eyes came from. She let go of her boys to sweep Patty up in a tight hug that smelled of vanilla and cinnamon. "Will told me all about how kind you were to him the day . . . that terrible, terrible day." She stepped back, still holding Patty's hands. "I'm beholden to you."

Patty blushed. She'd never experienced such a full-on and sincere embrace except from her godmother, and Patty was still uncertain how to end those Aunt Marjorie encounters gracefully. "It was my pleasure . . . I mean, I was happy to . . . I mean . . ."

Mrs. Ferguson gently patted Patty's face. "That's all right, sweet pea, I know what you're getting at. And you fill my heart." She squeezed Patty's hands. "You're part of my nightly blessings now." She smiled, and a lovely set of laugh lines rippled up her cheeks and crinkled around her eyes. "I'm sorry we won't have time for a proper chat. There's a vigil at the National Cathedral in an hour with some of Jimmy's friends and their families. To remember those lost." Mrs. Ferguson pulled in a sudden, deep breath in a moment of heart-piercing sorrow that ravaged her honest, open face. Another moment and she had contained the beast. She smiled. "I wanted to make sure to meet you in person to say my thanks."

Tucking one hand back into the crook of Jimmy's arm and the other into Will's, Mrs. Ferguson concluded, "You come visit me. Stay long. We have lovely Junes in Carolina—just about as pretty as your sweet face. And I make a mean wild-strawberry and rhubarb pie."

"Mama's pie is *the best* in the county," agreed Will. Then in a shyer voice he added, "See you tomorrow, Patty. I've missed you—guys." He shifted his eyes to include Abe in his comment.

Then the three Fergusons turned to walk along Constitution Avenue in the rose-tinted shadows of the lowering sun, watching for a taxi they could hail. The brothers sticking close to their mama, leaning down toward her to hear whatever she was saying. She looking up into their faces with unabashed devotion. With some shame, Patty knew what her mother would mutter right about now and what Patty almost thought as well: *Going to church in a hand-knitted cardigan, canvas lace-up shoes, strands of her gray hair loose from pinned-up braids, flying about in messy wisps, no makeup except a hint of lipstick? How tacky.*

Yet watching Will's mama, Patty thought her perhaps the most dignified woman she'd ever met.

"All right. The Temptations!" Julius turned up the radio and an R&B song filled the bubble of Simone's Beetle.

He sang along, in a rich tenor, pointing at Simone: *"As pretty as you are, oo-oo . . ."*

Laughing, Simone sashayed in her seat in time to the slow-slide dance beat, her face lit up off and on as the passing streetlights along Independence Avenue shone through the Bug's windshield. She was beaming.

Simone reached a red stoplight in time to face Julius as he tapped her shoulder and belted out, . . . *"and baby you're so smart, oo-oo, you know you could have been a schoolbook . . ."*

A jazzy saxophone and piano took over the song as the light changed to green. Simone shifted into first, and the VW bolted toward the Capitol, all spot-lit and aglow.

Grinning, Julius looked back at Patty. "One of my favorite songs. They could have written it for Simone. You know she's probably going to be valedictorian of her class."

Simone shrugged. "Oh, I've just got easy teachers this year."

With some surprise, Patty recognized that nice-girl credo: Downplay being smart. That sounded like something she'd say—not at all like Simone. Not that she bragged. She just didn't ever hide how much she read or knew.

Shifting again, the Bug jolting, Simone added, "Senior year will be a lot harder."

Julius gave Simone a playful pretend shove. "Say what? You've got some of the most infamous teachers grade-wise now. Face it. You're a total brainiac. And I love that about you."

Patty caught her breath at Julius's unabashed adoration and . . . respect . . . such respect for Simone. As they turned right onto Pennsylvania Avenue, Patty wondered what song Scott might sing to her. She searched her memory of past scenes together. Dances. Driving to the movies. Ice cream sundaes at the club's canteen. She couldn't remember his ever serenading her. Or complimenting her brains. Patty frowned. She was just forgetting something, obviously.

Again, turning around in his seat to address her face-to-face, Julius said, "Thanks again for inviting me to Mr. Henry's tonight."

"Oh my gosh, thank *you*. I couldn't have come if Simone hadn't driven. I was afraid I'd be interrupting your alone time." She smiled toward Simone, catching her gaze in the rearview mirror. Simone had been pretty mum about Julius ever since Patty's mother had shown such obvious disapproval at the Picasso exhibit of the two of them dating. But Simone's expression seemed even more defensive somehow. Oh! Oh dear. Patty realized Simone might be thinking she meant "alone time" as code for sex. Patty had managed to offend her again.

Sugar! Patty squirmed, knowing that trying to explain she hadn't meant *that*—while Julius was with them—would only make things more awkward.

Julius seemed oblivious to the friction between them. "Are you kidding? A chance to hear Roberta Flack sing? I'm down with that."

"Abe heard the rumor she was in town and might drop by to play a set," Patty explained. "He's really excited about celebrating his birthday this way. I hope she actually shows. She's so big-time now, she might not."

"Yeah, but Mr. Henry's is where she got her start." Julius thought a moment. "You know, when she was a teenager and attending Howard University, she used to sing gospel at local Baptist churches. Mom says we heard her during a service when I was little, but I can't remember." He pulled out a small, flat square package tied in a bow. "Even if she doesn't show, I got him Roberta's latest single, 'Killing Me Softly with His Song.' She covers Dylan's 'Just Like a Woman' on the B-side. Good stuff."

"You got Abe a present?"

"Sure! Simone told me it's the brother's birthday! Birthday boys deserve presents."

Patty hadn't gotten Abe anything.

"A spot!" Simone whipped into a tiny space beside one of the city's many tree-filled mini-parks. "Lucky, lucky, lucky."

The three popped out and crossed the street.

"Abe said if we didn't see him waiting at the door, he'd gone ahead upstairs to grab a table," said Patty as they reached the corner of Sixth and Pennsylvania. Milling around the front of the brown-brick building were about a dozen young men, a few with dates, most stag. No Abe. Julius pulled open the door to an overwhelming smell of French fries, Old Bay–seasoned crab cakes, and spilled liquor. He held it for the girls to pass through and into a very crowded tavern floor. They headed upstairs.

"The gang's here!" Abe shouted jubilantly as the trio surfaced in a quieter, wood-paneled room—a small stage and piano at the far end. He was sitting in a ring of upholstered chairs surrounding a coffee table, Will and his brother beside him. They rose instantly, Abe swaying a little as he got to his feet. There were two tall beer glasses—empty—in front of him.

"Will! I didn't know you were coming." Patty impulsively hugged him. Then, embarrassed, she quickly pulled away to introduce Simone and Julius.

"Please, take our seats," Will said, gesturing to big wingback chairs.

Flopping into one, Simone patted its arm for Julius to sit on, making Patty feel the need to do the same, suggesting Will follow suit. His face visibly reddening even in the lounge's dim lighting, Will perched awkwardly next to her. His brother took up post behind their chair. Abe fell into his.

"He started his birthday celebration early," Will explained.

Throwing his hands up in a touchdown V for victory, Abe shouted good-naturedly (shouting seemed to be his decibel level for the evening), "I'm legal! I can vote. I can drink. I can . . ." He brought his arms down abruptly, superstitiously not wanting to utter, "I can be drafted." But the thought teenage boys and their girlfriends and families had dreaded for the past decade lingered in the air. Thank God that was about to expire.

A waiter appeared to take drink orders. Again, Abe threw his hands up into that V. "I'm legal, man!"

Laughing, the waiter answered, "I know. I checked your license." He looked to the others. "What can I get you?"

"Fresca," requested Simone. "You can have a beer, too, Julius, if you want. I don't mind. I'm driving."

"You eighteen, kid?"

"Yes, sir," Julius answered. "But I'll have a Dr Pepper, please."

"Big spenders," the waiter muttered, rolling his eyes. "How about you, birthday boy? Another Rheingold?"

"I can't believe they've got a Brooklyn beer here," Abe said enthusiastically. "Yessiree bob! I'll take another. And keep 'em coming! Willie?"

"Just a Pepsi."

"Awwwww, c'mon, man."

"I'm still seventeen—until next month. Besides, someone needs to get you home in one piece."

"Right, right," Abe said, waving his hand. "Jimmy, what about you?"

Jimmy seemed to startle at the sound of his name. He just shook his head.

Leaning down, Will whispered to Patty, "Keep an eye on Abe, okay? I don't think he's ever had more than a few sips of beer before. It's going to his head fast. I can't stay too late. Jimmy and Mama leave for home on an early train tomorrow."

He glanced toward his brother, whose eyes darted warily around the room. "I . . . I'm worried this is overwhelming Jimmy. Crowds are . . . tough." Will's voice grew husky. "He was kept in solitary confinement mostly, able to communicate with others only by tapping on the wall. He—"

Not hearing Will's low voice, Abe interrupted in his jovial, bring-everyone-into-the-conversation way. "Jimmy was starting to tell us about the White House dinner. Go on, man," he urged, once again in a near-shout that prompted other patrons to look toward their corner.

Again, Jimmy seemed slightly surprised to be addressed.

"Was Tricky Dick a good host?" Abe asked.

Jimmy frowned. "You mean President Nixon?"

"Yeah, old gloomy Gus."

Will punched Abe's arm, amiable enough but definitely a warning to lay off. "Jimmy and the other POWs are grateful to President Nixon for getting them home," he said pointedly.

Patty noticed a few other patrons drawing in close to listen. Given the national obsession with the Watergate hearings, any conversation about the White House or Nixon these days seemed to attract eavesdroppers.

"Sooooo . . . who was there, Jimmy? Give us the lowdown!" Abe drained his third beer and slammed the glass back down to the table. "You're our inside man. What's the White House like?"

Jimmy blinked. Cocked his head as the waiter materialized magically and put another beer in front of Abe.

"It was real pretty, wasn't it, Jimmy?" Will prompted.

His brother nodded. Waited.

Will waited.

Nothing more from Jimmy.

Will took a deep breath and went on for him: "Mama told me all about it. Biggest dinner the White House has ever hosted. Thirteen hundred guests—too big for the White House itself. They put up a ginormous orange-and-yellow striped tent on the South Lawn. Hung gilded chandeliers. Put up white-cloth-covered tables, all decked out with flowers and candles and so much gleaming silverware it was hard for Mama to know which to use. All the ladies in evening gowns. The men in dress uniform. Big, three-course meal."

"Roast beef and strawberry mousse," Jimmy murmured.

Will smiled. "That's right. And the first lady was real nice to Mama, wasn't she?"

"Yes. Said her dress was lovely."

Will waited to see if Jimmy would add anything else. Jimmy's gaze was riveted to his brother's. "Tell them who you sat next to."

"Jimmy Stewart."

Simultaneously, Patty and Simone squealed, "Jimmy Stewart!" "I looooove him," crooned Simone. "He's the best of the old-time actors."

"*Rear Window*—my favorite Hitchcock," Julius chimed in.

Jimmy nodded. Silence.

Patty felt an inexplicable urge to help Will coax his brother to talk. "Isn't Mr. Stewart a veteran, too, Jimmy? Not just acting one, I mean. Didn't he serve in World War Two?"

"A bomber pilot," Jimmy answered. He smiled at Patty. Hesitant. But it was a real smile.

"Tell them what Mr. Stewart said," Will prompted once more.

"He wished us," Jimmy paused. His voice was so soft, they all had to lean forward to hear. The eavesdroppers inched closer. "He wished us peace. Calm. Happiness. Said we'd earned it." Jimmy nodded to himself, as if imprinting Stewart's wishes onto his soul, and looked back to Will, waiting for his next cue.

"Then Bob Hope hosted a USO show like he'd done for Vietnam base camps over the years. Right, Jimmy? Sammy Davis Junior sang? And Joey Heatherton?"

"Joey Heatherton?" Abe sat up and cat-whistled, completely breaking the spell of Will and Jimmy's call-and-response. "There's a babe and a half. Eh, guys?"

Patty had never heard Abe talk like that before and sighed with disappointment, surprising herself. Lord knows she'd heard her father and Scott make such comments. It just felt worse coming out of Abe's mouth somehow. So the product of those beers.

Will and Julius both scowled in unspoken apology to her and Simone.

But Abe didn't read the room. "Guys? C'mon. Don't you—"

Patty cut Abe off. "Did you get a chance to talk to any of the performers, Jimmy?"

Pulling up his sleeve, Jimmy pointed to a POW bracelet. "One of the trombone players . . ." he trailed off.

Will finished his brother's story, his voice husky with emotion again: "Totally by chance, one of the trombone players was wearing a POW bracelet with Jimmy's name on it. Just like mine." He held out his own arm, showing the nickel-plated wristband she'd first noticed at the inauguration. He glanced down at Patty. "The guy pulled his off and held it up—right before the band started their set—and asked if Private First-Class James J. Ferguson was present. Didn't he, Jimmy? You stood and . . ."

"People clapped."

"Then the trombonist gave you the bracelet, to mark the end of your ordeal."

"Yes."

"And President Nixon shook your hand, didn't he?"

Abe snorted. Way too loud. "I bet he did. Publicity hound." A murmur of agreement from a few longhair eavesdroppers who'd inched close to their circle of chairs. "Nixon's supposed love of God and country? It's all for show. All he cares about is covering his sorry ass. That whole POW event was staged to distract from the Watergate hearings. Makes me sick—using GIs as props."

Jimmy's face turned ashen, his eyes glazed over, and—just like that—he disappeared into that gaunt, gone aura Patty had witnessed before in front of the Old Senate Office Building.

Will glowered at his roommate.

"Abe!" Patty gasped. "For pity's sake." She pushed Abe's drink away from him. She'd seen plenty of confrontative, nasty drunks at her parents' cocktail parties. It'd be too awful if Abe became one. "You've had enough."

Abe blew a raspberry. "Whatever."

"Wow, and I thought I could be rude," quipped Simone. She leaned out of her chair to take Jimmy's hand and wiggle it, just for a moment, to pull him back to the room, like someone might gently wake a napping baby. "What else happened?"

Startling at Simone's touch, Jimmy looked at her, to Will, back to Simone, Julius, lingered a moment on Patty. Then he turned to Abe, focused, as his expression opened up—earnest, hurt, defensive—and said in a clear, strong voice, "I'm not a prop. I wanted to stop communists hurting innocent people. I went to 'Nam to help."

Now Abe seemed to startle.

But it was an onlooker who responded, his sarcasm as thick as the booze slur in his voice. "You went to help? Sure. By firehosing villages? Gunning down civilians?"

"Watch it, mister," Will growled, shooting to his feet, his hands balling into fists.

Julius put his hand on Will's arm, stopping him. "Don't take the bait. The guy's drunk and looking for a fight," he cautioned. To the man he said, "Sir, we'd appreciate your understanding this is a private birthday celebration."

"It's a free country. I've got the right to say what I want."

"You know," Simone said, gazing up at the interloper, who wobbled closer as she spoke, "I might have said something that stupid once upon a time. Being anti–Vietnam War, flower power, make love not war and all." She looked him up and down, glanced toward Jimmy, nodding slightly to herself as if in some kind of personal epiphany, before taking Julius's hand and adding, "Like he said, no one invited you and your obnoxiousness to this conversation."

"Oh yeah?" The man glowered, breathing hard, filling the air around him with the cloying sweet smell of liquor. He turned his glare to Julius. "Control your woman. Or I will."

Now Julius stood, stepping between Simone and the drunk. "Back off, man," he warned. "I suggest *you* control yourself. Why don't you go on back to your table and—"

But before Julius could finish, another sloppy, sneering voice, deep and guttural, came from behind the drunk: "Baby killer."

He threw the contents of his drink at Jimmy's face.

And as Jimmy cried out and leaned over rubbing his eyes against the sting of alcohol, the drunk hit him again with the cruel accusation, this time shouting: "Yeah, you, baby killer. How did that feel?"

Everything happened so quickly from there, it was hard for Patty to see who threw the first punch. It might have been Abe, who lunged forward, overturning the table, shattering glasses on the floor and shouting, "Shut the eff up, asshole!"

Or maybe it was Will, who hurled a guy who grabbed Julius by the collar.

Or Julius, who body-slammed the guy who had loomed over Simone.

Chairs knocked over. Grunts. Curses.

"Stop it!" the girls screamed. "Stop!"

But it wasn't their pleas that calmed the struggle or the bizarre cheers from onlookers. It was Jimmy eerily singing a hymn, standing rigid at attention, hauntingly detached from the fray: *"Oh God, to Thee we raise this prayer and sing, from within these prison walls..."*

The entire bar seemed to freeze.

Eyes closed, Jimmy sang on, clearly somewhere else in his mind, lyrics about withstanding the cruelty of captors. The words and music seeming to shield Jimmy against what was happening in front of him.

Two gladiator-big bouncers appeared, striding quickly and threateningly toward them.

"Out! Right now." One bouncer grabbed Julius and Will by their arms, the other Abe and the guy whose cruel sarcasm had ignited the brawl, dragging them to and then down the stairs. Simone and the buddies of the man who'd insulted Jimmy scrambled to follow.

Jimmy didn't move. Sang on: *"give us strength to withstand all the harm..."*

Patty grabbed his hand. Yanked. Urgent. "Jimmy! We need to go, Jimmy."

His eyes popped open. His gaze darted around furtively. "Where's Will?" Patty felt Jimmy coil. "Did the enemy get Will?"

"He's all right. They've taken him downst—"

"They?" Jimmy bolted.

The bouncers shoved Abe, Will, and Julius into the street, alongside their assailants. "Beat it or we'll call the cops," they warned, and headed back through the entrance just as Jimmy rushed out and past them. Unable to keep up with him, Patty shouted her plea, "Jimmy, stop! He's okay!"

Grabbing his little brother in a heartbreakingly relieved embrace, then holding him at arm's length, Jimmy repeated over and over, "Are you hit?" He turned Will around and around, patted him up and down. "Are you hit?"

People on the sidewalk stared.

"I'm okay, Jimmy," Will tried to reassure him. "I'm okay."

But Will wasn't entirely okay. There was blood trickling from the corner of his mouth, and one of those beautiful blue eyes was starting to swell. Someone had landed a hard couple of punches. Seeing the injury, Jimmy's sweet face turned primal.

Patty had never witnessed rage boiling up in a man before. Rage that was uncontrollable. It was terrifying.

Turning on his heel with a guttural roar, Jimmy charged the bar-goers who'd harassed him. Shoving to the ground one after another, he went straight for the man who'd called him a baby killer. Snatched him up by the throat.

"Jimmy!" Will cried out, and sprinted forward.

Julius pushed Simone toward Patty. "Stay here." He darted after Will.

"Help!" the man whimpered, gasping, coughing, as Will and Julius tried desperately to get Jimmy off him.

"Let go of him, man!" Abe stumbled into a run and threw himself on top of the struggling foursome, knocking them all to the pavement in a kicking, shouting mass.

Whooooo—whooooo—whooop-whooop-whooop. Rotating hell-red lights flashed along the faces of everyone. Cops.

"Oh no. No, no, no," Simone breathed. "Julius." Raising her hand, Simone called out, "Officer, wait! I can explain," as a policeman rushed past her. Within seconds he and his partner had yanked the boys up and apart. Clutching Julius and Abe, the cops marched them toward the police car.

"No, no, no, no." Simone stepped forward. "Officers, please."

"Stand back, miss."

The cop holding Julius shoved him hard—too hard—against their police car, commanding, "Hands on the hood."

Simone gasped as he kicked Julius's ankles. "Spread 'em."

"You're hurting him!" she shrieked.

"You want to come along for the ride to the station, girlie?"

"Pigs!" she shouted.

Patty grabbed Simone's arm, shaking her. "Shush. You'll only make it worse."

Simone snapped her mouth shut and pressed her lips tightly together.

Abe was put into the car. "This one's intoxicated," said the policeman handling him. He closed the door, locking Abe in, and turned back for Will and Jimmy, who were both still sprawled on the sidewalk.

"We've got to do something," Simone moaned.

"Stay here. Stay quiet," Patty warned Simone. "For once."

"Officer?" Patty made herself smile respectfully even though her heart was pounding. She walked quickly toward the policeman who'd deposited Abe without manhandling him the way the other had Julius. "May I speak to you, please?"

The policeman turned to look at her, not menacing but not inviting either. What should she say? What could defuse this awful situation? Her mind was racing. Being arrested could ruin Abe's and Will's and Julius's futures. Their getting into college. Julius's music scholarship. Abe running for office someday. Maybe even get Will and Abe kicked out of the page program. *Oh God. Think, Patty.* What would her father do? He convinced people in authority to do his bidding all the time.

Look at how they carry themselves, her father had once told her about assessing new patients or potential donors to Republican campaigns. *That reveals a lot. Use it.*

Patty took in a deep breath. Looked. Analyzed.

This officer was an older man. Probably a dad. Maybe even a grandfather. Not unkind in his expression. Maybe amused by teenage shenanigans. Solidly built, a bit of a limp. It was his slight hobbling that gave her hope. He might be a veteran. Korea, maybe. Surely that would make him sympathetic to Jimmy.

"I'm a little busy now, miss."

"I witnessed the whole thing, officer. These are my friends. Please. Please don't arrest them." She rushed to explain, words tumbling out of her—about Jimmy being a POW, about Will and Abe being congressional pages, about Abe celebrating his eighteenth birthday too much, about Julius being the one who had tried so hard to keep the peace and if anything was the one most blameless. She pointed to the gaggle of troublemakers, told him they'd called Jimmy a baby killer and thrown liquor in his face.

"Officer, please believe me. These are good boys. They're going to do good things for our country. And Jimmy. He only went after the guy who hit his little brother. Jimmy was held in Hanoi for months and months. He was at the president's White House dinner for POWs, in fact . . . he . . . he's just come home, officer. Just needs time to heal. To get his feet back under him. He's done his part for America. Now it's our turn. We need to do right by him. He's a veteran, after all." She smiled. "Don't you think, sir?"

The policeman had listened attentively—through her whole sermon. Now he stuck out his lip, considering.

Patty held her breath.

"Wait here." He strode over to his partner and talked, their heads bowed toward each other.

Finally, his partner nodded.

The officer opened the car door, hauled Abe out, and walked him over to Patty. "Get the birthday boy home, straight away."

"Yes, sir. Oh, thank you so much." She fought the urge to hug him in gratitude.

"I think you have a career in the law someday, miss. You argue a good case." The policeman turned to Abe. "And you, son, don't be a bonehead. You learned a valuable lesson tonight: You can't handle liquor. Leave off it. Next time, you won't be so lucky. You might not have such a lovely young lady to stand up for you."

"Yes, sir." Patty took Abe's arm, squeezing it in warning to keep his mouth shut.

The policeman put his hand to his cap in a little tip to her and then shooed all the spectators away. "Show's over. Move along now before I find a reason to arrest the lot of you."

People scattered. Including the gang that ignited the fight in the first place and might be tempted to start things up again once the police car drove away.

Satisfied, the officer pulled Jimmy to his feet, shook his hand, said something in his ear, and then clapped him on the back.

His partner returned Julius's wallet to him. "Go on about your business now."

They drove away.

Simone threw herself into Julius's arms. At first, he didn't respond. His arms stayed at his side, his gaze glued to the retreating police car.

"You're shaking," Simone murmured. "Julius?"

Slowly he put his arm around Simone's shoulder and glanced down at her, almost as if surprised she was standing there. "You okay?" he asked.

She nodded. "I am now."

He gave her a forced, reassuring smile. Then he looked to Patty and his expression changed. He seemed overwhelmed, first with fear, then relief. He swayed a little on his feet as he said, "Thank you."

Seeing Julius's raw, seesaw emotions, Patty suddenly understood—truly grasped—the gravity of what had just happened. God-awful images on the nightly news of past civil rights marches came back to her. Women, the elderly, young teens knocked down by the brutal blast of fire hoses and dragged away by police, billy clubs brandished—some clutching their heads and bleeding.

"Julius had family arrested during the protests following Dr. King's assassination," Simone began, "and—"

"—And." Julius squeezed Simone's shoulder to cut her off. "Let's just leave it at that for right now." He kissed her head. "I get too . . . mad . . . when I think about it." But after only half a breath pause, he continued anyway, his voice shaking with frustration and anger. "Dr. King taught us to answer hate with nonviolence, with civil disobedience, with disciplined, peaceful demonstrations. And they killed him for it."

Patty could hear Simone catch her breath at his words. Then, with her eyes still on Julius, Simone hugged Patty. "Thank you," she whispered. "I owe you. Big."

She pulled back but held onto Patty's shoulders. "I'm beginning to seriously like you." Simone held up her pinkie finger and said, "In the movies guys slice open their palms and shake hands to be blood brothers at a moment like this. I think we can make do with a pinkie pact." She wiggled her little finger, the one adorned with a peace-sign ring. "Just like Mom's political caucus, right? Sisters-in-arms against a common enemy—jerks."

Patty hooked her pinkie around Simone's.

When Simone let go, she turned to include the others, pointing to Patty and saying, "Hail, the grand negotiator, Ms. Patricia Appleton. What did you say to him anyway?"

"Yeah, Pats." Abe finally spoke, his voice stone-cold sober now. "You saved our butts. What did you say?"

"Honestly?" Patty suddenly felt a little quaky, all the adrenaline of the moment spent. "Just the truth."

"Ha!" burst out Simone. "You know what Gloria Steinem says about truth? It'll set you free. But first it'll piss you off." Then her face lit up with that bemused, wry smile of hers—the telltale sign she was about to skewer someone.

"What?" Patty asked, bracing herself. "What are you thinking?"

"Bella Abzug jokes that 'Women have been trained to speak softly and carry lipstick.' Of course, the cops wouldn't listen to *angry* me. You had to pull out the girlie, smiley charm to be heard." This time, though, unlike what she might have done before, Simone smiled as she spoke the harsh truth, no derision directed at Patty.

And this time, it was Patty who shrugged. "Yeah. Your shouting 'pigs' at them probably wasn't the best idea in that situation. That older officer was nice. I think he truly just wanted to keep the peace. Keep everyone safe. So . . . I just stayed polite with him. And we got what we needed. The boys *not* being hauled off to jail." She felt herself grin at Simone. "Just saying."

Simone's mouth dropped open, recognizing the playful jab of mimicking her. Then she laughed. "Hoisted on my own petard."

"Petard? See? Brainiac," Julius murmured absent-mindedly, like someone answers a rote "fine" when asked, "How are you?" He put his arm around Simone again, still seeming distracted, asking in a detached voice: "Shakespeare, right?"

"Yes," Simone answered.

"*Hamlet*, wasn't it? About . . . something about a guy with explosives being blown up by his own device and . . . a metaphor for those guys supposed to rat on Hamlet. Those two school buddies. . . ." He trailed off.

"Rosencrantz and Guildenstern," Simone picked up his train of thought. "You know, there's a new, absurdist play by a man named Tom Stoppard. Retelling *Hamlet* from the perspective of those minor characters. Debuted on Broadway a few years back. Maybe it'll come to the National. We could go see it together," Simone rambled on.

Patty could tell Julius wasn't really listening. Simone probably knew it, too, but seemed to want to do whatever she could to soothe his nerves.

Patty turned to find Will. He needed to put ice on that eye.

He had retreated to a tree-shadowed corner with Jimmy, their hands on each other's shoulders, talking, talking, talking. Slowly, Patty approached, not wanting to interrupt the moment of brothers reassuring each other that yes, they were in one piece. And together. She'd never much thought before about being an only child. Watching them made her heart hurt a little.

Will spotted her. "Patty." He breathed out her name. "Are you all right?"

His voice was soft, like a caress, and Patty felt herself blush. Thank God for the dim light. "Me? I'm fine." She tried to sound nonchalant. "How about you two?"

"We're okay now." He lowered his hand from Jimmy's shoulder to reach out and pull Patty in close, so close. "Thank you." Like Simone had, he whispered in her ear his gratitude as he held her. "I think another jail cell might have killed Jimmy."

He didn't let go.

She didn't want him to. If Jimmy hadn't spoken, breaking the trance, she might have stayed in Will's embrace for an hour. Happy. *What was wrong with her?* She loved Scott.

"I am beholden to you, Patty," Jimmy said—the same honest, heartfelt phrase his mother had used.

"You're so welcome, Jimmy. You know, you have a beautiful voice. What were you singing?"

Oh, the wrong, wrong thing to say.

Jimmy blanched, his face filling with alarm as he looked to Will. "Was I singing?"

Oh, she could have kicked herself.

"We better go," Will said. He leaned over to kiss Patty's cheek as if in casual goodbye, lingering there so only she could hear: "It was a hymn a POW air force colonel wrote. They sang it in the camp. To shore themselves up. To defy beatings."

Will's baby-face handsomeness was awash in far too-adult worries as he added, his voice hoarse with sorrow and confusion: "I . . . I don't know how to help Jimmy." He let Patty's hand drop away. He held her gaze as if he wanted to say something else. There were so many questions in that look. But all he got out was, "Can you make sure Abe gets home without causing another riot, please? I'm not ready to talk to him yet."

Then Will disappeared into the dark night, his arm protectively over his Marine brother's shoulders—just as a limo pulled up in front of Mr. Henry's. A gorgeous, majestic woman emerged, wearing a flowing kaftan richly embroidered with gold thread that seemed to gleam in the streetlights. She entered the pub. Cheers erupted inside. Roberta Flack had arrived.

"Daaaaaammmmmn," Abe moaned.

"Happy birthday?" Julius pulled out his gift.

"Thanks." Abe looked down at the 45 disc. "Serves me right." Then he glanced up. "What a screw-up. I'm sorry, Julius. Please accept my apologies, Simone. Patty?"

But Patty was still gazing down the street, wondering what would have happened, how she would have felt and reacted, if Will had kissed her for real.

TRIPLE WINNERS

JUNE 9: SECRETARIAT, A CHESTNUT THOROUGHBRED OWNED BY PENNY CHENERY, wins Belmont and BECOMES THE FIRST TRIPLE CROWN WINNER in 25 years. In a business dominated by men, Chenery had been DISMISSED AS MERELY A HOUSEWIFE dabbling in her father's stable. Her response: "YOU NEVER KNOW HOW FAR YOU CAN RUN UNLESS YOU RUN."

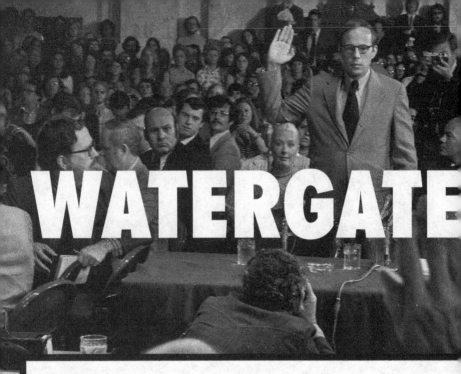

WATERGATE

JUNE 25: WHITE HOUSE COUNSEL JOHN DEAN TESTIFIES before the Watergate Committee for five jaw-dropping days. Americans are totally unprepared for the massive wrongdoing he reveals.

Refusing to "be scapegoated" by Nixon, **DEAN BRINGS A 245-PAGE STATEMENT**. He reads it aloud in no-drama monotone, occasionally adjusting his round tortoiseshell glasses. The hearing room remains hushed as **THE 34-YEAR-OLD GOES THROUGH A METICULOUS CHRONOLOGY**, meeting by meeting, in which he described the events and illegalities of the cover-up to the president, often with Nixon's top advisers, Ehrlichman and Haldeman, also in the room. Additionally, **DEAN TESTIFIES THAT NIXON** approved giving hundreds of thousands of dollars to the Watergate burglars to buy their silence and perjury.

Dean vividly recounts episodes like **HOWARD HUNT DEMANDING $125,000** or he "would have some seamy things" to tell, that **DEAN THEN URGED NIXON TO COME CLEAN** and tell the nation the truth. The president's reaction to Hunt's extortion, was, however, "You could get a million dollars. And you could get it in cash. I know where it could be gotten."

DEAN DROPS MORE BOMBSHELLS during the senators' follow-up questioning. When asked if Nixon ever used federal agencies for political revenge, Dean volunteers, "There also was **MAINTAINED SOMETHING CALLED THE ENEMIES LIST**. Rather extensive and continually updated"—opponents and critics Nixon suggested be targeted for IRS audits.

Everyone sits back, aghast.

The next day, **DEAN SUBMITS A WHITE HOUSE MEMO LISTING TWENTY "ENEMIES."** Democratic fundraisers, members of Congress, plus journalists like the *Washington Star*'s Mary McGrory.

In terms of national dismay, "Dean turned the lights on out there in the country," said CBS correspondent Lesley Stahl. **"EVERYTHING HE SAID WAS A JOLT."**

SIXTY MILLION AMERICANS stay glued to Dean's week-long, shocking testimony. **BEHIND DEAN SITS HIS STYLISH, SELF-POSSESSED WIFE, MAUREEN**, her platinum-blond hair pulled back into an elegant chignon. **HER UNWAVERING PRESENCE BUILDS SYMPATHY** for the recently married couple, for Dean being a young, star-struck attorney who simply followed orders from his hero.

Dean has no corroboration of his copious, comprehensive notes.

IT'S HIS WORD AGAINST THE PRESIDENT'S. Polls show only 50 percent of Americans believe him. The other half dismiss him as "a whiner," "a liar" out to save his own neck. One of the nation's most-read columnists, Joseph Alsop smears Dean's testimony as "the self-serving allegations of a bottom-dwelling slug."

DEAN GOES INTO WITNESS PROTECTION because of **THREATS TO HIS LIFE BY NIXON SUPPORTERS**.

HELP WANTED

NOW
NATIONAL ORGANIZATION FOR WOMEN

THE SUPREME COURT RULES in favor of a NOW complaint that newspapers' practice of running sex-segregated help-wanted ads—categorizing management positions as "Male Help Wanted" and clerical jobs as **"FEMALE WANTED"—WAS DISCRIMINATORY** and, therefore, banned.

CHAPTER SIX

JUNE

"That's what you're wearing?"

Simone had just come out of the bathroom into her bedroom, where Patty was waiting her turn. They'd blurted the question simultaneously.

"Oh my God, you sound like my mother." Again. Together in the same breath. Then: "Seriously?"

"Jinx!"

"Jinx!"

"Gotcha," Simone crowed. "Now you can't talk until someone says your name!"

Patty pretend-pouted. It'd been a long time since she'd done this verbal dance on the playground. But that was the game's rule.

"Just kidding," Simone said, elbowing her. "Say 'buttercup' and we're done."

"'Buttercup'? We always said, 'Pinch poke, you owe me a Coke.'"

"Wow. Pretty blatant capitalism for a child's game!" Simone pretended to be shocked.

"Not all of us are leftie hippie-dippies," Patty teased back. "Is *buttercup* a southernism of your mom's?"

"Probably. You know the only time she didn't live here in Old Town was when she went to Wellesley. And then Paris, of course, which, clearly, she adored. Look at my brothers and me, named for Simone de Beauvoir, Albert Camus, and any French Jacques will do, I suppose. Jacques popped out second. Mom didn't know she was having twins. *Quelle surprise!* She hadn't planned for a second boy name. Anyway, after college, she came straight back here. FFV-ties are strong."

"What the heck are FFVs?"

Snorting in her most unladylike manner, Simone explained, "First Families of Virginia. Ties to George Washington's family, on his mother's side for Mom. Daughters of the American Revolution bloodlines all the way. You'll meet a bunch of them today. Not for me though. I'm no debutante."

Obviously, thought Patty, looking at Simone's cut-off jeans, embroidered peasant shirt, and daisy macrame headband tied around her forehead. That's what Simone was wearing to a garden party viewing of the Triple Crown's Belmont Race?

Patty, by contrast, was clad in a pink eyelet sundress with crisscross straps over an open back, plus a straw boater with rose-colored ribboning she'd found in a shop on King Street. (She loved having that page salary!) Today's race wasn't the Kentucky Derby where fancy hats were required by tradition—that had run the month before—but she still wanted to wear one. Aunt Marjorie was even making mint juleps—simmering homemade simple syrup for the cocktail and plucking fresh mint from her small, bricked-in garden that morning.

The bathroom door slammed closed. "Dibs!" came a male voice from inside.

"Darn it," muttered Patty.

Simone's brothers were home from college for June and July, so she was sharing Simone's room on the weekends. It was uncomfortably crowded, and Simone's lava lamp gave her the creeps at night—so Patty was heading back to the Thompson-Markward Hall after the race. She and Abe and some of the other pages were going to the National Zoo on Sunday to see the giant pandas—Ling-Ling and Hsing-Hsing—which had recently arrived from China, a gift from the communist regime after Nixon's historic visit. Say what you will about Watergate, thought Patty, Nixon was exceptionally good at Cold War foreign policy. And that wasn't just her father saying so.

Flopping into her orange bean bag, Simone slowly unraveled a row of thread from her cut-offs to lengthen the fringe.

Patty couldn't help herself. "Aunt Marjorie is okay with your wearing that to her party?" Dot Appleton would lock Patty in the closet if she ever saw her wearing such a Haight-Ashbury flower-child getup.

"Nope." Simone pulled another row of thread. "She's not."

So, this was purposeful defiance. Why would Simone do that? Aunt Marjorie was sugar and spice and everything nice as far as Patty could tell.

Continuing to unravel her cut-offs higher up her thighs, Simone grumbled, "Here's the deal: I invited Julius to come today—in front of Mom—and she instantly said, 'Oh yes, please, I was hoping you'd come.' You know the way she talks. But Julius interpreted her not inviting him herself as meaning Mom didn't *really* want him to come."

Patty cocked her head in question. Aunt Marjorie had stood up for Julius at the National Gallery. She'd supported them at the exhibit, their holding hands. Put down those doyennes. Ignored the obvious disapproval of Patty's mother.

"I hear your wheels turning," Simone murmured. "Mom should have asked him directly."

"Maybe she just thought it was better to leave it up to you about whether you wanted him to come."

"Why wouldn't I want Julius to come?"

"I don't know. Maybe . . ." Patty wasn't sure why she felt the need to defend Aunt Marjorie, except her mind was suddenly rolling around the uncomfortable question of whether she'd judged her own mother as harshly without clear-cut cause as

Simone was now. "Maybe she was just being respectful of you—in case you didn't feel like you were at that point in your relationship yet to be bringing Julius to a family event. Or . . . or in case you'd had a fight or something and—"

"Yeah? Well, that's precisely what happened!" Scrunching down further into her seat, Simone angrily ripped more threads from her jeans. "Julius and I had an awful fight about it. Julius said he didn't want to come to this kind of thing anyway—a garden party of country club types. When I said that was dumb, it'd be good to shake everyone up, take the fight straight to the patriarchy, he asked why I was trying to fight a battle for him. If I just liked him to dabble in being a radical." She frowned. "Like I was some romance dilettante—using him to look rebellious and morally superior. I can't believe he'd think that about me. Now everything's weird between us." She kicked at the floor and muttered, "Thanks a lot, Mom."

Okay, Simone was being unreasonable—it wasn't Aunt Marjorie's fault things had escalated so much during her argument with Julius. And Julius was right—Simone did like to stir things up, just for the heck of it. She'd witnessed Simone's dinner table anarchy plenty now, starting with her dangerous needling of Patty's father the day after the inauguration.

Patty started to say so, but something about the misery all over Simone's face stopped her. It seemed like more than being mad—unjustly or not—at her mother. Simone looked devastated that Julius could think badly of her. All right then—it was pretty clear to Patty that no matter how much Simone might dismiss love's labels as part of her anti-establishment persona, she obviously *did* love Julius.

Well, Simone was going to blow it if she kept acting this way with Julius. Being so exhausting with her knee-jerk politics and righteous indignation. Pushing her boyfriend to do things that could be unpleasant for *him*.

"Maybe . . ." Patty began hesitantly. She thought about how hard, how unnerving, some of the moments she faced at the Senate were for her as one of the few girls in a sea of guys. "Maybe he didn't feel like stepping into a room filled with all kinds of judging going on about him."

Simone looked up at Patty. Scowled. Fidgeted. Got to her feet. Paced. Then, after muttering some oaths at herself, said aloud: "You're . . . right. You're right. I should have . . ." She stopped dead. For a long, slightly alarming moment, she eyed Patty, her expression shifting from arch and defiant to worried. Contrite, even? Finally, she said, "You look really pretty, Patty. Mom will love your outfit." She shrugged. "Seriously."

"Thanks," murmured Patty, surprised.

Simone stared at her for another few beats. "So will the Saints boys."

"Who?"

"My brothers' childhood buddies. And two of mine. The cotillion gang—they all went to private Saint-whatever prep schools. One's a total jackass you want to avoid. I'll try to point him out before he pulls anything—he's sure to zoom in on you. But the rest are basically okay. I'm heading to the Allman Brothers concert with my two pals this afternoon."

"You're not staying for the race?" Patty was stunned. First off, didn't Simone need to help her mother? Aunt Marjorie and Uncle Graham hadn't hired servers the way her parents did. And this race was feminist nirvana, wasn't it? The favorite to win was bred and owned by a woman—which was completely unheard of in the machismo business of horse racing. The newspapers had been full of it. "Don't you want to see Secretariat? He could be the first Triple Crown winner in twenty-five years."

"Nope. Do you know how cruel horse racing is to the horses?" Simone banged on the bathroom door. "Hurry up, *mon frère*.

I need to pee. And I want to call Julius before Mom's party starts." Tossing back over her shoulder to Patty, she added quietly, "I need to apologize."

The first guest arrived while Jacques, or maybe it was Albert—Patty really couldn't tell the difference between the twins—was darting around the front parlor, Simone thrown over his shoulder. She was shouting and giggling, in a better mood after chatting with Julius, while Albert—or Jacques—pelted her with needlepoint pillows from the Victorian settee.

"Children! Behave!" With a good-natured laugh, Aunt Marjorie tried to silence them as she went to answer the door, patting her French twist to tuck in loose strands, held only by old-timey tortoiseshell hairpins. No hairspray to keep it neat—something her own mother would never dare. Looking the least bit sloppy was a cardinal sin in the world Dot Appleton inhabited.

Slim moms in floral-print dresses and patent-leather flats spilled in, bringing a delicious scent of rosewater, magnolia, and lily-of-the-valley perfumes. Men in seersucker suits and bow ties followed. Rolling in after them were the Saints boys: Robert, Johnny, Luke, George, Mark, Paul, and Sam. Madras button-down shirts, khakis, Top-siders. The last two dared long hair, but as carefully groomed and trimmed as *The Partridge Family*'s David Cassidy.

They looked like her classmates and country club friends from back home, so Patty instinctively felt right at home with the cotillion crew.

Simone headed to the corner with the two boys with long hair, Paul and Sam, who had Grateful Dead T-shirts showing under their open collars. Obviously, her concert escorts.

"Girls, help me put things on the table, please." Aunt Marjorie motioned for Patty and Simone. Mini chicken-salad sandwiches, trimmed of crust, cut in diagonal quarters; bite-sized ham biscuits, the ham aged, marbled, and salty; crabmeat dip encircled by thin-cut French baguette medallions; teacakes and petit-fours she'd actually made herself. Simone and Patty laid them out on the dining room table, atop small labels for each dish—in perfect buffet flow from the side table. On it waited crisply ironed, monogramed linen napkins, silverware polished till it gleamed, and stacks of plates mixing three generations of family wedding china, mismatched and a few even chipped, Patty noted with surprise—something her parents would never do.

While they did that, Aunt Marjorie mixed Virginia Gentleman bourbon with her premade sugar syrup already fragrant with muddled mint leaves. She poured the elixir over crushed ice in silver julep cups, making them instantly frost over. Quickly, while they were still ice cold, Simone and Patty passed the cups on silver trays.

One of the of-age Saints boys took his and, as Patty moved to the next guest, pressed it against her bare back.

"*Sugar!*" Patty let fly, flinching away from the frost, grateful that her mouth sanitized what she really felt like saying since several parent-guests turned to stare at her.

"That's the one," Simone murmured to Patty.

"Geez, forgive my clumsiness! I didn't mean for that to hit your lovely skin, Miss—?" The jokester raised his eyebrows, waiting for Patty to supply her name.

"Sure you did, Johnny," Simone answered. She stepped between him and Patty, her tray blocking him.

"Sim." He looked her up and down. "You heading to a costume party?"

"No. You just come from one?"

Johnny drained his julep and set it down on Simone's now empty tray. "Deeee-licious. I suppose you're still drinking Shirley Temples?"

"Yup. Love 'em, too."

Johnny spread his feet, crossed his arms. "So, you rooting for this overblown Secretary, I suppose? Owned by the housewife?"

"The horse's name is not *Secretary*. It's *Secretariat*. Do you know what that means?"

Johnny smiled scornfully. "Couldn't care less. I'm rooting for Sham, the other record breaker in the race."

Patty knew the answer already, but she played along. She didn't like this guy. And she didn't like the way he was talking to Simone. "What does it mean, Simone?" she prompted.

The smile Simone tossed back at Patty was wonderfully wicked. "It means a governmental headquarters."

"That's a stupid name," said Johnny.

"Gosh, that's interesting." Patty made herself all wide-eyed. "How did they choose that?"

Delighted by their partnership in put-down, Simone began, "The owner, Ms. Chenery, was so grateful to her father's secretary for taking care of him when he was sick, she let her pick the name. You know, Ms. Chenery had to make a multimillion-dollar gamble to save the farm—picking which foal of two to keep *before* they were born. She chose by the mare, not the sire. Both colts' daddy was a famous *speed* horse. But Secretariat's mama had *distance running* in her blood, meaning her foal might be born with *both* talents. Everyone told Ms. Chenery she didn't know what she was doing—that mare was supposedly too old to birth a healthy colt."

"Wow," Patty chimed in. "And he's already won two races of the Triple Crown?"

Simone nodded, mischief still on her face. "Oh sorry, I digressed. The secretary once worked at the United Nations—which is a *secretariat*." She smiled sweetly. "So, you see, Johnny, everything cool about that stallion is born of women . . . or a mare."

"Yeah, well, we'll see, Sim. The Belmont is the longest, most brutal race of the crown. That's where horses who've won the Derby and Preakness fall apart." He smirked. "My dad says *Secretary*'s owner is aloof and arrogant. This race will take her down off her high horse." He sauntered off.

Simone linked arms with Patty. "You're a good wing-woman."

"I thought you said you didn't approve of horse racing."

"I don't." Simone shrugged. "But I read newspapers. If Secretariat wins, it'll be a terrific poke in the eye of the horse world's old-boys network . . . and blowhards like Johnny."

Simone had already left when the race ran. Secretariat not only won, but at a blistering pace and with a completely unheard-of thirty-one-length lead. The grown-ups had been loud in their cheers as Secretariat and his main competition, Sham, battled neck and neck for almost a mile of track. Then at the last turn, as Secretariat pulled ahead—by a nose, then a length, then two . . . six . . . ten . . . twenty . . . thirty!—they fell into stunned silence.

"Shazam!" exclaimed Uncle Graham, wrapping his arm around Aunt Marjorie's waist. "You were right, sweetheart. As clearly was Ms. Chenery. There's the power of women's intuition, eh, fellas?" The men raised their glasses to his toast, "To our beautiful wives and women's enviable sixth sense."

Aunt Marjorie smiled. Did a little curtsy.

Patty applauded, prompting the Saints boys to do so as well. Her father would never compliment her mother that way.

"Thank you, darling," Aunt Marjorie said, patting her husband's face, "but I think there also was some plain old savvy and daring—and knowledge of horses—that went into Ms. Chenery's success as well."

"Ho-ho, indeed!" Uncle Graham replied. "I stand corrected. To the ladies and their acumen!" He raised his glass again.

Wow, was all Patty could think.

The phone rang. Aunt Marjorie went to answer.

"Who was that?" Uncle Graham asked when she came back into the parlor. "Weren't they watching the race? Once in a lifetime, what we just witnessed."

"Jill," Aunt Marjorie answered quietly as she pulled two women aside, explaining that Jill Ruckelshaus had asked her to find a few more volunteers to stuff envelopes for a Women's Caucus mailing about the ERA. Would they help?

"Ruckelshaus?" Hearing that name, the men instantly knotted together to talk politics—not about Jill Ruckelshaus's effort for women's rights but about her husband and the increasing fallout from Watergate.

Said one, "Can't believe Ruck agreed to Nixon yanking him out of directing the EPA to temporarily head the FBI and clean up the mess of Director Gray confessing to burning Watergate evidence. If I were Ruck, I'd run for the hills. I'm thinking of leaving the Justice Department myself. If push comes to shove with Nixon, we're all worried about what unethical B.S. Tricky Dick and his henchmen might pressure us to do."

"But we need good men like you and Ruckelshaus to stay," answered Uncle Graham, "to right the ship."

"I'm beginning to wonder if that ship is rightable."

Another lawyer-type piped in, "It might all hinge on John Dean's testimony with the Senate committee at the end of the month. Did you read that Mary McGrory interview? She calls him 'the engine of impeachment.' He's claiming the president knew about the cover-up as early as September last year. If that's true..." The man shook his head ominously.

And so the conversation went, turning, as it always seemed to these days, back to Watergate and anxious speculation of what was coming next.

Time for Patty to return to D.C.

At 9:00 p.m. Patty was already in her nightgown, Clearasil applied to an annoying breakout on her forehead, and curled up on her residence hall bed. She'd finished her weekly letter to Scott—longing but not too needy, descriptive of the day's garden party without being too wordy, and definitely not mentioning Johnny, although maybe she should have. Maybe that would get Scott to visit her in D.C. next week the way he'd promised but had canceled for a graduation trip to the Bahamas.

Tap-tap-tap-tap. Knocking on her door.

Patty grabbed her robe. "Who is it?" she called. She barely knew her hallmates. Mostly clerical workers and paralegals in their twenties working for the government or downtown law firms. She really didn't want to present herself to basic strangers—even if female—lathered in white zit medicine, no matter how much they might walk the halls in curlers and PJs from the communal bathroom to their rooms.

Thump-thump-thump. Furious knocking now.

Alarmed, Patty rubbed off the Clearasil, unlocked the door, and opened it a crack.

Simone!

"Let me in," Simone whispered. "Hide me." She glanced over her shoulder.

"What in the world—"

"Hurry!" Simone pushed past Patty. "Don't you see them?"

"Who?" Patty looked down the empty hallway. "There's no one there."

Simone stared at her. "Are you sure?"

Patty looked again. "Nothing." Security at the house's front desk was good. Patty had always felt safe inside. "How did you get up here? Normally, the attendant would have called up to my hall for me to come down to get you."

Simone looked even more confused by Patty's question. "I . . . I must have been invisible. Which is good, because if I had been visible, they might have gotten me. But . . . you can see me." Simone held out her hands. "I can see me." She started pacing, rubbing her hands together, looking at them, rubbing. Until she bumped into Patty's desk chair. Simone let out a little shriek and jumped back, knocking into Patty.

Catching her, Patty held on, trying to steady her. "Simone, you're acting cuckoo."

Something about Patty holding her by the arm calmed Simone a little. Enough that Patty could get a good look at her. Simone's eyes were enormous. Her pupils nearly obliterated her hazel iris. "Good grief. Are you stoned?" *Of course she was*, Patty thought, furious. She'd been half expecting Simone to pull something like this. *Oh no.* If the house management saw Simone in this condition, Patty could be asked to leave. There were rules of conduct.

Disgusted, Patty let go. Simone fell to the floor. She crumpled into a ball, hugging her knees to her chest, hiding her face, rocking. "I didn't. I didn't. I didn't."

"Oh, come on, Simone. Don't lie. Clearly you took something. Are you really that mad at your mom that you wanted to add some stupid Ken Kesey psychedelic head trip to your list of rebellions?"

Simone's head shot up. "Oh my God."

"What?" Patty crossed her arms.

"My Fresca." A horrible thought was clearly registering. "Paul and Sam . . . I can't believe they'd . . . They had acid sugar cubes at the concert. They asked me if I wanted to trip . . . I said no way, I didn't do that junk, the music was trip enough, and . . ." She looked away from Patty, searching her memory. "I went to the porta potty. Had to wait. Came back and . . . It was hot. I drank my Fresca fast and chewed up the ice to cool down . . . and then . . . oh . . . oh God." She hid her face again. "How long will this last?" She started rocking again, keening. "They say it makes some people so nuts, they try to fly. Straight out a window . . . oh God . . ."

Patty fell to her knees beside Simone. She wasn't faking this. Her so-called friends had done this to Simone. *Bastards!*

Instinctively putting a protective arm over Simone's shoulders, she asked, "How long have you been like this?" Patty had no idea how much danger poor Simone could really be in. What could help? Could anything make it stop?

"Don't know," Simone murmured. "Is it still Saturday?"

Okay, Patty thought, Simone had been clearheaded enough to get herself here. Obviously looking for help. Maybe the effects were starting to wear off.

But Simone started shouting again. "Lock the window! Lock the door!" She looked wildly around the room, noticed the chair, flinched, stared, then cried out, "Do you see that?" Pointing, she wrenched away from Patty and scuttled backward, wedging herself into Patty's small, open closet. A little shriek. "Look out. It's growing. Come here! Come here, quick!"

As Patty crawled toward her, Simone lunged forward and dragged her into the closet. Pulling dresses in front of them, she whispered, "There. *Shhhhh.* It won't see us. Stay quiet."

"Simone," Patty whispered back, trying to reason with her. "It's just a chair."

Another little shriek. Simone was frantically brushing away scarves that had fallen off a hanger onto her legs. She kicked at them. "Get off! Get off me!" She shook Patty. "Snakes. Snakes." She rose to her knees and threw herself out of the closet to wriggle across the floor toward Patty's bed.

"Simone, stop! It's all right. There're no snakes. I promise."

But Simone couldn't be consoled. The bed was low to the floor, but somehow she managed to shimmy under it. "They can't see us here." Simone's hand shot out from underneath to grab Patty's ankle. "Come hide. Quick! Before they see you!"

There was no way Patty could squeeze herself under that bed. She crouched down. "Simone, there's nothing here."

"There is! Hide! Quick!" Her other hand shot out so that Simone had Patty by both ankles. She yanked—hard. Patty fell to her butt.

"Dammit!" Patty rolled away, rubbing her smarting bottom.

Knock-knock-knock. "You all right in there, neighbor?"

Patty knew that voice. The gregarious woman living across the hall. A longtime FBI secretary.

"Go away, go away, go away," Simone's voice squeaked from under the bed.

"*Shhhhh*," Patty hissed. This was bad. This woman worked for the law. If she saw Simone . . . oh God. "Everything's okay," Patty called through the door. "I was trying to . . . to . . . to dust the top of my window . . . I was standing on my chair and fell."

"Dusting the top of your window?" the neighbor asked with some surprise. Pause.

"Go away, go away, go away."

Patty held her breath.

"Well, dear, if you're into cleaning, you can come straighten my room anytime. Good night."

"Go away, go away, go away."

"Night! Thanks for checking on me," Patty said, her ear to the door, listening for the *click* of the neighbor's door shutting behind her across the hall. Hearing it, she darted back to the bed and knelt. "Simone. There's nothing to be afraid of."

"Go away, go away, go away."

Patty heard Simone bash her head against the wall. Once, twice.

This was getting worse. What should she do? She didn't have the skill to help Simone through this safely.

"Go away, go away, go away." *Bang, bang.* Simone's forehead against plaster.

"Simone, listen to me." Suddenly some of her father's stories about handling patients having a psychotic break came to her. Logic clearly wasn't reassuring Simone in the middle of her drug-induced delusion. Patty would have to play to it. "I'm going to go for help. You stay there, Simone, under the bed. Stay quiet. That way nothing can see you. But you must lie absolutely still. Okay?"

Silence.

"Okay?"

"Okay," Simone whispered. "But . . . hurry. Please. Don't leave me for long."

Simone was usually so sure of herself. Seeing her this vulnerable, so frightened, made Patty's heart break for her. She reached under the bed, took Simone's hand, squeezed it, and said, "I promise. I'll be right back. Hold on."

She raced down the hall to the pay phone. For a moment, Patty considered calling Abe's landlady to ask for him. Or even running down the street to bang on his door. Maybe he had friends who'd tried drugs; he always seemed so hip. But she stopped herself. Abe lived with a bunch of FBI trainees. She might as well call the cops on Simone.

Emergency room? How much trouble could Simone get into there? Would the doctors have to report her?

There was nothing to do but call Simone's house. And pray that Jacques or Albert answered the phone. They were college guys. They'd know what to do.

She dialed.

Someone picked up. Sounds of party chatter still going on. "Hello?" warbled a female voice. Aunt Marjorie.

Sugar! Patty panicked. Started to hang up.

"Hello?" Sounds of laughter. "I'm sorry if you can't hear me over the noise. People are just leaving. Hell-o-oh?" Aunt Marjorie called out in singsong tone. "Hell-o-oooh?"

From down Patty's hallway came another little shriek. "Patty? Where are you?" *Bang, bang.* No other choice. Simone was hurting herself. Patty told her godmother everything. Braced for condemnation, fury.

"I'm on my way."

Patty pulled Simone out from under the bed, as she sneezed violently from dust. Patty held on to her tightly, even when Simone tried to squirm away. She babbled—to distract Simone, distract herself. How much trouble was Patty in now with Aunt Marjorie? She rambled on about Scott, about Abe, even her weird flip-flopping stomach about Will. Senators. Mosaics at the Library of Congress. She put on the *Tapestry* album that Simone had lent her, dialed low.

By the time Aunt Marjorie rushed through Patty's door—thirty minutes later at most; she must have driven the distance from Old Town like an ambulance on the way to a hospital—Simone was whispering along as Carole King sang, *"Now ain't it good to know that you've got a friend..."*

Aunt Marjorie gathered Simone up.

"Mom?" Simone pulled her head back to focus. "Mommy?" Relief. "Oh, Mommy! I'm so sorry. I was so mad at you. About Julius. About—"

"Shhhhh, now, sugar. We'll talk about all that later. I need you to stand up. I need to get you to Dr. Mills, to make sure you're okay. He's going to meet us at his office."

Leading Simone toward the door, Aunt Marjorie reached out for Patty.

Patty held back in knee-jerk anticipation. Expecting a slap like the ones her father reprimanded her with sometimes. Or a terse rebuke that resounded with bitter disappointment in her. "I'm sorry," she said automatically.

"Oh, honey, for what? I am so grateful to you. For trusting me. Maybe Simone told you, I've always told my kids that if they get into trouble, call me. I'll always come get them. No questions asked. That we'll talk about whatever happened later, once they're safe." She took Patty's hand. "Are you all right?"

"Yes, ma'am," Patty murmured.

Aunt Marjorie studied her face. "For sure?" She smiled.

Patty nodded.

"All right. I'll call you in the morning. Thank you, thank you, thank you." She kissed Patty's hand.

When the door closed behind them, Patty fell onto her bed as Carole King crooned, *"If you're out on the road, feeling lonely and so cold . . ."* She burst into tears—of relief, of wonderment at Aunt Marjorie, and then in an inexplicable ache of loneliness and envy, for what, exactly, she didn't know.

The last week of June dawned miserably hot. Patty had heard about D.C. summer humidity, but breathing in air that felt like thick, wet cotton balls was beyond the awful she could have imagined. She wriggled a little, trying to unstick her bra and its biting wire from her skin without anyone noticing. Of course, everyone else in the Senate halls was already lathered in a thin coating of sweat, too, foreheads shining.

They were also in a total dither about who was coming that morning: John Dean, the White House counsel Nixon had fired the same day his top advisers Haldeman and Ehrlichman resigned—strongly implying Dean might be the mastermind of the Watergate break-in and cover-up. After that, Dean had told reporters he refused to be the scapegoat. Anticipation that he might drop some real bombshells during his testimony had made the nation hot to hear what he had to say. Patty had nearly been run over by the guards and staffers pushing trolleys, heavy with printouts of Dean's prepared statement, each as thick as a phone book. And then by the reporters who mobbed the trolley to grab a copy.

"A-holes," sneered Jake, who was loping along beside her and Abe on the way to their party's respective cloakrooms to get the day's assignments. "Where were these jackals last week during Brezhnev's state visit? President Nixon getting Soviet Russia's supreme communist to our White House for talks is way more important than whatever Dean the snake has to say." Jake looked like he was about to spit on the journalists, who were hungrily thumbing through Dean's statement. "Look at them. Like dogs with a bone. All they care about is getting Nixon."

Abe opened his mouth, but for once Patty beat him to the countermand. "I don't know about that. The *New York Times* ran a whole series of articles about Brezhnev's visit. The *Post*, too. You do read newspapers, don't you, Jake?"

Jake scowled. "They're all biased" was all he could muster before he strode away.

"Damn, girl." Abe grinned.

"You're a bad influence on me," Patty joked as she peeled off for the Republican cloakroom.

Given the hoopla, Patty was angling to run errands in and out of the hearings. She'd become obsessed with stubborn hope that the evidence would expose minion idiots responsible for Watergate while totally exonerating the president. The excuse "everyone does it"—if they did find Nixon knew of the cover-up—just didn't wash with her. She wanted the president—and by association all true-believer Republicans, like her father—to come out of this washing clean.

As she reached the cloakroom, Jake was coming out, his face lighting up to a sneer when he spotted her. "I volunteered you."

"For what?"

"One of Senator Baker's secretaries has a dentist appointment. They want help covering her phone. You're up."

They hardly ever asked male pages to man office phones when secretaries were out. Disappointed, Patty trudged her way to the minority leader's home office.

Phones were ringing wildly when she arrived. She could barely get in the door past an enormous pile of canvas mailbags and countless boxes stuffed with unopened telegrams.

"Ah, thank the Lord you're here!" one of the receptionists covered her phone's mouthpiece to say. She pointed to an empty desk, its phone jangling.

"Senator Baker's office," Patty answered, holding the receiver to her ear as she slid around the desk to its seat.

"You tell Baker to start asking some real questions at this hearing. Nixon's a crook. If Baker doesn't, all of us here in Memphis are going to assume he's in bed with Tricky Dick, sucking his—"

Patty dropped the phone. Red as a lobster.

The receptionist smiled reassuringly. "One of those, huh? Sorry, sweet pea." She picked up her next call. Nodding, she crooned into the phone, "I understand, sir . . . Yes, sir." She rolled her eyes and made a circle in the air with her hand in that universal gesture *yeah, yeah, for the love of God, wrap up*. "I'll be sure to tell the senator. Y'all have a nice day now." She hung up. "That's all you'll be needing to say today, I expect. No real calls coming through. Just bloodlettings."

Both their phones rang.

Gingerly, Patty picked up hers. "When is Baker going to grow a pair and stop listening to all them smug Ivy League assholes on the committee's investigation team, sticking their noses where they don't belong—"

Copying the receptionist, Patty hesitantly interjected, "I understand, sir." Big mistake.

"You understand? Where you from, girl? From the sounds of your voice, not Tennessee. You're probably doing one of 'em, aren't you? Yeaaaahhhh, bet you are. You don't want to find out how we do it to traitor bitches like you if me and my klavern boys have to come up there to shut this bullshit witch hunt down."

Patty dropped the phone, trembling.

"Okay, okay." The receptionist walked over to give her a big hug, enveloping her in sweet-as-honey perfume. "You've obviously got the jackpot phone this morning. If someone goes after you, just hang up."

"But . . ." Was it really okay to hang up on a constituent?

"Nothing about this day is going to be normal. Senator Baker told us to ignore the nutjobs—from both sides. And to not take garbage from anyone. He means it. Betty will be back before lunch. Can you last until then?"

Patty nodded.

The phones sounded again.

"All righty then." The receptionist gave her a squeeze, and they parted to listen to tirades.

For an hour the calls came in various degrees of outrage and language—only a handful of kind voices telling the senator to hang in there and find the truth, no matter where it led—most not. Patty marveled at the senator's support staff, how calm and respectful the women remained, no matter what was hurled at them.

When she didn't have the phone to her ear, Patty opened and sorted telegrams and letters into two huge piles: pro-Nixon and anti. Some as profane as the calls. But at least they weren't live. The pro pile was definitely growing bigger, reflecting Senator Baker's standing as that chamber's Republican minority leader.

Occasionally, Patty could overhear real conversations, ones that weren't just fielding abuse.

"Yes, sir." The receptionist's voice softened, less on edge with this call. Someone she knew, maybe a confidant of the senator's. "Yes, that's exactly what Senator Baker and our legal counsel think. They'll be cross-examining Dean, that's right . . . Mmm-hmm . . . Yes, sir. They figure they can weaken Dean's testimony if they push him to specify the time and place that he claims to have had meetings with the president. You know, make him look confused—or like he's fabricating." She laughed. "Yes, sir, mess with his mind, just like Senator Baker argued his cases as a lawyer way back when . . . The question? What did the president know and when did he know it . . . Yes, it is clever. The thinking is if they keep asking, it'll prove the president's aides acted on their own, without telling Mr. Nixon. Just like the president says . . . Yes, sir, I'll be sure to tell Senator Baker you called." She hung up and jotted down a few sentences on a pink telephone message note.

Another staffer emerged from an inner office. "Here's the information the senator wanted," he announced, holding up a folder thick with papers inside. "Can someone—" The phones erupted in chorus across all the desks again. "What a firestorm," he muttered, picking up the telephone closest to him—just as the absent secretary returned from the dentist, rushing in to grab up the phone Patty had been manning.

"Yes, sir," the male staffer began the litany. He waved the folder at Patty and jerked the phone away from his ear as a voice shouted through the line, "What's the matter with you people?" Patty took the folder and bolted—before another phone could ring.

She felt dirtied. Patty had been inculcated to expect bad things of Democrats, but she couldn't believe people who belonged to the party her father so passionately worked for could be so . . . so abusive . . . so foul. It wasn't right. She fought the urge to hide in a corner and scream. And then an almost flight-or-fight survival need to hear what John Dean was saying filled her. She prayed Dean's testimony would offer something to restore her faith in the political church she'd grown up in.

The caucus room was so eerily quiet when she entered, Patty felt the need to tiptoe.

John Dean sat at the witness table, in its blood-red leather chair, neat and tidy in a tan suit and button-down shirt even in the hot glare of dozens of TV camera lights—thirty feet worth of them. The room's vast windows were covered with black-out shades to facilitate the live filming, blocking out not only distracting sunbeams but any sense of the day's hour. The world felt suspended in time, in the drama of this slight, thirty-four-year-old man solemnly reading his sixty-thousand-word statement in a midwestern bland, matter-of-fact voice.

The hundreds of people in that room—the scrum of photographers sitting at his feet, the journalists jammed in at their tables, and the spectators crammed up in thick layers of bodies against the marble-cool walls—were all hushed. Dean's voice was punctuated only by the crisp sound of senators and reporters simultaneously turning the page of their copies of Dean's report in unison with him.

As Patty waded through cable lines and people manning the massive TV cameras to reach the row of researchers and committee staffers squished in behind the senators, Dean was saying, "The Watergate matter was an inevitable outgrowth of a climate of excessive concern over the political impact of demonstrators, excessive concern over leaks, and insatiable appetite for political intelligence."

She paused to listen, afraid of making noise.

". . . I was made aware of the president's strong feelings about even the smallest of demonstrations . . . when the president happened to look out the windows of the residence of the White House and saw a lone man with a large ten-foot sign stretched out in front of Lafayette Park. I ran into Mr. Dwight Chapin, who said that he was going to get some 'thugs' to remove that man from Lafayette Park . . . any means—legal or illegal—were authorized to deal with demonstrators" by Chief of Staff Haldeman.

News photographers leaned forward to snap shots of Dean as he shared that shocking anecdote, the clicks of camera shutters resounding like shotgun blasts in the room's trance-like quietude of stunned silence.

Patty made her way to the phalanx of committee staffers—she'd have to crawl over them to the intended recipient. Instead, she handed the folder to a fresh-faced, twentysomething man sitting at the end, pointed to the name written on the outside, and watched as the folder was passed down the line to a woman sitting directly behind Baker.

Her errand and reason to be in the room was done. Patty knew she should go back to the cloakroom for another assignment, but what Dean was saying now chilled her to the bone.

He was describing Nixon's personal attorney, Herbert Kalmbach, gathering "silence money" from presidential campaign contributions to buy the Watergate burglars' perjury.

Oh my God, she breathed. Patty had met that lawyer at one of her parents' parties. Had she heard right? Dean was saying Kalmbach funneled campaign donations—like money her father had coaxed out of people who believed in Nixon—to use as hush money?

Nothing was going to pull Patty from that tiny pocket of space she held now.

Breathlessly she listened as Dean confessed: to facilitating the payment of bribe money to the burglars; of being told by Nixon's top adviser, John Ehrlichman, to shred all "politically sensitive material" he'd pulled out of the safe belonging to Howard Hunt, the ex-CIA White House consultant arrested for masterminding the break-in.

Shredding what could have been important evidence? Wasn't that obstruction of justice? Patty's unease grew.

Inside Hunt's safe was also a briefcase of electronic bugging equipment.

Pausing, Dean straightened his tortoiseshell glasses, then read that Ehrlichman "told me to deep-six the briefcase. I asked him what he meant by 'deep-six.' He leaned back in his chair and said, 'You drive across the river on your way home at night, don't you?' I said yes. He said, 'Well, when you cross over the bridge on your way home just toss the briefcase into the river.'"

A collective gasp rippled through the hearing room. The committee senators rubbed their chins, shook their heads, and turned the page to Dean's next shocking revelation.

Patty reeled. Had her father heard any inkling of any of this? No. No way.

What did the president know and when did he know it? Dean laid it all out. With dates and times. Very specific. Nothing confused about them.

On March 13, said Dean, he informed Nixon of the burglars' increasing demands for money. "He asked me how much it would cost. I told him that I could only estimate that it might be as high as a million dollars or more. He told me that that was no problem." That he knew where the money could be gotten. In cash.

Again a gasp rippled through the chamber, echoing Patty's.

Dean continued: Hunt threatened "he wanted seventy-two thousand dollars for living expenses and fifty thousand dollars for attorney fees, and if he did not receive it that week, he would reconsider his options and have a lot to say about the seamy things he had done for Ehrlichman while at the White House."

Believing the president did not fully realize "the implications" of Hunt's extortion, Dean met with Nixon the next morning. "I began by telling the president that there was a cancer growing on the presidency and that if the cancer was not removed that the president himself would be killed by it . . . that perjury had been committed, and for this cover-up to continue it would require more paying and more money . . . that I thought all those involved must stand up and account for themselves and that the president himself get out in front of this matter." But, Dean added, Nixon "did not seem concerned."

In April—two weeks before Haldeman and Ehrlichman would resign and Nixon would fire Dean—he was summoned to the Oval Office. The president pointedly told Dean that he'd "only been joking" when "he had said that one million dollars was nothing to raise to pay to maintain the silence of the defendants." Dean added that he'd fleetingly wondered if Nixon was surreptitiously taping him that day, because the president's questions and comments were so leading.

During Dean's final conversation with the president—one week later—right as Nixon was plotting to smear Dean in the press, "the president called me to wish me a happy Easter," sending his best wishes to "my pretty wife."

All cameras and eyes in the hearing room—including Patty's—swiveled to Dean's model-beautiful, blond wife, who'd sat quietly behind Dean through hours and hours of his sworn testimony. Wearing a golden, long-sleeved dress belted at her small waist, her hair swept back into a neat chignon, Maureen Dean didn't blanch at her husband's words. She stayed frozen in her breathtakingly regal, self-possessed, marble-still posture. Whatever despair or shock or anger she'd felt when all this intrigue was happening—or at that very moment as sixty million Americans watched her on TV—was completely masked.

Just like . . . like Dot Appleton. Patty felt herself run cold again. How many times had she witnessed her mother looking just like Maureen Dean did right then? Standing slightly behind and to the side of Patty's father while he spoke with other powerful men, her mother intent and hushed and inscrutable. Showing absolutely no reaction or emotion.

Had her mother too been witness to things awful enough that she'd learned to be that . . . impenetrable?

WATERGATE

After John Dean's shattering testimony, **AMERICAN OPINION DIVIDES INTO "PARANOID JOHN DEAN BELIEVERS"**—as satiric columnist Art Buchwald calls them—**AND THOSE LOYAL TO THE PRESIDENT**.

"As a public service," Buchwald offers 36 tongue-in-cheek "Handy Excuses for Nixon Backers." These include:

Everyone does it.
The press is blowing the whole thing up.
Only thing wrong with Watergate is they got caught.
What about Chappaquiddick? (repeated five times)

One line is particularly pointed: **ARE YOU GOING TO BELIEVE A RAT LIKE JOHN DEAN OR THE PRESIDENT OF THE UNITED STATES?** After all, Dean had no corroboration of his testimony other than his own meticulously detailed notes.

Until former White House deputy assistant Alexander Butterfield appears before the Senate Watergate Committee.

Asked, **ARE YOU AWARE OF ANY LISTENING DEVICES IN THE OVAL OFFICE?** the decorated air force fighter-pilot pauses for a long five seconds, his jaw visibly clenching, then answers, **"I WAS AWARE OF LISTENING DEVICES, YES, SIR."**

Those eight words—revealing **NIXON HAD BEEN TAPING PEOPLE WITHOUT THEIR KNOWLEDGE**—change everything. Dean's claims can be either confirmed or debunked—by Nixon's own voice.

THE DOJ SPECIAL PROSECUTOR AND THE SENATE WATERGATE COMMITTEE SUBPOENA THE TAPES. Nixon refuses to hand them over, claiming executive privilege, setting off an unprecedented constitutional crisis.

UNDER OATH

During his testimony in front of the Senate committee, Nixon's former White House adviser John **EHRLICHMAN IS ASKED ABOUT THE NOW-RELATED PENTAGON PAPERS MISTRIAL**. He admits approving **THE BURGLARY OF DANIEL ELLSBERG'S PSYCHIATRIST** to look for damaging mental health reports on Ellsberg. But he **CLAIMS IT WAS JUSTIFIED BY NATIONAL SECURITY** concerns and, therefore, within the constitutional powers of the president.

ALSO CALLED TO TESTIFY IN JULY IS NIXON'S PERSONAL LAWYER and a leading fundraiser, Herbert Kalmbach. He admits to **OVERSEEING A SECRET $500,000 SLUSH FUND** to finance dirty tricks sabotage of Democratic candidates, plus $220,000 in hush money to pay off the five burglars and their handlers. Kalmbach **CLAIMS HE BELIEVED THE MONIES WERE PURELY "HUMANITARIAN"**—for defense costs and support for defendants' families. "It was incomprehensible to me" that Dean and Ehrlichman "would ask me to do an illegal act." **AND YET, KALMBACH MADE SURE THE MONEY WAS DELIVERED CLANDESTINELY**: in hundred-dollar bills, stuffed in brown paper bags, left in hotel lobbies or airport luggage lockers.

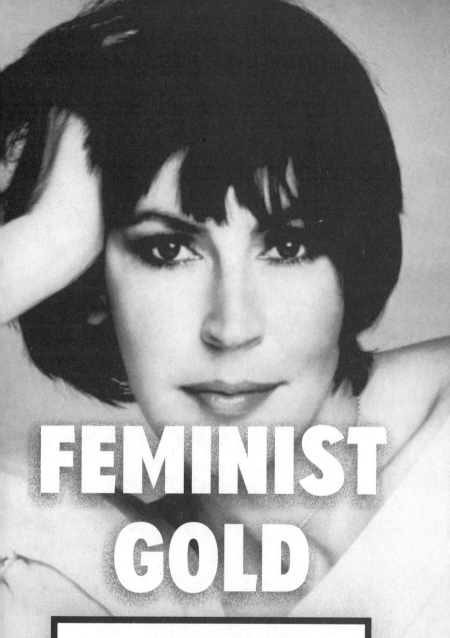

FEMINIST GOLD

Helen Reddy wins a Grammy for **"I AM WOMAN"—THE FIRST EXPLICITLY FEMINIST SONG TO BECOME A GOLD RECORD**. Of its chorus, **"I AM STRONG. I AM INVINCIBLE. I AM WOMAN,"** Reddy explains that she felt it important to make a "positive statement. I can't bear all those 'Take me back, baby! (or) I'll just die' songs that women are supposed to sing."

CHAPTER SEVEN

JULY

"I swear you could hear a guillotine drop," quipped Abe, describing the stunned silence of the Senate hearing room during John Dean's testimony the previous week. He turned away from gazing over the Potomac River toward the Lincoln Memorial to look at Julius as he elbowed him. "Ha ha. Get it? Like a pin, but . . . a bit more consequential, you know, like—"

"Yeah, man. We got it," Julius answered with a slightly forced smile.

"Just trying to lighten the mood. Everyone seems so uptight," Abe grumbled, looking back toward the Mall and its direct lineup of the Lincoln Memorial, the Washington Monument behind it, and the Capitol in the distance. He squirmed a bit, his butt scrunching up his corner of the blanket he was sharing with Patty, Simone, and Julius.

They were picnicking, waiting for D.C.'s legendary Fourth of July fireworks from the Virginia side of the river, on the hill with the marines' Iwo Jima Memorial. Best viewpoint in the city, one of Senator Baker's staffers had told Patty. Other pages sprawled on adjacent blankets, including Jake—much to Patty's annoyance. But it wasn't as if she could tell him he couldn't come to a public park.

After a moment, Abe asked, "Is everything okay?"

Patty waited for Simone to respond, very aware of the fact this was the first real date Simone and Julius had been on since their argument over Aunt Marjorie's Belmont race gathering. She knew Simone had called to apologize to Julius, and she'd seemed happy and relieved afterward at the party. So, Patty doubted that was the cause of whatever was going on. Maybe Simone had shared the betrayal of her cotillion buddies spiking her soft drink with LSD and Julius was angry about it. Clearly something wasn't right—they were both uncharacteristically absorbed in their own thoughts. Simone being that quiet was an unnerving phenomenon.

Patty was afraid to speak herself because her body was rattling with jitters and her voice was sure to be shaky. She'd been that way since seeing her parents earlier that afternoon. They were in town for a gathering of Republican heavy hitters, this time staying at the Watergate Hotel to watch the fireworks from the complex's rooftop.

"You've gained weight," Dot Appleton had said, frowning—the instant she opened the door and Patty stepped inside.

She'd led Patty to the hotel room's lavish bathroom. Even as wide as the sink counter was, her mother's makeup, bracelets, earrings, curlers, and medicines were strewn all over it. Patty had never seen her mother so disorganized. Normally her things were tucked into pretty, paisley-fabric cosmetic bags and stacked neatly out of her father's way.

In growing alarm, Patty had watched her mother riffle through prescription bottles, read the labels, drop and push the little canisters aside, their pills rattling, before finding what she was looking for. "Here they are. Your father prescribed them. Obetrol kills your appetite. Much more effective than the aminorex he gave me before." She poured dozens of little orange pills into an empty bottle. "I'll split my supply with you."

She'd taken Patty's hand—her own trembly and sweaty—dropping a pumpkin-bright tablet into Patty's palm. "Take one now. Before lunch. You won't gorge yourself that way."

"But—"

"That friend of yours, that Suzie, she's a perfect 35-24-35. Her mother bragged on it when we last played bridge at the club." Patty's mother eyed Patty's backside. "You know, Suzie's been spending a good deal of time with Scott on the court . . . and off." She nodded, her left eyebrow arched. "Take it."

Suzie, Suzie, Suzie. Patty was sick of hearing about Suzie. She'd popped the pill in her mouth, having to gag it down dry since her mother poured herself two pills and leaned over to slurp loudly from the tap's running faucet. Patty gaped. Her mother had always reprimanded her for looking like she'd been "raised in a barn" whenever she caught Patty doing that.

"Mother, are you all right?" Still haunted by Maureen Dean's set-in-marble enigmatic composure, Patty wanted to ask many more questions of her mother. But Dot Appleton had straightened up from the sink, all party business.

"Right as rain," she'd replied, brittle, as she looked in the mirror and patted her unmoving pouf of hair, flipped just at her shoulder. Once more taking Patty's hand, she'd led them in what presented as affectionate mother-daughter intimacy into the suite's living room, where several couples were already enjoying champagne mimosas.

Patty quick-skimmed the entourage, a little afraid of spotting Nixon's lawyer among them, worrying that if a man accused of helping to organize the finacing of the Watergate cover-up was in attendance, it would taint her father by association. Not there. Good.

A white-jacketed hotel waiter was laying out trays of enormous shrimps on a buffet table beside the balcony that stretched the length of the room. Patty fairly drooled at them. She was starving, in fact. She'd skipped breakfast at Thompson-Markward Hall, anticipating her mother's typical party feast.

"Look who's here," her mother sang out, chirpy as a canary.

"Princess!" Patty's father put down his Bloody Mary, stood up from a leather armchair, and embraced her. "Friends, you remember my daughter, Patricia. She's working on the Hill as a page. And getting more beautiful by the moment."

"Now, there's something easy on the eye," one of her father's closest political cronies half bellowed as he swaggered up to plant a cigarette-smelly kiss a little too close to Patty's lips. Her father didn't seem to notice. Just kept his hand on the small of Patty's back, propelling her to greet each of the twenty adults in attendance.

Yes, she was loving being a page, she automatically answered. Yes, Senator Baker was smart as a fox. No, she didn't run errands directly for "that backwaters bumpkin" Senator Ervin—he was a Democrat, and she was sponsored by Republicans. No, she'd never met Mrs. Nixon. That "loudmouth" Bella Abzug? No sir, she was on the House side. Patty actually hadn't met any congresswomen yet.

"You know what they say Gerald Ford's biggest job in the House is?" her father began a joke, waiting for his listeners to shake their heads in that prompt of unspoken no, what? "Keeping Bella from showing up in hot pants." He mugged a disgusted face. "Can you imagine?"

Ha ha ha ha.

Patty felt the dangerous urge to explain that his joke had a fatal flaw of incorrect Hill procedure and protocol—the Republican minority leader had absolutely no control over a Democrat. But her father was in the middle of adding a caveat. "Now, getting Gloria Steinem to come testify, wearing hot pants? Eh?" He grinned. "Seen the gams on that ballbuster? Sorry, girls." He bowed to the wives. "But it has to be said—what a waste of good legs."

The wives tittered.

Patty's mother offered a tight, frozen smile. Then she drifted to the balcony, gazing out at the two-year-old Kennedy Center for the Performing Arts right across the street from the Watergate complex.

"Is Mother okay?" Patty whispered to her father.

Looking over Patty's head to his wife, he let out an exasperated sigh. "She's got it in her head that she wants to tour that big Kleenex box of a building. Go hear the National Symphony Orchestra perform while we're here. Drip, drip, drip, water on stone. I don't have time. And besides, I don't want to spend my money supporting something named for a Kennedy. You'd think after all these years she'd know that." He shook his head and looked back to Patty. "That's something I know you understand, princess, now that you're initiated into Washington's ways."

That was the kind of compliment that before would have filled Patty with pride. But that morning the praise fell flat—maybe because it was based on comparison, linked to putting her mother down. Something she might not have noticed before. Or—Patty swallowed hard, feeling shame at the recognition—it might have made the comment even more positive in her mind, given her strained relationship with and her even more strained opinion of her mother. The image of Maureen Dean—so controlled, whatever hurts or embarrassment might be stewing inside her masked—rose up again in Patty's mind.

Without waiting for a response, her father turned to his guests to announce the buffet was open. "Please," he said, gesturing toward the balcony, "our Independence Day repast is served."

By the time Patty reached those brimming piles of succulent-looking shrimp, anticipating their delicious crunch, the thought of putting one into her mouth nauseated her.

The Obetrol worked that fast.

Feeling like she might vomit, Patty fled to the luxurious bathroom and locked the door just as her hands started to shake. And her mother had downed *two* of these pills?

Patty tried splashing water on her face—not thinking about how that would make her mascara run. Now she looked like some heroine in a Fellini horror film. *Sugar!* She scrubbed her face. Then reached for her mother's vast supply of makeup, scattering it clumsily. Blue shadow. Black eyeliner. *Sugar!* All squiggly. She scrubbed again. Reapplied, poking her eye with the mascara wand that wobbled as her hand shook.

She slid down the cabinet to collapse out flat, her face against the cool tile. *Stop spinning.* Patty closed her eyes against the floor seeming to rise and fall. That made the earthquaking worse. She opened them. Focus on something stable—like when she'd done pirouettes in ballet class to keep from getting dizzy before her mother made her quit, worried that ballerinas seemed to walk duck-footed. *Focus.*

Patty spotted a magazine lying by the toilet. Maybe reading would get her mind off the battle inside her body and help it calm down. A *Ladies' Home Journal*, Marilyn Monroe on the cover, touting an excerpt from an upcoming biography. The other teasers: "The Men We Marry: Exclusive New Report on American Husbands" and "You Won't Believe the Things You Can Make with Sheets and Towels!"

Patty turned to the first page of the Monroe article: "Marilyn Monroe! Hollywood's tragic 'angel of sex,' vulnerable child-woman, legendary love goddess . . . Now her life story is told as never before . . . by the perceptive lion of American literature, Norman Mailer."

Someone banged on the door. "Princess?"

Sugar! Her father couldn't see her like this. "Yes, Daddy?"

"Whatever you're doing in there, finish up. Your face is perfect as is." Then the command she'd heard him toss at her mother a thousand times. "Our guests are waiting."

"Be right there, Daddy."

Patty forced herself to her feet. Steadied herself on the cabinet. Her stomach wasn't revolting as much now—her body must be adjusting to the drug. Leaving her hopped up, but close enough to functional. Patty took the magazine with her as she left the bathroom, dropping it into her purse. *Suzie, Suzie, Suzie.* She'd read about Marilyn Monroe later. Men seemed to like girls who aspired to be kittenish sexy.

Abe's voice yanked Patty out of her flashback.

"Seriously, what's going on?"

He was quizzing Patty, but Simone answered. "Well, for one thing, my father quit his job."

That certainly brought Patty back to their picnic. "Oh my gosh, Simone. Why?"

"Remember John Dean testifying about Nixon having an enemies' list?"

Abe lit up. "Can you believe? An actual list of people the White House planned to screw with IRS tax audits? In retribution? I hope they get the sycophants who'd follow that order—"

Patty elbowed Abe. "Shhhhh. Simone's father is a prosecutor for—"

Simone held up her hand. "Let me." She shot Abe a sharp look. "For the IRS."

Abe shut his mouth mid-word.

"Was, anyway," said Simone. "Remember Mary McGrory was on that list?"

Patty didn't. But Abe did. "For sure. The columnist. Her stuff is great. She takes on—"

"Yeah, well," Simone interrupted, clearly not interested in Abe's political commentary. Patty stared at her with some surprise. Normally, Simone was eager to hear Abe's opinion, since she always agreed with it.

But what Simone said next explained: This time, the political was no longer theoretical. The impact of national controversies and power grabs had spilled down onto her family and completely upended it.

"When Dad heard Dean's testimony, and saw the names on that list, he realized his office might have been played. McGrory had been put through the ringer in an audit, focusing on her charitable donations. Including one to a Catholic charity to buy Christmas presents for kids." Simone paused. "I mean, c'mon." She shook her head. "At first, auditors claimed she didn't have proper receipts. She could have been liable for a thousand dollars in penalties. But, in the end, McGrory got a refund instead. That's how bogus the whole thing was.

"Given Dean's testimony, Dad realized Nixon and his henchmen had wanted to harass McGrory." Simone flipped her sheen of gold hair back over her shoulders with a defensive sigh. "Dad is an honorable man. So . . . he resigned. In protest."

"Damn," breathed Abe. "That took guts."

Patty stared at Simone. "But . . . what's Uncle Graham going to do now?"

"No idea." Simone's voice grew less combative and slightly anxious. "Dad was furious. He made a bit of a stink about why he was quitting. Don't think he'll be getting glowing references when he applies for new jobs." Simone paused. "My father worked for the federal government because he believed in service—not because the pay was all that good. My parents don't exactly have big savings put aside." She picked at the blanket. "My brothers are a little freaked out. It's in-state, fortunately, but they have college tuition due. And I'm hoping"—she looked to Patty—"to go to our moms' alma mater next year. Wellesley's not cheap. I'm really proud of Dad. But the fallout is a little . . . I don't know . . . scary." She shrugged. "Just saying."

"Is Aunt Marjorie okay?" Patty put her arm over Simone's thin shoulders.

Simone straightened up a little and smiled. "Mom is looking for a job herself."

"Wow. Really?"

"Yeah," Simone said, nodding. "She's not sure what a French major and decades of volunteer work will get her. She's never had an actual job. But she's looking. And kind of excited about it actually." Simone pulled away from Patty to ask, "Why are you all shaky?"

"Mother said I'm gaining weight," Patty admitted in a low voice, aware Jake and a few other pages were lolling within a few feet of her and might overhear. And embarrassed because she *had* put on a few pounds with all the cafeteria food she was eating. "She gave me Obetrol."

Jake suddenly sat up on his blanket. "Obetrol!"

Patty bit her lip. She should've expected that jerk to be eavesdropping.

Lunging for Patty's purse, which lay by her feet, Jake asked, "You got any with you? Nothin' better than obetrolling! Heightens everything." He stuck his hand in and rummaged. "I've run through the supply I stole from Mom's medicine cabinet. Aha!" He triumphantly held up the bottle of little orange bombs. "How much you want for these?" He eyed Patty. "You don't need them. Keep the curves, baby. You're looking good. Hey, maaay-be," he drew out the word, "you and I should both take some right now. Take a little walk together. Just as the fireworks start. Like I said—heightens everything."

Patty was so taken aback, she just stared at him. Was there any bottom to this guy's smutty presumptions?

"Shut the hell up, Jake," Abe shouted.

"Wait," said Simone. "You're Jake?"

"That's my name, don't wear it out," he answered in schoolyard banter. "Although, with you," he began, "I wouldn't mind your saying my name over and over and—"

"I've heard a lot about you," Simone interrupted.

"All good things, I'm sure." He gave her one of his sickening, once-over looks. "If Patty's going to be a prude, how about you?"

Julius glared at Jake. "Hey man, watch your mouth."

Simone put her hand on Julius's arm to steady him and said to Jake: "Good things? Not a one, I'm afraid."

Patty finally found her voice. "Mother takes two pills at a time. She's pretty petite. You might need three—to get the lift you want."

"What are you doing?" Simone whispered. Patty squeezed her hand to keep her silent.

"Go ahead, Jake," Patty urged.

He downed four. "Big guy," he bragged.

Twenty minutes later, as complete darkness fell, the effect Patty was hoping for happened. Jake ran to the bushes and puked.

Pop-pop-pop . . . ssssssss—BANG!

As Jake retched, the first fireworks shot into the air.

"Oooooh . . . " People applauded.

The cascade of exploded sparks—red, white, gold, green, blue—lit up the Iwo Jima statue of six bronze figures struggling to plant an American flag. An homage to marines photographed raising that flag in real life during one of the most terrible battles in the Pacific—an emblem of American resolve and courage during World War Two.

Gazing at the heroic figures, Julius sighed loud enough to be heard over the fireworks, seeming to come to a decision. "Okay, my turn. I was holding off, given how much upheaval is going on in your house right now, but I need to tell you something, Simone. The conservatory didn't grant me the scholarship."

"What?" she erupted.

Crossing his arms over his chest, Julius continued, his voice biting. "The guy interviewing me said the funds were earmarked for kids shooting for symphonic orchestras—you know, classical music careers. He said I had the talent, but 'Let's face it, kid, that's not really for you.'"

Simone gasped. "But . . . He said you had the talent! What the hell?"

"Ever seen a Black trumpeter in a philharmonic?" Julius threw out the question—sharp, like a slap.

None of them spoke, although the answer would have been no, they hadn't.

"The bastards," he muttered.

"But there must be a few, Julius," Simone insisted. "Or . . . or you could be the first."

Julius's answering smile was rueful. "I know you try really hard to understand what it's like, Sim. I love that about you." He paused, his silence implying that she simply couldn't, not really. "Yeah, I suppose I could be one of the first. But not there. Not after what that racist jerk-off said, or what I said to him."

"What did you say?"

"I told him there's a special place in hell—a dark, deep hole—reserved for assholes like him. That's what my mom says about dream stealers."

BANG! BANG! BANG! . . . sssssssss . . .

Another sky-rattling burst, explosion, and shower of rainbow sparks illuminated the six enormous bronze figures bent over, straining to shove a flag into an unyielding pile of rocks.

Julius kept his eyes on the statue. "Did you know there were nine hundred Black marines at Iwo Jima? Assigned as support troops, carrying ammunition and other supplies. But the fighting was so fierce as they hit the beach, they were firing rifles, too, not just carrying bullets to white soldiers. Wounded lay everywhere. They crawled through machine-gun fire to drag those boys to safety."

"No." Simone's voice was somber—reverent, even. "I didn't know that."

"My uncle was one of those nine hundred."

"You never told me that."

Keeping his eyes on the thirty-foot-tall figures being lit up sporadically in red, white, and blue bursts, Julius went on. "President Roosevelt issued an order in June 1941 to prohibit federal agencies and the military from racial discrimination. To create fair employment chances, in the armed forces, anyway. The Marine Corps had refused to recruit or train Black Americans until then. Of course, it wasn't until after the war that Truman banned segregation in the services. And," he gestured toward the statue, "I don't see my uncle's image anywhere in those guys."

He sighed again—a long, long exhale. "But . . . the military was ahead of the rest of the country. My uncle decided he could make a name for himself if he stayed in. Rose to the rank of lieutenant commander." Julius nodded to himself. "One of the first. That's how he made a difference."

Pop-pop-pop . . . sssssss . . . BANG!

He turned to face Simone. "I'm going to Virginia Commonwealth University instead. They have a good music department. I can join the ROTC. Get a full ride for four years in exchange for service after graduation. No college debt."

"Oh no, Julius—" Simone began.

"It's okay. I mean . . . it's not. God bless America, right?" He pointed his thumb toward the statue. "But honestly? I love jazz as much as I love classical. In the service, I have more of a chance to play both. I won't be limited. There's the Concert Band, the Army Blues, the Brass Quintet. And those ensembles are great. They play concerts in front of the Capitol every week during the summer. For free. For every American. My mom can come hear me there. Screw the conservatory. Their loss.

"And after that, maybe I become some kick-ass soloist—like Dizzy Gillespie. Ol' Herb Alpert played with the Army Band during the Korean War and then came out and started the Tijuana Brass . . . There's more than one way to take a hill . . . or plant a flag."

"But . . ." Simone looked frightened.

"Don't worry. It's peacetime now." Julius put on a little swagger—it didn't really suit him. "No one would waste a trumpeter as good as me on the front lines—like the Boogie Woogie Bugle Boy of Company B in that Big Band song. They built a whole jazz combo around him, remember?" Julius seemed to be carefully modulating his voice, forcing a shift to calculated nonchalant joking, then to affectionate teasing: "And this way, we can see each other more. I'll be in Richmond, only two hours away. Or one and a half hours, the way you drive, Ms. Lead Foot."

He took Simone's hand and turned back to watch the fireworks, signaling he was done discussing it.

Sssssss . . .ssssssss . . . BANG!

Patty glanced over at Simone. Her face glistened in the exploding light. Tears. Of relief? Regret? Anger? After a moment, Simone leaned her head on Julius's shoulder, and wrapped her arms around him, rocking them as one, gently, back and forth. "I'm sorry. So sorry, Julius."

Watching Simone embrace Julius, Patty's mind drifted to Will's brother. Remembering how Jimmy desperately needed to lay his hands on Will to make sure he was okay and safe after that bar fight. Terrified. *God, please, don't let bad things happen to Julius, too.* Then Patty felt that weird flip-flop in her stomach. Will. She really missed him. She turned to Abe. "Is Will coming back soon?"

Pop-pop-pop-sssssssss.

"He's not coming back to the Hill," Abe said quietly.

"What?" Patty's stomach lurched. "Why?"

Abe leaned in to whisper in her ear, "Will's brother tried to hang himself. Will had gone looking for him. Sensing something was off. They're so close, you know. Found him in the nick of time and cut him down. Will doesn't want to leave him." Abe pulled back and looked up at the fireworks, grim. "He'll finish high school in North Carolina."

Ssssssss . . . sssssss . . . BANG!

He glanced back at Patty. "Are you crying?"

"It's the stupid Obetrol," Patty muttered, wiping her face. Had to be.

Two weeks later, Abe and Patty once again sat shoulder to shoulder—this time having scored spots on one of the window ledges in the Senate hearing room to watch a surprise witness: Alexander Butterfield.

"Who is this guy?" they overheard one reporter ask another.

"Some air force colonel fighter-jock. Worked in Nixon's first term under Haldeman as an appointment aide."

"What's he supposed to be testifying to?"

"No idea. Everybody's mum."

Overhearing the reporters' consternation, Abe gloated. "I know," he whispered to Patty. "A little anyway."

He did always seem to know the skinny. Patty knew his ambitions and obvious place was in politics, but Abe could give Woodward and Bernstein a run for their money as an investigative reporter if he ever wanted to shift his dreams. "Sooooo?" she whispered back. "Tell."

Continuing to keep his voice low, Abe leaned in closer to her. So close, she was enveloped in the peppermint-like scent of Irish Spring soap he'd showered with that morning. "Seems a White House memo has surfaced that was addressed to Fred Thompson." Abe gestured to the Republican's chief legal counsel, who was just entering the room. "It was a detailed transcript of a conversation between Nixon and Dean—essentially *feeding* Senator Baker and Thompson quotes to use to discredit John Dean's testimony."

He pulled back to look Patty in the eye, to make sure she was registering what that implied. "That memo catches the Republicans on this committee with their pants down."

Patty made a face at him.

"No, seriously. And Pats, this doesn't make me happy to say: It proves Baker has been back-channeling with the White House. Before, it was just a rumor and worry. Nixon's staff trying to influence the Senate committee's line of questioning of witnesses—in a probe *about* that White House? And the committee—that's supposed to be unbiased and looking for truth—possibly taking those suggestions? Well, it's all kinds of wrong."

Abe let that sink in a moment before racing on, his voice lowered once more: "Baker fought the hearings being televised, you know, tried to limit them. He's a Nixon defender, hard-core." Abe stopped and grinned. "Like you."

Again, Patty made a face.

"But something about this memo has tipped his and his staff's attitude." He looked around, then lowered his voice so low she could barely hear him. "Remember I said it's a detailed transcript of a conversation between Dean and the president?"

She nodded.

"That means—"

It suddenly hit Patty. "Oh my God. That a secretary was taking notes when they met? That's great news, isn't it? A way to know for sure if what Dean is saying is true—or a lie to save his butt."

"That's the thing," Abe said. "No secretary was there."

"But . . . but how would they have a transcript, then?"

Abe raised his eyebrows. "That's the million-dollar question. Remember Dean saying he suspected Nixon might have been taping one of their last conversations, Tricky Dick's questions were so leading?"

"Yes, of course."

"You know how I hang around the committee's staffers as much as I can—they're the ones who do the research and write the questions the senators ask. The heart and brains of all this. They're . . . outta this world."

Patty smiled. Abe was their adoring shadow. He might have teased her at the inauguration for her idealistic notions, but in reality, he was the true believer in democracy, in its system of checks and balances. "Go on," she prompted with some fondness in her voice.

"Well, one of them told me that Senator Ervin is going to let Baker's minority counsel start the questions this morning."

"That's a first. Why?"

"To look totally bipartisan in whatever it is they've got with this witness. It feels like the Republicans have finally stopped thinking they have to circle the wagons, stick to party line, and defend Nixon no matter what. Between McCord and Dean's testimony, and whatever today's witness is going to reveal—the

Republicans seem shocked and disturbed enough to start asking real questions. Follow the truth. Wherever it leads."

The committee members filed in and sat down with loud squeaks of their chairs and thunderous rustling of dictionary-thick notes.

"Here we go," Abe muttered.

Alexander Butterfield raised his right hand and swore to tell the whole truth and nothing but the truth.

"Mr. Butterfield," the Republican counsel began, "are you aware of the installation of any listening devices in the Oval Office?"

Hands clasped together on the table, Butterfield blinked, blinked, blinked. Swallowed.

Patty and Abe leaned forward, waiting.

"Did he say listening devices?" the reporters gabbled.

The whole room seemed to hold its breath.

Butterfield adjusted his hands, bowed his head slightly toward the microphone and softly replied, "I was aware of listening devices, yes, sir."

Patty's mouth dropped open. Reporters in front of her looked around the room at the audience's amazement, then started scribbling furiously.

"From 1970 then until the present time," continued Fred Thompson, "all of the president's conversations were recorded?"

"That's correct."

Patty could almost hear a hundred people thinking *Ho-ly smoke* in the same breath. And the ground shifting beneath all of them.

Patty opened the door of a yellow taxi she'd hailed and slid in, yanking at her skirt to scoot across the seat's plastic covering without it rubbing the back of her thighs and creating an embarrassing fart-like sound. It'd just been too hot to drag on pantyhose that would have protected her from sticking. She'd made a choice to go bare-legged that her mother would never have allowed. But Dot Appleton wasn't there, was she?

"Seventeenth and L, please."

The driver nodded and hurtled off, Patty rolling down the window to survive the late July heat, still scorching even though twilight was approaching.

Her father was once again in town—totally out of the blue—and wanted to meet her for dinner. As the taxi pulled in front of Duke Zeibert's, Patty handed the driver three dollars. "Keep the change." Duke's was a major powerbroker restaurant, just a few blocks from the White House, where Washington lawyers, lobbyists, news broadcasters, administration staffers, and congressional types all went to see and be seen. She didn't want to look like she was some cheapo at the entrance to such an establishment. Especially since a man escorting a woman in what looked like a Chanel dress stood beside her door, waiting to nab the taxi.

"Good evening, little lady." A large, mustachioed man in a blue houndstooth sport jacket, his head bald on top but ringed with a wild mane of hair around his ears, stepped out from behind the maître d' stand. "You must be Dr. Appleton's daughter? He described you to a T—a pretty Ali MacGraw look-alike."

Patty smiled, although her father describing her the way her boyfriend did gave her a bit of a jolt. Had Scott first tagged her as resembling the *Love Story* movie star and told her father? Or the other way around? Patty would have never questioned the men in her life describing her looks the same way before, but now she felt a little weirded out by it.

"Follow me, please."

This had to be Zeibert himself, the way customers waved and waiters hastily made way for him to pass. She'd heard tales of muckety-mucks holding court at the restaurant, the most important among them seated prominently in front tables, close to the entrance—so she felt a little thrill when they reached her father quickly. And then even more when she saw he was talking to Senator Goldwater—the dean of conservatives.

"Princess!" He gave her a gin-laced kiss. "Senator, you recognize my daughter."

Goldwater eyed her through his thick, black-rimmed glasses as he slowly rose—one pants' leg hiked up, caught on one of the cowboy boots he always wore—and shook her hand.

Much to her disappointment, Patty could tell Goldwater had no memory of her. Despite the fact she'd repeatedly brought him glasses of his preferred club soda for near on seven months. "I'm a—"

"Wait!" Goldwater held on to her hand. "I do recognize you now. You're a page."

"Yes, sir."

He shook her hand enthusiastically before letting go. "And a mighty fine one, Dr. Appleton. You should be proud."

Dr. Appleton beamed.

The senator remained standing. But silent now.

Patty looked to her father. Weren't they going to sit down?

The tennis-court tan on her father's face seemed to fade a bit. "Well, thank you for your advice, Senator."

Goldwater nodded, smiled at Patty, and picked up his napkin to resume his seat.

Taking Patty's arm, her father led them to a small table in the back corner, where sat an emptied martini glass.

Their waiter quickly filled their water glasses and put Duke's signature pickles and onion rolls on the table. "Are you ready to order, sir?"

Patty hadn't had a chance to look at the menu yet, but her father ordered: "Crab cakes for my daughter and a New York strip for me—rare." He looked pointedly at the waiter. "Make it bloody. And another martini, heavy on the olives."

"Yes, sir."

Leaning back in his chair, Patty's father surveyed the room. "Quite a crowd tonight," he murmured. "Ah!" He stood suddenly. "Excuse me a minute, princess." Her father sauntered to a table of nattily dressed men, their white shirts, collar pins, and subdued ties in sharp contrast to the trendier wide lapels and thick, neon-bright ties most of the male diners sported.

He talked with them—his hands on the table, leaning over, intent—for quite a while.

Patty nibbled on a pickle. Dropped it. Took a bite of the hot onion bread. Delicious but pungent. Didn't want onion breath. She pushed that aside as well. Sipped her water. Fidgeted. Sipped some more. Listened to the boisterous, gossipy conversations swirling around her.

The restaurant fairly hummed with debate on the Watergate hearings that week: Butterfield's shocking revelation that Nixon had taped people without their knowing, Nixon defying the committee's demand to hear the tapes, Ehrlichman's contention the White House had the right to steal mental health records of "traitor" Ellsberg, and Kalmbach's admission that he'd funneled campaign donations to hush money for the Watergate burglars.

"That guy was about as clumsy with those payoffs as Inspector Clouseau," guffawed a cigar-sucking man to Patty's right. "Without the catchy *Pink Panther* theme song!" He took a long draw and blew out smoke like a self-satisfied dragon.

His tablemate laughed, but then said in a more serious tone, "The question I have is do donors know that's how he used their money. I'd be pretty ticked off if I found out my thousand bucks went to those shenanigans."

Listening, Patty turned her knife over and over and over, worrying. Had any of the donations her father solicited for Nixon's campaign ended up being misused? Accidentally, of course. Like that $25,000 check from a Midwest re-election chairman that mysteriously ended up—without his approval—in a Mexican bank account of one of the burglars. Patty didn't even consider asking if her father would *knowingly* channel money to unethical use.

As Dr. Appleton strode back to their table, several other people called out their greetings. Patty smiled, proud. So many people seemed to know her father. Here, in the nation's capital. He sat back down just as their waiter arrived with their plates and his martini.

"Who were you talking to, Daddy?"

"Oh, a bunch of lawyers." He changed the subject. "So, princess, tell me what you know. Primed and ready to be first lady?"

Patty beamed. She was going to have a whole dinner, just her, with her father. Here was her chance to impress him, prove that he'd been right to encourage her being a page. Maybe even have a serious, substantive conversation like Simone and Uncle Graham enjoyed. She'd start with what she'd witnessed that week at the hearings. "Daddy," she began as she cut into an enormous crab cake, crusty with herbed breadcrumbs, "you're a psychiatrist. What do you think about Ehrlichman sending Liddy to steal the mental health records of Ellsberg, the Pentagon Papers guy? And his saying national security considerations warranted that break-in?"

For just a moment, Patty saw an emotion she'd never seen register on her father's face before. Doubt. Then it was gone.

"Is this what I get for sending you to Washington?" he joked—sort of. "A daughter who questions the president's understanding of national security?" Dr. Appleton sawed at his slab of steak, still sizzling in its pool of blood. "The guy committed treason, princess, leaking *classified* Pentagon documents. He should rot in Leavenworth for life."

Popping a hunk of meat into his mouth, her father chewed for a moment, thoughtful. "Ellsberg probably would have been convicted—easily—if they'd left well enough alone," he muttered. "It was stupid overkill."

He took another bite. "I have wondered what Ellsberg's diagnosis was. Paranoia, perhaps. Narcissism. Delusional sense of grandeur. Clearly a risk-taker. Maybe acted in a full-on mania. Which could prove him *unstable* and, therefore, a clear and present danger to the nation. A classification, as I understand it, that allows the president to curtail individual rights." All this Dr. Appleton said more to himself than to Patty.

Draining his martini, he added, "Please tell me you've learned some useful things these past months on the Hill. Like party loyalty. Look what this guy Butterfield has done by not keeping his mouth shut. Of course, Nixon shouldn't turn those tapes over—there's sure to be all sorts of security issues being discussed on them that need to be kept secret—from the Russians, from the Chinese. All this dirt the Dems are trying to dredge up—it's a witch hunt. Just like President Nixon says."

Patty frowned. But it was more than that, wasn't it? Everything she'd witnessed as a page had opened her eyes to the fact things just didn't feel right about the campaign tactics of Nixon's re-election—the Watergate break-in and dirty tricks, the conspiracy to cover it up, that enemies' list. It all seemed such an egregious abuse of power. And simply ignoring it—or claiming the whole Watergate mess wasn't really all that bad—felt wrong. Cowardly. Even unpatriotic.

Wasn't loyalty to the country more important than loyalty to a political party or one guy? That's what she'd learned in the past few days, watching Senator Baker and the Watergate Committee Republicans pivoting and beginning to ask real questions.

And was it ethical for the White House to use Ellsberg's mental health against him? She wasn't being sassy; Patty just really wanted to know what her father thought, especially since he was a psychiatrist. These were the types of questions, the discussions and debates about political philosophy, that she was having all the time now with Abe, Simone, and Will—before tragedy took him away. The type of tragedy that might have been averted for Will's family if Nixon—and LBJ and Kennedy before him—had heeded the disasters and the strategic morass the Pentagon Papers were reporting to them that the Vietnam War had become.

Patty wanted to have these kinds of conversations with her father, to really connect with his passion for politics, to get closer to him and his thoughts. She considered how best to proceed. She really wanted to ask if he still thought Martha Mitchell was "delusional." Martha's accusations that White House people were involved in the Watergate break-in were turning out to be right. But Patty could sense that'd be a land mine. She'd ask about Democrats first.

"So," she began, "what's your opinion about what happened to McGovern's first running mate, Daddy? His having to withdraw from the ticket when it was leaked that he'd suffered from depression?" Patty couldn't help thinking President Nixon's campaign exploiting the disclosure and ridiculing the candidate for having a mental health condition was unnecessary. Cruel, even.

"Why are you asking all these questions?" Her father wiped his mouth with his napkin. "Would you want a guy who'd needed electroshock treatment and that lily-livered pacifist McGovern running the country instead of Nixon? We'd sure be going to hell in a handbasket then." In what felt a total non sequitur, he added, "Sometimes you have to get your hands dirty to make sure the right guy wins, Patricia. Everybody does it. Including those sanctimonious Democrats. I guarantee you FDR did similar things, or a lot worse."

Patty frowned. FDR? His presidency had ended nearly thirty years ago. How did that apply?

Snapping his fingers, then holding up his martini glass, indicating to the waiter he wanted another, Patty's father said, "Watch yourself. Nobody likes a nosy woman." He put his glass back down and pulled back into his more usual authoritative tone—slightly buffered with a patina of pleasant. "A little knowledge is good for a woman. But charm? Charm coupled with good looks?" He smiled at her. "That's the killer combo, princess."

Arriving with a third martini, the waiter announced, "There's a phone call for you at the desk, Doctor. I'm afraid we can't stretch a table phone back *this far*." Was that a smirk on the waiter's face?

Patty's father rose. "Bring us two cheesecakes, and don't scrimp on Duke's famous strawberry topping." He strode to the restaurant's entrance.

Her father was gone a long time. Long enough for Patty to push off the sticky-thick strawberry compote from the top of her cheesecake slice and take a few bites. Mostly, though, she played with the slab of sweet. She was trying to shed some weight without the Obetrol.

When he finally returned, her father was agitated, preoccupied. "Sorry, princess, I've got to go." He downed his last martini, threw a fifty-dollar bill onto the table, and took her by the arm to hurry them out the front door.

As he opened a cab's door for her, Dr. Appleton hugged Patty briskly. "See you soon, princess." He held up his pointer finger and added, "Be a good girl."

Then he stepped away to hail a different taxi for himself.

In the confines of her cab, Patty noticed a heavy, sweet scent her father's hug had left on her. Not the distinct, light, and lovely blend of jasmine and roses in Jean Patou's Joy that had been her mother's signature fragrance for years—elegant, expensive. Patty had always been a bit amazed her mother wore it, given that it reportedly had been Jackie Kennedy's favorite as well.

What was going on with Dot Appleton that she was changing her much-loved perfume?

WATERGATE

THE SENATE COMMITTEE WRAPS UP its public hearings. Whatever the senators do next hinges on hearing Nixon's secret recordings of John Dean. It was Dean's testimony—and Alexander Butterfield divulging that **NIXON SECRETLY TAPED ALL OVAL OFFICE CONVERSATIONS**—that finally pushed the committee co-chair Howard Baker and other Republicans into truly beginning to **EXAMINE NIXON'S CLAIMS OF INNOCENCE**.

Those tapes **WILL CORROBORATE DEAN OR PROVE HIM THE LIAR** so many people call him.

NIXON INSISTS THAT EXPOSING HIS CONVERSATIONS WILL HARM NATIONAL SECURITY, discouraging aides and visiting dignitaries from giving their honest opinions in the future. Unpersuaded, **JUDGE SIRICA ORDERS NIXON TO COMPLY** with the subpoena for nine specific tapes that, given their dates, Special Prosecutor Archibald Cox and his team have determined relevant to Watergate.

NIXON APPEALS Sirica's decision, stalling the proceedings.

On the day the Senate hearings conclude, **NIXON DELIVERS HIS SECOND PRIME-TIME ADDRESS REGARDING WATERGATE**. He takes a chiding tone: "I had no prior knowledge of the Watergate break-in. I neither took part in nor knew of the subsequent cover-up activities. That was and is the simple truth. We have reached a point in which a backward obsession with Watergate is causing this nation to neglect matters of far greater importance to all American people."

This time **HIS SPEECH FALLS FLAT**. His national approval sinks to 31 percent from a 69 percent high of that day in 1920 on which women of America were first guaranteed the right to vote.

NOW, THEREFORE, I, RICHARD NIXON, President of the United States of America, do hereby call upon the people of the United States and interested groups and organizations to observe August 26 1973, as Women's Equality Day with appropriate ceremonies and activities. I further urge all our people to use this occasion to reflect on the importance of achieving equal rights and opportunities for women and to dedicate themselves anew to that great goal. For the cause of equal rights and opportunities for women is inseparable from the cause of human dignity and equal justice for all.

WOMEN

As the battle for ERA ratification continues, **CONGRESS PASSES A BILL** sponsored by New York Congresswoman Bella Abzug designating **AN ANNUAL WOMEN'S EQUALITY DAY, TO COMMEMORATE** August 1920, **WHEN AMERICAN WOMEN WERE GUARANTEED THE VOTE**.

The women's movement is not without fissures. **MANY BLACK FEMINISTS FEEL THE FIGHT FOR FEMALE EQUALITY HAS FOCUSED TOO MUCH ON WHITE MIDDLE-CLASS CONCERNS.** To better address the double burdens of sexism and racism on Black women, **THEY ESTABLISH THE NATIONAL BLACK FEMINIST ORGANIZATION**. Attorneys Florynce Kennedy (right) and Eleanor Holmes Norton (left)—who also helped start the National Women's Political Caucus—are among the cofounders.

CHAPTER EIGHT

AUGUST

Thirty-two minutes left. Too soon to go down to the lobby. Patty paced her room, then stopped in front of her closet's full-length mirror. Checked the gauzy green scarf she wore like a headband, pulling her dark hair off her face, knotted to the side, and falling to her collarbone. Applied hot-pink lipstick. Fiddled with the three cloth-covered buttons running just below her dress's V-neck that closed the bodice of her dress. It was empire-cut, with a ribbon running just below her bust, emphasizing it. No immodest cleavage—just hugged her to advantage. She'd been really pleased when she found the dress at Woodies with how it flattered her figure, making her look a little sexy without appearing unladylike.

She especially liked its cut-out sleeves, rows of peekaboo diamonds running from shoulder to wrist. Smoothing the front of its mini length, she took one final inspection of the kelly-green dress. Wait. Would Scott think the color was loud? Patty turned, staring at her image from the side. Oh no. Was her tummy pooching out? She stood up straighter. Did her butt look big? Had eating nothing but cottage cheese at lunch not helped?

Patty rushed to her closet, riffling through dresses. Maybe she should change. She pulled out the sundress she'd worn to the Belmont party, then a blue shift and a red shirtdress.

Twenty-five minutes.

Laughter came from the hall as several other boarders passed her room, chatting. Their collective amusement reminded her of the sound of Simone's laugh when she thought something was ridiculous.

Stop. You look fine, Patty admonished herself. *Sit. Wait. Patience is a virtue.*

Picking up the *Ladies' Home Journal* that she'd taken from her parents' Watergate hotel room—"the magazine women believe in," as its cover tagline announced—Patty sat gingerly on the edge of her bed. Her dress's polyester blend wasn't supposed to wrinkle. But Patty didn't trust the label.

The magazine fell open to the feature on Marilyn Monroe and a two-page spread of the naked actress reclining provocatively, shielding herself only so much with a sheet. Punctuating the large photo was a caption in which author Norman Mailer compared Monroe to the most revered of stringed instruments to play—a Stradivarius: "Sex came up from her like a resonance of sound in the clearest grain of a violin."

Patty had read the article already, several times, absorbing Mailer's celebration of a woman who inspired all manner of dreams in a man and fulfilled them with a "whispery voice" and "a smile that promised 'take me.'" A woman who somehow combined girlish vulnerability with siren-sultriness, inspiring protectiveness as well as longing, Mailer had rhapsodized. The proverbial lady in the parlor but lusty minx in bed that men seemed to want.

After rereading that article to the point of almost memorizing it, Patty had practiced her version of the Marilyn Monroe smile, trying to capture that oxymoron of a look.

Now weirdly irritated by the spread, Patty flipped through front-of-the book columns like "Can This Marriage Be Saved," coming to a one-page profile of the vice president's wife. A mother of four and grandmother of two, Judy Agnew was still "as bouncy as a coed," the magazine gushed.

Patty turned the page, startling a bit at a sharp contrast to the Monroe article she hadn't noticed before: "Defending Yourself Against Rape—an excerpt from *Our Bodies Ourselves*." That unnerving book Simone had lent her.

Patty felt her face flush hot then cold as she read its blunt opening sentence: "Rape is sexual intercourse without consent, or violent sexual aggression" and then, a paragraph down, "because of the persistent myth that most women secretly want to be raped . . . men are often excused for their sexual aggressiveness because of their 'uncontrollable sex drive.'"

Patty had never before heard that awful word discussed—not out loud, not in her world, anyway—and unease rippled through her. How many times had Patty and her classmates laughed off the nuns' warnings about a girl's appearance prompting temptation with a dismissive shrug and the age-old "boys will be boys"? What about all those romance novels, those ripped bodices and Heathcliff-rugged and handsome bad-boy heroes? Femininity defined as being pleasing, diffident, waiting for men to act first. Then acquiescing, which every novel and movie she'd ever seen promised would bring joy and belonging. All from to-be-emulated smiles that—like Mailer described Marilyn's a mere ten pages later—"promised 'take me.'"

As if playing off her jumbled thoughts, the article went on to blame society's tolerance of rape, its mistaken belief it was an act of extreme passion not an act of violence and domination, on pop cultural fascination with "'sex and violence,' now an American idiom like 'love and marriage.' Many newspapers, magazines, and movies encourage people to groove on sadism . . ."

"Patty!" A knock on her door jolted her. "The front desk says there's a handsome gentleman caller waiting for you."

Sugar! Scott was ten minutes early.

Patty dropped the magazine like it was a hot potato and rushed downstairs.

When she caught sight of him, Patty felt her breath catch, her stomach lurch. She'd seen Scott two weeks before on a quick weekend trip home. But somehow today—leaning nonchalantly on the front desk, chatting up the middle-aged matron keeping watch on the lobby, he seemed even more gorgeous. And no longer a good-looking high school kid. A man. Tall, dark, and handsome, lean and muscular. Cleft chin, strong jaw, thick hair, and disarming grin like a young James Garner. Cocksure and charismatic.

The austere lady he was flirting with was totally enchanted, borderline-giggling at whatever he was saying. That's the way it always was with Scott. He left a wake of blushing women wherever he went.

And he was *her* beau. And now he was here.

Patty skipped up and hugged him from behind.

"Good grief," she heard the matron mutter at her less-than-prim arrival and embrace. Patty didn't care. She hugged her boyfriend even harder. He was here! Finally!

Turning, Scott kissed her on the head. "Hey, beautiful." Then he checked his watch. "Right on time."

She slipped her hand through his arm. He'd come to take her to Georgetown, to see its campus, having just moved into his dorm. She was beyond excited. "Shall we?" she murmured.

"Yes, we shall." Scott grinned, propelling her toward the door.

"Oh, Miss Appleton," the matron singsong'ed after them, holding an envelope up in the air. "You have mail." She wiggled it.

"Hang on a sec." Patty stood on her tiptoes to kiss Scott on the cheek, feeling the faint scratch of beard stubble that she hadn't noticed before. Yes, a man, all right.

As she went back to the desk, the matron whispered, as if in sorority-girl confidence, and yet loud enough for Scott to hear, "It's from North Carolina."

Patty knew only one person from North Carolina: Will. Through gritted teeth, she thanked the gossipy matron, snatched the letter, and shoved it into her purse.

Scott cocked his head. "Who's writing my girl from North Carolina?" he asked. Good-natured enough.

But Patty wasn't so sure that he'd appreciate a boy writing her. And given the way she and Will had parted—right after that terrible bar fight on Abe's birthday—how soft like a lover's voice Will's had been, how fervently he'd squeezed her hand before letting it go—Patty worried this letter might express what they had never spoken. An obvious tenderness for each other.

There was no way Scott would be all right with that.

"Oh, nobody important," she fibbed nervously. "Just a page who went home."

Scott squinted one eye and looked at her harder.

"Tell me all about your room." Patty linked her arm with Scott's again and looked up at him with her attempt at a Marilyn smile—did she get it right?—and careful adoration in her expression. Then she peppered him with distracting questions. "Is it wonderful? Is your roommate nice? Do you have a view of the river? Do you feel like a big man on campus?"

Laughing, Scott resumed their exit. "C'mon. I'll show you, Miss Inquisitor."

Patty fell in love at first sight. A self-contained citadel atop a hill on the edge of D.C.'s historic district, Georgetown University's campus was a gorgeous enclave of old trees, green lawns, and neo-Gothic buildings. Jesuit-based, founded in the late 1700s, it radiated an aura of scholarly contemplation and conversation. Scott's dorm, Copley Hall, even looked like a small castle—a beautiful five-story stone building with cathedral-style windows in its center entrance.

Standing in front, gazing up its staircase to massive, carved wooden doors, Patty murmured, "Oh, I could be really happy here. I should apply." She glanced at Scott. "They're accepting girls now, right?"

Scott made a face. "Only just. Started four years ago. Nobody likes them. A lot of libber types. Argumentative as hell. They'd make mincemeat of a nice girl like you in class."

Patty frowned. She was an A student. She could keep up. She started to say so—remembering Julius serenading Simone in her VW Bug, talking about how he loved she was "a brainiac"—but Scott put his arm around her, interrupting. "I was hoping you'd go to Trinity across town. That's where all the smart, pretty, Catholic girls go. Then we could see each other on weekends. Make up for all the time we lost this spring." He kissed her.

Patty melted.

Two freshmen men approached the dorm along the walkway. "They've brought a TV into the lounge for Nixon's speech," said a red-haired boy to the other. "You coming?"

"Cool beans," answered his companion. "You bet. I've watched every minute of those hearings. Witnessing history, man. I'm kicking myself now for not taking that internship on the Hill and filing papers all summer in my old man's law office instead. Could have seen it all firsthand."

They nodded at Scott in unspoken hello before jogging up the stairs to Copley's entrance.

Patty smiled with more than a tad of pride. *She* had seen it! "Can we watch the president's address, too?" She looked up into Scott's handsome face. "Pretty please?"

Scott assessed her for a minute. "I was planning for us to walk down to M Street. A beer for me. Ice cream for you. Maybe a little necking down by the river. It's supposed to be gorgeous at night, with a view toward the Lincoln Memorial."

"Oh, that sounds lovely. But . . . we can do that next time. Or after Nixon's address. Don't you want to hear what he has to say, Mr. Wanna-Be-President-Himself someday?"

"Well, yeah, as a matter of fact, I do. I just figured . . ." Scott trailed off and grinned. "I'm impressed. I'm not sure I could have dragged you off the tennis court before for a speech like this."

"But that's why I came to Washington to page, silly. Remember? You said that our being long distance would be okay because it would make me . . ." Patty smiled up at her beau, once more hoping her lips carried that Marilyn Monroe magic, before adding shyly, "the perfect wife for a man of ambition."

Scott seemed to startle just the slightest at her words.

Patty felt herself flush red and panic. "That's . . . that's what you said," she murmured.

"I did." Scott reclaimed his signature nonchalance and kissed the tip of her nose. "Sure you'll be okay among all those guys? You won't feel overwhelmed?"

Didn't Scott remember how few female pages there were—which made her selection as one even more impressive, demanding she be anything but overwhelmed? Patty made sure her voice remained sweet, not confrontational, as she said, "Not to worry. Don't forget I'm surrounded by boys and men all day on the Hill."

"Yeah." He put his arm over her shoulders and pulled her close. "I remember. It made me crazy jealous." Then Scott let go of her so abruptly, she staggered a little. He thought a moment. "I don't suppose there's any issue with your watching it in my dorm's parlor—in terms of violating any kind of rule. Sure." He checked his watch. "Let's get a seat." He held up a finger, like a teacher, before taking her hand and said, "Make me proud, doll."

She nodded enthusiastically.

Inside, Patty caught her breath at the baronial splendor of the lounge. With gleaming, herringbone parquet floors decorated with enormous Oriental rugs, dark paneled walls, exposed beams in the high ceilings, and stained-glass windows, the massive room felt like a set for some BBC Masterpiece Theatre production. Set up in rows in front of a TV that sat atop a tall dolly was a mishmash of rolled-arm, wood-carved, and metal folding chairs. Most were already filled with young men kibitzing about what Nixon might say, a haze of their cigarette smoke drifting up to the lofty ceiling.

A handful of other girls were already seated together. Patty seemed to be the only "date" among the women, which first made her feel special, but then made her wonder again about applying to Georgetown herself. She'd have to work on that with Scott.

The screen flickered to the president sitting in front of gold curtains and an American flag, holding a thick stack of papers. "Good evening," Nixon began. "Now that most of the major witnesses in the Watergate phase of the Senate committee hearings on campaign practices have been heard, the time has come for me to speak out about the charges made and to provide a perspective on the issue for the American people."

Everyone in the room hushed and leaned forward. Patty almost crossed her fingers in her hope that Nixon would be able to vindicate himself.

"For over four months Watergate has dominated the news media," Nixon read, his head bobbing up and down as he emphasized numbers. "During the past *three months* the three major networks have devoted an average of over *twenty-two hours* of television time each week to this subject. The Senate committee has heard over *two million words* of testimony."

"Nothing but a media circus," Scott muttered as the president put the first page of his speech to the side. Her boyfriend's words echoed Jake the jerk's—a troubling recognition that Patty had to make herself shake off to focus on Nixon's next words.

"It has become clear that both the hearings themselves and some of the commentaries on them have become increasingly absorbed in an effort to implicate the president personally in the illegal activities that took place."

Pausing, Nixon fairly glared at the TV camera.

"I had no prior knowledge of the Watergate break-in . . . I neither authorized nor encouraged subordinates to engage in illegal or improper campaign tactics." The president looked up from his notes to face his audience. "That is the simple truth."

Scott nodded, holding out a hand toward Patty in a silent, what-did-I-tell-you gesture. Inculcated by years at a Catholic prep school that pushed respect for authority as gospel and used guilt as a teaching tool, Patty slumped slightly in her chair, feeling chastised. She smiled dutifully and nodded back.

"My statement," the president preached on, "has been challenged by only one of the thirty-five witnesses who appeared—a witness who offered no evidence beyond his own impressions, and whose testimony had been contradicted by every other witness in a position to know the facts."

Patty frowned. Clearly Nixon was referring to John Dean. She'd watched the man give his forthright, six-hour-long statement. And the witnesses who followed him. What Nixon was saying wasn't true, not exactly. She squirmed in her chair. Why was Nixon fibbing?

She leaned over and whispered in Scott's ear, "Actually several of the recent witnesses corroborated at least part of what

Dean said." Like her father's fundraising compatriot, Nixon's personal lawyer, for instance, the man who'd admitted to turning campaign donations into hush money payments to the Watergate burglars. She ached to tell Scott about the uneasiness for her father that Kalmbach's revelations caused in her, even though she couldn't name exactly what she feared—she knew her father would never participate in something so egregious.

Scott pulled back and looked at her quizzically. "Dean's a worm."

"But—"

Scott shushed her.

Nixon went on, his voice—to Patty's thinking—growing a tad whiny: "I was told again and again that there was no indication that any persons were involved other than the seven who were known to have planned and carried out the operation . . . I was convinced there was no cover-up, because I was convinced that no one had anything to cover up."

"Oh, get real, man," the redheaded freshman groaned from a row in front of them. Several others nearby snorted and *pshawed* in concert.

Scott stiffened.

The president went on for twenty more minutes, justifying his refusal to obey congressional and court subpoenas. His secret tapes were "privileged," Nixon said, like conversations between "priest and penitent" or "man and wife," for him alone. If the general public heard these "blunt" exchanges, it would endanger national security.

"But they're only asking for the ones of meetings between him and Dean." The words just popped out of Patty's mouth.

This time Scott frowned and emphatically looked around at his new classmates before turning his gaze to her and raising his eyebrow archly, signaling her to be quiet.

Patty pressed her lips together as Nixon went on, blaming the civil rights and anti–Vietnam War protests for "a rising spiral of violence and fear" that established "the notion that the end justifies the means.

"We must recognize," the president chided, "that one excess begets another, and that the extremes of violence and discord in the 1960s contributed to the extremes of Watergate."

A long-haired freshman blew a very loud and very long raspberry at that. Someone else booed. Heckled a third, "Antiwar sentiment didn't make you a cheat and liar!"

A fourth student shouted at the dissenters: "Shut the f— up."

Suddenly, a low-boil hostility simmered through the room.

Nixon ended with reiterating his administration's policy goals and then, "I ask for your help to ensure that those who would exploit Watergate in order to keep us from doing what we were elected to do will not succeed . . . Thank you and good evening."

Scott stood and applauded, as did about a third of those in the room. The rest remained rooted in their seats, shaking their heads in disbelief and disappointment, or glowering at those standing—the tension between these new classmates as thick and sour as their cigarette smoke.

This is where Watergate has brought us, thought Patty sadly, looking around the room at the eighteen-year-olds who should have been flush with excitement and idealism and happy anticipation at sharing ideas in the communion a university was supposed to be—like she had felt at the inauguration. Instead, they were eyeing one another with suspicion and defensiveness and with a presumption of the other's stupidity.

Slowly, she rose to her feet, following her boyfriend's lead, and clapped her hands tepidly. The president hadn't answered the charges, had done nothing, really, other than act the misunderstood martyr and scold the country for being concerned about

Watergate and all it implied about his administration's political ethics.

But it was Scott's response that troubled her most. Hadn't he seen what she had? "You know," Patty began quietly, "all the pages have been talking about this. If President Nixon would just give the tapes with Dean to the Senate committee, a lot of questions would be put to rest." Patty noticed the redheaded freshman turn to listen to her, nodding as she spoke. "I'm hoping those tapes exonerate Nixon. It makes him look suspect to not turn them—"

Scott grabbed her hand to cut her off. "Want to see my room?" He smiled and added loudly, "Where I'll be having sweet dreams about you?"

Boys around them chuckled.

Patty blushed. "Sure!"

"C'mon, then, beautiful."

As soon as Scott ushered her into his narrow fifth-floor room, Patty felt uneasy. They'd snatched private moments before. It wasn't as if they hadn't made out, pretty hot and heavy sometimes, in his Porsche, or in the grass on the hill behind the club's eighteenth hole. And Lord, how she'd been longing for him to hold her. She'd missed him so much over the past months.

But something about the two single beds with their boy-blue linens, the scent of Old Spice cologne mixed with dirty athletic socks, the posters of the Rolling Stones, the Cincinnati Reds' Pete Rose, and Clint Eastwood as Dirty Harry made her feel vulnerably female in a very male domain. And she was disappointed by how he'd cut her off downstairs. Just like her father did her mother. And her. The whole point of Patty coming to the Hill as a page was to become a more worthy, more worldly, and therefore a more helpful political ally to her boyfriend and his dreams.

Didn't Scott want to hear what she'd witnessed? Or her opinions and analysis of what she'd seen?

Walking to the wide, double window, Patty gazed out at treetops to collect herself as Scott closed the door with a loud click.

"When did you start drinking lefty hooch?" Scott joked. Sort of.

"I—I haven't. I've just been listening. And there are a lot of things that don't add up, Scott. That just don't feel right." She bit her lip, tasting lipstick. Out of habit, she pressed them together in case the color had faded, to spread the gloss out evenly. Then she tried explaining herself again. "Actually, what I really mean is it's going to be important to gather all the evidence—tapes included—so Americans can feel confident they know the whole truth, and then decide what we as a country should do next. That's what democracy requires, isn't it? To be informed. And involved."

With a tight smile on his chiseled face, Scott strode toward her. Instinctively, she stepped back, bumping into a desk.

He took her hand. "It's great that you're so smart, Patty. I can use that. But you embarrassed me down there. When I start running for office, you need to not contradict my opinions." He pulled her to him.

Standing this close together, Patty had to tilt her head back to talk up to him, he was so tall. *Contradict?* That was one of her father's preferred words. Patty frowned slightly at the same time her heart began to pound at being in Scott's embrace. "But we can always talk about things—in private if you'd rather. Can't we?" she squeaked. "That's what makes us a team, a 'we, not an I,' like Daddy says. I've learned so much being here on the Hill. I want to share it with you."

"God, you're a stone-cold fox," he murmured, staring down at her. "Stop talking. Show me you're still my girl." He kissed her—with an insistence Scott had never shown before. It made Patty feel all kinds of new things.

She pulled back to catch her breath, but he held fast.

His lips went to her neck, and his fingers to the buttons of her bodice. "You're driving me wild," he breathed. One ... two ... three, with shocking confidence and ease, Scott had those buttons undone, and before Patty could react, his hand was on her breasts, scooping them up and out of her bra, out of her dress.

"Hey, man, what's doing?"

"Jesus!" Scott stepped back and Patty fell away, crimson with mortification as she yanked at the front of her dress, fumbling to tuck and button herself back in.

"We need to come up with a signal," Scott semi-growled.

"A sock standing upright on the doorknob perhaps?"

Scott's awkward laugh made Patty feel even sicker. "Doll, this is Mark." He put his arm around Patty and turned her to face his roommate. "See what I mean? Just like Ali McGraw, don't you think?"

"Oh, yeah." Mark smiled. Or was it a leer? Patty couldn't see straight in her haze of embarrassment. But she could smell beer on him from ten feet away. *Oh God.* What that boy must think of her.

"Give us a few minutes, okay?" Scott asked.

"Sure thing. Nice to meet you, ma'am." The guy did a fake tip of a fake hat and left.

"Next time I'll lock the door," Scott grumbled. He sighed. "Come on, I'll hail you a cab. You should go home. I don't think I can resist you and control myself if you stay."

Patty had no words. Dazed, embarrassed, confused, she just clung to her beau's hand as he walked her through campus, down a long hill and a neighborhood of ancient clapboard row houses to the bright lights of M Street.

Standing on the curb, he threw up his hand, whistled sharply, and a taxi pulled over immediately, picking Scott over at least half a dozen other people coming out of the restaurants and bars along that busy road and waving for a ride. He opened the door, pulling her in for one last ardent kiss, bruising her mouth with its force.

"That'll keep me for a while," he breathed, motioning for her to get into the cab. Scott stepped back, leaning over while holding the door ajar, to say, "I'm going to be jammed with orientation and the first days of class. I'll call next week."

Then he slammed the door shut and knocked on the taxi roof for the driver to pull ahead—before Patty could say anything.

Next week? In the darkness of the cab, Patty relived Scott's touch, trembling slightly as her heart filled up with a disorienting mixture of desire from that last kiss and dismay for being half naked in front of Scott's roommate.

Not until next week? That long? Tears stung her cheeks, rubbed raw by Scott's new five o'clock shadow stubble.

"You all right, miss?"

Startled, Patty looked up and caught the driver's gaze in the rearview mirror. He was older, his eyes kind.

"Yes, sir," she murmured, nodding.

"Where to, honey?"

Scott had forgotten to give the driver her address.

Snuffling, Patty managed, "Constitution and Second, please." She reached into her purse for tissues and felt instead Will's letter.

In the sporadic beams of streetlights, Patty read Will's brief but heartfelt note, explaining his decision to stay in North Carolina. His family needed him. If he was able to go to college, he hoped to attend NC State to study agriculture sciences and be twenty minutes from home. He was going to take over running the farm with Jimmy. He ended with *I'm sorry I wasn't able to tell you all this in person. And to tell you how I feel about you.*

The next sentence was scratched out so thoroughly, Patty couldn't decipher it.

I'll just say that the best part of my time in Washington was knowing you. You are so smart, Patty. So beautiful. And you were so kind to me when I most needed it. I've left part of my heart in your hands, and you will be that sweet "what-if?" I will treasure the rest of my life. Yours, Will

Patty held that letter to her own heart all the way to Thompson-Markward Hall.

The next Sunday, curled up in Simone's orange bean bag—Patty was beginning to like that hippie thing—she couldn't help herself. She'd been fretting over Scott for eight days now. Patty hadn't heard from him—not a word. Of course, he'd said it would be "next week" before he'd call. But how could he not reach out, after the way he'd kissed her?

A doo-wop, R & B girl group was playing on Simone's stereo: *"Tonight, the light of love is in your eyes, but will you love me tomorrow?"*

Patty recognized the tune. "I thought this was a Carole King song. I didn't realize it was just a cover."

"It isn't. She wrote it for the Shirelles. Just like she wrote the Beatles' 'Chains' and the Drifters' 'Up on the Roof.'"

"Is this a lasting treasure, or just a moment's pleasure?"

Opened up by the song's questions, and Simone having just confessed a few moments earlier how much she was missing Julius, Patty blurted, "Did you and Julius—you know—before he left last week for VCU?"

Sprawled on the floor, Simone sat up abruptly. "No."

"Please don't think I meant anything bad by that question," Patty said, rushing to get the words out quickly. "Not . . . not like I stupidly did before. You guys are so obviously in love—even if you're not going steady!"

"You need to stop relying on labels like *going steady*, Patty, to define what people feel." Ever since Patty had taken care of her that awful night of the concert, Simone had been far less defensive, less critical—with Patty anyway—and her tone carried no rebuke. "Why do you ask?"

Patty spilled. All of it—surprising herself that she wasn't worrying about admitting things she knew Simone would probably disapprove of—like the detail of Scott cutting her off during Nixon's address. As she did, Patty realized that maybe she and Simone were becoming what Aunt Marjorie hoped for—*real* friends.

"Oh, my God." Simone reached out to put her hand on Patty's foot. "Next time you see that guy, I hope he apologizes for not letting you say what you think."

Patty froze. Perhaps she'd been too quick to put Simone in the non-judgy friend category. Reflexively, she murmured, "Love means never having to say you're sorry," quoting the *Love Story* line that had become an omnipresent pop-culture slogan.

"Arggggh. I hate that movie!" Simone got up to change records, putting on the group Chicago. "The girl gives up her piano career, and what might have been international stardom—for a guy. A guy? And then she dies!" She lowered the needle to the record and turned to face Patty as trumpets led to the group's lead singer crooning, "'*You are my love and my life . . .*'"

"Love *should* mean you value your partner enough to say you're sorry when you screw up, Patty! Loving your partner as an equal. Not one being of service to the other." Simone scrutinized her.

"You're not thinking of going all the way with this guy, are you? Someone who's . . . so controlling? I know you see it as his being confident, suave, some kind of knight-in-shining-armor protector, but maay-be it's also just kinda, plain old domineering?"

Patty had planned to be a virgin on her wedding night. But . . . Scott's touch, that kiss. She blushed—yet again—remembering his voice: *You're driving me wild.* Wasn't that all about how much he loved her? Patty looked up at Simone, flushed and flustered.

"Oh no. You are, aren't you? Hold on." Simone went to her shelf and rummaged, finally retrieving an issue of *Esquire* magazine. "I see you sitting there, still all turned on by that guy. Before you do something that you might regret, there's something you should read." She flipped through its pages until she found what she was looking for and held the magazine toward Patty to take. "I'm still furious at *Esquire* for that stupid special pink issue last month that they claimed was 'about women' but really skewered feminists and made fun of Gloria Steinem. But Nora Ephron is always dead-on in her columns for them."

Patty startled at the title of Ephron's piece: "Fantasies." She tossed it back at Simone. "No thank you."

"Think you'll go to hell for talking about fantasies?" Simone asked with a small laugh.

The nuns certainly would have told her she would.

"Okay, I'll save you from damnation by reading it *to* you." Simone skimmed, looking for the right passage. "Here it is. Ephron writes that the way men and women treat each other won't change unless"—she held up a hand like she was sermonizing—"the 'romantic and sexual fantasies that are deeply ingrained, not just in society but in literature' change.

"Ephron admits to having what she calls an appalling fantasy since she was a preteen, about being so pretty, men would 'go mad with desire' just looking at her and want to rip her clothes off—her reel of imagination stopping there. She's pretty chagrined about it, but admits that in her fantasy nobody ever loved her for her mind."

Simone looked up from the magazine at Patty. "You hearing this?"

Patty blinked and shrugged.

"Okay, look. Ephron writes she has 'no desire to be dominated' but that she gets annoyed when her husband has trouble flagging a taxi or a waiter." Simone shook her head. "Ephron is about as feminist as it comes, and even she's shackled with these idiotic ideas of what being masculine or feminine requires of us. Why can't she hail the cab? Why are women supposed to want to be taken or ravaged like in some bad romance novel with all those ripped bodices?" Simone stuck her tongue out and her finger in and out of her mouth as if inducing vomit. "If Ephron struggles with this, that's how big the problem is we're dealing with, Patty."

Patty's mind went back to the Marilyn Monroe profile, the actress being eulogized as "a Stradivarius of sex"—the ultimate desirable woman, like the most responsive instrument to a violinist's touch. She frowned, tweaked again by unexpected, perplexing irritation and a new sense of unease with Marilyn's portrayal as a beautiful object to be played.

Simone's voice interrupted her musings: "Ephron's conclusion is really, really important: 'If society changes . . . where women are truly equal, where their status has nothing to do with whom they marry, when the issues of masculine/feminine cease to exist, some of this absurd reliance on role-playing will be eliminated.'"

Simone tossed the magazine down. "Just saying." She shrugged. "If *you* want to have sex, Patty, if you trust him, feel safe with this guy, that he wants you as you naturally are, like Carole King sings—not as some trophy or a piece of pretty clay he can mold to what he wants, when he wants—then go for it. But just think about what I've read you before you do. Oh, and for God's sake, make sure he uses a rubber."

Simone checked her wristwatch, not noticing the *What?!* look on Patty's face at the word *rubber*.

"Mom asked that I drive you back today. She's working the phones since it's Women's Equality Day. She gave me money to treat us to lunch." Simone grinned and put on her mother's slight Virginia drawl: "You'll feel better after a nice meal, sweet pea."

Patty managed a laugh over Simone's joking, motherly response to stress. She stood to gather her things as Chicago's "Just You 'N Me" ended: *"Ooh, baby, you're everything I've ever dreamed of."*

As Simone's Beetle raced along the GW Parkway—her eight-track blaring—Patty kept her gaze out over the Potomac, first spotting the Jefferson domed memorial, then the Lincoln neo-classical Greek temple. "Is your mother enjoying working for the Women's Caucus?" she asked.

"She loooooves it," Simone said, turning down the volume. "She had applied for a State Department job, given her fluent French. But she couldn't even get an interview. She was told she was too old. And that they wanted a man who would really commit long-term to the position. Implying that because she was a woman, she'd be fickle or change her mind about working." Simone's voice carried an edge. "Honestly, though, I think the work she's doing is so much better. She's thrilled to be involved directly with the movement. It's only part-time. The caucus has next to no money. But it's keeping us in groceries until Dad finds a new job."

Keeping them in groceries. Patty had never personally known anyone who had to worry about money before—not until Will. She couldn't imagine the awful uncertainty of her father not having a job. Maybe she should take Simone to lunch rather than her godmother treating them. Patty had her father's credit card. She turned away from the river to face Simone. "Is Uncle Graham having a hard time finding something?"

Simone nodded. "But cross your fingers. Dad's got an interview with the E.P.A. legal department. Mom set it up. Through Mrs. Ruckelshaus—you know, Mom's White House buddy who helped start the caucus. That's the way things work in D.C., she says—connections. Mrs. Ruckelshaus's husband was head of the EPA before Tricky Dick bounced him over to the FBI and now to the Justice Department."

She turned up her eight-track as a woman sang, *"You had me several years ago when I was still quite naïve . . ."*

Patty smirked. "If I didn't know better, I might think you were playing this song on purpose."

"Moi?" Simone shifted gears to slow for the loop exit to cross Memorial Bridge.

"Yes, you," Patty answered good-naturedly. "I'll play. Who is this?"

"Carly Simon. A song about a self-infatuated ex-boyfriend she's glad to be clear of."

"You said that we made such a pretty pair . . ."

Squirming inside, Patty turned the music off and asked quickly—as if she simply wanted to be easily heard, "Your father is okay with his wife setting up job interviews?" She could hear her own father's damnation of Uncle Graham as being "henpecked" for letting a woman direct him.

"Oh, for sure. He's stoked about the possibility of working to clean up the environment. Did you know there're so many chemicals in the Potomac River that photographers have been able to develop prints in the water? Faded and shadowy, but still . . ."

Patty made a face. "Gross."

"No kidding. It's why all eagles are borderline extinct. They aren't having babies. They eat fish. The contaminants in the fish get into the eagles' bloodstream so the females' eggs have shells so thin, they crush them when they sit to keep them warm." She paused a moment before adding, "I sure hope Dad's ex-boss doesn't try to blackball him somehow for protesting Nixon's going after his enemies through federal agencies like the IRS or the FBI or CIA."

"Allegedly," Patty murmured.

"Sure." Simone shot Patty a look of *are-you-for-real?* as she turned onto Independence Avenue. "I have to give Tricky Dick credit for the EPA, though," she said, subdued. "He signed it into existence. And hopefully the Endangered Species Act when it gets through Congress." She smiled at Patty in political truce. "So, where do you pages hang out for lunch?"

"Well, let's see." She thought a moment. "Abe's favorite place is the Hawk 'n' Dove."

Simone laughed. "That's clever."

"What?"

"The restaurant's name. *Hawk* for people supporting the Vietnam War and *Dove* for those who didn't. A place for all kinds, I suppose. Pretty politic." Glancing over at Patty once more, Simone teased, "That hadn't occurred to you before?" She gently punched Patty's shoulder. "Tell me again why you wanted to be a Capitol Hill page?"

As they entered the crowded, kitschy pub, Simone stopped dead, her face lighting up. "Oh my God," she whispered, grabbing Patty's arm. "Look over there. I can't believe it. Bella Abzug and Shirley Chisholm, together at a table. And that must be Congresswoman Burke, too." Simone pointed to a younger Black woman, who looked very pregnant.

Patty gaped. She didn't know congresswomen were allowed to be pregnant.

"Just a little over a dozen women in Congress. And there sit three of them! And the two most famous." She excitedly tugged on Patty's arm. "Can you introduce me?" Simone was still whispering, she was in such awe.

"I—I don't know them. I page on the Senate side."

Simone's face fell.

Don't be a baby, Patty reprimanded herself. Simone and her family had been so generous with her, she could manage to screw up her courage enough to walk over to a table and politely introduce herself. She'd seen her father do it a hundred times.

"Okay, come on." She pulled Simone along with her. But once they neared the table, Patty felt herself grow stupidly shy. She froze a few feet away from the congresswomen, arm in arm with Simone, the two girls staring.

It was Congresswoman Abzug who noticed them. Putting down her fork atop a salad she clearly was not enjoying much, the New Yorker broke into a warm, enveloping grin and beckoned the girls toward her. "Don't be bashful," she boomed in an accent that riveled Abe's in its thick, car-horn tone. "Waiting to be invited is no way to win the revolution."

Simone took Patty's hand and yanked her forward. "Congresswoman Abzug, I am such an admirer of yours," she gushed as breathless as an Elvis fan—very unlike the analytical, even cynical observer Patty thought she knew. "Congratulations on today. Your bill, I mean. Making today Women's Equality Day . . . You . . . you must be really proud."

"Thank you. I did it for you, you know. For all of us," Abzug answered encouragingly. "A celebration of suffrage and a call to mobilize. Never forget that it was only fifty-three years ago we won the right to vote in the first place. Think of that. When your grandmothers were your age. And there's still much to be done. Tell me about yourself and what you plan to do about that."

Amazed, Patty watched Abzug coax Simone out of her uncharacteristic hesitancy into chatting—bubbling, even. Brash and intimidatingly vehement, for sure, but "Battling Bella" appeared utterly sincere in her interest in the star-struck teenager.

As Simone and the congresswoman talked, Patty couldn't shake her father's derisive joke about Abzug in hot pants. But the more Abzug engaged with Simone and urged her to follow her dreams, maybe even think about becoming an advocacy lawyer like the congresswoman had been, the more Patty couldn't help liking the abrasive, big-personality woman. Given her father and his friends' vilification of Abzug, Scott's dislike of "libbers," Patty had expected strident and haughty—not charming and nurturing.

By the time she and Simone peeled away from the table, Simone was almost walking on air. And Patty was suddenly—shockingly—delighted by the mental image of Congresswoman Abzug in short hot pants and knee-high boots that could cause serious pain as she stepped on toes, like some raucous, avenging, and zaftig Wonder Woman.

Patty let out a small chortle. She was definitely getting Simone-ized.

Maybe that wasn't all bad.

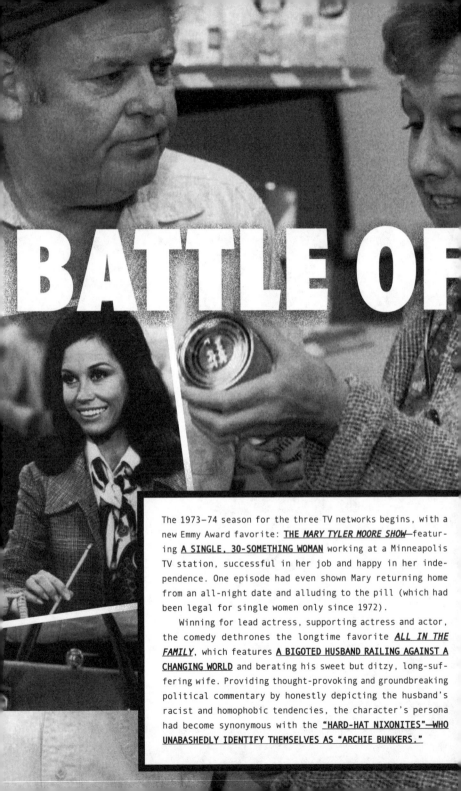

BATTLE OF

The 1973–74 season for the three TV networks begins, with a new Emmy Award favorite: **_THE MARY TYLER MOORE SHOW_**—featuring **A SINGLE, 30-SOMETHING WOMAN** working at a Minneapolis TV station, successful in her job and happy in her independence. One episode had even shown Mary returning home from an all-night date and alluding to the pill (which had been legal for single women only since 1972).

Winning for lead actress, supporting actress and actor, the comedy dethrones the longtime favorite **_ALL IN THE FAMILY_**, which features **A BIGOTED HUSBAND RAILING AGAINST A CHANGING WORLD** and berating his sweet but ditzy, long-suffering wife. Providing thought-provoking and groundbreaking political commentary by honestly depicting the husband's racist and homophobic tendencies, the character's persona had become synonymous with the **"HARD-HAT NIXONITES"—WHO UNABASHEDLY IDENTIFY THEMSELVES AS "ARCHIE BUNKERS."**

THE SEXES

BOBBY RIGGS, a self-proclaimed **"MALE CHAUVINIST PIG" AND FORMER NUMBER-ONE TENNIS STAR, CHALLENGES TOP-RANKED FEMALE PLAYER BILLIE JEAN KING** to a nationally televised match. The 55-year-old winner of six Grand Slam titles had turned into the consummate hustler in retirement, playing exhibition matches in which he wore costumes and clowned around and still triumphed over opponents. He'd also become **AN OUTSPOKEN CRITIC OF WOMEN'S TENNIS**.

He issued his challenge **JOKINGLY** (although many men across the nation took it seriously): **"I WANT TO PROVE THAT WOMEN DON'T BELONG ON THE SAME COURT AS A MAN** . . . Don't get me wrong. I am a big lover of women (in the bedroom and in the kitchen). But these days they want to be everywhere . . . This is Custer's last stand. The lobber versus the libber."

Riggs whips up publicity, turning their match into a dramatic **"BATTLE OF THE SEXES."** Thirty thousand fans crowd the Houston Astrodome, and **90 MILLION WATCH THE SHOWDOWN ON TV**, making it one of the most watched televised sporting events of all time.

Riggs spends the weeks leading up to the match gabbing on talk shows. King practices daily. **ON SEPTEMBER 20, SHE BEATS RIGGS: 6-4, 6-3, 6-3.**

CHAPTER NINE

SEPTEMBER

"Relax, Patty. Don't overread this. You take everything too seriously these days."

Scott was canceling on her—again.

Putting her forehead to the metallic front of the pay phone to hide her embarrassment as several hallmates passed by, Patty chewed on her bottom lip. She could hear the growing impatience in his voice. But she couldn't help it—she was so disappointed.

Given all the promotional hype and national chatter, Patty had been really excited to watch—*with* Scott—the proclaimed "Battle of the Sexes" tennis match between Bobby Riggs and Billie Jean King. It seemed the perfect way to reclaim tennis as a joint love of theirs. Especially after constantly hearing what great doubles partners he and Suzie had become while she was in D.C. *Suzie, Suzie, Suzie.*

This was the third time Scott had stood her up at the last minute. They'd gone out only twice since that night in his dorm room, the encounter that still made Patty blush and get a little quivery. How could she not read something into his canceling on her—yet again. "But I listened to President Nixon's Watergate speech with you at your—" she began.

"Yeah, I know," Scott interrupted. "And a couple of the guys who overheard you questioning the president have razzed me about getting my woman under control."

Patty's heart sank. She'd barely said anything that night about Nixon. "But—"

"I told them you make up for it in other ways," Scott teased. Then his voice grew serious. "This is a rush thing, Patty. You know how important my getting into the right fraternity is. Connections. For now, and for later. There's gonna be a lot of locker-room talk during this match. The guys are juiced to see Bobby take down Billie Jean. Me too. Trust me—you wouldn't like the conversation. I'm doing you, and me—us, really—a favor."

In the background came a voice: "Hey man, are you going to be much longer? I've got a girl to call too."

"Gotta go, gorgeous," Scott said. Then, with a laugh and what sounded like good-natured enough banter—"I'll call you after the match to console you when your girl gets trounced"—he hung up.

The dial tone buzzed in her ear. Panic bubbled up in Patty. Oh God, was she—what was the term he'd used—crowding him? Being silly? Clingy? Was it not okay for Patty to show her boyfriend that she wanted to spend time with him?

"Are you done with the phone, sugar?"

Patty startled at what sounded like Aunt Marjorie's comforting voice and easy affection. But it was a thirtysomething woman who lived down the hall, standing nearby, change purse in her hand to make her call. Was Patty imagining it, or did that woman look at her with pity?

"Yes, ma'am," Patty murmured, and handed her the receiver.

"Ma'am? Please, I'm not that old!" The woman pressed down the tongue of the receiver cradle to stop the phone's loud dial tone as she added in a gently sympathetic tone, "Some of us are going to watch the tennis match in the parlor tomorrow. Big color console TV down there. Join the party. A few of us have even dared to make little wagers with our office colleagues." She began dialing. "Let's hope Billie Jean comes through for us."

As Patty headed for her room, she heard the woman say into the phone, "Tommy! Is that you? What a big boy you are to answer the phone when Mommy calls!... Say what, darlin'? The alphabet song?... You do?... Go ahead, I'm listening..."

Surprised, Patty slowed and glanced back at her. She had a child? Patty had thought the Thompson-Markward was exclusively for single women.

Another boarder leaned against the wall outside her door, clearly waiting for the phone as well. Patty had seen the two women together often, matched in their neat pertness and just-above-the-knee A-line skirts, sensible heels, and hair bobbed at chin-length with bangs. Traditional but still fashionable-enough pretty. Patty nodded in hello as she opened her door. The woman called for her to wait.

Patty paused.

"Donna is way too trusting," the woman said quietly. "She shouldn't be so open about her son. She could lose her job if her boss found out. They don't hire mothers at our law firm." She fixed her brown eyes on Patty's intently. "So please don't say anything to anybody."

"Of course," Patty reassured her. Who would she tell anyway?

Relieved, the woman smiled. "You're the Capitol Hill page, right?"

Patty nodded.

"Planning on going into politics?"

"Yes. Well, with my boyfriend. When we get married." She blanched. "I mean *if*... shouldn't be presumptuous." And recently it did feel more like *if* than *when*.

The woman laughed lightly—more in camaraderie than ridicule. "My advice, sweetie? Don't count your eggs until they're hatched when men are involved. The best thing you can do—since you're around lawmakers—is fill the ear of whomever you can about legislation that will help women work and support themselves with fair wages. Heck, run yourself. Or go out and campaign for passage of the ERA. That's how women, and single moms like Donna, will finally be able to be honest about themselves and still get a decent-paying job."

Down the hall, Donna hung up.

"My turn," the woman said, reaching out and squeezing Patty's arm in thanks before hurrying to preempt someone else nabbing the phone.

"You're sure it's okay for me to be here?" Abe asked, unusually hesitant as he walked in her residence hall's front door. He'd been lamenting that morning about not having a place to watch the Riggs-King match. The widow who ran his small rooming house didn't have a sitting area. And the communal kitchen didn't have a TV.

Hearing his disappointment, Patty had invited him to watch it with her. They had school early the next morning, so it didn't make sense for her to go out to Simone's. And she felt more than a little bit of I'll-show-you defiance of Scott as she suggested Abe join her. Patty and Abe were friends—why shouldn't they watch the match together? And maybe it'd be good to remind Scott that there were guys who *did* enjoy being with her.

"Yes, I promise, it's fine," she answered, putting her arm through his to walk them down the wide, toile wallpapered hall into the parlor with its traditional, Williamsburg-formal décor, a baby grand piano tucked in the corner. The big room was jam-packed. Women crowded onto sofas, balanced on the arms of chairs, sat crisscross on the floor in rows and rows—a sea of pastel-colored cardigans and a delicious aroma of multiple perfumes. Only a few wore jeans, flouting the common rooms' dress code.

No males.

"Aww, Patty." Abe stopped dead in the arched entrance.

Patty broke into a mischievous grin. She hadn't meant for it to happen, but what a great turnaround for Abe. "Give you a chance to feel what I do every day on the Hill," she teased.

The secret mother named Donna looked up and waved to Patty, beckoning them into the room. "Come in, come in. Look, ladies," she said, pointing to Abe, "a sacrificial lamb."

Without missing a beat, Abe laughed and bowed, even as Patty noted some of the women not being so inviting in their looks. "Into the lioness's den," he joked.

They found a spot in the back, perching against a window with ceiling-to-floor brocade and gold-tasseled curtains—just as ABC's notoriously bombastic sports announcer Howard Cosell began the broadcast, announcing that the night's purse was a winner-take-all one hundred thousand dollars.

Everyone in the room gasped. "It would take me twelve years of working at the FBI to earn that amount," said one of the secretaries.

Waiting for the opponents to make their grand entrances to the packed Astrodome, Cosell filled time, describing what an extravaganza the night had become, thanks to the unabashedly male-chauvinist PR campaign waged by Bobby Riggs, the "biggest hustler perhaps in all of history." Cosell broke off when thirty thousand fans exploded into cheers as Billie Jean King entered.

Abe and Patty and all the women surrounding them joined in, clapping enthusiastically.

"Are you truly rooting for Billie Jean?" Patty whispered.

He nodded. "Affirmative! I don't like guys who claim victory before they win it, or what my mom calls BTOs."

Patty looked at him quizzically.

"Big-time operators. And Riggs sure is one loudmouth operator. Besides, when in Rome"—he gestured to the room of women and then to the TV as King was brought into the arena like

Cleopatra, on a chaise carried by bronzed University of Houston football players clad in miniskirt togas and gold chestplates.

Riggs arrived in a chariot pulled by "Sugar Daddy" cheerleaders.

Cosell commented on King wearing a new "gown"—quickly correcting himself to say "dress"—designed for the match. He didn't mention its color—white with a tinge of menthol green, a purposeful if subtle bow to the Virginia Slims Women's Tour and its cigarette sponsor. King and eight other female players had started the women's-only tournaments in 1970, boycotting the United States Lawn Tennis Association in protest of its awarding male winners prize money that was eight times the amount given women.

He simply noted that King was a "very attractive young lady," adding, "sometimes you get the feeling that if she ever let her hair grow down to her shoulders, took off her glasses, you'd have someone vying for a Hollywood screen test."

That's a nice compliment from the typically grouchy announcer, thought Patty, right before the thirtysomething secretary—Donna's friend and coworker—groaned loudly, setting off a ripple of similar exclamations of irritation across the parlor.

"Maybe she should play in high heels," one of the women jeered. "Because obviously what she should *really* care about is going to Hollywood and becoming a pinup."

Patty felt herself flush a little, realizing only then how patronizing Cosell's comment was. He wasn't saying anything about Riggs's looks.

As Riggs and King warmed up, the broadcast switched to a pre-match interview with King, in which a male reporter asked her how important "the feminist thing" was.

More groans in the room. "The feminist *thing*?"

Shh-shh. Others leaned forward to hear King's answer.

"I think that the women's movement is really making a better life for more people than just women," said King.

Everyone in the parlor nodded approvingly and leaned back, ready for the contest to begin.

"Cross your fingers that Billie Jean doesn't fall apart against Riggs like Margaret Court did," Donna worried. "That was terrible." She shook her head. "I'll never hear the end of it from my boss if King loses, too."

Many murmurs of fretful agreement.

"Wow," Abe said more to himself than to Patty. "I didn't realize that tonight was so loaded for you guys." He perused the faces around him before leaning into Patty to whisper solemnly, "Feel it? How much these women need King to win?" He paused, once more gazing slowly around the room. "I know you've said you aren't some bra-burning libber. But—damn—look around you, Pats. At the anxiety these women are feeling. Over a tennis match. Whether you want to be a trailblazer or not, you are. You should be proud of yourself." He smiled at her with that odd shyness he had sometimes that Patty couldn't figure out, and said, "I know I'm proud to know you."

A little flummoxed, Patty started to repeat that she hadn't come to Capitol Hill to make some feminist statement. But then she noticed the woman sitting beside them nervously chewing on her fingernails, and the woman jammed up beside her, bobbing her foot furiously. Abe was right: The sense of apprehension in the room was thick. If Riggs beat King, it would give fuel to every jerk like Jake to continue claiming male superiority, that women couldn't keep up—just like Jake constantly implied about Patty's worth as a page.

Was she embracing all that being a page offered *and* demanded of her? She thought back to Simone saying how jealous she was of Patty seeing Congress at work firsthand. Her hallmate urging

Patty to lobby senators to protect women's rights so that young mothers like Donna didn't lose their jobs when they had children. Bella Abzug warning there was so much still to be done.

Yes. They were right—at least in terms of being the best page she could be, for herself, but also for other girl pages following her. Nodding to herself, she joined Abe's clapping as he shouted, "Let's go, Billie Jean!"

A wave of faces turned around to stare at Abe suspiciously.

"Now, now ladies," Donna called out. "This is how change happens. One person at a time won over to our cause. Boys can be feminists, too, you know." Once again, she smiled warmly at Abe. "Welcome to the movement, friend!"

Perhaps not knowing how to turn off the firehose of hoopla, the players just started the match without warning—Billie Jean King serving.

It was stunning how quickly thirty-thousand-plus spectators could silence.

Along with everyone else in the room, Patty held her breath as King bounce-bounce-bounced the ball, threw it into the air with her left hand, and swung her racket up with her right to quick hit the ball—hard.

Thunk!

Her first serve of the night caught the top of the net and dropped flat to her side of the court.

The parlor crowd let out a collective groan.

She looks scared, thought Patty.

King's next serve was softer, careful, and well placed in the corner of the service box, but her return of Bobby Riggs's lob went long over the baseline. She lost her opening serve, the point going to Riggs.

Love-15.

Not an auspicious beginning. The women surrounding Patty sat back, hands to their mouths.

Riggs flubbed his next return, hitting the net.

15-15.

A good serve, a smash return from King to Riggs. The TV crowd roared. But King's sizzling ball had landed "just an eyelash" over the line. Again, the point went to Riggs.

15-30.

After a solid next serve, King hit a blistering low ball, sliced to the corner.

Beautiful, breathed Patty. How many times had she tried to swerve her return like that, adding a killer underspin to the ball? You had to be crazy good to manage it.

Riggs didn't even try to reach King's ball—just called out, "Atta girl!"

"Oh, shut up," grumbled Donna's friend.

"He's just trying to psych her out," said Abe. "That's what he does—he lobs as much lip as balls when he plays. They call him a junk and bunk artist. Ever watch his other matches?"

"Never," laughed Donna's friend. "I suffer through enough male swagger every day at work."

The women around her nodded.

"He'll stop shouting 'Atta girl' when he starts losing," Donna quipped. But she still squirmed in her seat anxiously, and breathed: "Make him stop, Billie Jean."

Next serve, King sent a zinger, but then hit the net on her return—an unforced error on her part that lifted Riggs up into a tie score.

Deuce.

If Riggs managed to break King's serve in the very first game, it could be a big blow to her confidence. *Talk about getting off on the wrong foot*, thought Patty. The parlor crowd shifted and fidgeted.

Two more long, back-and-forth volleys.

Advantage King.

If she won the next point, the first game would go to King. She played it safe and sent Riggs a soft serve, but then rushed to the net, risking Riggs sailing one of his signature "moon-ball" lobs behind her that she couldn't possibly backpedal fast enough to get. Instead, in bravura, Riggs tried to slam it past her. King lunged and returned a pinpoint-accurate ball to the far-right corner of Riggs's court, then to the left, running him ragged until he finally missed.

Game to King.

An unspoken *Thank God* communal sigh of relief filled the parlor as the TV went to commercial break with the tune *"Anything you can do, I can do better..."*

The women spoke in almost-whispers as they waited for the match to come back on: "She looks spooked." "Wouldn't you be, in front of all those people?" "She's not playing her usual game." "If she stays this tentative, he'll beat her."

But King didn't stay tentative.

After the commercial, she came back onto the court with steely resolve on her "almost-Hollywood-screen-test-worthy" face. Riggs served. King rushed the net, managing to sprint back to catch up to Riggs's clever high lob to the right-hand corner and whack it toward him in a scrambling backhand. Then she dashed to the other side of the court to hit Riggs's return—zinging it past him with such velocity, Patty wondered if Riggs felt the wind of it on his leg.

Squeals of delight and vindication from the parlor women almost drowned out Cosell opining on King: "Walking back to the baseline, she's walking more like a male than a female."

The parlor women booed Cosell.

"Never mind, ladies!" sang out Donna. "That's the Billie Jean we know. She's back."

And there Billie Jean King would remain, dominating most of the match from then on with her savvy corner shots and speed.

It would take a while for the male commentators to recognize it. One woman—Rosie Casals—sat in the announcers booth with Cosell and another legendary tennis player, Gene Scott. She was a regular on the circuit herself and King's doubles partner on the Virginia Slims Tour. Each time Cosell expressed surprise at King's stellar placement of the ball, Casals would counter with comments about King's skills. "Billie Jean can really get to the ball. If Bobby doesn't put the ball away, Billie Jean is going to hurt him."

"Rosie Casals, who tells it like it is," Cosell added, as if in apology to the TV audience for her bluntness.

Casals was undeterred. She pushed Gene Scott to back up her statement that King had one of the sport's greatest volleys—as good as any man's.

He good-naturedly admitted that he'd "been killed" by it when playing mixed doubles against King in the past. But he held to his belief that the male volley would dominate.

But it wouldn't. Not that night, anyway, not in that Battle of the Sexes.

Billie Jean King would send Riggs all over the court for two hours with her strategically placed volleys that forced Riggs to run and run, wearing him out—to win in three straight sets.

Relieved tears on her face, Donna stood and started singing the Helen Reddy hit that the Australian star had performed at the Astrodome right before Billie Jean King entered the arena: *"I am woman, hear me roar..."*

One after another, every woman in the parlor rose to join in. As much as she itched to add her voice, Patty held back out of deference to Abe—not wanting to look like she was gloating.

But Abe elbowed her. "Go ahead. You guys are entitled. And

don't worry, my masculinity is totally intact. In my neighborhood, I grew up on trash talk!"

With a grateful laugh, Patty jumped in: "... *no one's ever gonna keep me down again...*"

When she walked him out, Patty asked, "Where did you learn to think like that, Abe?"

"Like what?"

"Like ... so respectful." She paused. "So okay with women being ... *mmm* ... strong."

Abe grinned. "My mom. She's a marcher. She marched for civil rights. Joined the college kids marching for peace after Kent State. Marched in NOW's Women's Strike three years ago that shut down Fifth Avenue. She's a schoolteacher, too. Civics."

"Ha!" Patty smiled. "Civics. Suddenly everything about you makes sense."

Abe laughed at himself a little. "Yeah, the apple doesn't fall far. But you think I'm opinionated?" He snorted. "She's so outspoken, she was targeted by Red Hunters—like Nixon—during Senator McCarthy's reign of terror. She got hauled in front of a Loyalty Review Board for starting a petition to stop book banning in school libraries. Almost lost her job."

"Oh my gosh, that's ... terrifying."

Abe grinned. "Maybe to others. Mom's fierce. She's still out there knocking on doors for left-leaning candidates from school board to Congress."

"What does your dad say about all her activism?"

"Oh, he loves it! Even though they don't always agree on policy." Abe rolled his eyes as he added, "Dad even votes Republican sometimes—God save him."

"Hey!" Patty swatted him playfully. "Watch it. We Republicans backed the ERA."

Abe laughed. "Yeah, I know. So, there's hope for you guys."

"Your dad lets her have such different opinions?"

"Lets her?" Abe guffawed again. "There's no 'letting her' about Mom. And honestly, nothing's better than a ringside seat to my parents' debates. My dad says this country was formed by debate. *E pluribus unum*—from many opinions comes one path, for the common good."

Patty mulled that over for a moment. "My father and my boyfriend say it's vital for a couple to have 'a united front.' Scott says that'll be really important when he runs for office."

Abe frowned. "You know, Pats, Will and I used to talk about how we see you running for Senate someday."

"Really? That's very kind of you two," she demurred.

"Nothing kind about it—fact." He cocked his head. "Think about how you defused things the night I was such a jackass at Mr. Henry's. You're stronger than you think."

Patty looked down the street, toward the Capitol. "I hadn't considered it before." She hesitated. "Scott thinks I'll be a perfect first lady when he becomes president—that's what he always says." She paused, thinking, *Did say*.

"Haven't seen this boyfriend around."

"He's . . . he's just getting settled into Georgetown."

Putting his hand on her shoulder, Abe said quietly, "If I were lucky enough to have you as my girl, Patty, I'd make sure I caught at least a glimpse of you every day." He paused, and in the shadows of the street, Patty couldn't decipher his expression since he immediately switched to jesting. "And Will? That boy would be crooning beneath your window. Sappy John Denver songs, of course, but hey, his heart would be in the right place." Abe dropped his hand and turned to leave. "See you tomorrow, Pats."

Patty went upstairs, hoping Scott might call the hall phone—since he'd promised to do so to rib her if—*when*, he'd claimed—King lost. He'd always been a good sport when they'd lost their doubles matches, sincerely congratulating the winners. She'd really admired that about him.

But Scott didn't call.

Like millions of American women in the days following that match, Patty felt a new confidence and sense of vindication. Even when Jake dismissed King's win with "She got lucky."

Patty flat-out laughed at him. "Nothing lucky about a 6-4, 6-3, 6-3 score."

So that's probably why Jake took such pleasure a few afternoons later—while she sat on the Senate floor steps, awaiting the next senator's finger snap—in handing Patty a note in pretty, florid penmanship that read, *If you're going to take a position that rightly belongs to a deserving young man, the least you can do is sit in a more ladylike posture.*

Aghast, Patty looked up at Jake. "Where did you get this?"

Jake smirked and pointed up to the gallery of spectators. "One of the guards handed it to me as I came back in from running files to Senator Doyle's office. Seems you've offended a group of ladies watching from above." Jake scanned the balconies. "Ah, I bet that's them." He waved to a klatch of women wearing tailored shirtdresses, scarves tied and knotted at their throats, and minimalist bouffants.

They responded by crossing their arms across their bosoms.

"Gosh. Seems the ladies don't like you," Jake said.

Patty straightened, crossed her ankles together, and tucked them to the side, creating a modest, clamped V angle with her legs. *Pretty is as pretty does.*

It was an incredibly uncomfortable position on a step.

Patty crammed the note into one of the pockets Simone had sewn to her jacket for her. Simone would probably stand up and flip the bird at those old witches. But Patty stayed rooted, refusing to look up at her coven of detractors, while she waited to be called by a senator to perform some chore. She wasn't going to be knocked off her job.

Jake sat down beside her, stretching out his legs and resting his elbows on the step behind him—totally comfortable. "So, how *did* you get this page-ship, Patty? I've always wondered. Bat your eyelashes at someone? Or even—"

Snap.

Patty stood, smoothed her jacket, and walked with a new, hard-won dignity to Senator Thurmond's desk. If Billie Jean King could ignore all the foolish things said about her—no, *misogynistic* was the word—Patty could, too. So what if some women didn't like her deportment? Patty knew the truth: She did her job as a page well. That self-recognition felt good.

When the sergeant at arms asked to speak to her the next day, however, Patty's heart started racing. Had the old biddies complained to him, too?

"Your father is here," the man informed her flatly. "He'd like you to meet him at the Reflecting Pool, by President Grant's monument, at noon. You may leave the chamber fifteen minutes before that."

Even though she was relieved there was no mention of her supposed lack of decorum, Patty's heart continued to double-time. Why was her father in town without telling her beforehand? "Is something wrong?"

"He didn't say." The sergeant at arms went back to his papers.

For an hour she worried.

At 11:45, Patty raced down the steps of the Capitol's west side, dashed across the wide and serene swath of green lawn that separated the Houses of Congress from the Mall where military bands—and ideally Julius one day—played free concerts during the summer, and then darted—dangerously—between tourist buses and taxis to cross First Avenue.

"Daddy?" she called, not seeing him at first.

"Here," he answered.

Patty found her father sitting by the four bronze lions flanking the statue of General Grant atop his horse. He was gazing toward the Smithsonian Castle, munching a sandwich.

"Good lord, princess, you're a mess."

Patty's hands shot to her hair to push it off her forehead, beaded with sweat from her pell-mell run. "Is everything all right, Daddy?"

Her father wiped his mouth before answering gruffly, "Of course. Why wouldn't it be?"

Taken aback by his defensiveness, Patty fell silent and simply shrugged.

Which seemed to irritate her father even more. "For pity's sake, Patty, don't revert to acting like a toddler. Haven't these months on the Hill taught you how to field questions?"

Suddenly Patty's mind blurred with the memory of crying over something at dinner and spilling a full glass of milk in her nervousness, its flooding across the dining room table and onto the antique Oriental rug, while her father shouted, "Use words, damn it! Don't be a ninny."

She bit her lip.

"Well?"

"I have learned. A lot. About how senators make laws. When to push, when to listen." Her father didn't seem any happier with her answer. Patty chattered on nervously, switching to the Watergate hearings. "It was really informative to watch the hearings—how evidence is slowly brought to light during testimony. And how it's not so much the headliner witnesses who give up the truth as lower-level staffers, like Colonel Butterfield, and . . ."—the worry she hadn't been able to effectively name surfaced—"and people who were just trying to get the president re-elected and got caught up in the cover-up, like Mr. Nixon's lawyer getting pulled into funneling campaign money to—"

Abruptly, her father stood and asked, "How's Scott?"

This conversation was almost making Patty dizzy with its sudden turns. "He's good." Then she made the mistake of admitting she hadn't seen much of him. "He's been really focused on settling in at Georgetown." Her standard answer at this point.

Her father had been pacing a little and stopped to face her. "Scott certainly seemed to have no trouble this summer mixing social outings with school duties. I saw him plenty at the club with that knock-out Suzie while he was supposedly packing to come to Washington. You better step up your game to keep that boy on the line."

In the past, Patty would have simply accepted her father's warning. Now, somehow, she found his mixed metaphors—and their obvious message—annoying. Even a tad insulting. Which must have leaked out in her question: "You know, Daddy, I don't think I've ever heard you say—what about Mother made you fall in love with her?"

"I don't think I like your attitude, missy." Her father glowered at her. "You might wish to reconsider your tone. I'm sure you don't mean to sound insolent."

"I . . . I didn't mean anything, Daddy." Patty retreated to careful. "I honestly wanted to know what qualities attracted you—traits I might have? Or could replicate?"

He seemed to think on that for a long, long moment.

Was it really that hard to remember? Patty started to feel slightly queasy. Her stomach was rumbling with hunger, too. Her father hadn't thought to bring a sandwich for her, and in her worry that something was wrong, she hadn't stopped to pick up anything to eat.

Finally, her father replied, his voice caustic: "Nothing that she shows much of today." He looked out over the Reflecting Pool. "Did you know she's doing work with the STOP ERA women?" He didn't wait for an answer.

"Initially, I'd thought it would be good for her. Some actual involvement for once. That ridiculous libber amendment was thought to sail right on through this spring when it came to our Illinois General Assembly. But Phyllis Schlafly rallied busloads of housewives to go to Springfield. Completely charmed the legislators with their best home-baked bread while the libbers shouted and stomped their Birkenstocks and shook signs in the legislators' faces. Your mother got to experience the power of voters lobbying their representatives. Figured it'd help her understand why what I do is so important.

"But now?" Her father's tone returned to irritated. "Now, the ladies are targeting other state capitols. More meetings. Endless clucking. Your mother is constantly baking banana bread. The house reeks of overripe bananas. Fruit flies in the kitchen. Disgusting."

He resumed his pacing. "She's also taken to spending hours out in the garage, in her studio. Painting God knows what. Wandering back into the house, covered in pastels or charcoal, smelling of turpentine. Lost in daydreams over nothing that I can tell."

He checked his watch, winding its stem as he talked. "She's been waking me up in the middle of the night—drenched in sweat, blibber-blabbering nonsense. She doesn't seem to understand that I need my rest to be able to focus on my patients. I've had to give her stronger sleeping pills. I hope her taking the flurazepam along with her Valium will improve things."

Frowning slightly, he gazed at Patty. "I always thought you were a lot like her. In her youth. When she was so beautiful."

Beep-beeeeeeep. Beep-beep-beep. Beeeeeeep.

Her father turned and waved at a baby-blue Cadillac paused on the curb by a statue of President Garfield. "There's my ride," he announced.

"Where are you going, Daddy?"

"Meeting." Dr. Appleton pulled an envelope from his suit jacket pocket and handed it to Patty. She could feel cash in it. "For your birthday next week. Eighteen. You're a woman now." He seemed to mull that over for a moment. "A voter." He shook his head slightly—in disbelief? Then he gave Patty his usual brisk, goodbye hug. "See you at Thanksgiving, princess." He loped to the car and got in.

As it drove away along First Street, passing between the Capitol and the Grant Memorial, Patty could see a blond woman behind the wheel.

AGNEW RESIGNS

OCTOBER 10: In another unprecedented and startling scandal, Nixon's most trusted hatchet man for attacking liberals and antiwar demonstrators, **VICE PRESIDENT SPIRO AGNEW RESIGNS** amid overwhelming **EVIDENCE OF HIS TAKING BRIBES** and evading taxes. **TO REPLACE AGNEW, NIXON NOMINATES** Minority Leader of the House **GERALD FORD**.

WATERGATE

WILLIAM RUCKELSHAUS

RICHARDSON

COX

OCTOBER 12: THE U.S. COURT OF APPEALS UPHOLDS JUDGE SIRICA'S ORDER that Nixon turn over the nine subpoenaed tapes. "The President," the opinion reads, "is not above the law's commands."

But **NIXON DEFIES THE APPELLATE COURT AS WELL**.

On Friday, October 19, **HE COUNTERS** with the "Stennis Compromise," suggesting the tapes and **WRITTEN SUMMARIES COMPILED BY WHITE HOUSE STAFFERS BE GIVEN** to Mississippi "Dixiecrat" John Stennis, chairman of the Senate Ethics Committee. After listening to verify the transcripts, the senator would turn over the written summaries—**NOT THE TAPES THEMSELVES**—to Judge Sirica, the Senate Watergate Committee, and the special prosecutor.

NIXON'S PROPOSAL IS ALMOST LAUGHABLE. The elderly Stennis is well-respected but notoriously hard of hearing, still recovering from being shot during a mugging. Even so, the Senate Watergate

Committee chairmen, Ervin and Baker, agree. **SPECIAL PROSECUTOR ARCHIBALD COX, HOWEVER, REJECTS IT.**

FURIOUS, THE NEXT DAY, NIXON DEMANDS COX RESIGN.

COX DECLINES.

Nixon then immediately orders Attorney General Elliot Richardson to fire Cox. **RICHARDSON REFUSES AND RESIGNS IN PROTEST.**

Next, the deputy attorney general—husband of White House consultant and feminist Jill **RUCKELSHAUS**—is ordered to fire Cox. He **ALSO REFUSES AND RESIGNS**.

Finally, that night, Nixon demands that his solicitor general, Robert Bork, fire Cox. **BORK COMPLIES.**

The press and the nation are astounded. "In the simplest terms, an investigator appointed to investigate scandals was fired, because he insisted on investigating scandals," says NBC anchor David Brinkley in a breaking-news broadcast that night.

Thirty minutes later, **NIXON SENDS THE FBI TO SEAL COX'S OFFICE**, essentially seizing all evidence the special prosecutor and his staff had amassed about the cover-up. The FBI also seals the Justice Department offices belonging to Richardson and William Ruckelshaus.

"IT FELT LIKE A COUP," says *New Yorker* reporter Elizabeth Drew. **"IT WAS TERRIFYING."**

THE PRESS DUBS NIXON'S SHOCKING ACTIONS ON OCTOBER 20TH "THE SATURDAY NIGHT MASSACRE." Public outrage is swift and enormous. Telegrams of protest flood congressional offices, overwhelming Western Union. **CROWDS SURROUND THE WHITE HOUSE** fence line, calling for passing drivers to **HONK FOR IMPEACHMENT**. The result is cacophonous.

FOR THE FIRST TIME IN OVER 100 YEARS—when President Andrew Johnson was impeached in 1868—members of **THE HOUSE OF REPRESENTATIVES DRAFT RESOLUTIONS CALLING FOR IMPEACHMENT HEARINGS**.

CHAPTER TEN

OCTOBER

"Horse!" the drum major called, his breath misting in the cold Friday night October air.

"Better scooch over," Simone warned Patty as he snapped his arms up in an expectant U-shape, his whistle clenched between his teeth. Simone and eighty or so of her fellow high school musicians quickly rose and whipped their instruments to their lips.

Tweet-tweet-tweet-tweet. The drum major blasted in brisk 4/4 cadence and the band kicked into a fast, jazzy fanfare, swinging their horns in unified dance.

Duuuu-whee. Sweep to the right—rest.

Duuuu-hoo. Sweep to the left—hold.

Laughing, Patty ducked as a trombone swung over her head—froze—then swung away—froze. Ducked again as the instrument came back in repeat.

All around her, spectators on the home side bleachers of Simone's high school came to life with the music. Jumping to their feet, the crowd step-slid to the right, step-slid to the left. Cheerleaders bounced, shaking their pom-poms—first to the right—wiggle—then to the left—wiggle. Standing by the bench, some of the football players turned around to bow and straighten in rhythm, making the crowd cheer even louder.

Patty had never seen anything like it—not at her girls' school, not at Scott's all-boy prep. A collective dance of hundreds. And so enthusiastic!

When the song ended, the fans didn't sit back down. A few even shouted "Again!" But the time-out on the field was over and the band had to quiet so the offensive team could hear their quarterback call the play.

"That was so much fun," Patty exclaimed.

Simone smiled, still a little winded from the tune. "Aren't you glad you came rather than staying in D.C. and mooning over that guy?"

Patty grinned back at her. "Actually, yes!" Scott and his new frat pals were "bonding" at a remote lodge in the Blue Ridge Mountains over the three-day weekend. But Patty wasn't feeling deserted as she might have. She and Scott had had a good date the weekend before.

They'd gone to see *The Way We Were*—starring Barbra Streisand and Robert Redford. Streisand's character, Katie, was strong-willed, an ardent activist. More than once, Scott muttered she was "loud" and "she better watch it" or Hubbell, Redford's character, would get fed up with "her making trouble." Eventually, even though Katie's opinionated personality was painted favorably in the movie, she did, in fact, lose the love of her life. Hubbell left her.

Before Patty would have completely agreed with Scott and been drowning in heartbroken tears at the end of the film like all the other women in the movie theater, tacitly blaming Katie's lack of self-control for the tragic break-up. But Patty couldn't help feeling bothered by Hubbell, who clearly loved and admired Katie yet couldn't handle her smart and, yes, forceful personality. Maybe that was the point? That Hubbell was at fault? If that's what the filmmakers were trying to say it was pretty subtle. The theme song—about bittersweet memories and remembering the laughter—beautiful for sure—didn't clearly proclaim such feminist revelation. Fleetingly, she wondered what Carole King might sing about the movie.

Toward the end of the film, Scott had nibbled on Patty's

earlobe, his breath smelling sweet of buttery popcorn, and whispered, "I know you'll never get crazy like that on me."

Crazy. There was that word—the adjective that tainted women as unpredictable, unhinged, unhelpful, and plain old aggravating. Like Martha Mitchell, the wife of Nixon's onetime attorney, now under serious scrutiny for his part in Watergate. Like Patty's mother. What the heck? For a moment Patty considered asking Scott if he'd ever heard a man described with that particular adjective.

But Scott adding, "I know I can count on you to be there for me," stopped her cold.

"Yes, you can," she'd whispered back, daring to initiate a lingering kiss. He'd seemed to like that she had. And the rankling thoughts disappeared.

"Next time, come to a pre-game bonfire," said Simone, interrupting Patty's musings. "The football players pound on an old, junked car painted in the opposing team's colors. It's a ridiculous display of brute, Neanderthal aggression, but the pep band plays. It's not an official school event, so we can jam the Temptations or Marvin Gaye, even Creedence. It's the best."

"Hey Simone," one of the saxophonists called up to her. "Look who's coming."

"He made it!" Simone shoved her piccolo into Patty's hand before darting down the bleachers to launch herself into Julius's arms. He spun her round and round and then kissed her.

"Hey!" the drum major shouted. "That's a demerit, Simone! No PDA when in band uniform."

The trumpet section booed their leader. "C'mon, man. Leave 'em alone. It's Julius."

"Them's the bandmaster's rules," the drum major countered. "You know that." He turned back to Simone. "You clean drums this week."

Grinning, her arms still around Julius's neck, Simone answered gleefully, "Well worth it!" She kissed Julius again. Longer.

"Ooooo," the piccolo and flute section pretended to swoon.

"Sim!" The drum major looked exasperated. "Quit it. Please don't make me have to give you two weeks of cleaning." The kid genuinely looked stricken at having to discipline her.

As if he could, thought Patty, with an indulgent fondness that surprised her a little.

The trumpet section jokingly booed their leader again and started to razz him about necking in the parking lot with his baton-twirling girlfriend.

"Okay, okay," the drum major said, holding up his hands and laughing at the situation he was in. "I know what. I'll let Simone off"—the band cheered—"if our superstar can get through the 'Bumblebee' the way he played at senior concert last year."

"Ju-li-us! Ju-li-us!" the band chanted.

"I need a trumpet," he answered as Simone unfurled herself from him.

A skinny boy stepped down to hand Julius his own instrument, with an elaborate bow of adulation.

Julius buzzed his lips and warmed up with one quick scale, his tone rich and beautiful, despite the cold. "How fast?" he asked the drum major, with a watch-what-I-can-do grin.

"Ooooo." The band laughed and applauded his bravado.

Simone glowed. There wasn't any other word for it.

"This fast," said the drum major mischievously, snapping his fingers in a wildly fast beat.

Julius grimaced. "Oooooh—kay."

The drum major held up his hand, waiting until the ball was snapped and in play before saying, "Ladies and gentlemen: Rimsky-Korsakov's 'Flight of the Bumblebee'!"

Julius let loose with a breakneck cascade of notes that swirled and climbed and dove, humming and zinging, just like the buzz of a bee in urgent flight. It was a staggering performance. He didn't stumble, didn't crack a note. Patty had heard that trumpet solo performed once before by the Chicago Philharmonic. Julius's rendition was just as good.

What had the scholarship guy at the conservatory said to Julius? That a classical career clearly wasn't for him? What an idiot.

No. Use the real word, Patty admonished herself. One that before she might have hesitated to utter—her father and his friends' defensiveness ingrained into her own thinking—but there was no other word for it, was there? That guy denying Julius a scholarship because he didn't fit a long-standing mold? What a *racist*.

Stomping on the bleachers while they clapped, the band members rocked the stands in admiration.

Julius bowed. Then he called out to his old classmates, "Want to hear something even better? Convince Simone to play *Stars and Stripes*."

"Sim, Sim, Sim!" the woodwinds cheered.

She shook her head.

"Please?" Julius urged her.

"Sim-Sim-Sim!"

Patty waited until Simone smiled—shyly! modestly?!—to make sure she really wanted to play before Patty scampered down the bleachers to hand back her piccolo.

Simone didn't wait for a countdown. She sailed into a lightning allegro performance of Sousa's wickedly high and complicated piccolo solo with its sudden octave jumps and grace notes. As she finished with the flourish of a long-held high note trilled and trilled and trilled and trilled, her friends applauded until she came to a stop, pulling in a long gasp of replenishing air.

Julius went down on one knee, his hand to his heart, calling out, "The astonishing Simone Conroy, folks."

Awwwww. Every girl in the stands sighed, enchanted.

But directly behind Patty, two clarinetists worried. "Daaa-mn. They're so boss. But . . ." the voice hesitated. "Simone and Julius better watch their backs tonight."

"I know," her friend responded. "I mean . . . I'm obviously thrilled for them. You too. We've been figuring out how to get along and respect each other for two years now since the city combined our schools. We're cool. But—"

The first speaker finished her thought: "—But I bet some of our opponents won't appreciate a Black dude kissing a white chick in front of a couple hundred people. I don't see a whole lot of brothers over there in the visiting stands."

Patty caught her breath. A few months ago, she'd had the exact same concern for Simone and Julius about their showing affection when they were at the Picasso exhibit. That it would invite trouble from onlookers. But now, hearing someone else say it aloud—and after witnessing that incredible, straight-out-of-a-movie scene of affection and mutual respect between Julius and Simone—teenagers having to worry about the outside world's opinion of who they were felt so very, very wrong. "That sucks," popped out of her mouth.

"No kidding," one of the voices behind her answered.

Patty turned to find two female musicians, one Black, one white. "What are you afraid might happen?" she asked, her worry for Simone and Julius resurging.

"Damn, girl," one of them answered. "Haven't you been in the parking lot after one of our games against some of these peckerwoods?"

"No, I'm just a friend of Simone's. This is my first game."

"Well, it isn't pretty," said the other. The two friends put their arms over one another's shoulders, each protective of the other. "A lot of rocks thrown sometimes when the opposing school isn't integrated. Cracked my windshield once. That's why we're always careful."

Her friend nodded. "It is what it is."

"But . . . it shouldn't be." Again, Patty felt more than planned what blurted out of her. She could imagine Simone's indignant tirade against the situation. "No one should have to be careful about who they're friends with or who they love."

The girls grinned at her. "Right on, sister," said one.

"Friend of Simone's, did you say?" asked the other.

"Yes. That's right."

"That figures," the two said at once, laughing.

Later—in the middle of the night, Patty startled awake, roused by noise in the bathroom connecting Simone's room to her brothers', where Patty slept.

Singing. Loudly. *"You make me feel . . ."* Simone. Doing Carole King. At 1:00 a.m.

"What the heck?" Patty mumbled as she got out of bed.

Half asleep, she pushed the door open to find Simone standing in front of the mirror, trying to tie a long leather and beaded band around her neck.

"Geez Louise!" Simone jumped in surprise. "What are you doing up?"

"You were singing."

"Oh! Sorry," Simone apologized distractedly, dropping something off her hippie necklace with a thud to the thick-piled, orange bathmat at her feet. "Shoot!" She crouched, rummaging.

Patty spotted it first: a class ring. Not the one Simone had just gotten. Big. A boy's. "Oh! Oh my gosh. Is . . . is that Julius's? Does that mean you two are—"

Simone waved her off, sitting down cross-legged. "It isn't some engagement ring, Patty. But . . ." She smiled dreamily and trailed off.

Patty plopped down on the floor next to her. Simone was acting weird. "What's going on with you?"

"I did it," she whispered, suddenly hugging Patty.

"Did . . . what?"

"Said yes to making love."

"What?" Patty pulled away, like she was burned.

"Oh, don't be the old Patty and all scandalized," Simone teased her, drawing her legs up to hug herself. "We haven't done it yet. Although I was ready to. We were at the river, the top down on the Bug, under the stars. Julius's kisses were so gentle and . . . and the way he touched me was . . . so solicitous . . . you know, wanting to know if I was liking it." She trailed off again. Smiled. "All about love."

Patty could feel herself blushing hot enough to light a match, but hanging on every word, too, almost desperately wanting to know what she should expect if she and Scott ever went for it.

Still dreamy, Simone talked on, more to herself than to Patty. "He did this thing . . . I'd read about it in *Our Bodies, Ourselves*. Saw the diagram. But I had no idea . . . about how . . ." She seemed to suddenly remember Patty was sitting there and glanced up. "Oh my God!" She laughed and hugged Patty again. "You look like that Edvard Munch painting, *The Scream*. It's okay. I'm okay. It . . . honestly? . . . it was lovely. I was completely ready. But he said we should wait."

Patty pulled back. "*He* said to wait?"

"Yup. That we should wait until we were in a safer, really romantic place. And that he wanted me to be absolutely sure."

She leaned against the sink. "I've really, *really* missed him now that he's away at college. Like . . . my heart hurts. Then tonight, being with him? Remembering how all kinds of wonderful it is to be around him. I feel like I can be completely myself . . . Sooooo." She held up Julius's ring. "I gave him my ring. Not in some dumb, high-school 1950s he's-mine-and-you-better-watch-it-girls kind of way. More like . . . like . . ."

Now it was Patty's turn to laugh—gently—at Simone. "Face it, you're head over heels about Julius. You don't have to label yourselves, but you're essentially going steady. And I think it's terrific. You love him. Why not show it, Simone? You're always quoting Shakespeare, so think what Juliet says: 'That which we call a rose, by any other name would smell as sweet.'"

Simone gave her signature shrug and stood, moving to the door of her bedroom. Before exiting, though, she looked back at Patty. "Thanks for being happy for me, Patty. I mean it."

Patty stood as well, feeling a little spark of Simone's wicked humor take her, in this odd wee-hour bathroom role reversal. She tossed Simone's previous words back to her: "Remember—just be sure to have a rubber." Then she clapped her hand over her mouth, stunned at herself for using that word.

"Ha!" Simone pointed at Patty with glee. "The lady hath grown a merry and witty soul."

"And who said that?" Patty asked.

Simone threw open her arms: "Me!" Then she disappeared, once more singing.

The next morning when she got up, Patty found Aunt Marjorie in the little sitting room off the kitchen, alone, immersed in the morning's papers. Uncle Graham was already running errands, and Simone was still asleep. An all-caps, double banner headline screamed across the front page of the *New York Times*: "NIXON

TO KEEP TAPES DESPITE RULING; WILL GIVE OWN SUMMARY; COX DEFIANT."

Patty was instantly drawn to the bold, startling headline, just as she now always checked the AP and UPI wire machines when passing them on her way in and out of the Senate chambers. She'd turned into a total news junkie, like Abe. Like Simone. Without saying good morning, she leaned in to read the section her aunt was holding:

COURT REBUFFED

Washington, Oct. 19—President Nixon refused to obey an order by the United States Court of Appeals to turn over the subpoenaed Watergate tapes and told Special Prosecutor Archibald Cox to drop his inquiry.

Instead, the newspaper reported, *Mr. Nixon would personally edit a summary of the recorded White House conversations, have it verified by an independent authority, Senator John C. Stennis, and furnish it to the Watergate grand jury and the Senate Watergate committee.*

"What the heck," Patty breathed. Nixon was thumbing his nose at the Court of Appeals? And ordering the special prosecutor to drop the case? She could hear Abe's expletives now.

"Oh!" Aunt Marjorie startled. "I didn't see you there, sugar. Good morning. There's coffee in the percolator and some biscuits keeping warm in the oven. Help yourself."

"Thanks," Patty murmured, but she remained rooted, reading the next few paragraphs:

Mr. Cox indicated strongly that he would defy Mr. Nixon's directive . . . "For me to comply with those instructions would violate my solemn pledge to the Senate and the country to invoke judicial process to challenge exaggerated claims of executive privilege."

However, the leaders of the Senate Watergate committee—Senators Sam J. Ervin Jr. and Howard H. Baker Jr.—agreed to the President's compromise after returning to town for a 40-minute meeting in the White House this afternoon.

Patty straightened up, stunned. Senators Ervin and Baker agreed to *not* getting the tapes themselves, only a summary—after all those jaw-dropping hearings? When John Dean's claims that Nixon had known and participated in the cover-up hinged on being verified by those tapes? The country was supposed to rely on the president and his staff to transcribe and authenticate conversations that could implicate them? That required a heck of an honor code from them—which, considering the campaign's dirty tricks, seemed highly unlikely.

Senator Stennis was an upright gentleman—everyone in the Senate held him in high regard—but the guy was almost totally deaf. Would he be able to hear muffled conversations on a tape? Would he hold up under the strain? The elderly senator was visibly fragile when he did show up at the Senate, still recovering from being shot back in January.

Patty frowned. Again, she could well imagine Abe's outrage about this arrangement not feeling kosher. Not at all.

Wait. A forty-minute meeting in the White House yesterday? Both senators had been out of town. Ervin in North Carolina, Baker in Chicago. That meant they'd been *summoned*. Wow. Patty could hear Abe now: Nixon must have really put the screws to those guys.

According to the newspaper, Baker hailed the plan as being "in the best interest of the country." The old Patty concurred—wholeheartedly. But the new Patty wasn't so sure. She agreed more with Baker's fellow committee Republican, Senator Weicker, quoted as calling it "a hollow deal, to release a summary of the evidence rather than the evidence itself. The nation deserves the truth rather than politics as usual."

Patty flopped down beside her godmother on the chintz-covered love seat.

"Doesn't sit quite right, does it?" Aunt Marjorie folded up the paper. "All this was announced late yesterday evening. On a

Friday night at the beginning of a three-day weekend. Your uncle Graham speculates they did it that way to slide it through, when people are out of town, hoping no one notices." She handed the paper to Patty and reached behind her to the side table where everyone dumped their keys to pick up a small envelope. "By the way, here's your mama's weekly note." She stood. "I'm heading for another coffee. Like some?"

"Yes, please." Patty had grown accustomed to—and liked—the informality in Simone's house of sometimes eating in this cozy room while reading or watching TV, feet tucked up comfortably. Her parents never allowed food beyond the dining room. For probably the hundredth time, Patty wondered how it was that her mother had been best friends during college with this woman who was so different from her.

Patty tore at the tightly sealed envelope to get it to open. On the front of the note was one of her mother's quick-sketch watercolors—of their black cat, Cassatt, gazing out a window.

Inside was Dot Appleton's usual recitation of her doings: several charity teas, some fairly pointed gossip sprinkled in about what the ladies wore and said. No questions about how Patty was, no sentimental claim of missing her. But at least there wasn't her mother's usual reprimand for not having written home more. This note was unusually sparse, a bit rambling, without her mother's typically pitch-perfect formal grammar and penmanship. Sloppy, even.

Remembering her father's recent and alarming condemnations of her mother—that she was acting *crazy*—Patty looked at the note more closely. The little watercolor was smudged. Her mother's handwriting looked a bit wobbly, definitely not marching across the page in her typical evenly spaced lines. There were even words scratched out, a few basically illegible. The note looked hasty. Anxious. Although there was that predictable water dot beside *Love, Mother*, that tiny dab of her perfume.

Patty held the letter to her nose. A lovely hint of jasmine and roses. Jean Patou's Joy. Well, at least her mother had gotten rid of that overly sweet and heavy cologne she'd been experimenting with. Maybe things would start getting back to normal. Maybe?

But what *was* normal in marriage? The seemingly total symbiotic bond between Aunt Marjorie and Uncle Graham? Or the... the... What would Patty call her parents' relationship that, on the surface at least, seemed perfect? Until coming to Washington, Patty had always held them up as being the model of what she wanted—a successful husband, a king in his community, a provider of social prestige and all sorts of niceties. Her mother a much-admired handmaiden-queen.

Without invitation, one of Simone's records started playing in Patty's mind. Carly Simon's "That's the Way I've Always Heard It Should Be." Despite its slow ballad style and graceful piano accompaniment, Patty had found the song cynical, its lyrics disquieting. About getting married, having kids right away, nice houses and lawns, but the couple's children hating them *"for the things they're not."* And the kicker before the final chorus: *"Soon you'll cage me on your shelf—I'll never learn to be just me first, by myself."*

Trying to shake off the disheartening rhyme, Patty settled her gaze on a lovely Monet-style painting of an overflowing garden that hung over the fireplace. She lost herself in it, methodically absorbing its images to push away the song. The scene was colorful and soothing. Tall delphinium, foxglove, lilies, and peonies, trumpet vine entwined along a white picket fence with a beckoning open gate. Riotous and wonderfully messy. The kind of cottage garden that invited playful hide-and-seek.

It made her smile.

"Your mama painted that." Aunt Marjorie stood in the doorway, a tray with mugs and a plate of steaming biscuits in her hands.

"Really?"

"Mmm-hmm. Lovely, isn't it?" She put the tray down on an antique trunk that served as a coffee table and rejoined Patty on the couch. "She gave it to me for graduation. It won first prize in the Wellesley student art show."

"She didn't keep it for herself?" Patty asked with surprise. She would if she'd won a blue ribbon.

"I think she might have given it to me partly as apology for not spending that year in France with me," Aunt Marjorie answered with a small sigh. "We'd planned to go together, you know. But she met your father the summer before we were to leave—this devastatingly handsome medical student who pursued her as if there was no tomorrow. She fell in love and backed out the week before we were to leave for Europe." Again, a sigh. "He had big plans—not just medicine but politics. He wanted her by his side. And . . . I think she was afraid she'd lose him if she was gone for months."

Staring at the painting, Aunt Marjorie mused, "It was like she and I were together in that beautiful garden, full of sunlight and possibilities, and Dottie went out that gate and disappeared down a path I just couldn't see . . . but maybe I feel that way because it all happened so suddenly. A real whirlwind romance. Like in storybooks. The wedding was announced a month before our graduation, and the day after getting our diplomas, your parents married in a gorgeous ceremony that Dottie had managed to pull together to perfection—in just a few weeks. We'd expect nothing less of her, right? Candlelit ceremony and dinner. String quartet . . ."

She went silent for a long, long moment before nodding toward the painting and forcing herself back to chatty. "Dottie also knew how much I loved the Impressionists. She too. Especially Berthe Morisot, the one French woman among the initial group. She'd always planned on naming her first daughter Berthe. Like I named Simone for the writer, Beauvoir." Aunt Marjorie laughed. "What a pair of starstruck Francophiles, *oui*?"

Patty squirmed around to sit on her feet as she faced her godmother. "Oh my God, Mother was thinking of naming me Berthe? Yikes!" She gave a little laugh.

"Oh no, she didn't because of the other baby that—" Aunt Marjorie broke off.

Patty stared. "What other baby?"

"Dammit, Marj," her godmother muttered. "Me and my big mouth. So, I'm guessing you never knew your mama had a miscarriage just a few months after they got married?"

Patty's mouth dropped open in astonishment. No, she didn't.

"Oh dear. I shouldn't have said." She gazed at Patty solemnly. "But . . . maybe better for you to know a little more about your mama. I get the sense that sometimes it's hard for you two to understand each other?" She waited for Patty to respond.

Patty felt herself flush and just shrugged, picking at her pajamas.

Aunt Marjorie patted her hand and said in a quiet, careful voice, "She lost the pregnancy early on. She'd jokingly been calling the baby with both female and male names: Berthe-Bert. So, out of superstition, I suppose, the name didn't come up with you. It took her years to conceive again, so she wasn't taking any chances with karma."

Once more Patty's godmother slipped into pensive: "She's never quite been the same since that miscarriage. Some women sink into a terrible depression after one, you know. That maelstrom of hormones and the sadness combined . . . I still see glimmers of my comrade-in-hijinks, the whip-smart, easy-to-laugh, confident gal I grew up with at college." Aunt Marjorie added, more to herself than Patty, "We just need to coax that Dottie back out of the shadows."

Maybe sensing she'd made Patty uncomfortable, Aunt Marjorie stood, kissing her on the head. "Eat some biscuits now, sugar. The special prosecutor is going to hold a press conference explaining why he's sticking to his guns. I know how involved you've become in Watergate, working on the Hill. Want to watch?"

Patty nodded, relieved to change topics. She needed to mull over everything her godmother had shared before she could ask questions about it.

As she snapped the TV on, Aunt Marjorie threw out a final shocker, softened with affection: "I'm still working on your mama's politics, by the way. To pull her into the moderate feminist fold with me. I have faith. Once upon a time, Dottie was head of Wellesley's Young Democrats, after all."

That night, Simone had just finished making Jiffy Pop and plopped down next to Patty—the butter inside the tinfoil smelling slightly scorched—as the helicopters in the opening credits of M*A*S*H started thumping across the TV screen.

Through a mouthful of popcorn, she asked who was Patty's crush between the two main men at the fictional Korean War mobile army surgical hospital. "So, are you a Hawkeye or a Trapper kind of girl?"

"Oh, Hawkeye, of course," Patty answered as she dug into the popcorn, pulling out a handful. She popped one kernel into her mouth, savoring the salt. "I mean, come on, those azure eyes on Alan Alda? What about you?"

"Trapper. Better one-liners. And Elliott Gould in the original movie? To die for."

"But Hawkeye's the character who's soulful."

"Aha!" Simone elbowed her playfully. "I knew you were a closeted bleeding heart."

Patty laughed. "Okay, okay. What about *Star Trek*. Captain Kirk or Dr. Spock? Wait." She held up her hand. "I can guess. You'd go for Spock."

"Of course. Spock's got the Vulcan mind meld. And those pointy eyebrows!" She wiggled her own eyebrows playfully.

"And Julius is okay with this?" Patty teased.

"Oh, he's got his own way of mind melding," she countered, softness in her voice.

"Why aren't you seeing him tonight? He's still in town, right?"

"He wants some time with his mom. I'll see him for lunch tomorrow before he catches the Greyhound back to VCU. Besides," she said, pulling a tartan throw blanket over both herself and Patty, nestling into the soft cushions, "tonight's the best night of TV: *M*A*S*H*, then *The Mary Tyler Moore Show*, *Bob Newhart*, and *Carol Burnett!*"

Nodding, Patty scrunched down to get comfortable as well. These were all shows she might have to fight to watch at home. *M*A*S*H*, for sure. Her father did not approve of its sardonic, gallows-humor comedy—originally a not-so-subtle commentary on Vietnam.

For a fleeting moment, Patty wondered if Will could bear watching the show's depictions of war's brutality, what he might be doing that night in North Carolina.

"Awwwww," Simone cooed as Hawkeye sat at the bottom of a bed, reading aloud to amuse an injured five-year-old Korean civilian brought into the hospital. "Okay, you're right," she said. "He's got the soul."

In a singsong voice appropriate for a picture book, Hawkeye was reading an off-color novel—all the adult patients listening raptly—to the little patient, who smiled adorably, not understanding a word. "Ha!" Simone chortled. "A rapscallion soul, I'd say."

"We interrupt tonight's regularly scheduled program for a special news report."

Hawkeye and the set of the 4077th disappeared.

The girls booed. Simone chucked a pillow at the TV.

"Wait," Patty said, sitting upright. "This may have something to do with the special prosecutor."

She knew her father hated Archibald Cox and his prosecutor team investigating Watergate. Called them Cox-suckers. But

Patty had been awfully impressed earlier that day by the courtly, soft-spoken man during his press conference. He'd entered, holding his wife's hand—she carrying ladylike white gloves and handbag—and sat down at a cloth-covered table all alone, no staff, facing a room stuffed to the gills with reporters.

As Cox talked, he had come off as modest and self-effacing. Not like the fire-breathing, liberal-demon, out-to-get-Nixon-at-whatever-cost zealot some Republicans painted him as. He'd even begun by apologizing to reporters for bringing them indoors to the National Press Club on such a beautiful Saturday morning. Cox also admitted that as he considered what he should do—in reaction to Nixon's unprecedented defiance of an appellate court order—he'd worried whether he was getting "too big for his britches" in going eyeball to eyeball with a president of the United States. Wondered if what he saw as principle might be vanity.

But in the end, Cox said, he'd decided he had to stick by what he felt was right. The nation's conscience and the law were at stake. He could only hope to awaken a sense of principle in the American people by standing his ground. There was clear evidence of "serious wrongdoing on the part of high government officials to cover up other wrongdoing," he'd concluded, and only the tapes could unequivocally prove or disprove the allegations.

His arguments had made complete sense to Patty. And to the press corps listening to him.

The TV screen flickered to Dan Rather, the anchor of the *CBS Evening News*. "Good evening. *The country tonight is in the midst of what may be the most serious constitutional crisis in its history.*"

"Mom! Dad!" Simone shouted. "Come quick!"

As Rather announced that Nixon had ousted Archibald Cox, the screen shifted to stock footage of the bow-tied special Watergate prosecutor in front of floor-to-ceiling shelves filled with law books.

"Are you kidding?" groaned Uncle Graham from the hallway door. "Nixon's just thrown the rule of law out a West Wing window."

"Attorney General Elliot Richardson has quit, rather than carry out the president's orders to fire Cox."

Aunt Marjorie slipped past her husband to roost on the sofa's rolled arm, as Rather went on to share that Richardson's deputy, William Ruckelshaus, "in a moment of constitutional drama" had also refused Nixon's order to fire Cox and was himself fired by the president.

"What?" she gasped as a pleasant-looking, bespectacled man—the husband of her heroine Jill—was shown trying to get to his car as two network reporters shoved microphones in his face.

The TV images shifted to a policeman ushering a young staffer out of Cox's suite of offices, grasping her upper arm with one hand and holding up his other to block cameras. The newscaster narrated, *"Half an hour after the prosecutor was fired, agents of the FBI—acting at the direction of the White House—sealed off the offices of the special prosecutor, the offices of the attorney general, and the offices of the deputy attorney general.*

"All of this adds up to a totally unprecedented situation, a grave and profound crisis in which the president has set himself against his own attorney general and the Department of Justice. Nothing like this has ever happened before."

More footage of the special prosecutor's legal clerks and researchers filing out, grim faced. They squinted in the TV camera floodlights as their office door was slowly shut from the inside by police and FBI agents rummaged through things atop their desks.

More film clips of Richardson's limo driving away, being chased on foot by photographers, bulbs flashing. Rather shared that after Richardson and Ruckelshaus had refused to fire the special Watergate prosecutor, Nixon had elevated Solicitor General Robert Bork—the number three man in the Justice Department's hierarchy—to be acting attorney general. Nixon then ordered Bork to fire Cox, and Bork did.

"Who the hell is Bork?" muttered Uncle Graham.

The phone started ringing loudly as Nixon's press secretary was telling reporters that President Nixon had "discharged Archibald Cox because he refused to comply with instructions."

"He's an independent prosecutor! The president has no authority over him," Uncle Graham was fairly shouting at the TV now, he was so aggravated.

"Dad," Simone whispered. She'd answered the kitchen phone and now stood at the door, its long cord stretched out taut, her hand over the lime-green receiver. "Dad," she hissed a little louder. "It's a reporter. Asking for you."

"For me?"

He looked at Aunt Marjorie, who stood up, her face suddenly pale. "Go ahead," she said with a nod, and then turned the TV's volume down.

As he passed, Patty reached out and touched his arm—without hesitation, without worrying whether this dad, this adult man, would be angered by a kid trying to advise him. She'd witnessed too many ambushes around the Senate. He needed to be honest but careful. "If the journalist asks anything you're uncomfortable with, say you're off the record, Uncle Graham. That's what Hill staffers do when a reporter nabs them in the hall. But you have to make that stipulation *before* you answer."

He smiled down at her as he answered the call: "This is Graham Conroy . . . Yes, I am a legal counsel at the EPA . . . Yes, I know him, but only a little. I just joined the agency." Uncle Graham paced as he talked. "Yes, a man of absolute integrity . . ." He smiled and nodded. "Yes, he's known as Mr. Clean—fondly and with admiration." Uncle Graham's smile disappeared. "Yes," he answered cautiously, "I did resign from the IRS in disagreement over some audits."

There was a long pause and Uncle Graham turned to look at Patty. "My next statement is off the record . . . No, I will not be identified as an 'unnamed source' or as 'a former IRS prosecutor.' If I answer, it is solely on background. No attribution of any kind. Agreed? . . . All right. Yes, I have heard there may be—I emphasize *may be*—some issues with the president's back taxes." He nodded. "You're welcome."

He hung up, exhaling a long breath. "Thanks for the tip, kid," he said to Patty.

"That was impressive, girlfriend." Simone playfully swatted her.

Well, there was one, clear-cut good reason she could list for being a Capitol Hill page—protecting Simone's dad from a media gaffe that could have serious blowback for him.

Immediately, the phone rang again.

Frowning, Uncle Graham answered, "I have no further comment . . . Oh! Hold on." He held the phone toward Aunt Marjorie. "This reporter's looking for you. Wants to ask about Jill."

"Me? Oh no," she said, shaking her head.

"Go ahead, Mom," Simone urged. "Your opinion is as important as Dad's." She grinned at her father. "Just saying."

"Just remember what I told Uncle Graham," Patty breathed. Aunt Marjorie—talking to reporters. Wow.

Uncle Graham whispered, "She's asking whether you think Jill's special assistant job at the White House with the Office of Women's Programs will be in jeopardy."

"What? Why would it be? That would be so unfair. So . . . vindictive of Nixon."

Uncle Graham made a face of *yeah well?*

Aunt Marjorie straightened up tall in Simone-like indignation. "Give me that phone."

Pulling off one of her snap-on earrings, Patty's godmother put the receiver to her ear. "This is Marjorie Conroy . . . Yes,

I work at the Political Caucus—part-time . . . I certainly hope nothing would happen to Mrs. Ruckelshaus's position in the White House. Her efforts to place women in professional-level government posts is essential to improving job equality by providing federal role models to the business community at large. She has nothing to do with the Watergate investigation . . ." Aunt Marjorie rolled her eyes. "Of course she is very supportive of her husband . . . I'm sure she agreed with his decision to not fire Mr. Cox . . . No, I would *not* say she is frustrated with the administration as a feminist. I'd say determined and persistent . . ."

Aunt Marjorie shook her head and then said, putting sweetness in her voice, "I'll just quote something Mrs. Ruckelshaus said to reporters this summer when asked the same question: 'If you were crossing a river and had asked an alligator to take you across, it isn't smart politics to comment on how scaly his back is.'" She let out a little laugh. "Yes, jumping to a new alligator is always an option. The hope, of course, is that one day soon we don't need to ride a darn alligator at all. That we're already to the other side . . . Yes, you may quote me . . . You're welcome."

After hanging up the phone, Aunt Marjorie picked up her sky-blue leather address book. "Excuse me. I need to activate the phone tree. We better figure out the best way to express our expectation that nothing bad will happen to Jill as a result of tonight." From the kitchen came the sound of dialing—decisive and impatient. "Hello, Betty? Marj here . . . Can you believe it? . . . I know. Listen, we need to discuss . . ."

In the sitting room, Patty, Simone, and Uncle Graham watched. He beamed. Simone grinned. "That's my mom," she said proudly.

Patty wondered if her parents had even watched the news that night.

WATERGATE

NATIONAL OUTCRY AGAINST THE SATURDAY NIGHT MASSACRE IS SO SEVERE, Nixon backpedals, appointing a new special prosecutor and agreeing to turn over the nine tapes. **NIXON MAINTAINS HIS INNOCENCE**, saying he welcomes the examination, "because people have got to know whether or not their president is a crook."

But in yet another shocker, **ONE TAPE IS FOUND TO CONTAIN AN 18½-MINUTE GAP**—right in the middle of a conversation between Nixon and his former chief of staff, three days after the Watergate break-in.

THE ONLY PERSON WHO CAN EXPLAIN IT, SAYS THE WHITE HOUSE, IS NIXON'S DECADES-LONG SECRETARY, ROSE MARY WOODS. She transcribed the tapes.

WOODS IS CALLED TO THE WITNESS STAND. More adviser than secretary, Woods had been named one of the nation's 75 most important women in a *Ladies' Home Journal* list that included *Washington Post* publisher Katharine Graham. Nixon's daughters call her Aunt Rose.

She will be questioned by **THE ONLY FEMALE ATTORNEY ON THE SPECIAL PROSECUTOR'S TASK FORCE, 30-YEAR-OLD JILL WINE-VOLNER**.

Under oath, Woods **CLAIMS SHE ACCIDENTALLY DAMAGED THE RECORDING** when she'd reached to the far end of her desk to answer her phone, pushing the record button without realizing it and leaving her foot on the tape machine's pedal while she talked.

Woods's tape recorder and headphones are brought to the courtroom. **WINE-VOLNER ASKS WOODS TO DEMONSTRATE.**

Woods puts her foot on the recorder's pedal. The tape begins to whir. But as Woods reaches for her headset, resting on the witness stand's ledge, her foot comes off the pedal. **THE TAPE STOPS TURNING—MAKING ANY ERASURE IMPOSSIBLE.**

THE CROWD IN THE COURTROOM GASPS.

If that small reach caused Woods's foot to lift and stop the tape, there was no way the petite secretary could have stretched across her desk to pick up a phone on its far end and kept her foot on the recorder's pedal, especially for 18½ long minutes.

WINE-VOLNER HAS CAUGHT WOODS IN AN OBVIOUS LIE.

Reporters race out to a hallway bank of pay phones to call their newsrooms.

No matter how much her boss and other lawyers praise Wine-Volner's deft examination of Woods, **NEWS AGENCIES GLOSS OVER HER CREDENTIALS** and professional savvy. They instead **DESCRIBE WINE-VOLNER AS "THE MINISKIRTED LAWYER" WHO BROUGHT DOWN THE PRESIDENT'S SECRETARY**.

FIRSTS

YVONNE BURKE BECOMES THE FIRST MEMBER OF CONGRESS TO GIVE BIRTH WHILE IN OFFICE.

LITTLE LEAGUE BASEBALL ALLOWS IN GIRLS, WHEN NEW JERSEY JUDGE SYLVIA PRESSLER rules in favor of a sex discrimination lawsuit brought by NOW, after eleven-year-old Maria Pepe was forced off her Hoboken team. Maria aged out of the league before the case could make its way through the courts. But the judge's ruling allowed these Hoboken girls, and others across the country, to try out and play.

IN HER DECISION, PRESSLER WRITES: "Little League is as American as the hot dog and apple pie. There is no reason that part of Americana should be withheld from little girls. THE SOONER LITTLE BOYS BEGIN TO REALIZE THAT LITTLE GIRLS ARE EQUAL and that there will be many opportunities for a boy to be bested by a girl, THE CLOSER THEY WILL BE TO BETTER MENTAL HEALTH."

CHAPTER ELEVEN

NOVEMBER

Smothering a cough, Patty rested her head on Scott's shoulder to gaze up at him as he talked. She wished they'd been able to get seats in the nonsmoking section of the plane. But to sit together on their flight home for Thanksgiving necessitated their being smack-dab in cigarette stench and haze. Even so, sitting next to Scott, holding his hand for two hours—listening to him describe his courses, his professors, his classmates—had been worth putting up with stinging eyes and a scratchy throat. She marveled that the foul fog didn't seem to bother Scott at all.

"Which class is your favorite?" Patty asked.

"Poli-sci. It's just an intro survey, but it's fascinating. The professor's on to global, post–World War Two politics now. Learning a lot about Eisenhower. Always admired him, of course, being our allied commander during the war. But Ike is really interesting in today's context. Clearly Nixon gleaned a lot from being Ike's VP—about recognizing hidden enemies and containing the communist threat but knowing how to work with them at the same time. Eisenhower with Stalin's generals. Nixon negotiating the Strategic Arms Limitation Treaty with Brezhnev. Calming relations with China enough to open up trade between us."

Patty shifted a bit, thinking about Abe describing his mother almost losing her teaching job during the Red Scare and the conspiracy theories of McCarthyism—which had happened under Eisenhower's watch.

After their conversation, out of curiosity, she'd done some reading. Patty had been embarrassed to realize she knew little about Senator Joe McCarthy's "anti-communist" hearings—so infamous and polarizing that eventually his own Republican colleagues would vote to censure him. She was shocked to learn how many Americans were ruined solely by innuendo and ginned-up public opinion. Things as minor as having donated to causes deemed "subversive" by McCarthy's committee being enough to get Americans blacklisted. "Loyalty Review Boards" that his fear-mongering rhetoric had spawned across the country. Firing librarians for shelving "Red-leaning" novels as innocuous as *Robin Hood*. (The hero took from the rich to give to the poor—supposedly making readers susceptible to communist thought and lawlessness in general.)

"What do you think of Eisenhower's handling of Senator McCarthy? He didn't really push back much against McCarthy's unfounded accusations against innocent Americans."

Scott pulled away to look down at her. "Don't start acting like that Katie character," he teased, referring to the radical activist in the movie they'd seen—*The Way We Were*. "Because her anti–Red Scare politics and big mouth nearly ruined Hubbell's writing career."

"Of course not!" Patty answered, surprised and hurt by his reference. But she made herself keep the conversation light: "I will remind you what Katie told Hubbell—that he'd never meet anyone else who would love or believe in him as much as she did." She playfully batted her eyelashes.

"All right, all right," Scott replied, "I'll take that part of it." He laughed, putting his arm over her shoulder. "It's all a matter of the right amount of spice, doll. Girls who are too serious too often are a drag."

Patty watched a pretty stewardess with a pixie haircut come down the aisle, retrieving passengers' trash in preparation for landing. She wore the National Airlines much advertised uniform: a Uhura *Star Trek*–style hot pants outfit with an ironically modest mock-turtleneck on a not-so-modest dress ending just below her butt, the hot pants' shortie-panties the same hot pink—revealed whenever she leaned over the slightest bit.

Right before she reached Patty's row, a man handed back emptied mini-bottles of booze and then stretched his arm across the aisle to block her moving away as he slurred, "I'll fly you anytime, baby"—echoing the airline's signature ad campaign of a sweet-faced stewardess below the headline "I'm Cheryl. Fly me."

Patty felt her stomach lurch at the man's raunchy joke. The stewardess's reddening face and downcast eyes threw Patty back to how Jake's gross overtures had nauseated her with a sense of being defamed and alarmingly, suddenly, vulnerable. Bearing witness to the attendant's discomfort, Patty filled up with the same vomit-worthy feelings.

"Excuse me, please," said the stewardess.

"Aw, come on, hon. Coffee, tea, or me, eh?" The man leaned out of his seat, way, way too close.

In a movement that looked painfully practiced, the stewardess took hold of the man's sleeve with her fingertips to lift and drop his hand onto his armrest. Somehow nonconfrontational, avoiding making trouble.

Patty caught the flight attendant's eye and did her best to silently convey her sympathy. Her face still burning red, the stewardess gave Patty a tiny thank-you-for-noticing smile, and continued down the aisle.

"Scott?" Patty turned to her beau, wanting him to say something like Abe might have. Or Will. About what a jerk the passenger was.

"Hmm?"

She frowned slightly. "Did you see that?"

"What?"

"That . . . that guy accosting the stewardess. 'Joking'"—she made imaginary quotation marks in the air—"he'd fly her. You know . . . *fly* . . . like the ad implies."

"Pretty clever double-entendre, that ad," Scott answered, stretching to relieve the stiffness in his long legs. Noticing Patty's shocked expression, he said, "Yeah, yeah. I saw the guy. A complete a-hole. But she signed up for it, Patty. No one's holding a gun to her head to keep this job. Or put on that uniform." He checked his watch. "Should be landing soon."

Patty stared at him—feeling another surge of queasiness. That's exactly how she would have judged—hard—the stewardess in the past. Now, thinking of the young mother in her residence hall, who needed to keep her job even to the point of not admitting she had a child, her next question just popped out: "What do you think about the ERA?"

Again, Scott pulled back to be able to look her in the face. "That's a non sequitur."

Not really, thought Patty.

"Why do you ask?" Now his voice was defensive.

Careful. Don't end the flight with an argument, she cautioned herself. And truth be known, Patty wasn't sure exactly *why* she had asked her question right then. "Well . . . Aunt Marjorie's so for it, working with the Women's Caucus to push for passage, but Mother's fighting it with the STOP ERA housewives. I've been thinking about it because of going home—worrying I'll get caught between them somehow. Trying to decide what to say if Mother demands to know my opinion." Not that her mother ever really asked Patty what she was thinking.

Scott's reply was quick, automatic. "What I think is this: The ERA was part of the Republican plank at the convention. The party supports it. Nixon supports it. It's harmless enough. Throws a bone to the ladies. So, I support it."

"You're aware that STOP ERA women are trying to change Republicans' minds? Convince them to switch their votes? If the Republican Party withdrew its endorsement, would you still support the amendment?"

"Of course not," Scott answered without a moment's thought. "I go with the party."

Patty blinked, blinked, thought. Unquestioning loyalty to the opinion and edicts of party superiors. She'd have said the same thing before... before witnessing the Watergate hearings, before knowing Abe, before spending so much time with Simone and Aunt Marjorie, before seeing Uncle Graham pushing back, sticking to his own personal sense of principle.

"What's your father's opinion?" Scott's question jolted her back to their conversation.

"I'm not sure," Patty murmured. "I should ask." She paused. "You know, I've been worrying about Mother a little."

"Since when do you worry about your mother?" Scott asked with a laugh. "All you've ever said about her is that she drives you bonkers—for as long as I've known you."

Patty winced. Felt the little nudge of worry she'd experienced when Simone was so angry at Aunt Marjorie about Julius and the garden party—wondering if she'd ever been that unfair in her judgments against her own mother. And, oh God, did Scott think her frustration with her mother was ugly of her? She searched his face, but all she saw was amusement. So Patty continued, rather than pivoting to safer conversation. Her anxiety about what she was going home to was that high. "Last time I saw Mother she was on diet pills that were making her unbelievably jittery. A total space cadet. And Daddy says... Well, he complained she's keeping him awake at night and that's she aggravatingly highstrung and—"

"The big M," Scott interrupted.

"Excuse me?"

"Menopause. Makes all women nuts, my dad says. Your father has my mom on a regimen of Valium and sleeping pills, too."

"I didn't know your mother was a patient of Daddy's."

"Aren't all the moms?" Scott joked. "Maybe I should be a psychiatrist first, and make lots of dough, like your dad, and then run for office—so I can afford to campaign in style. I've always wondered why your father never ran for anything. I asked my old man recently and he said, 'Dr. Appleton prefers being the guy behind the curtain, pulling the strings.'"

Patty wasn't sure she liked the image of her father as some manipulative Wizard of Oz.

Ping. "*Ladies and gentlemen, we're about to begin our descent into Springfield...*"

The stewardess made her way back down the aisle, saying, "Buckle up, please," scooching quickly past the booze-bloated man.

Patty was surprised to find her father awaiting them at the baggage carousel. She'd expected her mother.

"Princess!" He hugged her briskly, then shook Scott's hand heartily. "The college man returneth!" Her father almost seemed happier to see her beau than her, Patty thought with a little torque of jealousy.

The two men marched out to the parking lot—tall, squared jaws, strides matched, commanding. Patty followed, noting how many female heads they turned as they went. Her momentary pang of envy was replaced with a swell of pride.

On the thirty-minute drive to drop Scott at his house, her father must have asked a hundred questions about Georgetown before reaching the front door of Scott's baronial Tudor–style family home.

"I'll see you at the party," Scott said to Patty, putting his hand on her shoulder and squeezing it before sliding out of the back seat. "Thanks so much for the lift, Dr. Appleton."

"Things seem fine between you two," Patty's father said as they drove out of the long driveway.

It was more statement than question, so Patty simply nodded and waited for him to quiz her about the Hill, like he'd just engaged Scott. Like the last time she'd seen him. She'd been storing up answers. Careful ones about the Saturday Night Massacre to tease out his reading of the night's unprecedented events. But she wasn't apprehensive this time. Patty couldn't imagine her father not agreeing with how outrageous Nixon's firing of a special prosecutor was. A whopping three-quarters of polled Americans disapproved of the president's actions.

But all her father said was "We need to stop by the liquor store. Your mother managed to forget our order. And then we'll have to swing by the bakery to pick up her damn cake. I swear the woman can't remember a thing these days," he groused. Each Thanksgiving weekend, the Appletons hosted a holiday cocktail party on Friday night. Sometimes it coincided with her mother's birthday—as it did this year.

At the liquor store, Patty waited in the car, glum, dreading what she'd find at home even more now, given her father's disgruntlement. Dot Appleton *never* forgot party supplies—she choreographed her events meticulously, completing tasks days beforehand.

Ker-choo, ker-choo, ker-chooooo. Patty was hit with one final cigarette-smoke-congested sneezing fit. She rummaged in her purse. *Sugar.* Out of tissues. Thank goodness her mother always put a Kleenex box in the car's glove compartment—that is, if she'd remembered.

Popping open the compartment, Patty found the usual thin box of tissues. Okay, her mother was put together enough to keep to her usual housekeeping chores, at least. Oh! Patty's hand slid from the tissue to a small, flat bag with a gold-embossed logo—the Tiny Jewel Box, Washington's famous, expensive, and infamously snobby jewelry shop. With a quick glance toward the liquor store to gauge how much time she safely had to snoop, Patty pulled it out.

If her father had purchased her mother something pretty, it would put to rest some of Patty's fears. She snapped open the box.

"Oh . . . my . . . gosh." Nestled on royal-blue velvet was a gorgeous, matching set of earrings and a choker necklace. The earrings were a cascade of mother-of-pearl discs, long enough to reach her mother's collarbone. The choker was also mother-of-pearl, a fan of discs, punctuated with tiny carved doves. Very mod, shimmery, youthful. Completely unlike the Chanel-style pearls and button earrings her mother typically wore. She'd look . . . *sexy*.

Blushing a little at the thought of her parents being *sexy*, Patty still smiled with relief. Things couldn't be that bad between them if her father was giving her mother birthday presents like that. Hastily, Patty closed its lid and tucked the jewelry box back into its bag and then the glove compartment, just as her father appeared, flanked by two stocking clerks carrying boxes.

But the fabulous jewelry never appeared. Not during their Thanksgiving dinner at the club, not at their cocktail party, which was perfectly orchestrated despite her father's complaints. Instead, with everyone gathered round, champagne flutes in hand, Patty's father presented Dot Appleton with an antique Limoges tea set—elegant, bone-thin china—but definitely *not* sexy.

Her father must be saving the necklace and earrings for Christmas. It was far too intimate a gift in this setting, after all.

Raising his glass, he toasted, "To my wife, in honor of her hostessing abilities, which equal the nineteenth-century French marquise this tea set once belonged to, and in celebration of her forty-ninth birthday, which, I believe, is the age she has chosen to remain in perpetuity. Here's to your frozen beauty, my dear." He paused, mugged an "oops" face, but Patty recognized his telltale subtle smirk. "Frozen in time," he corrected himself and bowed. "As stunning, twenty-seven years later, as the girl who captured me."

"Hear, hear," cheered the gathered, lifting their crystal en masse to take a long sip as one.

"Captured? Did your parents have a shotgun wedding I don't know about?" Scott joked.

Patty swatted his arm. "Of course not. I'm sure Daddy meant to say, 'captured his heart.'" Like all the adults that evening, her father had been drinking pretty heavily. Patty glanced around the room to see if others had overheard and misinterpreted her boyfriend's jest. But she was overreacting. Everyone used the phrase "to catch a man." It was the mantra of womanhood. The guests had all downed the sparkling wine and returned to light-hearted tête-à-têtes. Nothing worrisome or gossipy.

Although Simone's voice whispered in Patty's mind: *As if "captured his heart" is any better. Captured? Just saying.*

Patty listened to the ripples of conversation. Only a few splashes of Watergate speculation here and there. So unlike Simone's home. Lots about the new tennis bubble and "that delicious" new pro, critiques of the latest Ferrari, complaints about taxes being so high and going to "do-nothing" welfare mothers.

Patty had never felt like an oddity in her own world before. Now, it was like she wore old, ill-fitting clothes that scratched and pinched.

After the last guests left and the kitchen crew had cleared and cleaned, Patty lay awake for a long time listening to the nighttime quiet, mulling over her parents' parallel silence with each other. They used to talk more, didn't they?

Finally, around 2:00 a.m., she got up and wandered down the sweeping staircase, heading to the kitchen for graham crackers and a glass of milk to dunk them in. The milky ginger taste always helped her fall asleep.

An eerie light spilled into the dining room.

Through the doorway she could see her mother—backlit by the glow of the open refrigerator, holding a washcloth packed with ice to the back of her neck, her negligee drenched in sweat, hunched close to the cool, and breathing hard.

"Mother! Are you all right?"

Dot Appleton turned, her face pale and drawn. "You're home," she murmured.

"I . . . I've been home, Mother." Patty's alarm skyrocketed.

Her mother frowned. Thought a moment. "Yes, of course. Of course you have been." She closed the refrigerator door and sat down at the table, running the ice-filled washcloth along her neck as it dripped all over her and onto the bright yellow Formica.

"Do you have a fever, Mother?"

She shook her head as she pulled an ice cube from the cloth to suck on, her breathing beginning to calm. Patty stared. Dot Appleton had always forbidden chewing on ice—it ruined the teeth, she'd said, and looked cheap.

After a long moment, her mother swallowed the crunched-up cube and answered, "Hot flashes . . . Like being picked up and hurled into Hades." She smiled wanly. "Your aunt Marjorie calls these 'personal summers.' Maybe for her. I wish I could adopt her Pollyanna attitude about the change of life."

Her washcloth's ice had completely melted at this point. Patty's mother stood to drop it beside the sink before pouring bleach over something and turning on the faucet to run and run and run as she stared down into it, unmoving. Slowly, Patty came to the counter to stand near her, startled to see a bloody sheet in the basin.

"Change of life," her mother muttered. "I'll say."

Quickly rising, the water threatened to overflow. Patty reached over to shut off the faucet. Her mother didn't look up. "Change of everything . . . You know, after watching that ERA debate with Marj and Simone, your godmother gave me a copy of Betty Friedan's cursed book, the *Feminine Mystique*. Trying to change my mind to her way of thinking. I read it. I wish I hadn't. It . . . bothered me. Her talking about yearning . . . the Freudian doctrine that imprisons us with its claim women can have no greater destiny than to glory in their own femininity, and that if we aspire to more than running a good household, we must have confused sexual identity, penis envy, be neurotic . . . 'the problem that has no name,' as Friedan calls it."

Dot Appleton let out the water, watching it drain. "Your father did not approve of my reading that book, I can tell you." She poured more Clorox onto the stain to rub and rub the cloth.

Surely the bleach stung her hands, worried Patty, although her mother didn't seem to flinch, her ruby-red, salon-perfect fingernails a sharp contrast to the sheet that was regaining its white little by little as she scrubbed. "When I heard that Friedan was going to debate Phyllis Schlafly at Illinois State University, I decided to go. To support Phyllis. But also . . . to hear Friedan.

"There she was on stage—the woman whose words so unsettled me . . . the proclaimed mother of the women's movement . . . She seemed so angry and abrasive. Of course, Phyllis goaded her . . . but still. Do you know she called Phyllis—and she might as well have been spitting on every housewife in the audience, including me, when she said it—a traitor to our sex, an Uncle Tom . . . Friedan came across as everything Phyllis paints her as being—a rejected, middle-aged divorcee, alone and unhappy. It . . . it terrified me. Because . . ." her voice dropped to a whisper, "I do feel some of the things Friedan described in her book, God help me."

Patty's mother stopped scrubbing and turned to look at her daughter with such anguish, it took Patty's breath. "Betty Friedan is not that much older than I am . . . What would I do if your father . . . Phyllis says the ERA would do away with alimony . . . would let husbands throw cast-off wives out of their own homes, the family havens the wives created . . . What would I do if . . . if . . ." She shook her head, dropped the sheet back into the sink, and wandered out of the room, staggering back up the stairs.

Horrified, Patty watched her disappear. If her mother kept acting like this, her father might indeed leave her. The line from that Geritol ad, about the woman who was the perfect mother, housewife, and still desirable woman—"My wife, I think I'll keep her"—shouted through her head. Would her father want "to keep her"—like this? *Snap out of it, Mother!*

But suddenly Patty was drawn up short by the memory of some of her own revelations recently. How often her father cut off Patty, too, embarrassing and disappointing her, cowing her, even, making it impossible to explain herself. How different Uncle Graham was with Aunt Marjorie. And that beautiful but haunted, painfully self-contained visage of Maureen Dean.

What had Aunt Marjorie said about Patty's mother? Something about disappearing down a path her godmother just couldn't see. How her father had pursued her "as if there was no tomorrow." That didn't sound like Patty's mother had "captured *him*."

The beautiful painting hanging in Aunt Marjorie's home—of a garden overflowing with new life blossoms that Dot Appleton had painted when she was just a few years older than Patty—rose up in her mind. Its messy cheerfulness and explosion of color so very striking, so . . . out of character for the mother she knew.

Then her thoughts jumped to how often her father had implied her mother was overwrought, distracted, pestering him with selfish, thoughtless requests—and yes, *crazy*. Expecting Patty to think the same. Another of her father's complaints thundered through her mind—his grumbling that her mother was spending too much time in her studio, "painting God knows what."

Suddenly, Patty wanted to see what.

She rushed to the garage, took the stairs two at a time to the apartment above it, pushed the door open—to turn round and round staring. Astonished. Seeing the mind's eye of a woman she realized she barely knew.

Piled willy-nilly were pencil sketches of Patty as a child she'd never seen before—mirthful, playful, belly-laughing. A lovely mother-daughter portrait of Patty sitting on Dot Appleton's lap as they read a book, in easy, comfortable affection that Patty only now remembered the long-ago feel of, looking at her mother's sketch of it.

Vibrant pastels of the woods behind their house, in spring and summer, rich with a dozen shades of green, dappled light, and starbursts of wildflowers along the paths—ruby, cobalt, violet. Delightful miniature watercolors of soft-fur squirrels, opulent feathered birds, glistening frogs, and skinks with emerald and sapphire stripes sliding down their backs. Bigger paintings of gold-rose dawn and fading peach twilight, azure ponds reflecting even bluer sky, swaths of sun-ruptured storm clouds. Close-ups of hands, their veins made to look delicate—balletic, even—instead of bulgy. Studies of eyes that somehow conveyed sorrow as well as wonderment.

Why weren't any of these hanging in the house? They were beautiful. So full of life, of empathy and understanding of the unique splendor of nature, the essence of other beings—all from the cool, walled-off, critical Dot Appleton!

Patty felt her eyes well up with tears of admiration, of confusion.

On easels by the window, she found what clearly were her mother's current works: a startling-stern pencil portrait of her father, his face handsome, but haloed with smears and erasure scratches. And a truly disturbing self-portrait, Dot Appleton's features blurred into a yowling, catlike face, thick lines running over it, like . . . like cage bars. There was writing scribbled on the back. Patty squinted at the almost illegible handwriting. "The Panther," a poem by someone named Rainer Maria Rilke. *"His vision, from the constantly passing bars, has grown so weary that it cannot hold anything else . . . and behind the bars, no world . . ."*

Patty's breath snagged. She hadn't comprehended before, in the kitchen, what her mother had meant. But standing in her studio, knee-deep in her self-revealing creativity, Patty came to understand her mother's reaction to Friedan's book. It wasn't just "unsettled." It was a self-loathing and anger, a paralyzing fear of a "change of life," or perhaps of existing trapped as a shadow of what was or what had been hoped for but never grasped.

Patty hated the heart-stopping epiphany.

Hated it even more after what happened next when her father drove her to the airport Sunday morning for her return flight to Washington. Scott had taken a late flight out the night before to make an audition for a campus barbershop quartet group. "Your mother is down with one of her headaches," explained her father as he opened the car door for Patty. Dot Appleton hadn't even come out of their bedroom to say goodbye, which was unusual enough, even with what she'd witnessed in the kitchen, to make Patty wonder if her father had just given her mother another sleeping pill to shut her up during the night.

They rode in silence until Patty spotted the edge of the airfields and dared to say, "Daddy, I saw that gorgeous, super-cool jewelry in your glove compartment. I know you must be saving it for Mother's Christmas present, but maybe it would give her a real lift if you gave it to her beforehand. I think—"

"What the hell are you doing, going through my things? Is

that what they're teaching you on the Hill with those Senate investigators sticking their noses into the president's business?"

Patty's father pulled up to the curb in front of the airport terminal, slamming the brakes, lurching them forward. Before she could say anything, he reached across Patty to unlatch her door. "Come back for the holidays, my good girl." He did everything but push her out onto the pavement.

Tears almost blinding her, Patty retrieved her suitcase from the trunk. She barely closed it before her father gunned the car and roared away.

Patty caught a taxi when she landed at National Airport, told the driver to wait as she dropped her suitcase at Thompson-Markward Hall, then asked to be taken to Georgetown University, straight to Scott's dorm. She needed him—the young man she hoped to marry, the young man who was linked to a time when her life felt stable and definable, the young man who could offer all Patty had been convinced she wanted for her future.

That errant sweet perfume. The phone call at Duke Zeibert's restaurant that made her father pay the bill and leave so hurriedly. The blond woman who picked him up in the blue Cadillac outside the Capitol. His mysterious meetings. The hip jewelry.

Her father must be having an affair.

Patty had barely made it through the flight without screaming.

Scott would understand her panic. Her confusion. Her hurt. He would make it better.

When Scott opened his door, surprised to see her, Patty flung herself at him. Explained in a torrent. "What should I do? Should I tell Mother?"

Scott led her to his bed to sit down. He paced a minute, then stopped, turned, crossed his arms across his chest. "What your mother doesn't know won't hurt her, Patty."

"Wha-what?"

He sat down beside her. "Listen, you don't know for sure that he's screwing some other woman, do you?"

Patty startled at Scott's language, the coarse imagery of it. She hadn't before imagined the actual act her father might be doing. "No," she said hesitantly.

"Then think about not telling your mother as being for the greater good. Why blow up a decades-long marriage? Your dad's a good provider. I don't see you or your mother wanting for anything. And mostly their relationship is good, right? Sometimes men step out for . . . a change of pace. They get bored. Especially if their wives aren't . . . you know . . . reciprocating enough in bed. Doesn't mean anything. So even if your suspicions are true, why let one mistake totally upend your lives? She doesn't need to know."

"You mean cover up?"

"Just . . . keep quiet. It's not like you're actively trying to cover for your father. And maybe there's a logical explanation for all this, Patty. You do overthink sometimes. Get a little overly emotional. You don't know that he isn't going to give that necklace and earrings to your mom. It just sounds like he was pissed you got into his things. That's kind of like him, isn't it?"

Patty nodded slowly, remembering. She could think of a dozen incidents—like the time he'd spanked her when he found her in his closet bureau, pulling cardboard sheets out of his laundered shirts to use for an art project. She had invaded his privacy then, too, without asking permission.

Tears fell down Patty's face again. She didn't know what to think.

Gently, Scott kissed away her tears. Held her, rocked her soothingly. She kissed him back, looking for redemption, for belonging. In her boyfriend's embrace, Patty no longer felt lost. She was protected.

And then she was not.

This time Scott didn't stop when Patty protested that his insistence was frightening her.

"Trust me," he crooned as he pushed her flat to the bed. He was on top of her before she could roll away. Muscular, heavy.

She wanted to trust him.

Scott took her hand, kissed its palm, whispered into her ear, "I want you, Patty. We're meant to be together." She felt herself believe him.

But then he shoved her hand—that just a moment before he'd held so tenderly, so reassuringly—down his pants—abrupt, crude, rough, to rub himself. "Feel what you do to me," he demanded, his voice suddenly harsh. "You're driving me crazy. Have a heart."

Desperate now, Patty tried to pull her hand away. Not this way. This wasn't how she wanted her first time to be. But Scott was strong. Too strong. She couldn't get loose.

"Don't be a tease. You know you want it."

It was over before she really knew what was happening. Over except for a sudden searing pain and blood.

"That's my girl," Scott murmured, then fell asleep on top of her.

Patty managed to crawl out from under Scott as he slept. Hands shaking, she pulled her panties and pantyhose from around her knees back up to her waist. Managed to button her blouse closed enough, even with the now missing buttons. Left without a word, without a note.

Walked, no, staggered down O Street to Wisconsin Avenue—too disheveled, too distraught, too desecrated to step into a streetlamp's spotlight to hail a cab. *Don't look up. Don't look anyone in the eye. They'd see. They'd know.*

Down to M Street, left onto Pennsylvania. *Don't look up.*

Patty stumbled her way past the White House, lit up like a fairy-tale castle, down Seventeenth Street to Constitution Avenue. Past the National Gallery, full of beauty, to the gleaming Capitol Building.

Four miles in the cold, growing shadows of night. Keeping to dim edges. Holding her coat collar up against her face. *Don't let anyone see.*

Almost there. Almost. Patty turned left onto Second Street to the fortress of the Thompson-Markward Young Women's Christian Home. *Oh God.* If anyone spotted her approaching on dark streets without a male page escort, they might report her. The Senate's sergeant at arms could claim she'd broken her promise to never walk alone at night, to never endanger herself or cause the page program trouble by getting hurt. They could send her home.

Don't look up. Don't speak to the desk attendant.

Patty stood in the shower until the hot water ran out. Stayed in the cold until she was shivering so much, she dropped her bar of soap repeatedly.

Thought of Will, his gentleness. His bittersweet good-bye note. That "sweet what-if." Abe's good-natured laughter as women teased him about Billie Jean King schooling Bobby Riggs in their tennis "Battle of the Sexes." Julius turning the spotlight from himself to Simone at the football game. His saying they'd wait until Simone was truly ready.

Men didn't have to act like Scott.

Back in her room, still dripping from the shower, Patty opened the little writing desk by her bed. She pulled out one of her mother's hand-painted notecards that she'd given Patty to use in writing home—this one a delicate watercolor of a swallow-tail butterfly—and penned a one-sentence note to Scott that she never wanted to see him again.

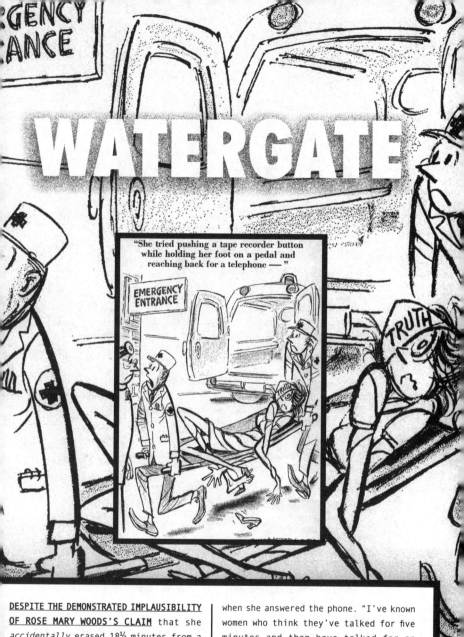

WATERGATE

"She tried pushing a tape recorder button while holding her foot on a pedal and reaching back for a telephone —"

DESPITE THE DEMONSTRATED IMPLAUSIBILITY OF ROSE MARY WOODS'S CLAIM that she *accidentally* erased 18½ minutes from a subpoenaed tape, **NIXON'S ADMINISTRATION MAINTAINS THE STORYLINE.** A week after Woods was caught in her **NOW INFAMOUS "ROSE MARY STRETCH,"** Nixon's new chief of staff keeps the blame on Woods. He insinuates that Nixon's loyal secretary is simply confused about what happened when she answered the phone. "I've known women who think they've talked for five minutes and then have talked for an hour," he quips.

JUDGE SIRICA RECESSES HEARINGS UNTIL A PANEL OF AUDIO FORENSICS EXPERTS CAN EXAMINE THE TAPE AND DETERMINE WHAT TRULY CAUSED THE GAP in the crucially important conversation between Nixon and former Chief of Staff Haldeman.

EXHIBIT NO. 48

August 16, 1971

RETRIBUTION

MEMORANDUM

SUBJECT: Dealing with our Political Enemies

This memorandum addresses the matter of how we can maximize the fact of our incumbency in dealing with persons known to be active in their opposition to our Administration. Stated a bit more bluntly -- how we can use the available federal machinery to screw our political enemies.

After reviewing this matter with a number of persons possessed of expertise in the field, I have concluded that we do not need an elaborate mechanism or game plan, rather we need a good project coordinator and full support for the project. In brief, the system would work as follows:

-- Key members of the staff (e.g., Colson, Dent Flanigan, Buchanan) should be requested to inform us as to who they feel we should be giving a hard time.

-- The project coordinator should then determine what sorts of dealings these individuals have with the federal government and how we can best screw them (e.g., grant availability, federal contracts, litigation, prosecution, etc.).

-- The project coordinator then should have access to

NIXON IS ALSO IN TROUBLE WITH THE IRS, which asserts that the president **MAY OWE $235,000 IN BACK TAXES**. He also paid no local or state tax in either D.C. or California for several years. This charge of misconduct the public easily understands. Watergate is complicated and confusing. But a wealthy politician—even if a self-made man—cheating on his taxes? That revelation hits law-abiding Nixonites hard.

Once again, John Dean pulls back the curtain on the president's mindset. Called in to testify before the Congressional Joint Committee on Internal Revenue Taxation, **DEAN REVEALS A SECOND WHITE HOUSE ENEMIES LIST**. This one has more than 100 names. He also shares a 1971 memo with the header: "How we can **USE THE AVAILABLE FEDERAL MACHINERY TO SCREW OUR POLITICAL ENEMIES."**

(99)

DECEMBER 6: REPUBLICAN MINORITY LEADER GERALD FORD IS SWORN IN AS VICE PRESIDENT. FEMINISTS ARE PLEASED. Ford was the Republican who helped Democratic Congresswoman Martha Griffiths cajole enough bipartisan signatures on a discharge petition that **FINALLY WRANGLED THE ERA OUT OF COMMITTEE TO A SUCCESSFUL FLOOR VOTE**. Plus, his outgoing and candid **WIFE, BETTY, IS A TRUE AND VOCAL ADVOCATE FOR THE WOMEN'S MOVEMENT**.

A NEW V.P.

CHAPTER TWELVE

DECEMBER

"Whatcha reading, Pats?" asked Abe as put his lunch tray on the wide cafeteria table and sat down across from her. "Looks like it's got you pretty riled."

Patty glanced up. "How can you tell?"

"I know you. You're chewing on your lower lip. You never do that unless something's got you going." He nodded at the *New York Times* she had spread out in front of her. "So, what is it?"

"A profile of Jill Wine-Volner, the special prosecutor who questioned Rose Mary Woods."

"Savvy lady. That was one deadly cross-examination."

"I know! But look at this." Patty pointed to the headline, "A Lawyer in Miniskirts," running below a large, full-length photo of the prosecutor—smiling, swinging her briefcase, her unbuttoned raincoat revealing her fashionable mid-thigh skirt and black, high-heeled boots. "The woman just blew open the doors on Watergate, getting Nixon's secretary to demonstrate how ridiculous her claim is of *accidentally* erasing the tape. And the main thing the *New York Times* cares about is her skirt?"

Abe sat back, grinning. "Look who's become the feminist!"

Ignoring his teasing, Patty went on, "It doesn't stop with the headline and photograph. The text is unbelievably insulting. The reporter interviews Wine-Volner's husband and quotes him about three times more than her! *She's* the subject of the article."

"Well, journalists do like interviewing secondary sources to give background flavor—"

"But all his quotes do is . . . is denigrate her. I can't believe what the jerk said about his own wife! Sort of complimenting but putting her down at the same time." Patty's voice caught in the throat. She didn't know why exactly the article was upsetting her so much. Except, reading the husband's statements, they just sounded so . . . similar to things her father might say about her mother.

"Her husband is quoted saying he is 'amazed' by 'the variety of things' she can do 'all at once' and 'fairly well.'" Patty frowned and shook her head. "That she is 'quietly competent,' has 'a reasonably stable personality,' and is 'extremely level-headed up to a point.'"

Again, Patty looked up at Abe, her face hot with indignation. "*Reasonably* stable? Level-headed *up to a point*? Good grief. And the reporter quotes Wine-Volner only once! About her skirt length! Saying . . . oh, darn it, where is that? It's buried. Wait—here it is." Patty snapped the paper to straighten it up and read, "'*My hemline is irrelevant . . . The question is, Do I ask good questions?*'"

Angrily folding the paper up, Patty breathed, "Darn tootin' she asked good questions! I need to show this to Simone. She's going to blow a gasket."

Abe laughed again. "Who wrote this dreck?"

Patty hadn't checked the byline before, she was so incensed. Looking, she went even more ballistic. "Are you kidding me?" she exploded loudly enough that the table next to them all turned to stare. "It was a woman." How could a *woman* write such drivel about another woman?

Hmpf, Simone's voice sang into Patty's ear: *How can Phyllis Schlafly say all that merde about Gloria Steinem and my mom and scare—on purpose—housewives like your mother?*

Abe waited for Patty to ease down. "You know, Pats, doesn't matter what B.S. people write about her, Jill Wine-Volner did something that'll change history, I bet. Seriously. Because of those 'good questions' she asked, Judge Sirica ordered that the tape be examined for tampering. Word is, according to committee staffers, there could be as many as five separate erasures."

"Five?" Patty gasped.

"Yeah. That's no accident. Like someone listened to the conversation, said, 'Crap! That sounds bad,' erased the exchange, listened some more, backtracked, and erased something else incriminating. On and on for a total of eighteen and a half minutes." Abe sighed in exasperation and shook his head, adding, "How stupid do they think the American people are?"

A few months ago, Patty would have found a way to defend Nixon, or to explain away such unethical actions with some contextualizing excuse, like Art Buchwald's "Everyone does it." But the facts, piled up, one atop another, month after month, were just too damning. She stayed silent in tacit agreement. How stupid indeed.

Sometimes people just had to face uncomfortable, even awful truths. Sometimes people you believed in, believed to be filled with integrity and noble purpose, believed had other people's best interest at heart as their guiding principle—just didn't. Sometimes it was just all about them—*their* egos, *their* desires, *their* power. She'd certainly learned that in the hardest of ways.

Submerged in her own maelstrom of thoughts, she vaguely heard Abe say, "Fool me once, shame on you; fool me twice, shame on me. Right, Pats?"

She nodded absently.

But what about when the fooling was done so subtly, so incrementally, wrapped in seeming gallantry and compliments or inspiring promises? What felt at first like a soft morning mist drifting in, all cozy, bringing sweet smells and subdued birdsong, that slowly built up, billowing thicker a little at a time, into a totally enveloping fog. Even then still a caressing, protective cocoon—until something horrible, something irrevocable happened. Harder to find your way out then, after being fooled a hundred times.

But . . . it had to be done. No matter the cost. Like her decision about Scott. She'd held to it, even when he called her hall's phone, even when he showed up at her residence hall's reception desk. She'd refused to speak to him both times. He didn't bother to try again.

Patty's hands started trembling as her mind raced into a worry that had been gnawing at her: How would she explain her breakup with Scott when she went home for the holidays? Where everyone had anointed them as being perfect for each other, and Scott as the catch of the century. What would *he* say about *her*? She clasped her hands together to hide their quaking and made herself listen to Abe's words.

"I'm beginning to feel sorry for Rose Mary," Abe talked on. "I'm going to stop making fun of that ludicrous stretch of hers. Although I did a boffo impression of it. Even had my housemates, those macho FBI trainees, laughing at it the other night. Nixon's men are just throwing that poor woman in front of a moving train, counting on her loyalty to a man she's worked for for twenty-some years." He stopped and grinned mischievously. "Can you imagine putting up with Tricky Dick that long? She probably deserves a Purple Heart or hazard pay."

Then Abe sobered and regained his sympathy. "God knows she's going to have a tough time finding work after this—if she can at all." He paused. "I think I read that she's single, no children—I hope she has savings."

Patty stared at him, amazed.

Squirming, raising an eyebrow, Abe asked, "What?"

"You're a good guy, Abe," she answered quietly.

"Thanks!" He smiled ruefully. "Maybe someday being a good guy won't be the kiss of death with girls. You all do seem to prefer those Butch Cassidy and Sundance Kid bad boys."

"Oh, you must have had plenty of girlfriends back home, haven't you?"

"Not really." He paused. "And not the one I want," he murmured, barely a whisper.

But Patty heard and understood. And her reaction knocked the wind out of her.

She felt herself recoil, as if threatened. Over nothing. By one of her closest friends. What was wrong with her? Panicked in a hundred ways, including alarm at not being able to control this out-of-the-blue fear, her expression must have been as wild-eyed as a spooked horse, given the hurt on Abe's face. This boy who had been so good to her. But she couldn't help it. Knee-jerk revulsion and fright bubbled up like acid in her throat.

She hadn't told a soul what had happened with Scott. Couldn't. Couldn't think about it without the shakes. She'd been antsy in general in the weeks since. Instinctively shied away from men passing too close in the halls—but they were strangers. How could she be this unnerved by a friend?

"Sorry, Patty," Abe murmured. "I didn't mean to step over a line. I know you're with Scott."

Patty shook her head way too vehemently.

Abe frowned. "Paaats," he said her name slowly, a question in it. "Are you okay?" He leaned over to touch her arm and she shoved back in her chair, out of reach.

"I . . . we . . ." She stood, forced a smile. "You're going to have plenty of girlfriends, Abe. Lovely ones. Maybe"—she paused, telling herself to ease up, make light of it, for Abe's sake—"maybe just lose those sideburns so girls can really see that"—she might have said *handsome* before, and Abe was that, but Patty chose words that meant more to her now—"that open, honest, caring face of yours."

"Patty," he rose, too, again saying her name softly, like one might speak to a spooked horse about to bolt. He could tell something was seriously wrong. He was right, Abe did know her.

"I'm okay," she croaked. "I'll see you on the Senate floor. I need to run to the ladies' room." She fled. And barely made it to the toilet before vomiting.

A week later, a few days before the holiday recess, Patty was carrying a message through the Senate office building, dodging staffers loaded down with wrapping paper, cookie tins, and the makings of ginger ale punch for office parties. Despite Watergate, Nixon had still held the annual lighting of the National Christmas Tree and the Pageant of Peace—fifty-seven smaller trees circling it, one for each state plus the six territories and District of Columbia. The mood throughout Washington was undeniably festive and less frantic than it had been for months.

Relaxed chatter spilled out of the offices into the hallways, where people were strolling rather than dashing in the usual congressional hair-on-fire urgency. Patty got stuck behind a group of young secretaries, walking four abreast, chatting—typically an unspoken no-no of blocking traffic. She started to scoot around them until their gossip caught her ear.

"Well, girls, in the latest scuttlebutt, I hear investigators have discovered that a large amount of money may have been given to Rose Mary Woods from a campaign slush fund," announced a petite woman wearing very high heels but still reaching only the shoulders of her friends. Her stiletto pumps clacked percussively on the marble floor.

"What?" "Are you serious?" "For her legal expenses?" her three companions chorused.

"Maybe? She had to retain her own lawyer, remember? The White House counsel wouldn't go with her when she testified. Poor old bird. I mean, I don't agree with what she's accused of doing. But you know how we all do things sometimes out of loyalty to our bosses, figuring they know whether something's right or wrong—to keep our jobs."

Her companions nodded, compulsively looking over their shoulders as they did. One of them noticed Patty shadowing them and smiled in that unspoken sisterhood among congressional staffers.

Patty smiled back, flattered the woman thought her old enough to have a real job on the Hill.

"If the money wasn't for legal expenses—" began one.

"You mean Woods might have been—" said another.

"Bribed with hush money?" a third blurted.

"Maaay-be?" answered the high-heeled secretary, lowering her voice. "Think about all the cash that ended up in the Watergate burglars' bank account. But I don't know anything for sure."

"These guys need to get their you-know-what together," said the worker who'd smiled at Patty, "and stop being so darn stupid. I don't know about your office, but we've had to field so many calls from constituents worrying that the money they gave in good faith to re-elect the president ended up being used for some pretty unethical stuff. Now they doubt us, too."

"Yeah, my office as well," added the tallest in the quartet, her ponytail swinging as she turned to talk down their flank, accentuating the pique in her voice. "I had to waste oodles of time trying to track down how every penny of a check to CR(EE)P from one of our biggest donors was used. He's a lovely older gentleman, sounds like Gregory Peck's Atticus Finch when you talk to him. A man of the highest integrity, big supporter of my senator.

"He'd handed his whopper check to Nixon's personal lawyer. You know, the guy who testified that he'd put together half a million bucks from re-election donations to fund CR(EE)P's 'dirty tricks' campaign—that got delivered in laundry bags at secret drop-offs."

The petite secretary let out a scornful laugh. "They're all nothing but a bunch of Double-O-Seven wannabes." She lowered her voice. "But it's coming home to roost for a bunch of them now. One of the senator's friends was called in front of the Watergate grand jury—evidently the special prosecutor's looking way beyond the White House staff for possible indictments. Maybe as many as sixty people. Mostly about campaign money."

The group stopped abruptly in front of an office as one of the secretaries peeled off with "Well, the new year's sure to be interesting! See you ladies in 1974!"

Patty nearly bumped into the women she'd been eavesdropping on so intently. "Excuse me," she murmured as she slipped past them, ducking her head, feeling clammy and flushed with sudden anxiety.

She hadn't thought about her father's political acquaintance, Herbert Kalmbach, for weeks. Caught up in her horror that her father must be having an affair—of course, she was no longer sure if her suspicions were correct, given Scott's questioning her thinking before . . . before . . . Patty felt a wave of nausea as an image of Scott's face—too expectant, too close—rose up in her mind. She stopped and put her hand on the wall to steady herself. Closed her eyes, tried to breathe.

For God's sake, don't faint in the halls of Congress, she could hear her father's gruff voice. *Calm down.*

But her mind whirled on.

Maybe she'd misinterpreted her father's mysterious meetings in Washington during the summer. Maybe it wasn't an affair but . . . but what?

She quick-replayed her father's working the room at Duke Zeibert's restaurant in July. His lingering at a table of lawyers in serious conference. His curt, belligerent pronouncement to her as they ate: "Sometimes you have to get your hands dirty to make sure the right guy wins, Patricia." His annoyance with her asking his opinion about the break-ins, both at the Democratic National Committee and the office of Daniel Ellsberg's psychiatrist. "Is this what I get—a daughter who questions the president's understanding of national security? Watch yourself. Nobody likes a nosy woman." Then his brushing her off entirely in September, abruptly changing the subject to Scott when Patty had described what she'd witnessed at the Senate hearings.

Deflection. Sanctimonious, indignant, guilt-inducing, counter-accusation. Just like Nixon and his men did whenever they were asked about Watergate.

"Oh my God," Patty murmured. "Oh my God." As many as sixty people. Beyond the White House inner circles. Being questioned about campaign money. Could that be what her father's mysterious meetings had been about? "Oh my God."

Her wave of nausea turned into a tsunami. Patty raced to the ladies room.

And there, kneeling on the cool floor, her head in the toilet—yet again—another horrifying possibility came to her.

She never threw up like this. Not this much over being upset. Patty remembered one of the club's newlyweds rushing off the tennis court to vomit in a trash can, saying it was the heat, but a week later announcing she was pregnant.

Oh no. Please no. She began counting the days in the month.

Patty struggled to her feet. Found a pay phone. Called the one person she knew she could trust with this—if it were true. "Simone," she whispered, her voice shaking. "I'm in trouble. Can you come get me?"

Shivering as the December sun set early, bringing that bone-chilling cold of winter darkness, Patty waited where she'd told Simone she could probably find a parking space, or at least pull over safely: in front of the Folger Library. She sat on the same stone bench where she'd tried to comfort Will in the spring when he learned of his brother's death in Vietnam. Beneath the enormous, carved-stone Greek mask of tragedy.

And just as Will had that terrible morning, Patty gazed at the nine stone-relief Shakespeare scenes along the building's creamy wall. Will had been transfixed by the assassination of Julius Caesar. Her gaze drifted from Titania, nestled up to an ass-headed man, to Queen Gertrude, hovered over by her duplicitous brother-in-law-now-husband, to the three witches luring Macbeth, to a graceful Juliet leaning into her Romeo for an almost kiss as her bumbling but doting nurse looked on. A foolish romantic; a myopic, weak mother; three dangerous hags; an idealized ingenue; and a comedic, middle-aged idiot to be laughed at—classical literature's five faces of womanhood.

She closed her eyes. *Don't be that way.* That cynical—at eighteen years old.

But, oh, Patty had seen so much—so much that had shaken her beliefs to their core since she'd sat on that bench with Will in what felt like years ago now. She'd tried then to reassure him—when he'd shaken his fist at the heavens, blaming himself for somehow suggesting to God that He take his older brother if that one-for-one exchange of life was necessary to let Jimmy survive. She'd reassured Will that God surely didn't think that way. Even managed a semi-joke about what one of the nuns at her old school would say, that she'd chide Patty for being woefully prideful if she thought she could bargain with or tell God what to do.

Will had actually laughed a little, a brief relief to his tears.

But Patty could find no comfort for herself now. If what she feared was true, God must be punishing her for her sins. Nice girls didn't find themselves in this kind of trouble. Nice girls never went beyond first base. Nice girls didn't let a boy feel them up. If they did, they got what they deserved—that's what the nuns and everyone else she knew said.

If he were sitting here again, what would Will think? Would he think she was a slut?

Covering her face with her mittened hands, Patty remembered how harshly she'd judged Simone in June—even as she'd held Simone tight to help her survive LSD-induced hallucinations—that Simone's rebel attitude and hippie clothes invited people to assume she'd be fine with someone dropping acid into her soda. People could judge Patty the same way—think she'd encouraged Scott, acting like what Norman Mailer called Marilyn Monroe—a vulnerable "child-woman" with "a smile that promised 'take me.'" *Oh God.* Patty could hear the accusatory questions: What were you doing in his dorm room in the first place? You turned to him for comfort, what did you expect from a full-blooded American boy?

Don't be a tease, he'd said, right before . . . right before—

"There you are!"

Patty took her hands away from her tear-stained face.

"Oh my God, you look terrible!" Simone sat down beside Patty. "What happened?"

No longer alone in the darkening night, Patty fell apart. She began sobbing incoherently.

Simone let her cry. "It's going to be okay." She hugged Patty. "Whatever it is."

"But it's not. It's not going to be okay." Finally, through coughs and gasps and half sobs, Patty told, ending with "I shouldn't have . . . I shouldn't have gone to . . ."

"Jeeeee-suz," Simone breathed. "Patty, *you* did nothing wrong."

"I let him kiss me. I let him touch me. I . . ."

"It's not your fault. Listen to me." Simone shook her a little, gently. "Feminists are starting to use a term called 'date rape.' That's what happened to you. You were with someone you trusted. He took advantage when—"

"But they say rape"—oh, God the word itself was so horrible—"they say it can't happen in a marriage. That once a woman marries, she's in essence consented. And when you're dating seriously—"

"Bull hockey!" Simone exploded. "Women *always* have the right to say no." Then: "What are you looking at?" she carped at two Hill-types who'd stopped to stare at her when she shouted.

Patty buried her face in Simone's shoulder to hide herself.

"Come on, let me get you home. Where we can really talk about all this without bystanders."

Nodding, Patty let Simone pull her to her feet. And then—without warning—she vomited again, right at the toes of Simone's purple suede boots.

"Whoa!" Simone jumped back.

"Oh, God, I'm so sorry."

Cocking her head, Simone put her hand to Patty's forehead. "No fever. Do you feel . . . oh . . . ooooooh." She took Patty by her shoulders to look her squarely in the eye, sympathy all over her freckled face. "Are you—?"

"Maybe?" Patty groaned.

"Are you late?"

"Yes."

"Is your period ever irregular?"

"Sometimes."

"*Merde*," breathed Simone as she took Patty's hand. "Okay. Okay. Okay." She thought a moment. "Let's get home. Mom will know what—"

"No! No-no-no-no." Patty stumbled backward. She couldn't tell Aunt Marjorie. Not about this. She tried to jerk her hand free. "Let go." She'd run away. Where no one knew her. "Let go of me!"

Simone held fast. "No way, Patty." She grabbed her other hand, too. "Remember how you held on to me when I thought monsters or secret agents or zombies or whatever the hell the LSD was telling me had followed me into your room?"

Slowly, Patty nodded.

"So . . . I'm not letting go either." Gently but firmly, she led Patty to her VW, talking, reassuring. "Mom's not like that. She never yelled at me about that night. Just got me to the doctor and talked to me about how to protect myself in the future." She opened the car door. "You had my back, Patty. I've got yours. Please get in. It's going to be okay."

Soothed, somewhat, Patty did.

As Simone slid into the driver's seat and turned over the ignition, her fury flared. "Son-of-a-bastard! I've never even met this guy, and I want to run him over with the car for you." She pulled out, whipped the car around in a sharp U-turn, and hurtled along Constitution Avenue. "Bastard!"

Patty covered her mouth. "Maybe drive a little slower, please."

"Sorry!" Simone decelerated and drove more carefully, though still muttering oaths. "I wish you had called me that night, Patty. I'm so sorry you've been dealing with all this alone. I know we haven't always agreed on things. But this"—she shifted into a lower gear as she rounded the Lincoln Memorial, then reached over to briefly squeeze Patty's hand—"this is what friends are for.

I don't know how you feel about my opinionated self, but you're definitely a friend of mine. Maybe even my closest, given everything we've been through together now." She tried a little joke: "Bar fights, elephant hallucinations, bad clothing choices, sex critiques." She gave her characteristic shrug. "Just saying."

Tears fell down Patty's face again—this time, though, tears of relief, and of *belonging*. "Who'd have thought?" she murmured, smiling at Simone. "Our own little bipartisan caucus."

"Ha! I get to be our Gloria Steinem then."

As they crossed Memorial Bridge like they had so many times over the previous twelve months, the eternal flame flickered into view once more.

"Patty," Simone began cautiously, "I'm really sorry to spring this on you now, given . . . you know . . . But before we get to Alexandria, you better be prepared. Your mother showed up just as I was leaving. Driving your station wagon, filled with suitcases and easels."

Patty clung to Simone's hand as they entered the chintz-bright sitting room looking for their mothers—terrified of what she'd find and what she had to tell. But what Patty saw waiting for her was not what she anticipated. Not at all. She'd expected her mother to be collapsed on the sofa or in Aunt Marjorie's arms, muddled or vacant, completely lost.

Instead, her mother stood gazing at the lush, prize-winning garden scene she'd painted long before, cradling her cat Cassatt in her arms. Her face was ashen and tear-streaked, her mascara smeared, her hair unsprayed, unteased, and yanked back with a scarf—but she was clear-eyed. Present. Tall. Aunt Marjorie was beside her, arm around her waist, saying, "Look, Dottie. Look what you can do."

"Mother?"

The women turned as one, still linked, and Patty heard her godmother whisper, "And look, Dottie, look at your daughter. You did that, too. Brought an exquisite young woman into the world."

Then Aunt Marjorie stepped back. Probably expecting Patty's mother to embrace Patty. But she only managed a small smile and, "Patricia. I have something to tell you."

Simone squeezed her hand, a silent *tell her*.

"Not yet," Patty whispered.

Crossing the small room to the love seat, her mother put Cassatt down and patted the flowered cushions. "Come, sit by me."

Aunt Marjorie motioned for Simone to take one of the armchairs by the fireplace as she lowered herself into the other one. Once the four were nested in that conversational circle, Patty's mother spoke, her voice shaky but coherent.

It had been a long time since she'd heard her mother speak that lucidly, that matter-of-factly, and at such length. Which made Patty realize just how often her father had interrupted Dot Appleton or ignored her or simply bullied her. Enough to cause her mother to question herself so much that her thoughts came out truncated, wary and defensive, her words carefully stripped of revealing emotions or the opposite, riddled with angst. All of which Patty had before interpreted—condemned—as haughty and distant, cold, maybe even a little nuts. Justification for the walls she'd put up against her mother. The revelation made Patty's soul ache, like a gate was creaking open in her heart.

"Your father has gotten himself into some serious trouble with the Watergate investigation," her mother began, putting her hand atop Patty's. It was trembling, but her grasp of Patty's was steadfast. "He himself didn't wittingly do anything wrong with the campaign contributions that he handled during the president's re-election. Your father learned of the misuse of the money after the fact. But you know how your father is—whatever it takes for his candidate of choice to win. He didn't think what happened was all that bad—in terms of 'intelligence gathering' on opponents. Everyone does it, he kept saying. What about LBJ, what about Chappaquiddick, you know, those kinds of party-line deflections.

"So, when the FBI first questioned your father—as they did many finance chairs across the nation—he evidently evaded their questions or gave vague answers or turned their questions around on them, misleading the agents. As you know, your father is quite good at redirecting conversation to the way he wishes it to go." She paused. "Blue smoke and mirrors. Like a magician. You know, making you think you're seeing things that aren't there. Making you second-guess everything, especially yourself."

"Like that 1940s movie *Gaslight*," muttered Aunt Marjorie. "Making that poor wife think she was delusional. Damn him." She held her hand up in apology for interrupting. "Sorry. I've just been . . . so angry for you, Dottie. For a long time now."

"No, it's all right," Patty's mother murmured. "I need to see things for what they are." She nodded to herself before continuing. "Your father assumed Watergate would simply go away, dismissed in the public's mind as the 'third-rate burglary' and politics as usual that Nixon's people kept portraying it to be. *What Americans didn't know wouldn't hurt them*, he said."

Patty blanched at hearing the exact same phrase Scott had used when suggesting Patty keep secret her father's possible affair from her mother. They really were frighteningly similar, those two. She could see that now. It made her skin crawl a little that she'd found that attractive in Scott.

Her mother continued, "But your father hadn't counted on the Senate Committee staffers or the special prosecutors being as smart or as persistent as they are. Or other campaign workers being forthcoming. Comparing witness statements, the investigators began to doubt your father's and called him in front of the grand jury. Under oath, he took the Fifth. Stonewalling more than anything. He's now facing a misdemeanor charge as pressure to get him to tell what he knows, to confirm information the investigators have from others.

"I told your father that ours was an honest house. That he needed to come clean." She paused and drew in a long, rattling breath. "Your father laughed at me. Said, '*Your* house?' It was his house. He had paid for it. He owned it. And how dare I question him or tell him what to do. That I was merely an ornament in *his* house and . . . and . . . no longer an attractive one either . . ." She stopped. Looked away out the window, haloed in embarrassment.

Patty felt herself reel—mostly with astonishment at the fact that none of this surprised her. It fit. She stared at her mother's profile—still elegant, still beautiful, even in anguish. Her mother deserved to know what else Patty suspected her father of. The total, uncomfortable, awful truth. So that her mother had all the facts before deciding what she should do next.

Patty blurted out what she had witnessed—the jewelry, the phone call, the hint of perfume on her father's coat, the car driver who picked him up.

"A blonde?"

Patty's mouth dropped open. "Yes. You knew?"

"I suspected. I noticed blond hair on his sweater when I took it to the cleaners. She . . . I doubt she was the first." Patty's mother paused. "I recently read about a California study of male psychiatrists. Fifty-one percent admitted to having sexual intercourse with a female patient. Eighty percent of them said they'd done so with multiple patients—some claiming it was therapeutic for them. 'Casanovas of the Couch,' the study dubbed them." She trailed off, sighing.

Revulsion burbled up in Patty, as bitter as her vomit. Her father wouldn't do something like that. Would he? Those women were exploited when they were most vulnerable, just like . . . like . . . Patty shook her head to make herself focus on what her mother was saying.

"Anyway . . . The D.C. woman's existence came out during our argument. He threw her at me as comparison. Proof that I wasn't as supportive of him as I should be. Told me he'd met and been romancing a 'very pretty young thing' who worked at the U.S. District Court, where Judge Sirica presides. Trying to pick up information, he claimed, to protect *us*. Then he stormed out.

"That was right after Thanksgiving, the day you'd left for D.C." She paused. "I didn't see or hear from your father until two days ago when he returned home. Didn't explain where he had been. Said he"—Patty's mother paused with a surprising smile of wry amusement before adding—"forgave *me*—as long as I pulled myself together."

She glanced over at Aunt Marjorie, who rolled her eyes and shook her head.

Taking another deep breath, Dot Appleton went on. "In his absence, I stopped taking the new tranquilizer he'd been shoving at me. Coming off that has not been pleasant." She pulled her hand away from Patty's to clasp hers together to steady them. "But it allowed me to think clearly, for the first time in a long time. I . . . I don't like who I've become with him. As a person, or . . ." She managed another small smile at Patty—this one so sincere, so direct, so much of an unspoken apology that it made Patty tear up. "Or as a mother. So I left. And here I am."

Patty struggled to swim through the flood of information that washed away everything her life had been.

What came next to replace it?

"Sooooo," Aunt Marjorie filled the silence. "Patty, honey, you and your mama are going to stay with us for a while. Which will make this Christmas really special. Alexandria has just announced plans to turn the old, deserted torpedo factory down by the river into an art center, with studios and galleries. Dottie and I were discussing this as you came in. I'm going to tell my friends on the city council about what a phenomenal organizer your mama is. And artist. They'll be thrilled to snap her up, I'm sure, to charm some DAR types into getting involved and making some wondrously large contributions. Then, Dottie, you can decide what you might like to do with *all* your talents. Betty Friedan says, 'Who knows what women can be when they are finally free to be themselves.'"

Patty shot a nervous look at her mother, worrying she might react badly to Aunt Marjorie mentioning Betty Friedan, given how upset she'd been by the *Feminine Mystique*.

But all she said was "Thank you, Marj. You've . . . you've always been there for me."

"When you've let me," Patty's godmother answered, looking like she might cry herself. "All right then." She stood. "I need to feed everyone. No one can think straight on an empty stomach. Simone, come help me, please."

Simone didn't budge, looking to Patty, her expression asking if Patty wanted her to stay, as a shield. Then raising her eyebrows in an unspoken *tell her*.

"Come along, sugar." Aunt Marjorie wiggled her fingers at Simone, like mothers do at lollygagging children on a playground. "Let's leave them alone. They have a lot to discuss."

"It's okay," Patty said, nodding at Simone.

Aunt Marjorie closed the kitchen door behind them as they exited.

Awkwardly—they'd never been a cuddling mother and daughter, not like Aunt Marjorie and Simone—Patty hugged her mother.

After a moment, Dot Appleton softened, and put her arm over Patty's shoulders to pull her in close. "I'm sorry. This is going to undo so much. This isn't what you deserve, darling. Especially not now. We should be planning for your college. Not worrying about . . . divorce lawyers . . . Oh God." She swallowed loud enough that Patty did so as well in chain reaction. "Please don't let Phyllis be right about women being left high and dry." She trailed off.

Darling. Patty hadn't heard her mother call her that since she was little. A dance of childhood memories, like those her mother had sketched—happy, playtime ones—suddenly waltzed through her mind.

Then: *College.* Oh no, what about college?

After that horrific night with Scott, Patty had started wondering about maybe going to law school, like Jill Wine-Volner. Like "Battling Bella" Abzug. She'd made herself reread that *Ladies' Home Journal* article about rape victims. It made clear that women needed advocates—people who knew the law and how to argue it, how to change it. Just like Aunt Marjorie had said about what getting more women elected to state legislatures and Congress could do. And hadn't that policeman said Patty had made a good case when she'd convinced him to not arrest Julius and Abe, Will, and Jimmy after that terrible bar fight at Mr. Henry's? That he thought she could have a career in law someday?

It had been just a glimmer of an idea. But one that had lifted her battered heart when she really needed hope in her future. Would Patty have to give that up before she'd really had a chance to think it through? Now that her father's financing of their day-to-day lives might stop. Now when he might be in trouble himself. Now that she maybe was . . . was . . .

Another wave of nausea rolled over Patty. She bit it back. "Mom?"

Her mother pulled back just a little to look Patty in the eyes, just as surprised by Patty's using *Mom* instead of *Mother* as Patty had been at being called *darling.*

"There's something I need to tell you." Patty stood, paced, finally stopping by the fireplace, hesitated. But bolstered by how all the hard-to-face revelations within that cozy room had been accepted with love, with friendship, with empathy, Patty managed to tell the horrors of that night in the dorm and what she now feared. Without breaking down. "I'm sorry," she whispered.

Her mother shot to her feet. "Oh no. No, no." She moved toward Patty.

Patty backed away. No? What did *No* mean?

"No. No, no, no. *You* should not be sorry." Patty's mother caught her up into a tight embrace.

The two of them stayed like that a long time in front of Dot Appleton's long-ago painting of an overflowing garden with its flower-bedecked open gate, Patty feeling her mother's heartbeat against hers, her mother straightening her spine, pulling them both a little taller, balanced together.

"*R-E-S-P-E-C-T. Find out what it means to me . . .*" Aretha Franklin suddenly belted through the house. "*Sock it to me . . .*"

"What in the world is that?" Patty's mother whispered.

A Simone-worthy blunt—but affectionate—*ha!* popped out of Patty. "Just Simone and her music. She's anything but subtle."

"Let's sit down." Her mother closed the door leading to the hallway as Aretha sang on, *"You're runnin' out of foolin' and I ain't lyin'"*—muffling the music a little, so they could hear each other. She led them back to the love seat and they sank down into it, leaning against one another.

"I'm scared, Mom."

"I know." She brushed Patty's hair off her forehead and kissed it. "I know." She clasped their hands together again and thought a moment. "Seems we both have choices to make. We'll take yours on together. Tell me what you are feeling and thinking. And we'll go from there."

THE WHITE HOUSE

WASHINGTON

August 9, 1974

Dear Mr. Secretary:

I hereby resign the Office of President of the United States.

Sincerely,

Richard Nixon

The Honorable Henry A. Kissinger
The Secretary of State
Washington, D.C. 20520

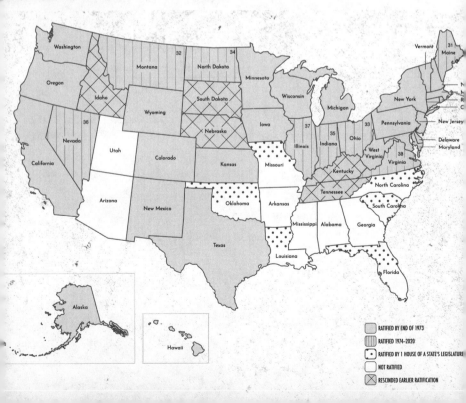

EPILOGUE

1974 AND BEYOND

WATERGATE

January: The panel of forensic experts appointed by Judge Sirica determines the 18½-minute gap in the June 20, 1972, tape recording of Nixon and Haldeman consists of five, and possibly nine, separate erasures. The gaps were created by hand—suggesting someone methodically listened-erased, listened-erased. No accident.

Calls for Nixon to resign skyrocket. The House Judiciary Committee holds serious conversations about impeaching Nixon as he continues to deny knowledge of how the erasures occurred and resists the special prosecutor's demand for additional tapes and evidence.

In his State of the Union address, Nixon reverts to his alarmist rhetoric: "Five years ago, our cities were burning and besieged; our college campuses were a battleground; crime was increasing at a rate that struck fear across the nation."

At the end of his prepared statement, Nixon closes the manila folder containing his remarks and waits for the applause to subside, then says, "I would like to add a personal word with regard to an issue that has been of great concern to all Americans over the past year. I refer, of course, to the investigations of the so-called Watergate affair . . . The time has come to bring that investigation . . . to an end. One year of Watergate is enough.

". . . I was elected for the purpose of doing a job and doing it as well as I possibly can. And I want you to know that I have no intention whatever of ever walking away from the job."

The year will prove him wrong.

March: A grand jury indicts seven members of Nixon's former staff for Watergate-related crimes and names Nixon an "unindicted co-conspirator."

April: The special Watergate prosecutors subpoena 64 additional tapes. Nixon ignores the subpoena and instead provides edited transcripts that shock the public with the vindictive tone, foul language, and misogynistic, anti-Semitic, and racist comments repeatedly made by Nixon and his aides, even with much of it marked through. *Expletive deleted* becomes a new catchphrase.

May: The House Judiciary Committee begins impeachment hearings.

July: The Supreme Court unanimously rules that Nixon must surrender the tapes, denying his claim of executive privilege.

The House Judiciary Committee adopts three articles of impeachment against Nixon with a bipartisan vote, for (1) obstruction of justice, (2) misuse of power and violating his oath of office, and (3) refusing to comply with congressional subpoenas.

August: Nixon releases transcripts of conversation between himself and Haldeman on June 23, 1972—which become known as "the smoking gun," proving his knowledge of the cover-up. In it, he and Haldeman agree to tell FBI Director Patrick Gray to stop the FBI's investigation of the Watergate burglary, claiming national security concerns. Seeing these transcripts, Republicans on the House Judiciary Committee who had voted against impeachment the previous month announce they will change their vote to yes.

Arch-conservative GOP Senator Barry Goldwater, a longtime friend and supporter of Nixon, says, "There are only so many lies you can take."

Putting country over party, Goldwater goes to the White House to tell Nixon he must resign for the good of the nation, that he no longer has enough Republican votes to survive impeachment.

August 8, 1974: Nixon resigns. He leaves the White House the next morning on Air Force One helicopter, still giving his iconic V-for-victory wave.

Gerald Ford becomes president, saying it is time to heal "the internal wounds of Watergate, more powerful and poisonous than foreign wars."

In the end, 69 people are indicted and 48 convicted in the Watergate scandal, the charges ranging from contempt of court to perjury to illegal campaigning to obstruction of justice; their jail times vary from one month to four-and-a-half years in federal prison.

Ford pardons Nixon.

THE ERA

January: After months of new ERA state ratifications being stalled by the STOP ERA movement, Maine and Montana pass the amendment in January.

February: Ohio ratifies, bringing the number of states adopting the amendment to 33. Only five more states are needed for the ERA to be added to the U.S. Constitution. But there are no more ratifications during 1974.

In 1975, North Dakota ratifies. In 1977, Indiana.

Phyllis Schlafly's STOP ERA campaign keeps rolling, combining forces with other conservative groups like the anti-abortion Pro-Family Forum started by Texan Lottie Beth Hobbs. Their coalition grows into the Moral Majority, which sweeps conservative Republican Ronald Reagan into the presidency in 1980. Schlafly doesn't stop lobbying states to block the ERA until its time limit runs out in 1982, just three states short of the 38 needed to add it to the Constitution.

Many of Schlafly's dire claims of what the ERA would cause if passed—more and more women "forced to work" for economic reasons, exhausted by trying to juggle their roles as mothers and wives with full-time jobs, many choosing to not have children because of financial pressures and lack of childcare support—have come about anyway. However, they happened without the protections that would have been guaranteed by the ERA of equal pay and opportunity, and the right to make personal reproductive-health choices.

Witness the data found in the 2020 census: American women still made less than men in the exact same jobs. White women: 83 cents to a man's dollar. Black: 64 cents to the same dollar. Latina: 57 cents. The median annual salary for American men was $61,420; for women, $50,980. A woman would have to work 40 extra days to earn a man's wage in the same job.

According to the Columbia Law School Center for Gender & Sexuality Law, the ERA's explicit guaranteed equity regardless of sex/gender would also protect a woman's reproductive rights and access to abortion.

In Justice Ruth Bader Ginsburg's dissenting opinion on *Gonzales v. Carhart* (2007), she wrote that a stereotyped, gendered notion of citizenship in which women were "regarded as the center of home and family life, with attendant special responsibilities that precluded full and independent legal status under the Constitution" denied equal citizenship.

"Those views are no longer consistent with our understanding of the family, the individual, or the Constitution," wrote Ginsburg, adding that full and equal citizenship in the workplace and in public life "is intimately connected to a person's ability to control their reproductive lives."

Since the ERA's deadline passed, three additional states have ratified it: Nevada in 2017, Illinois in 2018, and Virginia in 2020—bringing the total number of ratifying states to the required 38. For the amendment to become part of the Constitution, however, Congress would need to re-extend its deadline. (The ERA is one of the few amendments to have been subjected to a finite ratification timeline.) So far, despite several recent proposed resolutions, congressional Republicans—once staunch ERA advocates—have blocked debate to consider a floor vote to re-extend the deadline and pronounce the ERA as accepted law.

AUTHOR'S NOTE

> "WATERGATE SHOWS THAT THE SYSTEM DID WORK. PARTICULARLY THE JUDICIARY AND THE CONGRESS AND ULTIMATELY AN INDEPENDENT PROSECUTOR WORKING IN THE EXECUTIVE BRANCH."
> —BOB WOODWARD

> "THE PRESS DID ITS JOB."
> —CARL BERNSTEIN

> "THE POLITICAL LESSON OF WATERGATE: NEVER AGAIN MUST AMERICANS ALLOW AN ARROGANT, ELITE GUARD OF POLITICAL ADOLESCENTS TO DICTATE THE TERMS OF A NATIONAL ELECTION."
> —PRESIDENT GERALD FORD

> "DURING WATERGATE, [THE CONSTITUTION] WAS INTERPRETED AGAIN SO AS TO REAFFIRM THAT NO ONE—ABSOLUTELY NO ONE—IS ABOVE THE LAW."
> —WATERGATE SPECIAL PROSECUTOR LEON JAWORSKI

> "ANY WOMAN WHO CHOOSES TO BEHAVE LIKE A FULL HUMAN BEING SHOULD BE WARNED THAT THE ARMIES OF THE STATUS QUO WILL TREAT HER AS SOMETHING OF A DIRTY JOKE. THAT'S THEIR NATURAL AND FIRST WEAPON. SHE WILL NEED HER SISTERHOOD.
> . . . AND THOSE OF US TAUGHT THE CHEERFUL AMERICAN NOTION THAT PROGRESS IS LINEAR . . . HAVE HAD TO LEARN THAT NO WORTHWHILE BATTLE CAN BE FOUGHT AND WON ONLY ONCE."
> —FEMINIST GLORIA STEINEM

It's hard to adequately convey how riveted Americans were by Watergate—the piece-by-piece unearthing of the Nixon administration's political dirty tricks and exploitation of presidential authority. How in 1973 we hung on every broadcast, every hearing, every newspaper report.

How ripped apart we'd been by Vietnam, the distrust and "generation gap" it wrought that split families, how callous we were to our returning veterans. How the nation, especially our youth, still reeled from the horrific assassinations of Martin Luther King Jr. and Bobby Kennedy, both in 1968, just five years earlier.

How threatening a woman in a miniskirt—having a choice, having an opinion, and wanting a career—seemed to be.

And how telling the truth—or demanding it—could somehow be divisive.

The year 1973 was all that. A wild maelstrom that technically didn't end until August 9, 1974, when Nixon resigned the office whose power he had abused, and Gerald Ford, his calming replacement, announced, "Our long national nightmare is over."

And yet, here we are, fifty years later, in similar storms.

You've heard the adages about history: That it rhymes. That those who cannot remember the past are condemned to repeat it. They swirled in my mind as I wrote this docudrama novel. Those and Gloria Steinem's statement "The truth will set you free—but first it will piss you off."

That's for sure.

In the history of 1973 and its tipping points lies an irony, both inspiring and unnerving: Truth finally prevailed during Watergate. Eventually, the nation *listened* to facts, put country and ethics over party or individual ambitions, and saved itself from people bent on retaining power by any means—coercive, illegal, subversive of our democratic election process. During the very same months, however, hyperbole, fearmongering propaganda, and flat-out lies took hold about the Equal Rights Amendment, that somehow guaranteeing equal rights to women would destroy the American family.

This novel was the idea of the insightful, brave editor Elise Howard. When she first suggested I follow my previous "political history" novels—*Suspect Red* on McCarthyism and *WALLS* on Cold War Berlin—with a look at Watergate, I was immediately interested. I'd been a young teen growing up just outside D.C. during Watergate. As a high school freshman I had, like the character Simone, marched with my piccolo in the massed band for Nixon's frigid inaugural parade. And, like many journalists of my vintage, I'd been glued to the Senate hearings and ended up deciding my life's calling—choosing between music and writing—because of my admiration for Bob Woodward and Carl Bernstein's unyielding pursuit of truth, vividly showing how critical to democracy a free *and responsible* press corps is.

During Watergate and the simultaneous debates around the ERA, political revelations often inspired personal epiphanies.

Although I did not become an investigative daily beat reporter, I was a staffed magazine writer for two decades, focusing primarily on "women's issues" and what in the 1980s and '90s were almost taboo topics—things like domestic violence, sexual assault, mental health. These reporting experiences informed and enriched—I hope with empathy and substance—my portrayal of Patty and her mother and the challenges they faced given the constricting societal attitudes about women that held firm throughout the 1970s despite feminist protests.

Even though I had lived through (as a teenager) the decade's sexism and far-too-slow-to-fade objectification and marginalization of women, I was still shocked by just how debasing and overt the jokes, overtures, and assessments were when re-hearing them during my research's deep-dive into 1970s pop culture. Tragically, as recent #MeToo revelations prove, there are still miles and miles to go to expunge the attitudes that allow, even feed, violence against women. I hope this narrative provides a drop of revelation into that stream of change.

I admit to hesitating at first to take on this novel. I'd explored the impact of "tribalism," inflammatory rhetoric and hate labels, disinformation, and lies on teens in *Suspect Red* and *WALLS* by creating "everyman" characters on opposite ends of the political spectrum coming to understand and respect one another. McCarthyism and the raising of the Berlin Wall both offered intrigue and espionage that could legitimately sweep fictional teens into some suspenseful plot action. With Watergate, it was hard for me to see at first how to do that without stepping on the toes of the real-life families of Watergate's players, almost all well known to history.

But then I remembered Capitol pages—the Hill's messengers, firsthand witnesses to all that happened in Congress. Perhaps fictional congressional pages could be my way in.

As I was figuring that out, a beautifully acted and disturbing bio-pic series aired, *Mrs. America*—about Phyllis Schlafly and her STOP ERA crusade of homemakers who rose up against the feminist movement and the ERA's momentum. Seeing it, Elise and I realized that 1973 was *also* the year that the ERA was working its way toward ratification, state by state, and meeting unexpected opposition from frightened *women*.

It became clear this novel should be layered with both ground-shifting, nation-defining moments and the questions about us as a people they raised.

Again, the congressional pages offered an authentic, plausible springboard. In mid-1971, three progressive-minded senators sponsored three teenage girls as pages, breaking two centuries of boys-only tradition. In 1973 there were still only a handful of female pages, and none were in the House until that May. They were—whether they had planned to be or not—symbols for women's liberation.

Several 1970s pages, male and female, were kind enough to talk to me, as did the gracious and truly inspiring Jill Ruckelshaus—a speechwriter, cofounder of the National Women's Political Caucus (NWPC), ERA activist, White House liaison for women's issues, and wife of a deeply honorable man in the Nixon administration. Her life blessed me with a linchpin character who genuinely connected Watergate with the women's movement.

Please know, however, that my fictional characters are just that—amalgamations of my reading, interviewing, and imagination, fashioned to be archetypes found in Washington during 1973. (On the other hand, the hearings and court testimonies, televised talk shows, news reports, and Senate floor debates included in chapter scenes and photo essays are quoted directly.)

I am not an expert on Watergate, Second Wave Feminism, or the fight for the Equal Rights Amendment—just a reporter of barebone factual details and the political/cultural milieu that would prod and buffet an idealistic, trusting, eager-to-please, traditional "nice girl" like Patty. There are many books, memoirs, documentaries, and historical docudramas that explore those topics in compelling and comprehensive depth. Please see my Selected Sources for suggestions.

I will, however, expand a little on a few people mentioned in the narrative:

THE CAPITOL HILL PAGES: In the 1939 classic film *Mr. Smith Goes to Washington*, an earnest young page in knickerbockers explains the lay of the land to the main character and frequently saves him from embarrassment—a wonderful encapsulation of pages' earned wisdom and the aid they've given our elected representatives for 200-plus years. Ever since Congress has met, it has had young people serving as runners. During the 1800s, the boys were usually around twelve years old, often local orphans or sons of widowed mothers. Their congressional income helped their families and provided them schooling they might have had to forgo otherwise. They sharpened quills, filled snuffboxes, and chased bats out of the congressional chambers.

In the 1900s, pages became high schoolers recruited from all over the country for a prestigious front-row seat to history. Their ranks have included Microsoft founder and philanthropist Bill Gates, newscaster Cokie Roberts, former Facebook CEO Sheryl Sandberg, and political speechwriters and staffers, with a good number becoming members of Congress themselves.

Patty's day-to-day duties and experiences—answering those snapping fingers; delivering correspondence and legislative memos; her, Abe, and Will's schooling, the fact many pages in her day stayed in boardinghouses; the stipulation that female pages not walk city streets after dark without escort—are all factual details culled from interviews, articles, and yearbooks thoughtfully shared by 1970s pages.

Congressional pages were also included in many of the solemn ceremonies of governing—carrying, for instance, the leather-bound electoral boxes to be opened for the official count and certification of presidential elections.

The House page program was discontinued in 2011. The Senate program continues.

One of the greatest pleasures in writing this book was interviewing **JILL RUCKELSHAUS**. She was incredibly generous with her time, in sharing her vast wisdom hard-won from fifty-plus years advocating for women's equality and reproductive rights, and in her enduring hope in the power of women uniting for common good. As a devoted leader of the NWPC and its bipartisan quest to groom women to run for office at all levels, Ruckelshaus has long and eloquently urged what feminists have now learned the hard way post-Dobbs: Tweets, impassioned Oscar speeches, and cultural representation are great, but they do not have the same power as legislative seats and votes.

In a 1972 article about the surprising and influential presence of female delegates at the Republican convention nominating Nixon for re-election, *Time* magazine described Ruckelshaus as a "soft-spoken" woman, the "Republicans' answer to Gloria Steinem." One gets the sense that such comments on her bearing and appearance—that she was "pert and pretty," had "Windex-blue eyes," had an ability to charm naysayers, and was the antithesis of a "noisy libber"—annoyed Ruckelshaus but that she tolerated them to get the job done. "Why bother poking a pig?" she recently said. "I found noisy voices and agitation were needed to start the conversation and quieter ones to bring consensus."

In many ways, as a well-educated, moderate Republican with a post-graduate degree from Harvard and a mother of five, she was the most unimpeachable voice against Phyllis Schlafly's claims that feminism and the ERA were undoing the traditional American family.

She'd moved to the Washington area in 1969, when her husband, Bill, became the first head of the Environmental Protection Agency. Her suburban Maryland kitchen quickly became a gathering spot for NWPC strategizing as her young children darted about. Word of mouth grew their numbers—which is exactly how Patty's godmother, Aunt Marjorie, could hypothetically meet the iconic feminist and get involved in supporting the ERA. That allowed Jill Ruckelshaus to become a never-seen but wonderful influence on my characters—especially Patty and her mother, who had a longer journey to take to reach self-redefinition.

By 1973, Ruckelshaus had become the White House special assistant on women's rights, working to improve the shocking statistic that only 3 percent of all elected and appointed jobs were filled by women. She chose to give up the position, however, after her husband, then the deputy attorney general, resigned in protest during the infamous Saturday Night Massacre and Nixon's demand that he fire the Watergate special prosecutor.

That did not stop Jill Ruckelshaus's advocacy and activism. Gerald Ford made her head of his Presidential Commission on Women's Rights, and in 1980, Democrat Jimmy Carter would appoint her to the U.S. Civil Rights Commission.

Right before the historic National Women's Conference of 1977, knowing they had a hard battle ahead of them against anti-ERA and anti-choice forces, Ruckelshaus spoke to an NWPC gathering with stirring words that hauntingly apply to today: "Sisters, you are all here because you are smart. You are committed to an idea that is much larger than ourselves or the length of our lifetimes. You want to elect women to public office because we want to gain some control over the issues that affect our lives.

"We want the women of America to understand what it is to be raised female where we have met the government and it is not us. Somebody is making laws in this country that affect our legal rights, even our basic right to control our own bodies. And there are not enough of us among those somebodies.

"We've learned that we have to win our fight, then win it again four years later, and four years after that . . . We are in for a very, very long haul. I am asking for everything you have to give . . . your youth, your sleep, your patience, your sense of humor . . . In return I have nothing to offer you but . . . your pride in being a woman and all your dreams you've ever had for your daughters, and nieces, and granddaughters."

KATHARINE GRAHAM: It's not a stretch to speculate that without the *Washington Post*'s quiet but steely publisher, the country may never have known the full truth of Watergate and the scandal would have slipped into obscurity as the nonsensical "third-rate burglary" the White House painted it as being. Woodward and Bernstein did the stunning reporting, Ben Bradlee the editing—but the reports would never have been printed without Graham braving the ire of a president known to be singularly vindictive about "screwing his enemies" and the very personal and vile threat the former attorney general and Nixon's campaign director, John Mitchell, made against her.

She'd already stood up to the White House earlier, printing sections of the Pentagon Papers even after the administration got an injunction stopping the *New York Times* from circulating the damning report on the Vietnam War. But that was a more clear-cut risk, standing up for First Amendment rights. Watergate's details were murky at first, disconnected, and—given Nixon's overwhelming win in the 1972 presidential election—so implausible that few believed them. The *Post* was overwhelmingly denounced. "If we hadn't been right, we'd have been dead," Graham said matter-of-factly.

Bernstein still chokes up relating this anecdote: After he and Woodward reported that Mitchell—while the acting attorney general, the highest law enforcement official in the land—controlled a secret Republican Party fund used to finance clandestine political espionage against Democrats, a subpoena server arrived at the *Post*. Sent by CR(EE)P, the Committee to Re-elect the President, he demanded the reporters' notes. Bradlee called Graham, who responded that Bernstein's notes were not his to turn over. They were hers. If anyone was to go to jail, it would be her. The subpoena server left empty-handed.

"It shows you the courage of this great publisher," says Bernstein.

It was not a role Graham ever expected to play. She only inherited the reins of her family's newspaper after her husband died. But she more than rose to the daunting responsibility. The first twentieth-century female publisher of a major American newspaper and the first woman Fortune 500 CEO, Graham was posthumously awarded the Presidential Medal of Freedom by Republican George W. Bush. Her memoir, *Personal History*, won a Pulitzer Prize for her candid portrayal of both her husband's mental illness and suicide and her personal journey through the momentous change in women's roles that the fight for the ERA brought.

Frankly, there are no more resonant icons for females proving women's capabilities during and connected to Watergate than Katharine Graham and **_JILL WINE-BANKS (IN 1973, JILL WINE-VOLNER)_**, the only female lawyer on the Watergate special prosecutor staff. At that time only 4 percent of American attorneys were women. Wine-Banks's savvy cross-examination that caught Nixon's secretary in a jaw-dropping lie—about the cause of an 18½-minute erasure in one of Nixon's taped conversations—is a touchstone that made all the difference in the nation's understanding that a "third-rate burglary" had evolved into a conspiracy of calculated moves and lies to hide wrongdoing. It was a moment when loyal "Nixonites" began to break from blind loyalty. (That court testimony is referenced in Chapters 11 and 12.)

Today, a much-quoted legal analyst and co-host of the podcast *Sisters-in-Law*, Jill Wine-Banks recounts in *The Watergate Girl* what it was like to be a highly skilled but young and attractive woman lawyer in the national spotlight, delegitimized by the press describing her as a miniskirted bombshell. At one point during the thirty-year-old's razor-sharp questioning of Rose Mary Woods—when the Oval Office secretary's response was particularly hostile and heated—Judge Sirica reflexively chided them both, "All right, we have enough problems without two ladies getting into an argument." In her memoir, Wine-Banks recounts that she managed to maintain her cool despite the judge's patronizing comment and the resulting spectator laughter. Such was the requirement to always be "ladylike" in 1973.

Interestingly, Wine-Banks adds that her home was burglarized—twice—during her stint as a Watergate prosecutor. The second time, after Woods's testimony, the police called in the FBI. The agents informed Wine-Banks they could tell that a bug had been removed from her telephone during that break-in.

MARTHA MITCHELL: The tapestry of Watergate is thick with a vast multitude of players, major and minor, and some nonpolitical issues threaded throughout. Attorney General Mitchell's wife, the vivacious and colorful "Mouth of the South," Martha was legendary for her gossipy, late-night telephone calls, and purposely shocking sound bites. An ardent campaigner for Nixon, a frequent guest on talk shows and *Laugh-In*, Martha called White House reporter Helen Thomas immediately after the Watergate break-in to say the administration was trying to silence her. During the call, Thomas heard a scuffle, and then the phone went dead. Martha would later claim she was held down and drugged by her husband's protective detail.

Much has been made recently of Martha's tragic life story. Julia Roberts played her in the 2022 miniseries *Gaslit*. After her claims that Nixon had to have okayed the cover-up and his campaign's other political espionage—long before there was any kind of connection made to the White House—Martha was smeared by Nixon's people as "crazy," overwrought and confused, and not to be believed—a disparaging label sadly common in the 1970s for women who insisted on saying "troublesome" things or appeared upset when they said them.

I bring her into Patty's story briefly in Chapter 3, to further embroider the novel's backdrop of contemptuous, sexist attitudes about women's acumen and "emotionality" that feminists were fighting and women like Patty's mother, Dot Appleton, were trapped in.

With Martha, her well-known love for a cocktail didn't help. But she kept talking—at first trying to protect her husband as it became clear to her that Nixon would turn on his old friend and law partner to pin the break-in's planning on him. She was, of course, correct—as John Dean revealed during his testimony—that Mitchell was to be scapegoated for the break-in and campaign dirty tricks, Dean for the cover-up.

When Martha died in 1976, alone, ravaged by cancer, someone planted an enormous banner of flowers at her graveside funeral that spelled out "Martha Was Right." And the psychology field coined a term, "the Martha Mitchell effect," to describe a mental health professional mistakenly dismissing—as delusional—a patient's seemingly paranoid but totally correct perceptions of real events.

MAUREEN DEAN stood by her new husband, John, as he testified before the Senate and the nation, as he was convicted of obstructing justice, and as he served four months of a four-year prison sentence (granted leniency for his cooperation with the Watergate special prosecutor). In October 2022 they celebrated their fiftieth wedding anniversary. She co-wrote the screenplay for a 1979 miniseries based on her husband's book, *Blind Ambition*, starring Martin Sheen. Maureen also penned two novels, *Washington Wives* and *Capitol Secrets*.

Her husband became an investment banker, frequent television commentator, and bestselling author of eleven nonfiction books. John Dean has often shared that as "Mo" helped type his sixty-thousand-word statement for the Senate hearings and learned *all* the illegalities the White House staff engaged in, she vehemently declared that if they had only told their wives first, none of it would have happened. The women would have talked sense into them.

During Watergate, Washington had two newspapers, morning (the *Post*) and evening (the *Star*). **MARY McGRORY** was a *Star* columnist, winning a Pulitzer Prize for her commentary that so aggravated Nixon, she became the only woman on his primary "enemies list." Coincidentally or not, she was subjected to an invasive IRS audit, a retribution Nixon was caught on tape suggesting be done to his critics. McGrory would one-up Wine-Banks when the two met for lunch with columnist Art Buchwald, according to *The Watergate Girl*, telling Wine-Banks that she had been burglarized—and possibly bugged—as well. But three times to the lawyer's two.

Congresswoman, lawyer, and activist, an organizer of the 1970 Women's Strike for Peace and Equality and platform battles for the ERA at the Democratic National Convention, plus an NWPC cofounder, **BELLA ABZUG** was a formidable, boisterous, and omnipresent national figure throughout the 1960s and '70s. "She's fierce and intense and funny," said her friend and ally Gloria Steinem. "When she argues with you, it's because she takes you seriously." Representing New York (1971–77), Abzug spearheaded the bill declaring an annual Women's Equality Day. She authored legislation stopping credit companies from denying a woman's application for a loan or credit card unless her husband or father cosigned, pushed for abortion rights and programs to support working women such as national day care, and introduced the first gay and lesbian rights bill. Her nickname "Battling Bella" fit her, as did her signature wide-brim hats that she began wearing as a young attorney representing union workers—so her opposing counsel would not mistakenly assume she was a secretary there to take notes.

The first Black woman elected to the U.S. House of Representatives, **SHIRLEY CHISHOLM** served six terms from 1969 to 1983, introducing more than fifty pieces of legislation. In 1972, she became the first woman to run for the Democratic Party's presidential nomination. During that campaign she was initially blocked from participating in televised primary debates. After suing, she was permitted one speech. Even so, despite those hurdles and a surprising lack of support from the male-dominated Congressional Black Caucus, Chisholm entered twelve primaries and won an impressive 10 percent of delegates to the national convention.

After she retired from the U.S. House, Chisholm remained a tireless crusader against the double discrimination of race and sex facing Black women, cofounding the National Political Congress of Black Women.

At the twentieth anniversary gathering of the NWPC, which she also helped found, Chisholm shared with the attendee audience a story about one of the first lunches she ate as a congresswoman in the members' private dining room. A Georgia congressman arrived at the table where she sat, lunch tray in hand. He told her she shouldn't be there. It was only then Chisholm realized she had mistakenly sat at a table meant for his state's delegation. There were no reservation markers delineating tables according to state that she could see, and there were six empty chairs at the table. She apologized and reassured the congressman that the next day she would find the correct New York table, but right now she wanted to finish her lunch.

He didn't budge.

"He was determined not to sit down beside me, and I became determined not to move. . . . So I decided to use my home-grown psychology. I gentled my voice and said,"—here Chisholm adopted a soothing, motherly tone—"'I know you're hungry, aren't you? I understand that you are uncomfortable sitting here with me.' I pointed to an empty table. 'You go on over there and enjoy your lunch and if anybody bothers you, you tell them to come see Shirley Chisholm.'"

Delighted laughter followed her anecdote. After waiting for it to subside, Chisholm gestured to the other veteran feminists on stage with her. "We did the best to our abilities, in spite of snide remarks and epithets muttered about us. We knew we were about the business of bequeathing a legacy for future generations to come. You are here today to carry it on."

THE FEMININE MYSTIQUE: Author Betty Friedan is often referred to as the mother of the 1960s women's movement. She had help, of course. But her gut-wrenchingly honest book was indeed the explosive treatise that ignited countless women's epiphanies about their frustrations, aborted hopes, and inherent right to have the same opportunities as men. In a March 4, 1973, *New York Times Magazine* article celebrating its tenth anniversary, Friedan recounted the origins of her book that rocked the world of American housewives—a survey of her Smith College classmates of 1942. "Each of us thought she was a freak if she didn't experience that mysterious orgiastic fulfillment waxing the kitchen floor as the commercials promised . . . if we still had ambitions, ideas about ourselves as people in our own right."

She cited the fact that in 1963 nearly half of all women in the United States were already working outside the home to help pay the mortgage and buy groceries, "betraying their femininity, undermining their husband's masculinity, and neglecting their children by daring to work for money at all—no matter how much it was needed." Her classmates shared that they resented the guilt they felt for . . . well . . . feeling, for having their own sexual needs, for being angry that they were paid half what a man was, and for anonymously "writing the paper for which *he* got the degree and the raise."

When Friedan shared these findings with women's magazines for which she had been writing regularly, hoping to sell an article about her survey and classmates' reality, she was met with hostility. Turned down and told that only "the most neurotic housewife could identify" with the reactions she was describing, Friedan decided to write a book instead. At the time of her death in 2006, more than three million copies had been sold.

In that 1973 *New York Times* article, Friedan urged women to beware untruths told by the STOP ERA crusade and people trying to limit women's freedoms by claiming it was to protect American families. To not be frightened by independence, and to not resort to alienating "man-hate" rhetoric. To her, men were also victims, saddled with a "masculine mystique" that left them feeling emasculated when "there were no bears to kill."

Most will remember **NORA EPHRON** as the witty screenwriter/director of the romantic comedies *When Harry Met Sally* and *You've Got Mail* or female-driven movies like *Julie and Julia*, but her earlier career was as a searingly blunt columnist, writing poignant and pointed essays about the condition of womanhood. She, too, was a trailblazer. She worked briefly at *Newsweek*, when women were not allowed bylines of their own, instead serving as researchers for the exclusively male reporting staff. She participated in a 1970 class action lawsuit against the newsmagazine—spearheaded by civil-rights attorney and equal pay activist **ELEANOR HOLMES NORTON**—to push the publication to allow women to be reporters themselves (this episode is dramatized in the Amazon Prime Video series *Good Girls Revolt*). Ephron went on to write for the *New York Post* and *Esquire* magazine. In a Watergate connection, she was briefly married to Carl Bernstein.

Holmes Norton would also become a founding member of the NWPC and the National Black Feminist Organization. President Jimmy Carter would appoint her the first woman head of the Equal Employment Opportunity Commission, and in 1991 she was elected to Congress as the District of Columbia's delegate, where she has served ever since.

Ephron's wonderful essays, her droll observations on things like body image and cultural stereotyping/expectations—which unnervingly still ring so true today—would certainly have fueled the ideas of a liberal young woman like Simone and startled conservatives like Patty into rethinking society-dictated definitions of worth and femininity.

At this writing, the legendary feminist, activist, and author of a half dozen empowering and eye-opening books, NWPC cofounder, founding editor of *Ms.* magazine, and winner of the Presidential Medal of Freedom, **GLORIA STEINEM** is ninety years old. She is still speaking, still urging unity among women as the way to achieve rightful change. At the 2017 Women's March on Washington, half a million people hushed to hear her impassioned words: "Thank you for understanding that sometimes we must put our bodies where our beliefs are. Sometimes pressing 'send' isn't enough."

She urged her listeners to remember the United States Constitution "begins with 'We, the people.' . . . We will not be quiet, we will not be controlled . . . God may be in the details, but the goddess is in the connections . . . Introduce yourselves to one another and decide what we're going to do tomorrow and tomorrow and tomorrow."

Finally, I must thank Kayla E. for her exquisite photo essay design that punctuates Patty's individual journey so powerfully with the events and debates that defined 1973; editors Cheryl Klein and Krestyna Lypen as well as art director Keirsten Geise for their exceptional hard work on a complex novel they inherited; and my incredibly supportive, wise, and diplomatic agent, Katelyn Detweiler, a gifted novelist herself.

As always, I am so grateful for the love and steadying counsel, the artistic sensibilities, and deep compassion for humankind that my adult daughter and son, Megan and Peter—a theater director and a novelist/screenwriter/developmental editor—blessed me with as I wrote this novel. Their own resilience, brave honesty, and creative talents, their early and continuous reading of this novel, their astute suggestions and nuanced sense of story, were all critically important influences on its themes and character protrayals.

It is they who *really* showed me long ago—as children captivated by anecdotes of older family surviving World War Two—the power of story. It's how we humans have always found parable to make sense of ourselves—retelling past events in dramatized narrative, examining how people found courage within themselves or not. As such, *well-researched* historical fiction allows readers to walk characters' journeys with them, with concern, with surprise, with tears and laughter—learning history by osmosis.

When we humans feel something, we remember it.

I've also learned the power of presenting controversial issues in a past era rather than present day—it removes the heat of immediacy and readers' self-protective defensiveness, often prompting easier revelations and more productive discussion. I hope this look at Watergate, the ERA, and women's autonomy does that for readers grappling with similar questions today of personal agency, equity, integrity, and political divides as well as truth versus disinformation.

I *love* writing for young adults—and for this novel I extend that age range through twentysomethings, adhering to the 1960s grouping of the youth movement to those 30 and younger. I love their righteous indignation, the fact they want truth—and woe betide a writer who doesn't trust their intellect and ability to face hard realities or complex material—but truth wrapped with some hope. A tale with a little reassurance that if they follow their moral compass, they can stand strong against injustice and lies.

Frankly, looking at the morass we adults have created recently—the hate-filled tribalism, the stubborn and cowardly avoidance of uncomfortable truths—my hope rests on our younger generation, their open hearts and instinct to question *everything*. But if we want them to also find answers to their questions, we must gift them some historical context—our mistakes as well as our triumphs—to aid their analysis of today, teach them how to look for fact, *to think for themselves*, and then respect it when they do.

I smile as I write this last paragraph because I sense Simone whispering her usual summation in my ear, pushing me to add, with her characteristic shrug: "Just saying."

SOME SELECTED SOURCES

BOOKS

Bernstein, Carl and Woodward, Bob. *All the President's Men.* New York: Warner Books, 1974.

Conkling, Winifred. *Ms. Gloria Steinem: A Life.* New York: Feiwel and Friends, 2020.

Dean, John W. *Blind Ambition.* New York: Open Road Media; Reprint edition, 2016.

Ephron, Nora. *Crazy Salad: Some Things About Women.* New York: First Vintage Books Edition, 2012.

Gonzalez, Darryl J. *The Children Who Ran for Congress: A History of Congressional Pages.* Santa Barbara, California: Praeger, 2010.

Graff, Garrett M. *Watergate: A New History.* New York: Avid Reader Press, 2022.

Griffith, Elisabeth. *Formidable: American Women and the Fight for Equality 1920–2020.* New York: Pegasus Books, 2022.

Levine, Suzanne and Lyons, Harriet, editors. *The Decade of Women: A Ms. History of the Seventies in Words and Pictures.* New York: Paragon Books, 1980.

Povich, Lynn. *The Good Girls Revolt: How the Women of* Newsweek *Sued Their Bosses and Changed the Workplace.* New York: PublicAffairs, 2016.

Sims, Marcie. *Capitol Hill Pages: Young Witnesses to 200 Years of History.* North Carolina: McFarland & Co., Inc, 2018.

Spruill, Marjorie J. *Divided We Stand: The Battle Over Women's Rights and Family Values that Polarized American Politics.* New York: Bloomsbury, 2017.

Steinem, Gloria. *Outrageous Acts and Everyday Rebellions.* New York: Picador, 2019.

Wine-Banks, Jill. *The Watergate Girl.* New York: Henry Holt and Co. 2020.

DOCUMENTARIES

CNN Original Series. *The Seventies.* Playtone Studio. 2015.
CNN Original Series. *Watergate: Blueprint for a Scandal.* Herzog & Company, 2022.
Deane, Elizabeth, prod. *American Experience: Nixon,* PBS The Presidents Collection, 1990.
Ferguson, Charles, dir. *Watergate.* History Channel, 2018.
Kunhardt, Peter, dir. *Gloria: In Her Own Words.* HBO, 2011.
Lieberman, Jeff, dir. *Bella! This Woman's Place Is in the House.* PBS, 2023.
Lopez, Kamala, dir. *Equal Means Equal.* Heroica Films, 2016.
Lynch, Shola, dir. *Chisholm '72: Unbought and Unbossed.* Sundance Studio, 2004.
Mondell, Cynthia Salzman, dir. *Sisters of '77.* PBS, 2005.
Neyfakh, Leon, host. *Slow Burn: Watergate.* Amazon Prime, 2017.
Scheinfeld, John, dir. *Dick Cavett's Watergate.* PBS, 2014.

MOVIES/TV MINISERIES (PG-13)

Calvo, Dana, dir. *Good Girls Revolt.* Amazon Prime Video, 2015.
Faris, Valerie, dir. *Battle of the Sexes.* Fox Searchlight Pictures, 2017.
Howard, Ron, dir. *Frost/Nixon.* Universal Pictures, 2008.
Mandel, David, dir. *White House Plumbers.* HBO/Max, 2023.
Pakula, Alan, dir. *All the President's Men.* Warner Brothers, 1976.
Ross, Matt, dir. *Gaslit.* Starz, 2022.
Spielberg, Steven, dir. *The Post.* 20th Century Pictures, 2017.
Taymor, Julie. *The Glorias.* Roadside Attractions, LD Entertainment, 2020.
Waller, Davhi, dir. *Mrs. America.* FX Hulu, 2020.

PHOTO CREDITS

PROLOGUE: WELCOME TO 1973
Flower Power Festival, Woburn Abbey, Aug. 1967, Trinity Mirror/Mirrorpix/Alamy Stock Photo.

PROLOGUE: NIXON'S VIETNAM
"Now, As I Was Saying 4 Years Ago," 8/9/1972, ©The Herb Block Foundation.
"Get the Hell Out," Vietnam War Protest in DC, Oct. 21, 1967, Lyndon B. Johnson Library.
"Stop the War Now," Florida State U. students, Tallahassee, FL, 1970, State Archives of Florida, Florida Memory.
Cornell students making peace signs, Alumni Affairs and Development photograph files, #4-3-3857. Division of Rare and Manuscript Collections, Cornell University Library.

PROLOGUE: KENT STATE
National Guard personnel walking toward crowd near Taylor Hall, tear gas has been fired, Photo #1427, News Service May 4 Photographs. Kent State University Libraries, Special Collections and Archives.
Students surrounding to protect student hit by rifle fire, Photo #8723, McNees, Ronald P., Kent State Shootings Photographs from Various Sources. Kent State University Libraries, Special Collections and Archives.
Students running away from the firing at Kent State, May 1970, Everett Collection Historical/Alamy Stock Photo.
Texas students march holding names of slain Kent State students, Special Collections, University of North Texas.
Students, faculty, and local residents march from Carle Park to West Side Park, photo courtesy of the University of Illinois at Urbana-Champaign Archives, 0002165.tif.

PROLOGUE: BACKLASH RIOTING and A "SILENT" MAJORITY
Journalist being pushed off a ledge by workers, May 8, 1970, courtesy Municipal Archives, City of New York.

Student filmmaker after being assaulted by workers, May 8, 1970, courtesy Municipal Archives, City of New York.

Construction worker assaulting a man on Broadway, May 8, 1970, courtesy Municipal Archives, City of New York.

Hard Hat demonstration in support of Nixon and the police, May 20, 1970, courtesy Municipal Archives, City of New York.

1972 US presidential campaign button for George McGovern, Independent Picture Service/Alamy Stock Photo.

PROLOGUE: WATERGATE AND THE POST GOING IT ALONE; and "WOODSTEIN" KEEP DIGGING

Bob Woodward and Carl Bernstein, 1976, John Barrett/PHOTOlink.net/Alamy Stock Photo.

Address Book of Watergate Burglar Bernard Baker, National Archives and Records Administration #304966.

Katharine Graham, 4/4/1976, photo by Marion S. Trikosko/*U.S. News & World Report* Photography Collection, RBM Vintage Images/Alamy Stock Photo.

AG John Mitchell and President Richard Nixon at a press conference, Everett Collection Inc./Alamy Stock Photo.

"The Great Silence," 10/31/1972, ©The Herb Block Foundation.

Shredded Paper, public domain, Wikimedia.

PROLOGUE: WOMEN RISE UP, THE ERA, AND MS.

Supporters of ERA carry banner down Pennsylvania Ave., MVP History/Alamy Stock Photo.

Fannie Lou Hamer, at Democratic National Convention, 1964, photo by Warren K. Leffler, *U.S. News & World Report* Collection, Library of Congress.

Gloria Steinem, at Women's Action Alliance news conference, Jan. 12, 1972, photo by Warren K. Leffler, *U.S. News & World Report* Collection, Library of Congress.

Betty Friedan at protest outside Social Security Building, Federal Plaza, 8/26/72, Glove Photos/ZUMA Press Inc./Alamy Stock Photo.

Bella Abzug, Library of Congress Prints and Photographs Division.

Shirley Chisholm campaign button, 1972, Collection of the US House of Representatives.
1970s USA Ms. *Magazine Cover*, RetroAdArchives/Alamy Stock Photo.

CHAPTER ONE

Aerial of the Watergate complex and the mugshots of Watergate burglars Bernard Barker, Virgilio Gonzalez, Eugenio R. Martinez, James McCord, and Frank Sturgis, National Archives Special Access and FOIA Program.
Richard and Pat Nixon waving during Inaugural Parade, Jan. 20, 1973, Everett Collection Inc./Alamy Stock Photo.
Protester arrested at Nixon 1973 Inauguration, Everett Collection Inc./Alamy Stock Photo.
US Senator Joseph Biden takes the oath of office from his sons' hospital room, The Associated Press.
US Supreme Court group portrait, April 20, 1972, Alpha Historica/Alamy Stock Photo.
Attorney Sarah Weddington, Courtesy, *Fort Worth Star-Telegram* Collection, Special Collections, The University of Texas at Arlington Libraries.

CHAPTER TWO

US Capitol Building, courtesy Library of Congress.
Jill Ruckelshaus attending International Women's Year Reception at National Archives, courtesy Gerald R. Ford Presidential Library.
ERA March, photo by Howard Staples, courtesy MOHAI, *Seattle Post-Intelligencer* Photography Collection, 2000.107.232.26.01.
Phyllis Schlafly, STOP ERA demonstration in front of White House, photo by Warren K. Leffler, *U.S. News & World Report* Collection, Library of Congress.
Pilot Emily Howell Warner, courtesy National Air and Space Museum Archives, Smithsonian Institution.
Pacific Northwest Airlines Stewardesses, 1972, Everett Collection Historical/Alamy Stock Photo.

CHAPTER THREE

The Mod Squad *publicity photo*, August 1971.
Lily Tomlin, Laugh-In, *1967*, NBC Album, Alamy Stock Photo.

Letter from James W. McCord Jr. to Judge John Sirica, March 19, 1973, National Archives and Records Administration.
Mug shot of James McCord, National Archives Special Access and FOIA Program.
Martha Mitchell, July 29, 1969, Nixon White House Photo Office Collection, National Archives and Records Administration.
"Two Faces of Joy," photographer: Ben Oldender. *Los Angeles Times* Photographic Archive, UCLA Library Special Collections.
"Operation Homecoming," newly freed American POWs as they leave North Vietnam, US Air Force photo.
President Nixon greets former POW John McCain III, White House Photo Office Collection, #E0840-014.

CHAPTER FOUR

Acting FBI director Patrick Gray, May 1972, Courtesy CSU Archives/Everett Collection Historical/Alamy Stock Photo.
Haldeman, Ehrlichman, Nixon in the Oval Office, White House Photo Office.
Nixon advisers H. R. Haldeman and John Ehrlichman on Air Force One, 1973, photograph by Oliver F. Atkins, National Archives and Records Administration.
The Mike Douglas Show, with Douglas, NOW president Wilma Scott Heide, and anti-ERA activist Phyllis Schlafly, Everett Collection Inc./Alamy Stock Photo.
Pentagon Papers Defendant Daniel Ellsberg and wife Patricia, 1971, Courtesy of CSU Archives, Everett Collection Historical/Alamy Stock Photo.
G. Gordon Liddy, leaving US District Court, Everett Collection Inc./Alamy Stock Photo.

CHAPTER FIVE

Senate Watergate committee chairman Sam Ervin and ranking member Howard Baker, photograph by Senate photographer, courtesy of Senator Sam J. Ervin Jr. Library and Museum.
"Watergate Monopoly: The White House Game," 5/1/73, ©The Herb Block Foundation.

Ruth Bader Ginsburg, courtesy of the Digital Library of Georgia; UGA School of Law Sibley Lecture.

Air Force Lieutenant Sharron Frontiero, Maxwell Air Force Base, courtesy of the US Air Force.

Bella Abzug at press conference for National Youth Conference, 1972, photo by Warren K. Leffler, U.S. News & World Report Collection, Library of Congress.

American Express office, Amsterdam, 1971, courtesy National Archives of the Netherlands.

CHAPTER SIX

Triple Crown winner Secretariat led by owner Penny Chenery, 1973, courtesy Bob Coglianese Photos Inc.

Former White House counselor John W. Dean being sworn in to testify to the Senate Watergate Committee, June 1973, The Associated Press.

John and Maureen Dean in the Senate Watergate Hearing Room, Everett Collection Historical/Alamy Stock Photo.

"Late Returns" (Watergate TV hearings), 5/18/73, ©The Herb Block Foundation.

Boss dictates letter to secretary, 1970, INTERFOTO/Alamy Stock Photo.

CHAPTER SEVEN

Aerial view of the White House, Library of Congress Prints and Photographs Division.

John Ehrlichman testifying before Senate Watergate Committee, 1973, ©Keystone Pictures USA/ ZUMA Press Inc./Alamy Stock Photo.

"National Security Blanket," 5/27/1973, ©The Herb Block Foundation.

Singer Helen Reddy publicity photo, 1975.

CHAPTER EIGHT

"Above Any Office" (Sirica Ruling), 8/31/73, ©The Herb Block Foundation.

Judge John Sirica at his US District Court office, Danita Delimont/Alamy Stock Photo.

Nixon's proclamation for Women's Equality Day, 1973; courtesy GovInfo.gov.

Activist, feminist, and lawyer Florynce Kennedy, 1972, Underwood Archives, Inc./ Alamy Stock Photo.

Lawyer and feminist Eleanor Holmes Norton, courtesy Equal Employment Opportunity Commission.

CHAPTER NINE

"I Am Not a Crook," Nixon Hanging between Tapes, 5/24/74, ©The Herb Block Foundation.
All in the Family *scene, 1976*, Archive PL/Alamy Stock Photo.
The Mary Tyler Moore Show *scene, 1970, "Mary Richards" at her desk in the WJM-TV newsroom.*
Demonstrator in front of White House, supporting Bobby Riggs, Sueddeutsche Zeitung Photo/Alamy Stock Photo.
Billie Jean King at US Open, 1972, courtesy CSU, Everett Collection Historical/Alamy Stock Photo.

CHAPTER TEN

President Nixon at press conference, Everett Collection Historical/Alamy Stock Photo.
Caricature of VP Spiro Agnew, artist Edmund S. Valtman, Library of Congress Prints and Photographs Division.
William Ruckelshaus swearing in as EPA Administrator, 1970, courtesy Richard M. Nixon Presidential Library.
AG Elliot Richardson, courtesy US Department of Commerce.
Watergate Special Prosecutor Archibald Cox, press conference 1973, U.S. News & World Report Photograph Collection, Library of Congress.
Anti-Nixon demonstrators in front of the White House, Everett Collection Historical/Alamy Stock Photo.
"Mugging" (Sat. Night Massacre), 10/23/73, © The Herb Block Foundation.

CHAPTER ELEVEN

Watergate Prosecutor Jill Wine-Volner after questioning Nixon's secretary on the witness stand, The Associated Press.
"Something New for the House," photographer: Ben Oldender. *Los Angeles Times* Photographic Archive, UCLA Library Special Collections.
Little League tryout with girls, April 3, 1974, photographer: Bettye Lane, Library of Congress LOT 14193, no. 147, courtesy of Ms. Lane's heirs.

CHAPTER TWELVE

The "Rose Mary Stretch," 11/30/73, ©The Herb Block Foundation.

"Enemies List" Memo by John Dean, 8/16/71, part of US House of Representatives Impeachment Hearings, Resolution 803, National Archives and Records Administration.

Gerald Ford swearing in as VP, 12/6/1973, photographer: Warren K. Leffler, Glasshouse Images/Alamy Stock Photo.

Gerald Ford remarks when sworn in, courtesy Gerald R. Ford Presidential Museum.

Women holding sign supporting Betty Ford, courtesy National Archives and Records Administration.

EPILOGUE

"Listen, are you going to be loyal to the constitution or to me?" 1/31/1974, ©The Herb Block Foundation.

"Unindicted Co-conspirator," 7/14/1974. © The Herb Block Foundation

President Nixon's Resignation Letter, 8/8/74, courtesy of the US Senate, courtesy of the Center for Legislative Archives, National Archives and Records Administration, Select Committee on Presidential Campaign Activities.

Women's March in Los Angeles, 1/21/2017, Visions of America, LLC/Alamy Stock Photo.

Women marching to Supreme Court, photography by and courtesy of Alexandra Charitan.